Praise for M.
The Stephenv....

"An absorbing thriller, including a concise compendium of recent UFO history, written by the former head of the Mutual UFO Network (MUFON) Texas chapter, that presents new insights into the still-unexplained events at Stephenville, Texas, in 2008...what more could one want?"

- Jim Marrs, *New York Times* Best-Selling author
of *Alien Agenda* and *Our Occulted History*

"The Stephenville UFO event was one of the most extraordinary and important such events in recent history. Ken Cherry's novel explores the case and its implications in a creative and unexpected manner. Chillingly possible!"

- Whitley Strieber, New *York Times* Best-Selling
author *of Communion* and *Alien Hunter*

"As a journalist, I watched Ken Cherry devote months diligently attempting to uncover the series of peculiar sightings above the skies of Stephenville in the year 2008. His work was painstaking and precise. Now, he finally tells what he believes could very well have happened. Although this book is a novel, much of it is chillingly straight from the factual record. I know you will be haunted."

- Skip Hollandsworth
Executive Editor, *Texas Monthly*

"Get to the heart of the Stephenville UFO incident. Based upon eye witness reports and corroborative data, this fictionalized account puts you right into the middle of this ongoing controversy. Marc Slade Investigates provides you with all of the facts but will keep you turning the pages. A must read for the experienced UFO researcher as well as those newly interested in the field. "

- Rita Louise, Ph.D., author of *ET Chronicles:
What Myth and Legend Says About Human
Origins*

GÎT

Glannant Ty Publishing
Hamburg NJ USA / Carmarthenshire, Wales UK
www.glannantty.com

Marc Slade Investigates: The Stephenville UFO
Copyright © 2015 by Ken Cherry

First Edition: May 2015

Cover Design by Mark Johnson © 2015

Manufactured in the United States of America
Distributed by IngramSpark

10 9 8 7 6 5 4 3 2 1

ISBN-13: 978-0-9861675-7-7
ISBN-10: 0986167576

Library of Congress Number: 2015939562

To Pat...

....my wife and friend of 50 years, patiently transcribed many handwritten rewrites of my manuscript. The nearly year-long investigation of the Stephenville UFO impacted our family owned business greatly. Pat remained committed to the search for answers throughout the many disruptions.

ACKNOWLEDGMENTS

Special thanks to Nick Redfern for his introduction to this book and his many words of encouragement and advice.

Laurel B. Tague PhD. for her friendship, many hours of proofreading and encouragement when I needed it most.

Jim Marrs for his keen insights that led me to key pieces of information.

Becky Folger, Sharon Vining and Leena Peltoniemi PhD. for helping me to see past the pain of my physical rehabilitation and encouragement to finish what I had begun.

To the many dedicated Texas MUFON Field Investigators who gave generously of their time and talent in pursuit of truth.

To the more than 150 witnesses and confidential sources who contacted me personally to tell their story even at their own risk in more than a few cases.

A very special thanks to Mark Johnson and Irene Allen-Block at Glannant Ty publishing for believing in me and the importance of Marc Slade Investigates: The Stephenville UFO.

Many thanks to Dave Pavoni producer and The UFO Hunters for the investigative and scientific team they assembled in support: Bruce Maccabee Phd., Bill Birnes Phd., Ted Ackworth Ph.D.,William Puckett radar specialist and Pat Uskert gave critical assistance to the Stephenville investigation

FOREWORD

Marc Slade Investigates: The Stephenville UFO, you will already have surmised, is a work of fiction. It is, however, based upon events that are as real as they are astounding, amazing, and even other-worldly.

When the Texas town of Stephenville was hit by a wave of incredible UFO activity in January 2008, it wasn't just the people of the area who sat up and took notice of what was going on in the skies above them. The local media caught wind of what was afoot. Then the story went national. In no time at all, it was *global*.

The military was soon caught up in the controversy, too – chiefly as a result of its curious and conflicting statements on the affair. Witnesses were being interviewed on prime-time television shows. The UFO research community hadn't seen anything like this in years. And no wonder: there were reports of a huge UFO overflying the town, of attempts by the military to intercept the massive craft, of frightened witnesses, of government conspiracies, and even of the United Nations taking a secret and deep interest in what was happening in Stephenville.

From practically the day that the controversy began, one man was at the forefront of trying to figure out what was taking place in and around Stephenville. That man was Ken Cherry the Texas State MUFON Director at the time. He found himself plunged into a strange world filled with concerned eye-witnesses, insider whistleblowers, tales of cosmic cover-ups, and accounts of secret groups studying acquired alien technology. And that was just the tip of the extraterrestrial iceberg.

Although Cherry has publicly revealed a great deal about what went on during those crazy days and nights of early 2008, he has not revealed everything – which is why he has chosen to present the story you are about to read as a work of fiction. Doing so allows Cherry to use witness accounts, data from those aforementioned whistleblowers, and a variety of never-before-seen data, without compromising his sources.

Keep all of the above in mind as you read *Marc Slade Investigates:*

The Stephenville UFO. This is a story that needs to be told, that demands to be told. And Ken Cherry has done exactly that, in a unique, alternative fashion that works very well.

- Nick Redfern, author of
  The Real Men In Black

Marc Slade Investigates:

The **S**tephenville UFO

KEN CHERRY

-1-

Frank Carter was not a happy rancher. In fact, as he sat on the porch of his Stephenville, Texas farmhouse at 1:25 a.m., huddled under a thick blanket and armed to the teeth, Carter was practically spitting blood. He thought back to the events that led him to this current post.

Just the night before, Carter was jolted awake in the early hours by a bright white light that illuminated his second-floor bedroom like a Fourth of July celebration. For a few moments, Carter was disoriented and confused. That, however, immediately changed when he realized the light, whatever it was, was coming from right outside the window.

With adrenalin now surging throughout his body, and following the Texan instinct of "grab your guns and ask questions later," Carter flew out of bed. Just as he did – almost as if in response – the light winked out in an instant. Carter quickly threw on his jeans, boots and a jacket, grabbed his pistol, raced down the stairs, and headed for the front door – armed and ready to find the jerk that would invade a man's homestead in the middle of the night and the middle of almost nowhere.

At forty-four, still in good shape and a 10-year vet with the National Guard, Carter knew how to look after himself. Kids, burglars, or a bunch of crazy drunks, it didn't matter to Carter: someone was prowling around his property and they were going to account for themselves. Carter soundlessly unlocked and opened the door. Cold January air hit him squarely in the face. He stealthily circled the perimeter of his home – one which he had shared with his wife, Nancy, until breast cancer tragically took her two years earlier.

Everything was quiet and still; tranquil, even. The tall, silhouetted trees that stood at the edge of Carter's property swayed gently in the icy breeze. The stars above shone brightly in a cloudless sky. But there was something else, too: an itchy tingle of menace. Not really just a concern that he might find himself confronted by gun-toting burglars or a gang of crackheads, but that, as he would later recall, *things were just not right – not at all*. Something indefinable was afoot, and he was up to his neck in it, even if he didn't know exactly what "it" was.

About 200 yards away, a powerful light suddenly lit up part of the field and, for twenty or thirty seconds, systematically scanned the ground as if looking for something or someone. Whatever the source of the light, it couldn't have been more than a few hundred feet in the air. Puzzlingly, however, Carter couldn't see a damned thing in the sky. For a few moments, a bewildered Carter could only stand and stare in awe. His first thought, as he tried to rationalize the situation, was that the light was coming from a helicopter. But, if that was the case, where was the typical thump-thump sound of rotor blades? The answer was as simple as it was bizarre: there *was* no sound.

While Carter's mind raced to figure out his next move, the decision was taken out of his hands. The bright light suddenly disappeared, and the field was plunged once more into utter darkness. Carter caught his breath and instinctively raised his pistol, pointing it towards that same all-enveloping darkness. Had his eyes not been so keenly focused on his field, Carter just might have caught a fleeting glimpse of a large, black, oblong-shaped object that silently shot across the night skies above. Not to worry, unbeknownst to Carter, he was to get another chance the very next night.

"It was the damnedest thing," Carter said, the following morning, while filing a report on the night's events with Deputy Connor at the Sheriff Department on Glen Rose Road. As he paced around the room, sipping on a lukewarm cup of coffee, Carter added: "I stayed up all night, and it was only after I went to feed the cows – about 6 o'clock – when I saw two of them were missing, and I came to see you boys."

Four years previously, Carter had lost a calf. On that occasion, however, it was to a pack of vicious coyotes. That much was obvious from the graphic, tell-tale remains of paw prints, blood, flesh and bones that littered the expansive field dominating his ranch. But, this time, things were very different. In fact, they were downright weird.

As the thirty-something Connor pointed out after Carter finished telling his story, figures from the Texas Department of Public Safety showed that, in the previous year, more than 10,000 cows and horses were reported missing or stolen in Texas and Oklahoma. "It's a big problem Mr. Carter; no doubt about that, sir," the deputy added, in an efficient and businesslike tone.

"And how many of *those* cases included a silent airplane flying over a farm in the middle of the night?" asked Carter, his voice filled with frustration and fury – and a splinter of sarcasm. Connor conceded that Carter had a good point. He assured the rancher that an investigation would be launched but admitted the chances of getting his cows back were slim to nonexistent.

Carter thanked Deputy Connor and walked to the door, but could not contain himself from sharing a few, final, choice words: "You find those sons of bitches and you give me a call before you do anything else, right?"

Deputy Connor stood up and, in firm tones, replied: "Mr. Carter, that's not how we do things. I understand how you feel, but leave it up to us, sir."

The hell with all that, thought Carter, who wasn't just concerned about his two missing cows. Now he was also worried about the *rest* of the herd. What if those fuckers – whoever they were – came back again and took another two, and then another two? It was a question that preyed on Carter's mind the rest of the day. It was also what led him to his present post: out on the porch, peering into the inky blackness that threatened to swallow both rancher and ranch, with nothing but a bottle of Jim Beam for company. As for the cows, they were safely locked in their sheds.

Carter sipped from a shot glass and mused on everything that had happened a little less than twenty-four hours earlier. Okay, he thought, it might be possible to haul away a couple of cows by a helicopter. But a *silent* helicopter was too much. Unless, of course, the Pentagon had some seriously weird, top secret shit in its arsenal. Even so, why would the military want to steal *his cattle*? Questions flooded Carter's mind. Answers, however, failed to take form.

There was another issue troubling Carter, too: it wasn't just that he was hoping his mysterious visitors would return tonight, chiefly so he could fill them with a good supply of high-quality lead. Somehow, deep in his subconscious, Carter *knew* they were coming back. How he knew, he couldn't say. Worse still, he couldn't shake off the nagging feeling that, this time, they were coming for *him*. His instincts would prove to be correct.

Roughly ninety minutes later, and with two shots of his favorite tipple having been downed, Carter sat bolt upright in his chair. He gripped the solid, wooden arms tightly. It wasn't the sounds of unseen intruders that caught his attention. It was the exact opposite: the incessant noise of the countless insects in and around the field came to a sudden, deafening halt. Even the whistling wind fell silent. Carter felt the hair on his arms and neck rise. Goosebumps quickly followed. His mouth went dry, but not from the alcohol. *Something* was coming.

Carter slowly rose to his feet and took his pistol out of its holster. He was anything but a nervous man but, right now, you would never have guessed it. His breathing was shallow and fast, and his hands tingled – a sure sign of the beginnings of hyperventilation. "Get a damned grip," Carter hissed to himself in a panicky tone. He knocked back another shot of Jim Beam. And then another. Finally, after a few minutes, the anxiety subsided, giving way to a "bring it on, locked and loaded" mindset. His breathing and pulse slowed. The bourbon buzz was helping.

Carter tentatively took the eight wooden steps that led from his porch to the fringes of his field. After covering seventy or eighty feet, he stopped. For a few minutes, he stood still, letting his eyes get used to the dark. Carter saw nothing out of the ordinary. He checked out the tree-line: everything was just as it always was. And then he turned his attention to the sky. That's when he began to unravel.

Carter was confronted by the damnedest thing he had ever seen: one by one; the stars were going out – every single one of them. What the hell? After a few seconds, to his horror, Carter realized the stars weren't going out at all. Instead, a huge, black-colored aircraft of some kind, one that was flying unimaginably low and slow, was obliterating the stars from view. But this was no normal aircraft. To him it looked

4

like a gigantic monolith: a massive, black tombstone lumbering horizontally at roughly sixty feet off the ground and maybe only two miles per hour. Carter craned his neck to taken in the incredible spectacle. As he did, the huge, utterly silent craft did the one thing that he prayed it wouldn't do: *it stopped.*

It was then that Carter – looking like the proverbial deer caught in the headlights – could finally take in the sheer scale of the thing hovering above. It was breathtakingly huge: easily bigger than an aircraft carrier, longer than three football fields and twice as wide. It was also then that he lost it – completely. Driven solely by adrenalin and a primal sense of self-preservation, he fired off two bullets into the base of the vehicle. A metallic "clang" rang out and echoed briefly before a pervasive, eerie silence dominated once again. Carter did the first thing that sprang to mind: he made a run for it.

He had only sprinted for thirty seconds or so when something terrifying occurred: Carter felt like he was wading through mud. His legs no longer responded as they should have. He felt dizzy and disoriented. The piercing scream that rumbled up from his gut emerged from his parched mouth as a barely audible whimper. The last thing he remembered was being enveloped by a bright golden glow and a sense of falling forward. Then it was lights out.

It was around 7:30 a.m. when Carter finally came to, feeling cold and clammy. The first thing he saw as he opened his eyes was a blue sky. He instinctively squinted, groggily trying to get his bearings. Carter was deep in the heart of his field, flat on his back. He sat upright, painfully aware that his head was pounding, and his stomach was churning. He wished he could have blamed Jim Beam, but he knew this was no hangover. He struggled to his feet and thought of one thing only: his cows. Carter half staggered to their sheds and tentatively peered inside. Thankfully, all was good: each and every head accounted for. Quenching a raging thirst was the next thing on his agenda. Two large bottles of water and a pot of coffee solved that.

As he sat at his kitchen table, his nerves still jangling, Carter poured over what happened the previous night. He remembered everything: the silence, the stars vanishing, the huge craft, his ricocheting bullets, and his crazed race for safety. But what happened to him during that missing period, which he figured lasted about four hours? No answers emerged. Finally overcome by exhaustion and the need for sleep, Carter made his weary way to bed. Unfortunately, there would be no peaceful slumber that night.

Around 3:00 a.m., Carter awoke with a wild scream, soaked in sweat. His mind was jammed with disturbing memories: a sense of being lifted into the dark sky from the damp floor of his field, of being transferred to a small, brightly lit room, and of being confronted by a trio of hideous, black-eyed dwarfs that loomed over him as he lay strapped to a long table. Most baffling of all, in the corner of the room stood a man in a military uniform. It was unmistakably the uniform of some high-ranking Air Force officer.

Carter recalled hearing the man ask: "How much of this will he remember?"

"He will remember as much of it as you want him to," replied one of the terrible goblins...*in an American accent.*

Carter stared at his bedroom ceiling, praying for a safety-net in a world suddenly turned upside down and inside out. He knew next to nothing about UFOs. Like most people, he had heard about so-called "alien abductions." He'd watched a television show on the subject a few years back. Bunch of wild-assed crazies, in his opinion. Now, he didn't know *what* to think: vanished cows, missing time, something enormous hovering low over his farm, and now that nightmare. *Jesus.* There was something else, too. Something Carter wouldn't know until he went into town the next day.

He wasn't the only Stephenville resident whose life was forever changed that night by something that came from the skies.

Fifteen year old Bailey Kasten peeked through the blinds of the family home on Maple Lane, patiently awaiting a friendly arrival. Bailey's parents were out for the evening and wouldn't be back until late, which meant one thing: their house was as quiet as a mouse. Well, it was quiet until Bailey's best pal, Melissa Davis, came over. Cue cranked up music, a couple of shots of tequila (did Bailey's parents think she didn't know where they hid the liquor cabinet key?), and a chat about the kinds of things that have always interested fifteen year old girls. That included Daniel Thomas, the new boy in town that Melissa had her sights set on. Unfortunately for Melissa, it was a chat that was suddenly, and rudely, interrupted.

As the girls sat on Bailey's bed, excitedly chatting about sixteen-year-old Daniel, an almighty roar brought their conversation to a complete and immediate halt. To say it was deafening would be an understatement. It may have lasted just a couple of seconds, but the noise practically shook the house to its very foundations.

"Holy shit!" screamed Melissa.

"What the f..." began Bailey, when a second, thunderous boom battered their eardrums.

Despite the complete state of shock into which both girls were suddenly plunged, they both knew what was going on: a couple of military planes had just shot over the neighborhood. Both girls had seen and heard such aircraft on a number of occasions. It was no big deal. Until now, that is. Typically, they flew at heights guaranteed not to scare the shit out of the neighborhood. But tonight was not what anyone could call a typical night, to say the very least.

The girls charged out of the front door, into the street. It seemed like everyone on Maple was doing exactly the same.

"Did you hear that, Mr. Stein?" shouted Bailey to the old man who lived directly opposite. Stupid question: *of course*, Mr. Stein heard it. It was 8:15 p.m. and he was out in the street in his dressing gown, looking at the sky. The Timms family was outside too, doing their best to calm down their Rottweiler, Max, who was tugging on his chain and barking furiously.

"F-16s, I'll bet," said Gary Timms to his wife, Karen, both of who were standing in the middle of the road, scanning the heavens. "Kind of low for a night-time exercise, though," Timms added. He was not wrong.

After a few minutes of chit-chat and theorizing, the residents of Maple Lane returned to their homes. The only sound left was that of Max, still angry as a result of having his early evening, post-dinner nap in the yard interrupted.

On the other side of town, Bob Mott was taking his garbage to the edge of the road. Tomorrow was collection day. Mott was almost to the road when he, too, had his ears pummeled and battered. That Mott was already outside was fortuitous since he was able to make out a brief glimpse of the afterburners of no less than three aircraft already vanishing into the distance. There's some shit going down *somewhere*, Mott thought, before returning indoors. If only he knew the truth of it.

As for Alison Parks, she too couldn't fail to hear the noise as she pulled up in her driveway on Good Tree Street. As Parks got out of her car and slammed the door behind her, two fighter planes – she had no idea what kind – roared overhead. She instinctively ducked, wondering what was up. It was a thought going through the minds of just about every other resident of Good Tree Street, too.

Then there was the Watkins family: Rob, Jen and their ten-year-old son, Adam. They were heading northbound on Highway 108 when no less than five small objects, all bright white in color and flying in formation, shot past the Watkins' Ford Taurus just above the tree line, giving every indication they were on a mission. To where, and for what purpose, the stunned family had no idea.

"Were they UFOs, dad?" asked Adam, excitedly, as the objects vanished in the distance.

Ashen-faced Rob glanced at Jen and, after a few seconds of silence, replied: "They just might have been, son; they just might have been."

Meanwhile, over at Proctor Lake, some 24 miles from Stephenville, John Wilford's dogs were going crazy. Taking no chances, Wilford quietly opened the door of his home, pistol in hand. Thinking that maybe a wild animal was roaming around – perhaps a skunk or even a coyote – he shone his flashlight around the darkened, shadowy property. No luck there. Nevertheless, something had got the dogs riled; there was no doubt about that.

For no particular reason, Wilford turned his attention to the skies above. His timing was dead on: in the skies above his property were seven or eight brilliant white lights, all traveling at a high rate of speed and heading west. Some new gizmo of the military? Perhaps. But what puzzled Wilford was the complete lack of sound. Aside from a slight wind, there was nothing. Wilford continued to watch until all of the strange lights were lost from sight and then returned inside. He should have stayed awhile longer.

Around two minutes later, the unmistakable sound of a fighter plane flying low and fast shook Wilford's home. By the time he got to the front door, it was all over. Another piece of the puzzle and another mystified soul. Wilford spent the remainder of the evening wondering what he had seen and heard. He chuckled to himself and, with his mind still filled with the images of those glowing, white lights, even wondered if maybe aliens were there to steal the lake's fish population. Had he known what was due to unfold just a few hours later, Wilford might have considered his wild theory not so wide of the mark, after all.

Shortly after midnight, three young guys, Matt Pye, Robert Bishop and David Summers, arrived at the 4,500 acre Proctor Lake to do a bit of after-hours fishing. The lake was home to a wide and varied variety of fish, including Bass, Catfish, Gar, Crappie, and Suckers. And although Texas Parks and Wildlife placed limits on the number of fish that could be bagged per day, that didn't matter a damn to Matt,

Robert, and David. They didn't even have fishing licenses: just a large ice cooler filled with beer and a couple of bags of chips. It was going to be yet another fun night for the three, catching fish, having a few drinks and having a good time. No, it wasn't going to resemble anything like that at all. As fate would have it, the night was quite unlike any other.

Hunkered down in a secluded, shadowy part of the lake – one that was surrounded by trees and bushes - the three had barely dug out their rods and cracked open the first round of cold ones when something very strange happened. The air became filled with a deep, throbbing hum. It was also a hum that provoked an intense feeling of nausea in the three friends. Almost simultaneously, they stopped drinking and looked at each other. Their faces were filled with pure fear.

"What's that?" asked Robert.

"Dunno, I don't feel so good," replied David, his voice shaking.

Matt's contribution: he vomited.

Then, without any formal invitation, the source of both the hum and the attendant effect on the trio put in appearance. The shocked friends watched, pretty much unable to move, as a large, black-colored, triangular shaped object slowly descended from the star-filled skies and to a point where it hovered just above the lake and maybe sixty feet from where they sat. The water noticeably rippled, and at times even quietly bubbled.

That the craft descended in complete silence and appeared to lack any windows or engines only added to the sheer terror that the midnight anglers were already experiencing. If that was not enough to plunge Robert, Matt and David into states of unbridled fear, what happened next most certainly was: the black triangle began to move, inch by inch, in their direction, just like an apex predator preparing for the kill.

None of the three were able to move even a single limb by this point. What they did was to scream. Again and again. Uncontrollably. For months afterward, they thought long and hard about what might have happened next had something not intervened at that very moment. But, intervene something did. In a style that practically defied belief and comprehension, the craft rose into the sky and was gone. Whoever was piloting it clearly had good instincts.

Only ten or so seconds after the UFO made its exit, a General Dynamics F-16 shot across the lake, obviously in hot pursuit of its far quieter quarry and on the same flight path. It was a flight-path, Robert, Matt and David later calculated, that would have taken both the unidentified craft and the F-16 first through the town of Dublin and then on to Stephenville – which was clearly fast becoming the target of attention.

In total, more than fifty separate events were reported that night – to police, to local military bases, and to the Stephenville media. But it wasn't just the world of officialdom or the town's newspaper, that was given the lowdown on what was going on. Several astute residents, and particularly so those who swore they had seen numerous F-16's chasing down a bunch of alien invaders in Stephenville's skies, surfed the Internet in an effort to find someone in the Lone Star State who collected reports of UFO encounters. The local flying saucer sleuth, in other words. One name kept cropping up, time and again: Marc Slade.

-3-

It was shortly before 6:00 a.m. when Marc Slade's telephone rang out at his Grapevine, Texas home and jolted him out of a dead sleep.

"Mr. Slade? Mr. Marc Slade?" asked a slightly hesitant female voice.

"Yeah, who's calling?" Slade groggily replied, expecting – and bracing himself for - bad news. After all, why else would anyone be calling at 5:51 on a Tuesday morning? Turns out it wasn't bad news. Little did Slade know it at the time, but it was the beginning of an entirely new Chapter in his life; although not necessarily a safe one.

"My name is Sally Richardson. You don't know me, but I got your number from the AQUA website. I think I saw a UFO last night, here in Stephenville."

Slade was used to getting phone calls out of the blue, but right now? Come on! Slade was about to ask – as diplomatically as he could, given the time of the morning - if he could call back in a couple of hours. But what Sally had to say next stopped Slade in his tracks: "I'm sorry for phoning so early, but I have to leave for work in half an hour, and I'm pulling a long shift, so I wanted to tell you right now. Mr. Slade, it looked like the UFO was being chased by a bunch of military aircraft. My whole family and our neighbor saw everything."

Suddenly, Slade was wide awake: "Miss Richardson, could you just give me a moment?" He scrambled out of bed, grabbed a pen and notepad and returned to the phone: "Okay, let me have the details; just about everything you can think of."

And that's how the day began. It continued right up until around 11:00 p.m. that night, by which time – after having answered around forty calls - Slade knew he was on to something big. Exactly how big would become apparent alarmingly and astonishingly quickly.

Marc Slade did not fit the image that most people envisage when it comes to a UFO researcher. Slade knew very well what most people thought of those that immersed themselves in the field of flying saucers: male, socially-challenged, paranoid, nerdy, and – in an absolute worst-case scenario – living in mom and dad's basement, surrounded by books, files, maps and a large poster of Mulder and Scully adorned with the words: *I Want To Believe*. Oh yeah, and no girlfriend or wife anywhere in sight. Admittedly, there were a few characters Slade knew that fitted the bill to the absolute tee, but, largely, it was a very wide of the mark generalization.

Slade's exposure to and involvement in the UFO phenomenon was a notable one. He grew up with his family on a small, scrub-treed, rocky ranch in Duncanville, Texas, a suburb of Dallas situated to the south of the Big D. In those days, Duncanville was still ranchland, one of which was the ranch that Slade, his sister Jane, and his parents Kirk and Helen called home. As a kid, Slade was happiest playing, and exploring the nearby dense woods, with his fiercely loyal boxer dog, Trixie. Venomous snakes, bobcats, and tarantulas were everyday sights. For Slade, however, they were not to be feared: they were all part and parcel of the excitement of living on a ranch. Then, one day, during school break, everything changed.

After a few hours roaming the woods on a bright, summery afternoon Slade and Trixie entered a clearing, one which afforded a near panoramic view of the blue skies above. As he looked up, Slade was amazed to see a highly-reflective, disc-shaped object crossing the sky: an honest to goodness flying saucer. Suddenly, a military plane – a jet, no less – was on the scene, clearly chasing the strange invader. As the pilot closed in on his unearthly quarry, the young and transfixed Slade caught sight of a bright flash. Of course, it *could* have been caused by a reflection of the Sun, but even as a kid, Slade suspected the UFO had just taken violent, defensive action against its pursuer.

That probability was reinforced when the aircraft suddenly plunged into a steep decline; one from which it was clearly not going to recover. Only seconds or so later, the pilot ejected. Slade watched, near-hypnotized and fascinated, as the pilot gently drifted downwards, like a leaf falling from one of the many trees that presently surrounded

Slade. The rumor around town was that the pilot was found alive and well and hanging by his parachute from a tree on the other side of the woods.

There was nothing gentle about the final moments of the aircraft, however. It hurtled violently into the ground – fortunately in a desolate field on the edge of town. In no time at all, a military retrieval team was on-site to recover what was left of the aircraft from the significantly-sized crater that its speedy, fiery descent had created. The official line was that the aircraft had suffered a malfunction. Slade, however, knew better, even if he was just ten years of age at the time. And, for Slade, that's how it all began. Twenty-five years later – at the age of almost thirty-six – Slade still had his eyes on the skies.

After finishing his education, Slade, at the age of nineteen, entered the Marine Corps. He stayed with them for four years, traveled the world, saw his fair share of combat, and lived life to its fullest. Slade also got to hear a few UFO stories while serving in the military: sightings involving pilots, alien abductions, and even the occasional crashed UFO incident – hushed up by the government, of course – were the talk of Slade and his buddies. It was all good fun and gossip, but it convinced Slade even more that there was a very real – and very serious – mystery to be solved.

It was also at this time that Slade – as well as hitting exotic locations on behalf of Uncle Sam, and notching up a notable number of conquests of the female kind – started subscribing to a variety of UFO journals and newsletters, as well as buying just about any and all books on the subject he could find.

With his career in the Marine Corps finally at its end, Slade entered college: specifically the University of Texas Business School in Arlington, Texas. Three years later, he graduated Summa Cum Laude. There followed significant positions with Merrill-Lynch and Lehman Brothers, and a life-defining period in which Slade played the stock market – to the extent that, thanks to skilled advice and investments, he retired from the rat-race at the enviable and early age of just thirty-three. And it was then that Slade hooked up with AQUA: *A*lien *Q*uest *USA*.

The United States' largest independent UFO research body, one with chapters in every state, Phoenix, Arizona-based AQUA had been around for decades and boasted membership that included astronauts, scientists, military personnel, and even a couple of retired politicians. Slade quickly became a team-player with AQUA, to the extent that after just fourteen months he was offered the position of "State-Coordinator." Basically, that involved overseeing the work of the group in the Lone Star State, collecting and investigating Texas-based UFO encounters, and keeping the AQUA board fully up to date on his group's work, investigations and findings.

Conferences were a big part of AQUA, too, and particularly so the yearly gigs at Phoenix, at which the leading lights of Ufology would turn up – many of them brimming with egos and filled with extravagant demands for suites, Jacuzzis and breakfast in bed. Slade, however, liked to keep it simple and loose: never one for settling down and having a family, he discovered pretty quickly that conferences were the ideal places to nail chicks in a no-strings-attached atmosphere. The girls liked Slade's toned, still-fit body and his head of red-blond hair ("It's all due to my Celtic roots," he would tell them, true or not), something that made him a UFO player in more than just one sense.

In other words, Slade was dedicated to the task in hand – namely, trying to figure out what was behind the UFO phenomenon and what it wanted with us, the Human Race – but he was a regular guy too, one that was just about as far from the stereotypical image of the UFO geek as possible. And that's just how he liked it. There was, however, something that Slade *didn't* like. More correctly, it was *someone*: AQUA's head-honcho, and ex-NASA guy, Brian Anderson.

To say that Slade and Anderson butted heads on more than a few occasions was not an exaggeration. As a guy who went where he wanted and when, Slade despised the overly officious, bureaucracy-filled world of AQUA, in which getting something done required votes, meetings, round-table discussions and late night phone calls. It was, he thought, just another example of the self-important, huffing and puffing attitude of just about every UFO research group out there.

Anderson, meanwhile, was the polar opposite to Slade. Anderson was suits, ties and jazz music. Slade was jeans, t-shirts, and classic

American rock. On top of that, sixty-something Anderson – who grew up in a rich, powerful family in New Orleans, and who had a near-obsessive love of regulations and order - despised Slade's footloose and fancy-free approach to life. He had to admit, however, that Slade had whipped the Texas office of AQUA into shape and had created a solid, unified group of team-players.

Still, it was clear to Slade that Anderson and he would never see eye to eye. Slade suspected it was simply because Anderson – the definitive "old guard" - felt threatened by the new kid in town. Slade was partly correct: Anderson did see Slade as a threat, but not for the reasons that Slade thought. The real reasons were far more disturbing, as Slade would soon learn as he dug deeper into the Stephenville affair.

On the morning after the day in which Slade's telephone flat out refused to stop ringing, he put in a call to Anderson.

"Boss-man, you heard what's going on in Stephenville?" said Slade, with a buoyant tone of enthusiasm in his voice. Slade had once overheard Anderson telling one of his AQUA cronies how much he hated Slade calling him "Boss-man," something that ensured Slade used the now well-worn phrase whenever and wherever possible.

"Marc, how are you and what are you up to?" replied the cultured Slade, in quiet, deliberate tones.

"I'm getting my shit together for a trip down to Stephenville, that what I'm up to." Slade gave Anderson a brief rundown on the dozens of calls he had received the day before, carefully stressing the fact that the military seemed to have played a central role in the affair. There was, however, something odd: this was the first time in any conversation that the pair had had, that Anderson had not interrupted Slade. Was the old man finally in a good mood? Not quite.

"Marc, Marc, put on the brakes. It's all taken care of," said Anderson, when Slade finally finished. "We're handling this one. Bridges is going to be heading it." Bridges was Andrew Bridges, a retired Air Force guy who lived just a few miles from Anderson in Phoenix.

Slade, stunned for a moment, shouted down the phone: "What the hell do you mean? I've busted my ass on this for the last twenty-four hours! I've got the contacts and the leads, and I've got the people's trust and attention. I can be down there inside two hours and get the investigation moving. What's the goddamn problem?"

Anderson was – audibly, at least – unmoved. "We started getting reports and calls yesterday, too. The committee made a quick decision and decided Bridges is the man for the job, particularly as there appears to be a significant military link. As he's retired-Air Force, he's the perfect choice."

"And I'm retired Marine Corps, if I need to remind you," said Slade through clenched teeth, adding: "And when has the committee ever done anything quickly?"

"Marc," added Anderson, "the decision is made. I'm going to give you an address where Bridges will be staying in Stephenville – we already have a motel-room booked for him. He'll be arriving there in two days' time, around 9:00 p.m., I think. You will overnight all of your notes, names and contact information on the witnesses to Bridges after his arrival."

Slade's response was hardly surprising: "Like hell I will!"

Anderson's voice went from calm to cold: "Don't force my hand, Marc. You've done great things for AQUA, but you're not the only person in Texas who can run the ship. And I might remind you that any data you have acquired in the last day is ours. Remember that contract you signed? I suggest you check it."

"And I suggest you stick it!" Slade shot back. He slammed down the phone. Bridges flying in from Phoenix and a room already booked for him? Headquarters taking over the case? Demanding all of Slade's notes of the past twenty-four hours? Slade himself practically told to back-off? Screw this, Slade thought. It was time for a road-trip. No prizes for guessing where to.

-4-

Only a few seconds after Slade terminated their conversation; Brian Anderson made another call. This one was to a Washington, D.C. number that very few people possessed. Or, more correctly, a number that very few people outside of the Pentagon possessed.

"Yes?" said the elderly voice at the other end of the line.

"It's Anderson."

"What is it?" asked the man, clearly impatient already.

"It's Slade; that's what," replied Anderson, his voice filled with frustration and noticeable concern. "He's not playing ball."

"What do you mean by that?"

"I mean, he has made it very clear he's not going along with things. He practically told me what to do and where to go, and now he's refusing to hand over his notes to Bridges."

"*Jesus*, didn't I warned you about Slade when you got him onboard?" asked the man, in hostile tones. "And didn't I tell you we needed someone who could run the group down in Texas, but who we could control and use as we needed to? I *told* you he had that loose-cannon attitude."

Anderson cleared his throat: "Yes, well, it's always worked – until now."

"Yes, *until now*. Okay, leave it with me. We'll figure something out. Things can still go ahead as planned. It just means we might need to do a bit of tweaking."

"What does that mean, tweaking?" asked Anderson, with a degree of apprehension. Admittedly, he didn't get along too well with Slade, but he didn't want anything to happen to him. Anderson knew all too well what his Pentagon contacts could do to make things run their way, rather than anyone else's way. And it could get very, very messy – and very easily and very quickly, too.

"Tweaking means, exactly that, Brian: tweaking."

"Okay," said Anderson, hesitantly. "What should I do now?"

"You should wait for me to contact you again; that's what you should do. Got it?"

"Yes, got it." The phone went dead.

General Robert Fowler brought his fist down hard on his huge, burgundy desk: "Damn Slade to fuckin' Hell!"

Back in Texas, Slade was still seething from his phone conversation with Anderson. It was time to clear his head and try and make some sense of the situation. There was just one option available to Slade: he headed off to his favorite Mexican restaurant, *El Arroyo*, on Cooper Street, Arlington for an early lunch. A big plate of nachos and a couple of margaritas would do the trick and help settle him down.

As he sat and ate his lunch, checking out his waitress and sipping on his frozen, salted drink, Slade tried to get his head around what had happened just a couple of hours earlier. There had been a couple of previous occasions when Anderson and Slade had clashed on how particular cases should be handled, but this was the first time that he, Slade, had been forcibly removed from a case. And what made it all the more mysterious was that it was a damned, good case, too.

And bringing in Andrew Bridges made no sense either. Bridges knew Texas like Slade knew the far side of the Moon. In other words: not at all. Slade, meanwhile, was well acquainted with Stephenville. Ironically, he had dated a girl from there a few years back – and for a couple of months. As a result, he knew the town like the back of his hand. And being a fellow Texan would surely help in getting the locals to talk, instead of having a cigar-chewing outsider like Bridges blustering and strutting around.

Slade wasn't usually one for paranoia, but he had a feeling that there was far more to all this than merely Anderson being his usual prick self. Slade thought: this is the biggest case that the Texas Chapter of AQUA has had fall into its lap in years, and I'm being elbowed out of the picture? Something didn't add up. Or, not yet it didn't. Of only one thing was Slade certain: if he wanted the answers he needed to get down to Stephenville, quickly. After ordering another margarita and doing his utmost to get the waitress' number, of course.

By 2:20 that afternoon, Slade was fired up and ready to go. One of the most important things that Slade's time spent in the Marine Corps ensured he knew all about being prepared; at all times. In the event that situations developed out of the blue, Slade always had a couple of bags already packed: clothes, cameras, binoculars, night-vision equipment, and state-of-the-art audio-visual technology: the works. And if this was not a perfect example of a situation developing out of the blue, then *nothing* was.

There was something else, too: Anderson had alerted Slade to the fact that Bridges wouldn't be getting into Stephenville until around 9:00 p.m., on the following night, which meant it would likely be the morning after that before Bridges stood any chance of getting involved in the case. Whether or not that was a slip of the tongue on the part of Anderson, it didn't matter. What *did* matter, however, was that Slade could be in Stephenville in about ninety minutes – the afternoon traffic notwithstanding, of course – and he could make good headway with the people who had called him and get moving way before Bridges' feet even touched Texas. There was, then, no time to lose. Slade loaded up his distinctive, yellow Corvette and hit the road to Stephenville - as did a white Honda Civic that kept a respectable distance behind Slade for the entire journey.

While most drivers would be oblivious to the fact, Slade knew when he was being tailed. Hell, he knew before he had even hit the accelerator. Slade had a keen, eagle eye for detail and, on getting back home from *El Arroyo* he couldn't fail to see the Civic parked just four doors down, outside the home of his fellow baseball fanatic, Jim Tibbs. He knew that Jim – a single guy, just like Slade – worked in Richardson during the day, so what was the car doing outside, and who was the guy in the driver's seat, practically smothered by a large newspaper? Slade made a mental note to keep his eye on both car and driver.

After pulling out of his garage, reversing into the street and driving to the junction, Slade glanced into his mirror. Sure enough, the

Civic was already moving, keeping its distance, but not enough to convince Slade it was just a case of coincidence and nothing else. If Slade had any doubts that he was being followed, they completely vanished when he decided to make a couple of stops: one to grab a soda at his local gas station and the other to drop a letter in the mail to his parents (yes, there were some people who still couldn't get used to email and his folks were among them). The driver of the Civic was never far behind: pulling in at a Starbucks over the road from the gas station and finding a space on the car-park of the Walgreens that stood adjacent to the Post Office. Well, thought Slade, and echoing the famous words of Sherlock Holmes: The game is afoot. Whatever the actual nature of the game, Slade would surely soon find out.

Slade briefly gave thought to trying to outrun and outmaneuver his pursuer, but then thought better of it. After all, the only thing he knew right now was that someone was following him. Losing sight of the driver would tell Slade nothing about why he was being shadowed, never mind who was pulling the strings. Reeling the guy in would be a far better, and much more profitable, way of dealing with the situation.

Roughly halfway to Stephenville, Slade made a bathroom stop. Not that he needed to, he just needed to create the pretense of wanting the bathroom. What Slade did need most of all was a way to get a look at the license plate on the Civic. After pulling into the QuikTrip and parking his car, Slade dug into his bag: he pulled out a small pair of powerful binoculars and stuffed them into his jacket pocket. Slade strolled inside and made his way to the bathroom, waited a minute or two, then returned to stock up on a couple of big bags of chips – admittedly not the healthiest choice, but one of Slade's favorite vices.

Slade paid for the items – deliberately with cash. As the bored-looking kid behind the counter gave him his change, Slade purposefully dropped it. "Shit!" he cried, purely for effect.

"Need any help?" asked the kid.

"No, I'm good, thanks," replied Slade. While on his knees, pretending to look for a couple of quarters, Slade whipped out his binoculars and scanned the parking area for the Civic. There it was, way over on the right and with the license-plate in full view. Gotcha!

Slade memorized the number, stood up, and was just about to leave when the kid behind the counter said, with a knowing smile: "Sir, I saw what you were doing."

Slade grinned: "Girlfriend trouble. You know what I mean?"

"What kind of girlfriend trouble?"

"That's her husband. *That* kind of trouble. Our secret?"

"Sure, no problem," the kid laughed.

If there was one thing that Slade liked in a situation such as this, it was being in control. Slade had a good friend in the Dallas Police Department – Kenny – who Slade could guarantee to get the plate checked out, without causing any hassle for either of them. Slade made his way to his pride and joy – his Corvette, of course – scribbled down the license plate number and fired up the engine. In seconds, the driver of the Civic did likewise. When he was back on the highway, Slade pulled out his cell phone, clicked on his "Contacts" and dialed one particular number.

"Kenny; it's Marc. How's it going, bud?"

"Hey, my man, when are we going to hit the town again?"

"Soon, man, soon," Slade laughed. "Listen, I need some help. Can you run a plate?"

"Well, yeah, but I'm not on until 11 tonight."

That was good enough for Slade. He gave Kenny the number. "Thanks, Kenny. First *and* second round are on me."

"You know I'm not going let you forget that," laughed Kenny.

Yep, Slade knew it: "Thanks, I'll call you tonight. Around midnight okay?"

"Sure, bud."

It was coming up to 4:00 p.m. Eight hours from now Slade would hopefully know far more about his mysterious shadow. But, taking into consideration everything that had already happened in the past day and a half, Slade wondered if whatever Kenny had to say would make things any clearer or just make the waters even murkier. Slade hoped it was going to be the former. Deep inside, however, he just knew it was going to be the latter.

-5-

A t approximately the very same time that Slade was heading down to Stephenville, Corey Hanks was heading down eight flights of stairs in an underground facility situated a little more than ninety miles from that very same town. His final destination: a long corridor and a couple of rooms that had been his place of work for the past three weeks. The spotless, metal steps echoed loudly with every clunk of Hanks' heavy, black combat boots. Never mind his job: considering how much time he spent here, it might as well have been his home, too, thought Hanks, as he finally reached the lowest level. Why they didn't just install a fucking elevator, Hanks couldn't fathom – regardless of who "they" might be. As it turned out, there *was* a reason, as Hanks would eventually come to learn.

Hanks worked for Black Stone, the largest private security corporation in the United States. Created back in the mid-1950s, it provided a variety of services for the military, numerous defense contractors, the Pentagon, the intelligence community, and an impressively large number of powerful companies stretching all across the United States. Protection, security, and surveillance were the three, primary, official functions of Black Stone. Then there were the *unofficial* ones: industrial-espionage, computer-hacking, putting the heat on "troublesome characters" – as Hanks' boss, John Sinclair, had once memorably worded it - and even a fair bit of breaking and entering, if it was deemed necessary, as it so very often was.

Someone who served his country in Iraq from 2003 to 2004, and on home territory until 2006, Hanks was recruited by Sinclair just as he was about to leave the service. It was a strange set of circumstances. But, then again, so was everything else about Black Stone. At the time his life changed, Hanks was stationed at Fort Hood, Texas. He could still recall the events of August 5, 2006 as if they had occurred yesterday.

23

Hanks was drinking coffee and snacking on a ham and mayonnaise sandwich for lunch in the base cafeteria when a tall, gaunt, elderly man approached the table. Dressed in an expensive suit and equally expensive shoes, he asked: "May I sit?" There was something about the tone of the question that suggested it would be extremely unwise to say no.

"Sure," replied Hanks, slightly puzzled.

"I've heard good things about you, Mr. Hanks. *Very* good things," said the man, displaying a smile that was as emotionless as it was as cold as ice. "You're leaving the service next month, correct?"

"Correct, but who are you?"

"Sinclair, John Sinclair," replied the old man, in "Bond, James Bond" tones.

"Is that your real name?" asked Hanks.

"Very good, Mr. Hanks, very good," said Sinclair, this time beaming a genuine smile while carefully avoiding answering the question. He pulled out of a black briefcase a dossier titled *Hanks, Corey Andrew* and placed it on the table, right in front of Hanks, and clearly for effect.

"What's this about, Mr. Sinclair?" asked a now slightly irritated Hanks, as he finished off the last of his coffee.

"It's about offering you a job. A very well paid job, plus pension and medical insurance."

Well, that wouldn't be a bad thing, thought Hanks. Times were tough and up until a couple of minutes ago it even looked like Hanks might be returning to his dad's car-repair shop in Euless for work.

"Have you, by any chance, heard of Black Stone?" inquired Sinclair, in a quiet voice.

"Yeah, of course, I have. Security, right? You did a bunch of private security stuff when I was out in Baghdad: 2003."

"Indeed, we did."

Sinclair opened the folder and began to read: "You will be twenty-six years of age next month, you distinguished yourself very admirably in Iraq, you are an excellent marksman, and you will soon find yourself looking for work. Am I correct on all points?"

Hanks laughed: "Yep, you're not wrong, Mr. Sinclair."

And that's how it all began. In the years that followed, Hanks found himself involved in all manner of clandestine activities. Preventing a terrorist cell from kidnapping a leading virologist who worked at the Dugway Proving Ground, "securing" a series of compromising photos from the former mistress of a certain, famous political figure, and installing listening devices in the home of the editor of one of the nation's most influential newspapers were just three of them.

Given the level of work that he had become used to, Hanks had to wonder why he was now on a ten-hour, five-days-a-week assignment; one that involved little more than sitting outside a large steel door in the underground section of a bare and largely abandoned installation. Who looked after things on a weekend, he had no idea. Sinclair had assured Hanks that this latest job was no slur on his character, that everyone was completely satisfied with his work and that in a little more than a month he would find himself on a brand new – and far more gratifying – assignment. For now, however, it was a case of grinning and bearing it. But as for why, there was only silence.

After taking the final step of those eight flights of stairs, Hanks strolled along an approximately three hundred foot long corridor, one which had a width of about fifteen feet and a height of roughly the same. The walls and floor were both a dazzling, polished white. The very end of the corridor opened up into a large room; it contained an office, soda and snack machines, a wall-mounted telephone, a large couch, and on the far, right-hand side: a huge, silver, steel door, the type of door one would expect to see in the vaults of a bank. Except: this was no bank.

It had taken Hanks only a few minutes to figure out that life here was hardly conventional. On his first day on duty – "on duty" basically meant just staying alert and ensuring that no-one, *ever*, managed to penetrate that huge door – a Blackstone employee was waiting for him to arrive at the main gates. After Hanks had parked his car, the two shook hands and embarked on the fifteen-minute or so walk that, by now, Hanks had become so used to taking.

Aside from himself, the only other person ever on-site – so far as Hanks could tell - was Elliott. That was Elliot Newland. He and Hanks hit it off immediately. It turned out that, just like Hanks, thirty-seven-year-old Elliott was into horror movies and bone-crunching rock music. Elliott was also a UFO buff; with good reason, or so he claimed.

Practically every morning was the same: Hanks would be sitting in the office, pretty much doing nothing beyond keeping one eye on the corridor for any unwanted intruders, when around two hours later, along would come Elliott; his long hair waving and his equally long legs marching. Invariably he would be dressed in a Nine Inch Nails, Rob Zombie, or Motley Crue t-shirt, plus jeans and sneakers. For a guy who, it seemed, was doing some pretty serious and secret work for someone behind that steel door, Elliott was not your typical microbiologist, even though he *had* intimated that this was indeed his job.

Two or three times a week Elliott would crack a joke while punching in the code to open the "pearly gates," as he referred to that otherwise-immovable door. That joke generally revolved around ensuring that Hanks kept his distance until Elliott was inside and the door was secured: "We don't want you to see the alien body we've got on ice, now do we, Corey?"

Funnily enough, Hanks had an interest in the UFO phenomenon: it stemmed from an incident that had occurred to a couple of his buddies in Iraq in 2004. It was nothing special; just a few odd, low-flying lights that no-one could ever identify. But it was enough to make Hanks check out a few books and television shows on the subject.

On a couple of occasions, Hanks wondered if the entire assignment was a test of his loyalty. On the very first day, he had been explicitly told by his Black Stone contact never to open the vault (even though he had been given the code), unless it was absolutely necessary and a last resort-style emergency. Then there was the matter of Elliott sharing Hanks' passion for rock music and horror movies. And it was Elliott who had brought up UFOs. Come to think of it, Sinclair had mentioned once about how the company did security out at the Nellis Range, Nevada – a certain portion of which was better known to one and all as Area 51.

Was this all some screwed-up mind-game, one designed to see if Hanks might take Elliott's bait, and take a peek behind that formidable door, thereby alerting his bosses to a major flaw in his ability to follow orders? Well, if that *was* the case, Hanks wasn't going to fall for it. He would play the good soldier, do his job, and in a couple of weeks' time, move onto something bigger and better. It is strange how such well-thought out plans can go totally awry.

Since Elliott always wore sneakers to work, hearing him walking up the long corridor was always a difficult task, and particularly so when the air-conditioning was pumping out. But when, today, Hanks heard the unmistakable sound of shoes on concrete, he flew into action. He knew it wouldn't be Elliott; not just because of the shoes, but because of the time factor, too: Elliott never arrived before around 10:00 a.m., and right now it was only 8:45. Hanks already had one hand on his holster as he cautiously peered around the wall of the room in which he now spent so much of his time. His eyes almost popped. It was Sinclair.

"Not going to shoot me, were you, Corey?" asked Sinclair, adopting his customary fake smile. He always called everyone by their first names, which was odd in light of his detached manner.

"No sir, just staying alert," replied Hanks, forthrightly.

"That's good. Open the door, please."

"*Sir?*" said Hanks. "Shouldn't we wait for Elliott?"

Sinclair's face turned grim: "*The door: open it.*"

As Hanks tapped in the code and took a grip on the large metal handle and began to pull, Sinclair asked him: "Do you have any idea what you have been guarding the past three weeks?"

"No, sir," answered Hanks, as he released the handle and looked Sinclair firmly in the eyes.

A slight grin crossed Sinclair's lips: "None at all?"

Hanks offered a small laugh in return: "Well, only what Elliott keeps joking about."

"And what it is that Elliott keeps joking about?"

"That the bodies from Roswell are in there. You know; the UFO crash, 1947, New Mexico."

"Oh yes, I know. I watched *The X-Files*, too," said Sinclair. Hanks thought: my god, the old man cracking a joke. Whatever next? Quite a bit, that's what.

"But haven't you got that slightly wrong about Elliott, Corey?" asked Sinclair.

"No sir, that's his standing joke. I guess there's nothing else to say or do around here."

"No, Corey, Elliott has *never* told you anything about alien bodies being in the vault."

"Sir, he…"

Sinclair jumped in quickly: "I repeat, he has *not* joked about alien bodies; what he has joked about is an alien body: *just one.*"

Hanks' mind raced. Sinclair was right: Elliott *did* only ever talk about one body. The UFO subject was filled with people – some more credible than others – who claimed to know where "the bodies" were kept, but now that Hanks thought about it, very few people had made claims about knowing the alleged, final resting place of just *one* E.T. Even if it *was* just a joke on Elliott's part, that factor made Hanks wonder where things were leading.

Sinclair motioned Hanks to one side, his face became even grimmer than ever when he pulled hard on the door and said: "Come with me."

Hanks followed Sinclair into a room of around forty feet by thirty feet, which contained nothing but a bath-sized, metallic, freezer-like unit sitting on top of a series of metal struts and supports. The lack of pretty much *anything* else in the room begged a major question: what on earth was Elliott doing in such a place all day long? The door at the rear of the room suggested that whatever Elliott was up to, his work took him to the *other* side of that door. Hanks wondered: Just how big *is* this complex? Circumstances dictated that the question quickly evaporated from Hanks' mind.

"Take a look," said Sinclair to Hanks, as he pointed towards that solitary container. The walk, of around twenty-five feet, seemed to take forever. Hanks' legs felt like they were wading through mud. His mouth went dry. His mind raced: it's not possible. It can't be; not a dead alien. It just *can't* be. Hanks placed his hands on the sides of the container, took a deep breath, and slowly peered into the slightly misted glass top.

-6-

On reaching Stephenville, Slade's first stop was his motel: the Holiday Inn on Lockhart Street. Sure enough, the white Honda Civic was still faithfully stalking him. In one sense, that was a good thing. If the guy behind the wheel also decided to check in there for the night, it would give Slade the opportunity to perhaps do a bit of stealthy, middle-of-the-night sabotage on that damned car. Slade checked in for three nights, made a quick trip to his room, dropped off his bags, and called Sally Richardson – the woman who had got him into this mess in the first place.

"Hi, Mrs. Richardson, this is Marc Slade."

"Mr. Slade!" she replied, excitedly. "Thank you so much for calling back."

"Sure, no problem. I'm in town. Could we meet up, maybe tonight?"

"You can come over right now if you'd like to. You still have my address?"

"I sure do; sounds like a plan!" Things were working out nicely.

As Slade left the Holiday Inn, he couldn't fail to notice that the Civic was nowhere in sight. Whether that was a good or bad thing, Slade wasn't sure. Never mind, he had work to do. Twenty minutes or so later, Slade was sitting on Sally Richardson's couch, sipping on a welcome glass of sweet ice tea.

Sally's home was a spacious one, filled with designer furniture, cool artwork and quite possibly the biggest television set Slade had ever seen. Out back was a huge yard, one that was dominated by large swimming pool and a couple of soccer nets. A small white dog was fast asleep on a patch of well-worn grass. While Sally was busy in the kitchen rustling up a couple of bowls of chips and dip, Slade made a quick check of the family's bookshelves, which were situated on the right side of the room. Slade knew that a great deal could be learned from studying a person's books.

Just a few years previously, Slade had been given a great alien abduction-themed story by a guy in Fort Worth; a guy who swore he knew nothing about the UFO subject. Slade was, admittedly, impressed by the story told to him. It was one filled with tales of black-eyed aliens, missing time, and diabolical, genetic experiments. Slade quickly became far less impressed, however, when – on paying a visit to the bathroom – he caught sight of a huge bookcase standing against the wall of a cluttered bedroom. Slade groaned inwardly: on the top shelf he could see the familiar, iconic cover of Whitley Strieber's best-selling book, *Communion*.

A quick and quiet scan of the rest of the shelves revealed a ton of Brad Steiger's books, just about everything published on Roswell, a couple of Von Daniken titles, and dozens of other books on everything from the Men in Black to Area 51, and from the Face on Mars to the Bermuda Triangle. It wasn't long before the truth tumbled out and the guy's story came crashing to the ground: Slade's source was a full-on UFO obsessive, fantasy-prone, and just looking for a bit of excitement in his otherwise solitary life. Slade audibly sighed with relief that Sally Richardson's bookshelves were totally UFO-free.

"You like books, Mr. Slade?" asked Sally as she reentered the room, armed to the teeth with a bevy of snacks.

"I do, yes," he replied with a smile.

"Me and Andrew – my husband – we have always encouraged David and Christina, our kids, to read. And to get some exercise, too!" she added with a laugh. "We all ride bikes, swim in the pool and David's in a local soccer team. That's what led us to see the …whatever it was we saw."

"How's that?" asked Slade.

"Well, it was a chilly night, but David and Christina were kicking a ball around the yard; I was playing with the dog and Andrew was chatting over the fence with our neighbor, Jack. If we'd been inside we would have heard it all, but it would have been over before we could have got outside."

31

"You mind if we go outside so I can get an idea of how it went down?"

"No, not at all," Sally replied genially.

As they went outside, the little dog immediately woke, raced over to Sally, lay on his back, and demanded to have his belly rubbed. "Don't mind Buster, Mr. Slade; tickle his tummy, and he will be your friend for life." As a lifelong dog lover, Slade gave the little fellow exactly what he wanted. Then it was down to business.

Slade knew the most profitable way to get the facts was to simply sit back and let the witness tell their story, which is exactly what Slade did.

"It was Christina who first noticed it," Sally began. "She pointed to what looked like a group of satellites going over, right over the house, but very slowly. And I mean *really* slowly. But what was weird was they were flying in a rectangle formation, and they didn't seem to be that high either. Normally, with satellites they're on their own, right? Well, as we all watched it, Mr. Palmer – that's Jack – pointed out that it wasn't four objects in a formation, but four lights on the corners of just *one* object. As it was already getting dark, we were focusing on the lights and not realizing that between the lights was a solid black thing. But the weird thing is there was no noise; nothing."

Sally continued: "None of us are experts on aircraft, but you don't have to be to know that aircraft aren't rectangular! Well, we kept watching it until it started to fade in the distance. But as it did, there was this deafening sound and three planes came shooting over the street. It was like World War Three was starting. They were definitely military, and they were flying right in the direction of the object. But, as we watched the planes, we could see that the object was gone, which kind of made us think it had shot away when the planes got close. Now, this was about 7 or 7:15, but I mentioned it to a few friends at work and one of them, on the other side of town, heard a plane flying low and fast around 8:30, so maybe it came back. That's pretty much it: just a quick minute or so of looking at the object and trying to figure out what it was before the planes arrived."

Slade asked Sally to run through the story one more time, ensuring that just about every aspect of the encounter was covered. Slade developed a good, solid vibe, and even more when, a couple of hours later, he had the opportunity to interview both the rest of the family and Jack, the guy next door. The phone calls of the previous day were important, but there was nothing like sitting opposite a witness, gauging their reactions and assessing their mannerisms. Slade felt that quickening of his pulse that always kicked in when his instincts told him he was onto something major.

Slade hung out with the Richardson family until around 9:00 p.m. then made his way back to the Holiday Inn. On arriving, he carefully circled the entire car-park. Sure enough, there was the Honda Civic, parked just about as far from the entrance to the motel as was conceivably possible. Slade was pleased that, if nothing else, the driver was predictable. That would, at least, Slade surmised, give him the upper hand if things became dangerous – as he strongly suspected they might.

By the time Slade had unpacked his bags, taken a much-needed shower and cracked open a bottle of Jack Daniels, it was coming up to 10:30. In just ninety minutes, Kenny would hopefully be able to shed some light on the guy behind the wheel of that Honda Civic.

Given that Kenny had a busy job, Slade held off from calling until about 12:30. At least that way, Slade wouldn't be on his friend like a bold of lightning. Slade had to admit, however: that extra half an hour sure as hell went by slowly. Finally, it was thirty past the witching hour and the time had come.

"Hey, Kenny; it's Slade."

"Give me a minute but don't hang up," Kenny said, in a noticeable whisper. That didn't bode well, Slade thought.

After about forty-five seconds, Kenny was back: "Okay, I'm here."

"Where's here?" asked Slade.

"The bathroom. What the fuck are you into?"

"What do you mean?"

"I mean are you still just doing the little green men shit?"

"Well, yeah."

"And nothing else? By that, I mean nothing else that's even vaguely going to piss off someone in a suit and with a lot of influence?"

"Nope, not a thing. Kenny, what's going on?"

In even more whispered tones, Kenny replied: "That car: it's registered to Homeland Security; an office down in Houston. That's all I could find out. But I guess that's enough on its own, right?"

"Holy shit," said Slade, in startled tones. He didn't know what to expect, but it's safe to say he wasn't thinking about Homeland Security.

"Yes, indeed, my friend: holy shit."

Slade was about to say something else when Kenny butted in. "Marc," he began, "this is serious shit. You are being tailed by Homeland Security. You do know what that means, right? Whatever you're doing, you're pissing off someone big time. And Homeland Security is not the sort of agency to piss off."

Slade's mind began to race in different directions: "Kenny, thanks so much, pal. I'm gonna have to try and figure this one out alone. I don't want any of this getting back to you."

"If I could get into this deeper for you, man, I would. You know that, right?" said Kenny, in apologetic tones. "But, I can't go knocking on the kinds of doors I would have to knock on to get anything else."

Slade completely understood. His friend had already done more than enough. Kenny had done something else, too: he had convinced Slade that whatever was going on in Stephenville it just might turn deadly.

After hanging up with Kenny, the first thing Slade did was to turn off all the lights in his room. He walked to the window and carefully, and very slightly, pulled the curtain to one side. The external night-lights of the Holiday Inn afforded a good view of the parking area below Slade's window. Everything was quiet and still. It was clichéd and predictable, thought Slade, but it all seemed *too* quiet and still. Whether that was a good or a bad thing, Slade wasn't sure. Nevertheless, he was pleased he had brought a pistol with him.

For the next two hours, Slade lay on his bed, cross-legged, and sipping on Jack Daniels. He played over in his mind – time and again -

everything that had happened. First, there were the phone calls from the witnesses – around forty of them, no less, as many of who he intended to catch up with in person over the next few days. Clearly, a major event had occurred.

Then there was the previously-unheard of actions of that fucker, Anderson, telling him that Stephenville was out of bounds – like it or not. And now Slade had Homeland Security on his back. This made Slade sit up, take notice, and think of something else: Anderson was retired-Department of Justice and Andrew Bridges was ex-Air Force Intelligence.

Slade thought: just how "retired" and "ex" were Anderson and Bridges? Maybe they weren't – in the slightest. For as long as he had been with AQUA Slade had heard allegations that the organization was a front for people in government that secretly kept tabs on not just the UFO issue itself, but the research community, too. Slade had dismissed all the stories as paranoia run wild. But, just maybe, those same stories weren't so crazy, after all.

"Talk about trust no-one," Slade said aloud, as he took a final hit of Jack.

-7-

A brand new day brought with it a brand new atmosphere. Although Slade was still unable to shake off the uneasiness that came with the revelation that none other than the Department of Homeland Security was seemingly keeping tabs on his every movement, a hot shower, a tasty breakfast of eggs, bacon, jelly, toast, and orange juice, and a bright sun in the clear morning sky all helped to put him in a far better frame of mind. Even so, there was no doubt that Slade was now well and truly up to his neck in a world filled with uncertainty and, in all likelihood, danger. In fact, of just *one* thing only was Slade certain: what had begun as a regular, albeit very intriguing, UFO investigation was rapidly turning into something else entirely. And that didn't just go for Slade, but for the people of Stephenville, too.

As Slade tucked into his breakfast at a typical mom and pop-style diner (always his favorite kind of spot for a hearty meal), he couldn't fail to notice that practically everyone in the place was eagerly chatting about the UFO wave of the last couple of nights. There was a very good reason for that: the local newspaper was now hot on the trail of the aerial action.

"Did Aliens Visit Stephenville?" was the eye-catching headline that leaped off the front-page of the latest edition of the *Stephenville Journal*. Slade had picked up a couple of free copies from the front desk of the Holiday Inn and carefully read the three-quarter-page article as he ate. The writer, Jenny Abbott, had done a pretty good job: there were three or four witness accounts, a fairly detailed reference to the F-16 angle, and denials from staff at no less than three military facilities that they had anything flying around at the times in question. There was, of course, the obligatory and inevitable photograph of a "little green man," as well as a "take me to your leader"-style joke thrown in for good measure. But, thought Slade, as it was probably the biggest thing to have occurred in Stephenville for a long time, why not let the townsfolk have a bit of fun and bask in the fact that E.T. had put them on the map?

Speaking of the townsfolk, and with his breakfast now finished, it was time for Slade to get on the road and hook up with as many of the people who had phoned him just a couple of days earlier as was possible. And that's precisely what Slade did – and for roughly the next eight hours. First, there was Bobby Key. A car mechanic, Key, shortly after sunset on the first night that things got crazy, saw a curious, long line of white lights in the night sky and heard the roars of what he figured were at least a couple of jets flying fast and low. Ryan Clarke had seen what he described as a "large black square" moving low over the north side of town around 10:00 p.m. Mary Keel and her daughter, Joanne, had been visiting friends in Waxahachie and, roughly thirty minutes after Clarke's sighting, saw a gigantic, dark colored craft cross the skies at a distance of around a quarter of a mile from them. Jamie Masterson, after finishing her late shift at a local fast-food outlet, caught sight of a group of small orb-like objects flying silently over a field on the west side of Stephenville. And the list of witnesses went on and on, as did their extraordinary reports of encounters with what could only be termed the unknown.

Slade skipped lunch, chiefly to try and get as much work done as he could that day. As a result, and by 7:30 p.m., his stomach wasn't just growling. It was practically screaming to be fed; as in *now*. Not feeling like driving around town to find a good place to eat, however, Slade decided to head back to the Holiday Inn. After all, it had a good menu and a well-stocked bar, and – after filling his stomach – all Slade had to do was to take a walk up to his room and crash out. If only it could have been that easy.

As Slade pulled into the car park, he couldn't believe his luck – if luck is what it was; maybe it was one of life's strange synchronicities. Just getting out of a certain Honda Civic – none other than the very one that had been Slade's constant companion on his drive down to Stephenville – was a tall, black-haired man dressed in a dark jacket and pants, and an open-neck shirt. Finally, and under the light of the powerful illumination that lit up the parking area, Slade was able to get a good look at the forty-something guy who had been tailing him.

Slade thought quickly: play it cool; play it *very* cool. In a second, he made a mental note of the man, his appearance, and his dress and pulled into a parking space not too far from the entrance. Slade watched as the man walked into the lobby, not once turning around. After a few minutes, Slade followed suit. Slade glanced around the area. The staff aside, there was no-one to be seen, aside from a young couple checking in.

After quickly freshening up, Slade headed downstairs to the restaurant. Since it wasn't even a quarter full, he chose a table against the far wall, one which afforded him a perfect view of the entire restaurant. Slade was always planning ahead, just in case. It was a wise decision. Slade was about two minutes into his well-cooked steak, baked potato and Jim Beam when in walked none other than Mr. Homeland Security himself.

Slade's time with the Marine Corps had taught him how to assess situations and when to sit tight and when not to. Right now, at least, he elected to remain in sit tight mode; although his grip on that trusty, well-sharpened steak-knife increased significantly.

It was, perhaps, inevitable that the man should sit just two tables away from Slade, who thought: yep, close enough to keep any eye on me but not too close to make it obvious. After the waitress had taken his drink order, the man did an admittedly good job of feigning casualness and asked Slade: "What's the steak like tonight?"

"Pretty good, actually," Slade replied, feigning geniality. It was game on.

The waitress returned with the man's rum and coke and inquired about dinner. "I'll take the pork chop and the mashed potatoes," the man answered. The girl complimented him on his "fine choice," something she had no doubt done a thousand times in the past and headed for the kitchen.

For Slade, it was now or never. He could sit tight and try and figure out why Homeland Security was on his back, or he could put the ball solidly in his court. The latter was the only option if Slade was going to get to the bottom of things.

"Not having the steak?" he asked.

"No, been a while since I had a good pork chop."

"I figured it was for another reason."

"What's that?" was the reply, which was accompanied by a sudden and sharp frown.

"That Homeland Security's budget doesn't run to twenty-five dollar steaks."

The man took a deep breath and his jaw dropped slightly. For a moment, there was silence. Slade's words had clearly hit home and left a major mark. In a second the guy had recomposed himself. But, it was still a second too late. Kenny was right on the money about who this character was working for.

"I don't follow," the man bluffed in less than convincing tones.

"Sure you do," replied Slade, in authoritative fashion, and while clearly in control of the now-irreversible situation. "Your car: Homeland Security. The Houston office. You tailed me from just about my driveway to right here. Remember? I mean, it *was* only yesterday!"

Slade noticed the man was wearing a wedding ring and went for the jugular: "How about I return the favor and pay your wife a visit and do a bit of surveillance of the bodily kind while you're off playing your 007 games?"

The man glared at Slade but maintained his pretense: "Pal, you have me mixed up with someone else." He attempted to end the conversation with an abrupt three words: "Enjoy your evening."

Slade piled on the power: "*No*, I do *not* have you mixed up with someone else. And, yes, you *do* work for Homeland Security. Shall we stop with all the bullshit?"

"Sir, I have no idea who you are. I will say it once again and once only: you have me mistaken." The atmosphere couldn't have gotten colder if a new Ice Age had kicked in. There then followed a downright surreal situation in which Slade sat back, casually ate his steak and drank his whiskey. He had a fine time flirting with the waitress and was careful to display a shit-eating grin of mammoth proportions every time his nemesis glanced in his direction.

Slade knew that, before the night was over, Homeland Security – and whoever was likely at the top of the chain – would come to realize that they weren't dealing with some *X-Files* geek. While Slade certainly didn't have a clue as to why he was being watched – and watched very closely – he did know that sending a signal to whoever was responsible for this screwed-up affair placed him in a very commanding position.

After finishing his dinner, Slade stood up and, with more than a bit of sarcasm in his voice, said: "I'll be in the lobby about 8 o'clock tomorrow morning, and after breakfast I'll be doing a bit of detective work around town. You know, just thought I'd make it a bit easier for you. Try and keep up!" The only response: another glare.

Ten minutes after Slade was out of sight, the man flung a fistful of dollars on the table and left the restaurant, his pork chop only half-eaten. He entered the elevator and pushed the button for the fifth floor. Even in the few seconds it took the elevator to reach its destination, the man paced around its cramped confines. He practically jogged to his room, threw his jacket onto the bed, and took out his cell-phone and dialed.

"Harris. It's me, Simmons," he said.

"What's going on?" replied Harris, a man with a distinct and deep Bostonian accent.

"Slade's onto me."

Harris exploded: "I told you about keeping your distance! Slade is an ex-Marine, for Christ's sake! He's not your average Joe!"

"I'm not talking about *me* fucking up, Harris!" Simmons shouted down the phone. "He identified me - in the fucking hotel restaurant!"

"What do you mean, he identified you?" asked Harris, puzzled.

Simmons took a deep breath, one borne out of frustration and stress: "I mean he totally ID'd me: Homeland Security, Houston, everything!"

"*Impossible!*" Harris spit back.

"I'm telling you! He knows; the man *knows*!"

After a few moments, Harris – in somewhat calmer tones – said: "Well, that changes things somewhat and…"

"I'll say it does!" interrupted Simmons.

"Let me finish, Simmons. *Let me finish.* Clearly someone has been talking out of turn. Leave that to me. Get yourself back to Houston, and we'll figure out things from here."

"Okay, you're sure?" asked a somewhat relieved Simmons.

"Yes, I'm sure. I wouldn't have said so if I weren't."

Darren Simmons hung up and sat on the side of the bed: it had not been one of his best assignments. It had, however, been his strangest: watching a UFO freak? Hadn't the Air Force given up on all that stuff years ago? Simmons knew well enough not to ask questions of his bosses; only to deliver the goods. But even so: UFOs?

In his office at CIA headquarters in Langley, Virginia, Michael Harris – of the agency's Science and Technology Directorate – pondered for a while on this puzzling and vexing issue, and also on the fact that, in just a couple of days, Marc Slade had demonstrated exactly how much of a complete pain in the ass he really could be.

-8-

Despite the whirlwind events of the last few days, Slade felt more than satisfied with the way things were going. He had, after all, secured a solid body of witness testimony, pretty much confirmed that the military had given chase to one or more unidentified aerial objects over Stephenville, and determined that as a result of his actions, he was on the radar of at least one agency of officialdom. Some people might have reacted with fear and apprehension at the notion of being watched by "the government." Not Slade: he'd seen, and deftly and decisively handled, far worse in the Middle East just a few years earlier. There was, of course, something else he had to handle: the arrival, last night, from Phoenix, Arizona, of Andrew Bridges.

Slade had managed to briefly forget about Bridges while speaking with the locals about their encounters and while verbally jousting with Homeland Security. But, just like that pesky cockroach which refuses to roll over and die, it was inevitable that Slade would be hearing from Bridges soon. As it turned out, Slade didn't cross paths with Bridges, after all – at least, not right then. Instead, it was left up to AQUA's main man, Brian Anderson, to do all the dirty work. Slade was about to leave the Holiday Inn around 2:00 p.m. when the call arrived.

"Slade: it's Anderson," were the three, terse words that Anderson offered by way of a greeting.

"Well, hi there, Brian. How are things, good buddy?" Slade replied in cheery tones, ones that got Anderson even more riled than he undoubtedly already was.

"Slade, I'm not calling to chat. What I *am* calling to tell you is that you are officially off the case, and you are officially out of AQUA. Bridges got into town late last night. He's been going through the local newspaper this morning and called up the people mentioned in there, and guess what?"

"Well, I wouldn't rightly know. *What?*" Slade replied, his voice brimming with sarcasm.

"That *you* have already been in touch with them and that *you* have done lengthy interviews with them, too; that is what. You were *explicitly* told to stay off the case, that we wanted Bridges to handle this one, and that this was how it was going to be. You ignored every order, and so you leave me no choice but to inform you your time with AQUA is over."

Anderson's smug tones suggested to Slade that the leech was more than happy with himself and equally more than happy that Slade was no longer a thorn in his side. What Slade said next, however, took the wind right out of Anderson's sails.

"Suits me, Brian; after all, you've just cut me loose: I'm a free agent now. What I do here in Stephenville is my business." Slade knew he had just trumped Anderson. His lack of a reply, beyond slamming the phone down, made that very clear.

So, it had finally happened. Slade knew the day was coming. But, for it to have come at the very time Slade needed to be on his own was a godsend. He could now do exactly what he wanted and when. And, he wasn't answerable to anyone. Slade certainly wasn't going to make an effort to speak with Bridges if he ran into him in Stephenville – and the chances were that he probably would – but he wasn't going to make an effort to avoid him either.

In fact, upon thinking about it, Slade wondered if it might not be a bad idea to confront the man, after all. With Homeland Security now on the scene, Slade couldn't help but wonder if Bridges, as ex-Air Force Intelligence, might not be tied up with the guy from Homeland, the very guy who just happened to be buzzing around a couple of days before Bridges' arrival.

This suggested to Slade an even bigger issue: just maybe, Bridges, Homeland, AQUA, and Lord knows who else, were all one big happy family. By now, thought Slade, just about anything was possible. As he saw it, the best thing to do was remain visible and in the public eye. Slade might have considered it nothing but outright paranoia just a few days ago, but based on what had gone down, he now had major concerns about his safety. Not that Slade couldn't take care of himself;

quite the opposite, in fact. But it wouldn't hurt to make himself known around town to a more significant degree. He searched out his copies of the *Stephenville Journal*, phoned the main line, and asked for Jenny Abbott, the woman who had first unleashed the story of the Stephenville UFO flap on the town.

"Miss Abbott?"

"Yes, who's calling?" replied a bright and friendly voice.

"You don't know me, but my name is Marc Slade and I..." Slade was quickly interrupted.

"I know *exactly* who you are, Mr. Slade," said Abbott, with a chuckle. "You're quite the man about town, aren't you? Getting to know all our UFO spotters for your AQUA group, right?"

"Well," said Slade, slightly uneasily, "it's a long story, but the investigation is a personal one, now. No more AQUA."

"Right," said Abbott, thoughtfully, as she dragged out the word, clearly and astutely assuming there was far more to Slade's sudden departure from what she had soon come to learn was the United States' biggest UFO research society.

"Maybe we can do a profile on you, for the newspaper? Get your thoughts on what's going on here?" That was fine with Slade. And when Abbott added that she much preferred dealing direct with the boots on the ground and not with a bunch of bureaucrats, Slade knew he had done the right thing by making the call. Within thirty minutes, the two were chatting, over coffee, in the lobby of the Holiday Inn.

Slade liked Abbott: thirty-something, professional, looking for a good story, and not closed-minded or condescending on the UFO topic, she listened carefully and asked questions carefully, too. Not a bad looker either: brunette, leggy, nice smile. Of course, most of the questions were predictable: how did Slade get interested in UFOs? Did he believe aliens were visiting the planet? And, most important of all, were those same aliens hanging around in Stephenville? Slade knew it was important to balance the facts with a few light-hearted comments for local media outlets. He had to remember this wasn't an article for UFO enthusiasts: it was intended for the folk around town who were all agog with talk of flying saucer pilots coming to say hello.

Abbott explained that a full-page article would appear in the next issue of the *Journal*. Since the newspaper was a weekly, rather than a daily, however, there was a bit of a problem. Abbott's worry was that without regular updates, the story would stall, and the locals would lose interest. "Lose interest," Slade clearly understood, meant "not buying the newspaper."

So, Abbott had an idea: an online article at the *Journal's* website, one that would profile Slade (both man and UFO researcher alike), provide the readers with his thoughts on the sightings in and around Stephenville, and include Slade's contact information. This latter issue, Abbott said, would allow Slade to get on the receiving end of any new developments and allow him to promote those same developments via the newspaper's website.

Slade laughed: "Miss Abbott – I take it that it's Miss and not Mrs.?"

Jenny Abbott laughed in return and said: "Yes, it's Miss."

Good start, thought Slade. "I like the way you think, Jenny. I get something, you and your paper get something, and Stephenville gets something too."

"That's about it," smiled the town's burgeoning Woodward & Bernstein combined.

With work complete, Slade casually asked: "So, how about dinner tonight: got any plans?"

"Yep," she replied.

"Boyfriend?"

"Nope: writing and uploading the latest scoop on what E.T. wants with Stephenville," she answered while getting out of her chair and preparing to leave. Slade couldn't deny Jenny Abbott's enthusiasm. They shook hands, with Abbott promising to call Slade as soon as the article was posted, which was likely to be around 7:00 p.m., Abbott estimated.

After a fine Italian dinner - one which Slade would have preferred not to have spent alone, but which was actually not a bad thing, since it gave him the time to mull over all of the events that had gone on in the last few days – he drove back to his hotel and arranged to extend his stay in Stephenville for another week. Slade had a feeling he was going to need it. He was heading towards the elevator when his cell-phone rang.

"Marc; it's Jenny." That's good, Slade thought: first names on both sides in just a few hours. "Just wanted to let you know the article is online; front-page of the website. Hope you like it. See you later!" The phone was dead before Slade had a chance to utter even a single word.

On getting back to his room, Slade fired up his laptop and clicked on the link to the *Stephenville Journal's* website. Slade's picture dominated the right-side of the article. The photograph was a familiar one: it had been copy-pasted from his bio page at the AQUA homepage. Exactly what Brian Anderson might think about *that* bit of pilfering, a smiling Slade couldn't help wondering.

Slade knew that, in the light of the fact that Homeland Security was getting acquainted, it was all too likely that someone was monitoring his cell phone. Slade preferred not to go down the pathway to George Orwell's *1984*, but he couldn't ignore the possibility that any leads that developed from the article might not just reach his ears. It was a chance he had to take.

Twenty minutes after the article appeared, chaos erupted in Slade's room: it was as if the planet and its brother – maybe it entire family – had descended on Slade. New York, Los Angeles, Hong Kong, London, and Australia: the calls were coming in thick and fast. It wasn't just the people of Stephenville, or even Texas, that had heard of the Lone Star State UFO invasion: it was now the *world*, too. By midnight, Slade had done about fifteen brief interviews and spoken with four more witnesses, two of whom had very interesting stories to tell, one involving what sounded almost like Men in Black-style intimidation. They were all on his list for tomorrow. After quenching his thirst with a cold bottle of water, Slade hit the sack. It was twelve-thirty. Slade didn't know it, but in less than two hours he would be wide awake again.

The sound of Slade's cell-phone instantly woke him out of a dead sleep. "Hello?" he said, expecting a foreign accent and a faraway journalist. It was neither. It was a woman with an American accent who said she needed to speak with Slade as soon as possible.

"Well, how about now?" Slade replied, careful not to risk losing what might be a good lead. He looked at the screen of his phone. It read "Number Withheld." Typical.

"Mr. Slade," the woman began; her voice was both deliberate and sharp. "There's something you need to know about Stephenville and why it was chosen as the place for what's happening."

Puzzled, Slade asked: "*Chosen*? What do you mean by that?"

"Stephenville isn't just about UFOs, Mr. Slade."

"Then what *is* it about?"

"Mr. Slade," she added in careful and slow tones, "how much do you know about the Patriot Act, martial law, and the government's ability – its *legal* ability, I mean – to suspend the Constitution of the United States of America?"

Before answering, Slade reached over for the whiskey. The night had just got even more interesting.

-9-

"Okay, let's start over," said Slade, now wide awake and determined to take full control of the conversation. "You got my number from the website article, right?"

"Right," said his mystery caller.

"And you have something you want to tell me about the case that goes *beyond* the case?"

"Right again," was the brief reply.

"So, let's have it," said Slade.

For a second or two there was silence. There then followed what was without doubt the strangest question Slade had been asked in a long, long time: "Do you remember the day you passed your driving test?"

"Huh? What kind of question is that?"

"Could you please answer the question, and, without naming it, can you tell me if you remember the street on which the driving center stood?"

"Okay," said Slade, slightly exasperated by the whole cloak-and-dagger situation. "Yes, *of course*, I remember the place and the day. Who doesn't remember something like that?"

"Good," said the woman. "The center is no longer there. In its place is a well-known fast-food restaurant. Please meet me on the car-park at 9:00 a.m. I will come to your car." The phone went dead.

Slade hung up the phone, flopped back down onto the bed and said, in seething tones, but to no one in particular: "This is just getting fuckin' crazy." It was then that something occurred to Slade, something for which he cursed himself – and a lack of sleep – for not realizing: how had the woman known where he passed his driving test? Who was she? How did she know what his car looked like? What the hell is going on?

Slade thought carefully: clearly the woman was concerned that someone may have been eavesdropping on the call, hence her requirement that he not mention the particular location at which they would be meeting at 9:00 a.m. So, she was someone with a degree of knowledge of how the world of spies and spooks work. That, at least, told Slade something about her, even if it was just a nugget. But one nugget was better than none. There was another matter of potential concern, too.

If someone *was* listening in on the call, and if Slade was still under surveillance in town – whether by some Homeland Security goon or whoever – the chances were they would be tailing him all the way to Hulen Street, Fort Worth, which was where Slade got his license two decades earlier. As the drive to Hulen Street from Stephenville was only sixty-two miles, an astute eavesdropper would likely assume Slade would head off from the Holiday Inn around 7:30 a.m., thus ensuring enough time to cope with the extra flow of morning traffic. Slade had to find a way to ensure that any potential tail had no chance of finding him. That meant leaving way earlier than expected. It was time to mix things up a bit – immediately.

Slade jumped off the bed, quickly showered, shaved, dressed, exited his room and headed down to the lobby, keeping his eyes open and alert at all times. Aside from a bored-looking guy manning the desk, who casually nodded in Slade's direction, there was no-one around – it was, after all, nearly 3:00 a.m. Slade nodded back. He chose not to exit the hotel via the main doors: instead, he walked along the south corridor of the first floor, past an ice-machine and a small gym, and quietly opened a side-door to the car-park – a door which could only be accessed by using a room-key.

Slade scrutinized the dark, cold surroundings – and, just to be sure, he scrutinized them again. All was good. Being careful to remain in the shadows as much as possible, Slade made his cautious way to his car, with nothing but the occasional hoot of a solitary owl for company. It was times like this Slade appreciated all he had learned in the Marine Corps about the importance of stealth.

Slade quietly opened the door of his Corvette, got in and started the engine. Driving it as slowly as possible until he left the grounds of the hotel, Slade fully expected to see a set of headlights in his rear-view mirror in any second. It didn't happen. It didn't even happen as he left Stephenville. Slade felt that, for the first time in what seemed a lifetime, no-one was hovering in the background, watching his every move. He chose to take a leisurely drive to Hulen Street – the last thing he wanted or needed, was a speeding ticket. With no trouble at all, Slade found the spot where, as a teenager, he became legal on four-wheels: it was now a McDonalds. He pulled up at the far side of the parking area, turned off the engine, and promptly fell asleep.

A loud tapping on the driver 's side window of his car had Slade going from a state of dead sleep to wide awake in a millisecond. He shot upright, gathered his wits, and wound down the window. Slade squinted as a result of the morning sun, and was confronted by something that he was not expecting: a little old lady, around five feet tall, and wearing a long coat and a woolly hat. The sky might have been bright, but the temperature was downright chilly. She was holding a tray, on top of which were two large coffees and a couple of breakfast burgers. The woman moved to the front of the car and impatiently motioned Slade to open the passenger's door.

"Whatever you say, lady," Slade muttered, shaking his head. He was expecting something, but not *this*.

"Please take these, Mr. Slade, if you would," said the woman, now smiling widely. Slade held the tray, slightly astonished while his elderly visitor climbed in next to him.

"I have about thirty minutes, Mr. Slade, and then I have to be on my way," said the woman, and in a fashion so laidback and casual she might have been talking about the weather.

"And you are who, exactly?" asked Slade, still wondering if he really was awake, after all. That the coffee was hot and the burger more than adequate, suggested he *was* awake.

She gave Slade's right knee a friendly squeeze and replied: "I'm Gladys, and I'm the person who is going to tell you what you're up against."

"Okay, err, Gladys; I'm all ears," replied Slade. It had better be good, he thought.

"Stephenville, Mr. Slade, is, as I said on the phone, a test."

Slade asked: "A test of what?"

"Of public perception and of public manipulation," she replied, sipping on her coffee and nibbling at her food.

"You're talking about disinformation, right? Confuse the public about the truth of UFOs?"

"Well, in a way, yes; but something much worse than that. Stephenville is the first step in a process that will lead to the eventual deconstruction of the Constitution and the rise of a totalitarian police state."

"Lady, please!" Slade cried. "I've heard some things in my time, but come on! And, forgive me, but, what's your role in all this? No disrespect, but you look like somebody's favorite granny!"

The woman's demeanor changed: "Appearances can be deceiving, Mr. Slade; *very* deceiving. I have spent forty-five years serving my country at the highest level. I ate lunch with Nixon, dinner with Carter and played tennis with Oliver North. You will listen to what I have to say."

"Two presidents and the brains behind Iran-Contra: that's quite a résumé. I'm sorry; I apologize for my...uh...assumptions," said Slade, suddenly feeling like he was ten years old and in the presence of the school principal.

"We're running short on time, Mr. Slade, so I will get to the point. You know, of course, of the allegations surrounding Orson Welles' October 30, 1938 radio broadcast. That Welles' broadcast of H.G. Wells' *War of the Worlds* novel – a show that led many listeners to believe aliens really *were* invading – was a test by someone in government; a test to determine how the public might be deceived."

Slade certainly *did* know the story: so skillfully put together was Welles' Mercury Theater production, it convinced thousands of people – and particularly those who had tuned in specifically *after* the opening announcement that it was just a piece of fun and entertainment for Halloween – that the end was near, and that hostile extraterrestrials were about to trash the planet and everyone on it. Such was the scale of terror that gripped whole swathes of the nation, even the *New York Times* covered the story: *Radio Listeners in Panic, Taking War Drama as Fact*, was the headline on the October 31, 1938 issue of the newspaper.

"And you're saying that Stephenville is the start of a faked UFO invasion?" asked Slade, in slightly doubting tones.

"What I am saying," the old lady replied, her voice now filled with emotion, "is there are very powerful people in government – but who operate *outside* of government - who want to destroy this great nation. They want to put each and every one of us under an iron-grip of martial law and twenty-four-hours-a-day surveillance. And a UFO threat – one that will require we, the people, to surrender our freedoms in the face of an alien presence – is the next step in their plan. Except that the alien threat won't be real."

It sounded just too incredible to be true. Yet, what the woman had to say chilled Slade to the bone.

"It's simply not possible," said Slade, quietly.

"Mr. Slade," Gladys expanded, "the act of two aircraft flying into the World Trade Centers, and a third into the Pentagon on September 11, 2001, led to two major wars, the creation of the Patriot Act, and the complete surveillance by the National Security Agency of the nation's emails, phone calls, and social-networking habits. Three events, all on one morning, and America has been changed forever. If you think it couldn't happen again – but, this time, with bug-eyed aliens instead of men with dark skins and beards – you are so very wrong."

She continued: "Stephenville is the litmus-test. The town was chosen and targeted very carefully: fly in a few of our highly classified craft – some of a very weird design which could easily be passed off as UFOs -- and, in no time, what do you have? I'll tell you: you have a town full of people on edge, all looking for answers and, more importantly, all looking to the military and the government for those answers. What that creates is an environment ripe for manipulation."

Then it was time for the final revelation: "Can you imagine the next step, one involving another Stephenville, and then another and another? Strange craft in the skies, the nation on edge, panic in the streets, looting, perhaps a few more historic buildings destroyed and thousands of lives lost, and those men without conscience whipping everything into a state of frenzy. That will be the start of a steady process of erosion of our rights, martial law and an unending clampdown on American society – *forever*. And it all depends on how successfully things play out at Stephenville."

Slade was stunned: it sounded like unbelievable; paranoid sci-fi come to life. Gladys had made it sound so plausible. After pondering for a few seconds on everything he had heard, Slade looked up and asked: "So, why me? Why not go to the press? Or if these guys are outside the law of government, why not go to the FBI?"

"That's beyond my area of clearance, Mr. Slade. All I can tell you is that I was explicitly told to meet you here today and to share with you the facts. I was told to do a couple of other things, too."

Slade watched as Gladys pulled two items out of her pocket: the first was a folded piece of paper and the second was a cell-phone.

"For me?" asked Slade.

"For you," she replied, adding: "On this piece of paper you will find a phone number, and a name and address – in Washington, D.C. You will fly to D.C. tomorrow morning out of DFW International at 10:15."

Gladys dug deep into her pocket again: it was an envelope containing flight tickets and $1,000 in cash.

"This is for you. The phone is encrypted. You can't be traced by it, and it's secure from penetration. When you arrive, use the phone to call the name on that sheet of paper. Within forty hours from now you will have all the answers you need – to Stephenville, and to what may be coming next."

For a woman who looked to be in her late seventies, Gladys deftly and swiftly got out of the Corvette and said: "It was nice to meet you, Mr. Slade."

"Likewise, I think," Slade answered. He watched as Gladys got into the driver's seat of a nearby red Mini and vanished amid the morning traffic as she headed for I-20. From Stephenville to the end of the United States as we know it: what a way to start the morning.

-10-

Slade sat for a few moments pondering the revelations (*claims* might be a better term, he thought) of his septuagenarian whistleblower: a plan to turn the United States into George Orwell's absolute worst nightmare and tear up the Constitution, all thanks to a ruthless cabal of powerful manipulators using futuristic vehicles – derived from nothing less than back-engineered alien spacecraft – to deceive the public into believing deadly extraterrestrials are among us.

The more Slade thought about it, the more he knew deep down such a fantastic thing could indeed be achieved, providing that those running the show acted carefully. Gladys was right on target: just three aircraft crashing into buildings changed the face of America and forever altered the nation and its people. In view of that, Slade realized to his growing horror that there would be no need for gigantic armadas of craft to appear over just about every American city. Maybe only two or three battleship-sized craft – perhaps one over the Big Apple, another over Los Angeles, and a third over Washington, D.C. – would do the trick. And if those aboard the craft let loose with sophisticated, alien-derived weaponry and took the lives of hundreds of people or worse still *thousands*, in no time at all the nation would be in lockdown mode. Even worse: it might be in a *permanent* lockdown.

Slade pulled out his airline ticket and checked his flight-plan. He was flying out tomorrow. He had a full day after that to meet with Gladys' contact and was scheduled to return to DFW International on the third day. On top of that, not only did the envelope contain tickets and a grand in cash, it also contained reservation information for a five-star hotel for two nights in D.C. Someone was going to a great deal of trouble to get Slade on board – or to have him chasing his tail. He still wasn't entirely sure which. He knew one thing though: it was time to get back to Stephenville to prepare for his flight tomorrow.

To say that Stephenville had been turned into a circus by the time Slade got back to town was not an exaggeration. Slade had been so busy interviewing witnesses, fending off Homeland Security, and being on the receiving end of paranoia-filled tales from an old lady who rubbed shoulders with presidents, that there was something he had overlooked.

Slade did not know it, but after flying in from Phoenix, AQUA's Andrew Bridges had been a busy man; in fact, a very busy man. Only about fifteen minutes after leaving Hulen Street, Slade got a call.

"Hi Marc: it's Jenny; Jenny Abbott, from the newspaper."

"Hey Jenny, how's things?" asked Slade, finally pleased to hear a voice that he could trust – he hoped.

"You know your friend Bridges is here, right?"

Slade inwardly groaned: "Well, he's not exactly what I would call a friend, but go on."

"He has arranged a big meeting for tonight: at the Rotary Club in Dublin. We're promoting it at our website, local radio is on it, and it even got a mention on the morning news. It looks like we're going to get a good turn-out."

"Are you going?" Slade inquired.

"I sure am; there's going to be a big piece on it in next week's newspaper. Bridges has invited everyone who has had a sighting to come along and give AQUA the details. They're going to do a big report on the case and try and figure out what happened."

Slade didn't want to give away his suspicions about AQUA's motives – and, he suspected, Bridges' – and particularly not to a newspaper journalist, so he played things casual: "That's cool. We don't get along too well, but I'm sure he'll do a good job. What time does it start?"

"7 o'clock."

"I'll be there." Slade hung up. Well, this was going to be interesting.

As Slade got out of Fort Worth, he put in a call to Kenny. Taking no chances, he used the new cell-phone that Gladys gave him. It wouldn't hurt at all to play everything very safe. He knew Kenny's number by memory and dialed.

"Hello?" said Kenny.

"It's me, bud, Marc."

"That's funny, your name didn't appear. You got a new phone?"

Slade smiled and said: "Yeah; something like that. Listen pal, I need to ask you a big favor."

"Sure, go ahead."

"You won't believe what's gone on in the last two days."

"I'll bet I will," replied Kenny. "After the Homeland Security thing I'll believe just about anything!"

Slade outlined the plan: "Here's the deal: I need to lay low. I'm on my way back to Stephenville. And tomorrow morning I need to get out of town again and to the airport: DFW. But, I want to leave enough of a trail to make whoever might be watching think that I'm still in my hotel room. So, I wanna leave my car there and leave my phone in the room, just in the event that someone's tracking my movements by the phone."

"Things are getting that bad?" asked a clearly concerned Kenny.

"Things are getting that bad, my friend," answered Slade, in serious tones.

Kenny shot back: "What do you need from me? Just name it."

"Do you still get Fridays off work?"

"Sure do."

"Can you get to the hotel around 6 o'clock tomorrow morning and drop me off at the airport? If we leave early, chances are I won't be seen; and besides if anyone *is* looking, they're going to be looking for a yellow Corvette, not your Suburban."

"No problem, man. Meet you at the lobby doors?"

"I owe you far more than just one or two now, Kenny," said a thankful Slade. "See you in the morning, pal."

Slade spent the early afternoon getting everything together that he needed for the flight out of DFW: several changes of clothing, a camera, a digital voice recorder, and just about anything else he could think of. After all, he knew nothing about what might be waiting for him in D.C. After packing, Slade showered, had an early dinner in the hotel and took a drive down 377 to Dublin. It was time to see what Andrew Bridges was *really* up to.

When Slade arrived at the Rotary Club, the atmosphere was far less that of a sedate meeting and far more that of a Sunday football game: the place was heaving with people. And they all had one thing in common: UFOs. Slade pushed and jostled his way inside the foyer, carefully listening to the conversations that were going on around him: "…never seen anything like it;" "…as big as a battleship…" "…like something out of *Close Encounters of the Third Kind…*" and "…how could something that huge fly and not make any noise?" Everyone was sharing their stories with each other, waiting for Bridges to appear and get things moving. Camera crews from not just local channels, but from overseas too, were busy setting up their equipment, preparing for the big event.

A few moments later, an elderly man asked for everyone's attention and motioned them into a large room, one filled with around eighty or ninety chairs and a large stage. They should have got more chairs, Slade thought: at least sixty or seventy people were forced to stand, creating an atmosphere akin to that of a Saturday night rock concert at Dallas' American Airlines Center.

Anticipating there would be a rush for chairs, Slade managed to get himself a seat in the third row from the front. He saw Jenny Abbott standing to the side of the stage and caught her attention with a quick wave. She smiled and waved back. Slade thought: Probably been getting an exclusive interview with Bridges. It was then time for the main event.

When Bridges took to the stage, Slade instantly realized why he hated the man so much. It wasn't that he lacked polish as a speaker, but he was just too slick; like used-car-salesman slick. Sickly slick was a good way to word it. Bridges began by thanking everyone for coming. He then gave a fifteen-minute overview of the work of AQUA, and proceeded to explain why he was here: namely, to secure as much data as possible on the couple of nights of UFO activity in the form of witness reports, film footage, and photos.

Only once in his presentation did Bridges falter: it was when he caught sight of Slade who gave the old man a wink, and which clearly got his blood pressure boiling. It may not have been a coincidence that Bridges then quickly brought his speech to an end and announced: "Ladies and gentleman, we have AQUA staff on-hand all around the room to take your reports and I trust you will do your best to share your stories with us, AQUA, the most professional, respected UFO research group in the world." Slade almost vomited.

As Slade wandered around the room and checked out the tables that had been put to one side for AQUA's people, he couldn't help but notice that all of the people that Bridges had brought with him were male, none of them seemed to be older than thirty-five, they all sported crew-cuts and looked like the sort of people Slade had on his side in Baghdad in 2003. He edged closer to the nearest table and did his best to listen in on the conversation, without making it overly obvious.

Something very quickly stood out: the guy asking the questions – an unsmiling, barrel-necked character who looked like the typical spy novel assassin - seemed less interested in the details of the report he was getting from a family of five than he was in how they perceived the event.

The man asked them: "Did you feel frightened? Do you think what you saw was an alien spacecraft? Do you think aliens are dangerous? Did you think the town was going to be attacked?"

Had it been a one-off situation, Slade would have been inclined to think that the guy was just untrained in how to interview a witness about his or her UFO encounter. But it wasn't a one-off situation: all around the room, the questions were broadly the same: "Were you scared? Do you think extraterrestrials might pose a threat to the United States?"

He thought back to Gladys' words: "...The town was chosen and targeted very carefully...You have a town full of people on edge...which creates an environment ripe for manipulation."

Christ, thought Slade, this is *exactly* what Gladys warned him about. Bridges and his goons weren't there to investigate what was seen at all; they were there to see how effectively the event had affected the people of Stephenville, and if their encounters had them in states of fear.

And there was that other statement from Gladys: "Stephenville is the litmus test."

Slade could envisage it all now: when the meeting was over, Bridges would make a call to Brian Anderson, or, more likely, to some suit in the Intelligence world. He would tell them that, yes, the people of Stephenville *were* in states of anxiety. They had fallen for the alien ruse and it was now time to take the program to its next step.

Slade shuddered; he suddenly found himself very cold.

-11-

Despite the unbelievable nature of the situation into which he had been plunged, Corey Hanks instinctively knew what he was looking at: the body of a small, dead extraterrestrial entity, an *alien*. Hanks felt his stomach turn and his head spin. He gritted his teeth in an effort to fight off a bout of nausea and a growing sense of fear. But this was not the pristine corpse of some previously all-powerful creature. Rather, it was more correct to say that what Hanks was staring at were the *remains* of a dead alien. Suspended in a sickly, yellowish liquid was a severely pulverized body, one that was missing most of its right arm and the lower half of its right leg. Its jaw was severely mangled, and its stomach area showed signs of having been stitched back together. It looked like a semi-decomposed goblin possessed by the deranged brain of a hideous, malevolent demon. Hanks turned around and stared at John Sinclair, his mind filled with words that shock prevented him from speaking.

"Worry not, Corey," said Sinclair, clearly seeing the look of horror and terror on Hanks' face. "Everyone has that reaction the first time they encounter the unearthly in person; *everyone*. Some never get over it. People think they would be excited. But they're not; it's just pure fear. It's nothing to be ashamed about, however. Seeing an extraterrestrial on television isn't quite the same, is it?"

"I'll say," replied Hanks, in near-whispered tones.

"It's called culture shock," added Sinclair. "You're experiencing what everyone goes through when they see for the first time what you have just seen. Life will never be the same. The carefully ordered world in which you lived will never again be quite so orderly. You feel out on a limb, on the edge of a cliff. Am I wrong?"

"No sir, you're not wrong. You're totally correct," Hanks admitted, slightly sheepishly.

Sinclair motioned Hanks to the opposite side of the room, which contained just three things: a table and two chairs. "I'm going to tell you a story, Corey, which is made up of several parts, but which is, essentially, just one. It goes like this."

-As Hanks sat back and listened, near-hypnotized, Sinclair told him that elements of the U.S. Government and military had suspected that the Earth was being visited by extraterrestrials as far back as 1941: strange craft seen in the skies over war-torn Europe, pilot encounters; that kind of thing. It wasn't until the summer of 1947 when, as if by luck, a rancher stumbled upon the remains of an extraterrestrial craft on ranchland in Lincoln County, New Mexico, that the U.S. Government finally knew for sure, much to its consternation.

"You mean Roswell?" asked Hanks.

"I do," answered Sinclair. He continued that over the course of four days a large team of military personnel, from the old Roswell Army Air Field, recovered from the Foster Ranch the remains of five bodies of non-terrestrial origin and a large and widely scattered amount of strange debris. The latter displayed extraordinary properties: incredibly light, the wreckage could be bent out of shape, only to bounce back to its original form. Not only that, it was impervious to bullets. Several miles north of the debris field, a near-destroyed vehicle was found. Around forty feet long and delta-shaped, it had clearly exploded in mid-air, raining debris and bodies – and body-parts – down onto the desert floor. A hasty cover-up was put into place, one in which the military first admitted to recovering what, back then, was called a "flying disc," but quickly thereafter stating it had all been a big mistake: nothing but a weather balloon. Amazingly, the media bought the story until enterprising and persistent UFO researchers reopened up the cosmic controversy in the mid-1970s.

"It's beyond my scope of knowledge to tell you how many additional crashed craft we've recovered, but I know of three more. And then there are the 'donated' craft."

"Donated?" asked Hanks, his voice filled with amazement.

"Yes, donated: provided to us. I won't get into all the details, except to say a number of leading world governments have developed relationships with the intelligences behind the UFOs, even if they're not always eye-to-eye relationships."

Hanks started to ask what that meant, but Sinclair brushed his question aside: "What's important, right now, is the thing in that container. Do you know why it's here? Here in Waxahachie, I mean."

"No, sir; I can't imagine."

"Very well, here's the next part of the story."

Sinclair reeled off a fascinating tale of how, in the early, post-Roswell days, any and all alien bodies, technology and artifacts were taken to Wright-Patterson Air Force Base, Dayton, Ohio, for study. Over time, however, concerns developed that storing everything in one location was deemed potentially disastrous – and particularly so in the event of a Cold War-era confrontation with the Soviets. So a plan was formulated to spread the material far and wide: a well-preserved body at this base, the files on a 1956 alien autopsy at that base, the Roswell wreckage out at a certain, infamous installation in Nevada, and so on.

Plus, said Sinclair, the UFO research community was getting hot on the trail of the Wright-Patterson stories, and even none other than Barry Goldwater - a five-term Senator and the Republican Party's nominee in the 1964 presidential election – went public with the story of his failed attempts to see what the Air Force was hiding at Wright.

"Spreading the material all over the place, but still in highly secure places, was deemed the best approach," added Sinclair. "And all of that brings us back to right here, Waxahachie."

As Hanks listened, completely transfixed, Sinclair said that the old adage about the best place to hide something is in plain sight was absolutely correct: "There's actually far less going on at Area 51 than you might think. A lot of those stories are designed to get everyone looking at the base while most of the good stuff goes on elsewhere. That's the same for the bodies: keep spreading tales about Hangar 18 and Wright-Patterson, and they become the targets for the UFO enthusiasts, and the real places don't even come into play."

"And this is one of those real places?" asked Hanks.

"It is. And here's why: What makes this place almost unique in Texas, Corey, is not what is going on here right now, but what was *planned* to go on back in the early 1990s. Do you know what I'm talking about?"

"No, sir, I don't," Hanks admitted. It was time for another briefing.

Sinclair looked Hanks in the eye and asked: "Are you aware of the Large Hadron Collider?"

"Something to do with physics, right?"

"Very good, yes: its work is focused on research into particle physics and high-energy physics. But, what's more important to our conversation, right now, is not so much the nature of the Large Hadron Collider but its location: nearly six hundred feet below ground, in a seventeen-mile-long tunnel near, Geneva, Switzerland. And that's the important issue: deep underground."

Sinclair continued: "As people have short memories, I'll elaborate on the next part. In the 1980s, the Department of Energy researched the feasibility of creating the largest collider in the world: the Superconducting Super Collider, as it eventually became known. Had it come to fruition, it would have surpassed the Large Hadron Collider – both in terms of power and size."

All was going well, Sinclair explained, and the initial construction of the site began in the early 1990s – to the extent that by 1993, no less than fourteen miles of tunnel had been bored out, hundreds of feet below Waxahachie. Unfortunately, escalating costs, which ultimately reached the stratospheric level of $4.4 Billion, led Congress to deliver a decisive death-knell on the program. The project was officially closed down in October 1993.

Immediately afterward, the site was deeded to Ellis County, Texas. It remained unsold until 2006 when it was finally bought by an investment body overseen by none other than Johnnie Bryan Hunt, the brains behind the largest publicly owned trucking company in the United States. Then, in 2012, it became the property of a chemical company: Magnablend.

"Here's where it all gets interesting, Corey," explained Sinclair. "While the collider project was an entirely legitimate one, it also served another purpose. A deal was done – shall we say – between those in government that oversee the UFO program and the Department of

Energy to allow for the creation of a very deeply buried, fortified bunker in which certain UFO materials could be successfully – and very secretly, I should add – stored.

"And here's the wonderful thing about it all: no-one ever suspected that the massive tunnels and shafts were being built for anything other than the Superconducting Super Collider. Why would they? The people of Waxahachie, the local media, even Congress – who were carefully kept out of the loop on the UFO angle – would never know that *some* of the tunnels and shafts were being used for another reason."

"For the storage of bodies like that one?" asked Hanks, nodding in the direction of that old, battered corpse from another solar system.

"You have it exactly right, Cory," said Sinclair, adding: "Hidden well out of sight, but also – in a strange way – in full sight, too. No-one would ever compare this place to Area 51, solely because its primary goal – getting the collider project off the ground – was everyone's focus."

Sinclair added, with a smile: "What you see over there, that body, is just a small portion of what else is here, far below the collider tunnels; thing you've never dreamed of or even *could* dream of. Even the current owners don't know how to access the portion of the installation that you and I are now sitting in. *They don't even know it exists.*"

Hanks responded in the fashion he presumed his boss would approve of: "Sir, you have my word that none of what you have said will go any further than me. You know I'm 100 percent loyal to the company."

With a look on his face suggesting he was clearly relishing the situation, Sinclair said: "I'm afraid you have things the wrong way around, Corey. We *want* you to talk about what you have seen here, and we want you to talk about it *soon*. A man named Slade – Marc Slade – will be coming here in the next few days, although he doesn't know it yet. It's going to be your job to tell him all he needs to know."

Sinclair's face then suddenly changed from one of slight amusement to that of deadly – and even ominously – serious: "Corey, soon the entire United States and the rest of the world will know the truth. UFO disclosure is just around the corner, and you are going to play a major role in making it happen. The train is racing along the track, and nothing is going to stop it. *Nothing*."

Corey Hanks couldn't help but think there was something else Sinclair wasn't telling him, something deeply menacing.

-12-

Kenny was as good as his word. In fact, he was better: he arrived slightly ahead of time. From his room, Slade watched Kenny pull up and then hurriedly headed downstairs. He had gotten more than used to having a careful look around the parking area, but did so again anyway. By now, it was downright second nature. Fortunately, there was no sight of anyone acting suspicious or patiently waiting to get on his tail. But again, Slade couldn't figure out if he should be pleased or not. After all, if he *was* being followed, that suggested he was on the right track, and someone wanted him *off* that track. On the other hand, if he was now being left alone, did that mean he was being manipulated into a realm where he was essentially of no harm to anyone? Not only could Slade not figure it out, he couldn't let such questions dominate his mind and get in the way of whatever was coming next in D.C.

"Hey, bud!" said Kenny, as Slade opened the passenger door of Kenny's suburban.

"Finally, someone I *know* I can trust!" Slade joked.

"Except for when it comes to money and women, right?" Kenny shot back, with a grin. "So, what's been going on? You said things have been speeding up."

"That's the understatement of the year, pal," replied Slade, who proceeded to fill Kenny in on all that had happened since Homeland Security started snooping around. Hardly surprisingly, when Slade got to the part about the Constitution and martial-law, Kenny's face visibly paled.

"You think the old lady was on the level?" asked Kenny, after Slade told him all about the weird, early morning meeting on Hulen Street with the mysterious Gladys.

Slade gave Kenny a grim look: "I wish I could say she was full of shit, but I have a horrible feeling she's not. I think this is the real deal; I really do. What worries me most is how this is progressing so quickly. I mean, Jesus, it's only a bit more than a week since I got the calls from the people here in Stephenville telling me what they'd seen. And since then I've had that Homeland guy after me, a meeting with an aging, female Deep Throat, I'm off to D.C., and now I'm pretty sure AQUA is in league with whoever is pulling the strings on all this crap."

For a few moments, both men sat quiet, pondering on the potential enormity of the situation. It was up to Kenny to lighten things up: "Well, pal, if the world turns to shit, or you singlehandedly save it, there's only one thing we can do."

"What's that?" asked Slade, slightly puzzled.

"Van Halen!" Kenny hit "play" on his vehicle's CD-player and *Hot for Teacher* blasted out of the speakers. "Just like the old days: me, you, the beach, Van Halen, beer and girls!"

Slade laughed: "Yeah, you know what? You're right! Fuck it: if things do fall apart, we might as well go out singing!" Deep down inside, however, Slade was in no mood for singing or even for Van Halen. He knew this was far from being a laughing matter. Right now, he felt like one of those homeless loonies parading their placards adorned with: "The End Is Nigh." Maybe they weren't so crazy, at all.

As they exited off 360 and entered DFW International Airport, Slade said to Kenny: "I know this is gonna sound totally paranoid, but when we get inside the airport, don't drop me off at the American Airlines gate I'm flying from. Drop me off at one of the other terminals. If anyone knows what I'm up to and where I'm arriving, then let's not make it easy for them."

"Jeez, you *are* on edge," said a worried-looking Kenny.

"Wouldn't you be?"

True enough.

After thanking Kenny for all he had done for him, Slade cleared security with no trouble whatsoever. He grabbed a soda and a sandwich, to pass the several hours before his flight was due and made his way to the departure lounge. He found a seat near the window and dropped his backpack to the ground. He had deliberately only taken a bulging carry-on bag for the three days: the very last thing he needed was someone going through his luggage and planting God knows what in it: drugs, maybe; *anything* that could get him on a trumped-up charge with the cops and out of circulation for a couple of years. Maybe Kenny was right; perhaps his paranoia *was* getting out of control. But, even if it was, that didn't necessarily mean *they* weren't sniffing around.

Finally, it was time to board. Whoever was bankrolling this caper, they had put Slade in business-class, which was way better than cattle-class, he thought. With all that was going through Slade's mind, sleep was impossible. There was only one option: something cold, potent and guaranteed to relax the mind. And let's make that a double, please.

Although the flight to Dulles International Airport was not a long one – just a few hours, thanks to a non-stop flight and a Boeing 737 – it did give Slade plenty of time to ponder on what might be going down when his feet touched the ground in D.C. He tried to make some sense out of the little that he knew of the person he was going to meet.

Slade got the impression that pretty much everyone in the know – good or bad – was of a certain age and upwards. Gladys, Brian Anderson, and Andrew Bridges: none of them was under sixty-five. Gladys was clearly well passed seventy; she may even have been a healthy eighty. This led Slade to think that both sides - those looking to do the right thing when it came to UFOs, and those looking to use the phenomenon as a tool of control and fear - probably recruited people as they moved through the ranks, as the years progressed, and as they could be assessed for their suitability. Robertson had been with NASA, Bridges was ex-Air Force Intelligence, and Gladys was, well, who knew *what* she was. That Gladys was, however, apparently chummy with at least two 1970s-era presidents, suggested she knew her way around the corridors of power – and had done so for a very long time. In all likelihood, that would be the same for whoever it was that would be waiting in D.C.

Slade ordered another drink and looked out of the window at the cloud-filled, dull skies. It wouldn't be long now.

On de-boarding the plane, Slade made straight for the nearest exit. He walked outside, couldn't fail to feel the late afternoon, D.C. chill, and dug into his pocket for the cell phone that Gladys had given him the previous morning. Slade pulled out the piece of paper with the number he was to call. It rang out four times before it was answered.

"Yes, Mr. Slade," said the voice at the other end of the phone. But, there was something odd about this voice: not only did Slade hear the words down the phone, he heard them right behind him, too. He quickly swung around; ready to take whatever action was necessary.

"Forgive my little game, Mr. Slade," said a man of about seventy, who sported a white goatee beard and tightly-pulled-back white hair, which was held in place ponytail-style. While the man's face suggested he could be a fan of the Grateful Dead, thought Slade, his crisp, silver-gray, Armani suit was evidence this was no hippy.

Slade was already pissed: "I'm not in the mood for your games, Mr. whoever you are."

The man looked amused: "Mr. Whoever you are; that will do nicely."

"No, it will not," said Slade, angrily. "I want a name. I want some answers, not more of this *All the President's Men* crap."

"Will a name really make that much of a difference, Mr. Slade?" the man asked, softly.

"Probably not," admitted Slade, "but I want one anyway."

"Why not call me Mr. Drake? How about that? I quite like that, don't you?"

"Okay, Drake it is," replied Slade, shaking his head at the near-dreamlike world into which he had been unceremoniously dropped.

"I suppose you were waiting by the exit and followed me outside?" asked Slade.

"Well, of course, Mr. Slade. People *can* be so predictable at times. You've done a good job of specifically *not* being predictable this past week, but even you, sir, are not immune to the occasional error in judgment. No matter. Be thankful it was me who was waiting and not someone else."

"And just what does that mean?" Slade angrily demanded.

"It means, Mr. Slade, that there are opposing players in this game. It means there are warring factions. It means that sometimes those same warring factions cross sides when it suits them. It means not knowing who to trust. It means trying to figure out which side you, personally, want to be on when the storm arrives. And it also means taking great care at all times."

"That was quite a speech," said Slade, his tone brimming with sarcasm.

"It was meant to be. And..."

Slade interrupted and shoved his face into Drake's: "Look, let's quit the cloak and dagger stuff and get to the point, shall we?"

Drake looked impressed with Slade's forthrightness and said: "We shall, Mr. Slade; we certainly shall."

After a couple of minutes' walk to the underground parking area, Slade and Drake were heading off to a downtown hotel in Drake's black Mercedes.

"Nice choice of car you have, Drake."

"Thank you. A present from my employers," he replied, with a sly smile.

Slade thought: Yeah, and I wonder what you had to do to get it.

"And here we are," said Drake, as they arrived at a tall, gothic-style hotel that practically oozed old money and power.

"Good choice," Slade offered, with a smile.

"My employers are always generous, under the right circumstances."

"And this is one of those circumstances?"

"It is."

Slade checked in, while Drake – who seemed to be very well known to the woman on the desk – ordered a pot of coffee, a bottle of Jack Daniels, chilled cokes, ice, and a selection of appetizers from the hotel menu.

"My pleasure, Mr. Gray," said the woman, smiling widely at the sight of the twenty-dollar bill that Drake placed in her hand.

"Gray?" asked Slade. "*Gray?*"

"She gets easily confused," said Drake, dismissing the question with a wave of his hand.

"She's not the only one," Slade hit back. The pair made their way to the elevator and to Slade's room on the ninth floor. This was it.

-13-

Slade sat back on the couch in what was an incredibly spacious room for just one person, with a whiskey and coke in his hand, and listened intently to what his new ally had to say.

"What you're about to get, Mr. Slade, is the abbreviated history of why you are right here, right now, tonight," said Drake, sipping on his drink. "This isn't just history; this is *historic*."

Drake slowly walked the room, back and forth, as he explained the roots of the program that now threatened to provoke nationwide martial law and a radical overhaul of the country. It all began with something called the Robertson Panel, said Drake. Slade was familiar with it, but – and just like practically everyone else in the UFO research field – he had no idea that the work of the panel had, essentially, been hijacked by power-crazed maniacs intent on changing the face of America.

Nineteen-fifty-two, Drake said, was when the first step was taken that led to where things were at now, namely the planned destruction of democracy in the Land of the Free. Although admittedly, said Drake, such an agenda wasn't even on the cards back then.

July 1952, said Drake, had seen a wealth of UFO activity over Washington, D.C., something that deeply troubled the FBI and the Air Force. It worried the CIA even more - to the extent that the CIA's Assistant Director H. Marshall Chadwell noted the following in a classified report on UFO activity in American airspace: "Sightings of unexplained objects at great altitudes and traveling at high speeds in the vicinity of major U.S. defense installations are of such nature that they are not attributable to natural phenomena or known types of aerial vehicles."

From his black leather briefcase, Drake pulled out a copy of a formerly classified document that led to the creation of the Robertson Panel. He read it, verbatim, to Slade:

71

"The Director of Central Intelligence shall formulate and carry out a program of intelligence and research activities as required to solve the problem of instant positive identification of unidentified flying objects.

"Upon call of the Director of Central Intelligence, Government departments and agencies shall provide assistance in this program of intelligence and research to the extent of their capacity provided, however, that the DCI shall avoid duplication of activities presently directed toward the solution of this problem.

"This effort shall be coordinated with the military services and the Research and Development Board of the Department of Defense, with the Psychological Board and other Governmental agencies as appropriate. The Director of Central Intelligence shall disseminate information concerning the program of intelligence and research activities in this field to the various departments and agencies which have authorized interest therein."

Forty-eight-hours later, said Drake, the Intelligence Advisory Committee concurred with Chadwell and recommended that, "the services of selected scientists to review and appraise the available evidence in the light of pertinent scientific theories" should be the order of the day. Thus was born the Robertson Panel, so named after the man chosen to head the inquiry: Howard Percy Robertson, a consultant to the Agency, a renowned physicist, and the director of the Defense Department Weapons Evaluation Group.

Chadwell was tasked with putting together a team of experts in various science, technical, intelligence and military disciplines and have them carefully study the data on flying saucers then currently held by not just the CIA, but by the Air Force too – who obligingly agreed to hand over all their UFO files for the CIA's scrutiny. Or, at least, the Air Force *said* it was all they had, added Drake.

Whatever the truth of the matter regarding the extent to which the Air Force shared its files with Chadwell's team, the fact that there was a significant body of data to work with was the main thing. And so the team – which included Luis Alvarez, a physicist, radar expert (and, later, a Nobel Prize recipient); Frederick C. Durant, a CIA officer; Samuel Abraham Goudsmit, a Brookhaven National Laboratories-based nuclear physicist; and Thornton Page, an astrophysicist, radar expert, and deputy director of Johns Hopkins Operations Research Office – quickly got to work.

Drake stressed that the overall concern of the Robertson Panel was that the UFO phenomenon might be used by unfriendly forces to manipulate the public mindset and disrupt the U.S. military infrastructure – and specifically so on matters of a national security nature. Particularly significant were the panel's worries that faked UFO stories, spread by the Soviets, might result in, as, as the panel worded it, "mass hysteria and greater vulnerability to possible enemy psychological warfare."

It was this particular issue, Drake revealed, that led to the next development: the Robertson Panel recommended that some of the more influential UFO research groups of the day – such as the Civilian Flying Saucer Investigators (CFSI) and the Aerial Phenomena Research Organization (APRO) – should be watched and infiltrated due to, as the panel recorded in its files "the possible use of such groups for subversive purposes."

Drake was far from done. He handed Slade yet another page from the archives of the Robertson Panel.

"This document," said Drake, "is quite possibly the most important one of all. This is where we see the group realizing that to ensure the Soviets weren't able to manipulate the UFO phenomenon and put the American people into a panic, it would be necessary to 'educate' the population on the matter of flying saucers."

Slade studied its words carefully. Such a "public education campaign," the panel noted, "would result in reduction in public interest in 'flying saucers' which today evokes a strong psychological reaction. This education could be accomplished by mass media such as television, motion pictures, and popular articles. Basis of such education would be actual case histories which had been puzzling at first but later explained. As in the case of conjuring tricks, there is much less stimulation if the 'secret' is known. Such a program should tend to reduce the current gullibility of the public and consequently their susceptibility to clever hostile propaganda."

"Keep reading," urged Drake. "You'll see how this so-called education program was going to be achieved." Slade did exactly that. As the documentation noted:

"In this connection, Dr. Hadley Cantril of Princeton University was suggested. Cantril authored '*Invasion from Mars*,' a study in the psychology of panic, written about the famous Orson Welles radio broadcast in 1938, and has since performed advanced laboratory studies in the field of perception. The names of Don Marquis, of the University of Michigan, and Leo Roston were mentioned as possibly suitable as consultant psychologists.

"Also, someone familiar with mass communications techniques, perhaps an advertising expert, would be helpful. Arthur Godfrey was mentioned as possibly a valuable channel of communication reaching a mass audience of certain levels. Dr. Berkner suggested the U. S. Navy (ONR) Special Devices Center as a potentially valuable organization to assist in such an educational program. The teaching techniques used by this agency for aircraft identification during the past war [were] cited as an example of a similar educational task. The Jam Handy Co. which made World War II training films (motion picture and slide strips) was also suggested, as well as Walt Disney, Inc. animated cartoons."

Slade placed the document on the coffee-table in front of him. His thoughts were running wildly.

"Do you see what I'm telling you and what comes next?" asked Drake.

"Yeah, I do; only too well," replied Slade, his head full of rage.

"What we have here," continued Drake, "is a situation where the CIA was planning on using, and I quote, 'mass communication techniques,' psychologists, people skilled in the field of – and I quote again – 'the psychology of panic,' and even major media sources like Walt Disney. Of course, back then, the Robertson Panel was looking at a *benign* education, one designed to lessen the mystique surrounding UFOs so that the Soviets wouldn't be able to use the phenomenon to manipulate and terrorize the American people."

Drake added: "At the height of the Cold War all that made perfect sense. But, what we have today is *very* different: those scheming to change America are using the very same tools the Robertson Panel planned on using – Psychology, a study of how panic can be induced, the media, education, and propaganda – but not to *inform* the public, as was the case in the '50's, but to *deceive* them and *control* them. And the first step in doing so was to take control of the UFO research community – all of which brings us to NICAP."

NICAP – the National Investigations Committee on Aerial Phenomena – was the one organization more than any other, Drake said, that challenged the blanket of official secrecy which surrounded the UFO subject from the mid-to-late 1950s onwards. As a result, those within the CIA who were privy to the U.S. Government's deepest and darkest UFO secrets saw only one option available to them: NICAP had to be infiltrated, nullified, and, ultimately, exterminated.

"Do you know how many supposedly 'retired'-CIA people joined NICAP – seemingly innocently but clearly not?" Drake asked Slade. Slade did: he had read a number of papers demonstrating the suspicions of many in Ufology that NICAP was a front for the CIA. After all, that numerous "former" CIA people were allied with NICAP was surely not just a mere coincidence. Even Vice Admiral Roscoe Hillenkoetter, the first director of the CIA, was on NICAP's board of directors!

"Read this," said Drake, passing Slade a photocopy of a page from Richard Dolan's book, *UFOs and the National Security State*.

Slade took a look at Dolan's words: "John L. Acuff, an outsider to NICAP and not a UFO researcher, was suddenly elected to serve on NICAP's board. In May 1970, he became the new director. For some time, Acuff had been executive director of the Washington-based Society of Photographic Scientists and Engineers (SPSE). SPSE had already cooperated with NICAP informally in the area of photographic analysis. It was later discovered that SPSE had significant intelligence connections: many members were photo-analysts within the various intelligence components of the Department of Defense and CIA."

"And it's not just Dolan who has noticed all this. Patrick Huyghe – like Dolan, a good, solid, astute researcher - has made comments on this, too."

Once again, Drake was armed and ready with the evidence. Slade carefully digested what Huyghe had to say:

"After a flurry of Washington-area sightings in 1965, the agency contacted NICAP about seeing some of its case files on the matter. Richard H. Hall, then NICAP's assistant director, chatted with a CIA agent in the NICAP office about the sightings, NICAP's methodology, and Hall's background. The agent's memo on the visit suggests that the CIA had some role in mind for Hall, predicated upon his being granted a security clearance. Nothing apparently came of the suggestion. A later set of CIA papers reveals an interest in NICAP's organizational structure and notes that 'this group included some ex-CIA and Defense Intelligence types who advise on investigative techniques and NICAP-Government relations.'"

And, in 1979, Huyghe had written: "There are presently three former CIA employees on the NICAP board of directors, including Charles Lombard, a congressional aide to Senator Barry Goldwater, who is himself a NICAP board member and retired U.S. Air Force Col. Joseph Bryan III. Bryan feels, as he did back in 1959 when he joined the board, that UFOs are interplanetary. NICAP's current president is Alan Hall, a former CIA covert employee for 30 years."

As for the final outcome, serious mismanagement problems ultimately led to the downfall of NICAP: by 1980, it was as dead as the Roswell aliens.

"I guess you know where I'm going with all this?" asked Drake.

"AQUA? All of those ex-military, defense, intelligence people not being quite so ex, after all? A repeat of NICAP?"

"Exactly," replied Drake, "but with one major difference: there's no goal to destroy AQUA. They serve a very good purpose: they collect data on UFOs from the public, and from insiders who might want to blow a whistle or two. And, then, those people in AQUA who are linked with what we might call 'the project,' ensure that all the data makes its way to the movers and shakers in the UFO program."

Slade looked at the floor, his mind filled with regret and anger: "And I'm as guilty as AQUA for not realizing what was happening and for giving them all those damned reports over the last half a decade."

Seeing Slade's frustration and fury, Drake said: "Slade, all of this can be turned back. It *can* be done. It *will* be done. It *has* to be done.

Either that or the country as you and I know it is gone. There's no middle-ground: one side will win, and one side will lose."

Slade was just about to reply when Drake added something more: "There's one other issue that I need to tell you about: it's all to do with the United Nations."

-14-

"What I'm about to tell you now, Mr. Slade, gets right to the crux of not just *what* happened at Stephenville, but *why* it happened," said Drake, as he poured himself a second drink and added: "In fact, the *why* is the most important thing of all. What do you know about the so-called UFO Disclosure movement? And what do you think of it?"

Disclosure was something that Slade knew a great deal about, most of which he viewed through very doubtful and dubious eyes. For years, UFO researchers had been saying that "the government" was going to disclose all that it knew about a vast alien presence on Earth, as well as its origins and intent. That was fine, except for one thing: despite loud and vocal claims from the likes of researchers Stephen Bassett and Dr. Steven Greer - that disclosure was just around the corner - it never came; as in, *ever*. Greer had been making such assertions for more than a decade, and Bassett – who was publicly lobbying to get the floodgates wide open - was constantly pushing the date forward, year after year.

As Slade said to Drake, in answer to the latter's question: "It's an interesting concept, but it's like the boy who cried wolf: after a while, everyone gets tired of the message, or of the promise of disclosure, because it doesn't happen."

Drake smiled: "And you have hit the nail right on the head. But, despite what many of your saucer buff friends might think to the contrary, both Greer and Bassett *do* have credible contacts. And there *are* plans to disclose, and they are plans that have existed for more than twenty years."

"So, why hasn't it happened?" Slade demanded to know.

"Because, Mr. Slade, disclosure is multifaceted: there are different groups, with different agendas, and with different ideas on how disclosure should happen and why."

Drake explained there were two groups in government that had formulated plans to tell the world's population that the Earth was not the only planet on which intelligent life existed.

"There are those," said Drake, "who favor a benign disclosure. Tell the public everything: the abductions, the cattle mutilations, the missing aircraft, and the contact cases; be honest about the whole affair. Even admit to the lies and the cover-ups and the worse things that have been done to hide the truth; *far* worse things, I regretfully have to say. They believe that taking an honest approach, and just seeing where the cards fall, is the best way of dealing with what is a very difficult subject."

"But there are others who disagree, right?" Slade interrupted.

"Exactly," Drake replied, with a look of near-resignation on his face. "There are those who disagree. These are the people, the very powerful people, who take the view that humanity will not be able to stand disclosure – psychologically, I mean – if the full picture is revealed to them. So, this second faction has a different agenda, one in which disclosure is secondary to their main goal: the manipulation and control of society."

For decades – but certainly far more so since 9-11 – Drake said, and echoing the words of Gladys, plans had been in place to slowly, but surely, turn the United States into a full-blown surveillance state.

"If I told you the full extent of how closely the average American is already now watched, even you, Mr. Slade - with all the things you have experienced and seen in the last couple of weeks - would doubt me."

"I doubt I would doubt you," Slade quipped.

"Well, that's good," said Drake, "that's very good." He continued: "What this particular group wants is something so terrifying, so horrific, that it will make 9-11 look like nothing worse than a broken fingernail. So, they are going to play the ultimate card: create a faked alien invasion of the type that our mutual friend, Gladys, briefly told you about, and use the Patriot Act to enforce nationwide control; a form of control that will take things out of the hands of the government and into the hands of people who will ruin our nation and our people."

"So, what can be done to stop it?" asked Slade.

"I said to you, Mr. Slade, there are two groups in government that are in conflict over this. And I'm not exaggerating when I say in conflict: a disturbingly significant number of people on both sides have had fatal car accidents, suspiciously-timed heart attacks, and unlikely suicides in the last few years. What was previously a disagreement over how disclosure should progress is now counting down to all out, secret war between the two. But, what you may not know is that there's a third group that has a big stake in disclosure."

Drake suddenly sat silent, staring intently at Slade.

"Okay, who's the third group?" Slade asked.

"The third group, Mr. Slade, is the one that just might save us all: *the aliens*."

According to Drake, although the history of Ufology was beyond doubt littered with odd deaths, frightening cases of alien abduction, missing people, and occasional, violent and fatal encounters between military pilots and UFOs, the official verdict was that the aliens were, essentially, benign.

"There was a time," said Drake, "when we had a 'shoot first and ask questions later," attitude to the phenomenon. But it was always to our cost. We finally backed away and *their* hostility to *us* – which was in response to *our* hostility to *them* – stopped. It was, and still is, an uneasy truce; but one which has been largely maintained since the 1950s. But, now, one might suggest, the aliens are getting antsy. They want a smooth transition where human society accepts them with as little transitional stress as possible.

"At a very restricted level, there is contact; *ongoing* contact with the aliens. I won't tell you how it's achieved or where, but I will tell you that *they* have made it clear they want disclosure. If we don't do it, they will, and soon, too. But here's the problem: as I said, we *think* they are benign. Yes, we *think* they are benign."

"But you can't be sure?" Slade asked.

"No, we can't be sure. So, with the possibility that they – the aliens – have a plan up their sleeves we haven't yet seen, this has pushed both groups to try and move their agendas forward at a faster rate."

"So, what's stopping either or both of them, from doing exactly that and going public right now?" Slade wanted to know.

"Both plans – whether a benign release of data or one guaranteed to lead to martial law – require working with a perfect success rate. But, there are issues that need to be looked at further before either side can be confident of success: widespread civil unrest and protest, the entire population standing up against any more stringent loss of privacy, or of the nation collapsing into psychological shock, are all issues being carefully studied until the time is deemed as being right for the next move on the chessboard."

"And which side is winning?" Slade asked.

"Sadly, we – the people I am allied to – believe that the most likely outcome is going to be a totalitarian state. Here's why: Watergate."

As most Americans of a certain age knew, said Drake, Watergate was a major blot on the political landscape. It was a saga filled to the brim with conspiracy, illegal activity, shadowy characters, and a multitude of strange twists and turns. And, in the end, it led to the shameful resignation, on August 9, 1974, of none other than President Richard Milhous Nixon, himself.

"At the time," said Drake, "there was nationwide condemnation when it became clear that Nixon was involved in a plot to secretly spy on – and bug - the Democratic National Committee headquarters at the Watergate building, right here in D.C. And had he not resigned because of his attempts to cover everything up, Nixon would almost certainly have been impeached."

Drake continued: "So, there's a situation where, back in the 1970s, the president is, for all intents and purposes, forced to resign for one case of illegal bugging. Today, the *entire nation* is being watched: phone calls, Facebook, Twitter, email: the NSA is watching *everyone*. And who is doing anything about it? I'll tell you: practically no-one. If I had said to you, twenty years ago, that, in the 21st century, the phone-calls of everyone in the United States would be monitored, and hardly a single American would care enough to do anything about it, you would say I was insane.

"That's the disturbing thing: we are *already* sliding into a state of surveillance, where a steady erosion of civil liberties is accepted, and all but because of a state of nationwide apathy that prevents anyone from caring enough to take any action. We, as Americans, are *allowing* it to happen. And that takes us back to this issue of whether the American public can be deceived even further into accepting, and allowing, total state control of their lives, all thanks to a brilliant scheme to scare them into submission by a UFO threat."

Slade replied: "And you're saying that if, in a country of almost 320 million people, everyone's accepting the whole NSA thing, then they won't stand up against martial law and even more loss of freedom either?"

"That's exactly it. They – the group - are waiting to see just how far America can be pushed. And right now, America – as a people – is not pushing back. That's a signal they won't push when things get even worse."

"Well, there has to be something that can be done; there *has* to be," said Slade, with growing frustration in his voice.

"There is," Drake answered. "It's that United Nations angle I need to tell you about."

"Just a few days after everything began at Stephenville," said Drake, "a highly secret meeting was convened at the New York office of the United Nations; one that actually ran for three days and which specifically addressed Stephenville. While the U.N. does not have its very own UFO research program, it does follow advice and policy of those nations that *do* have such programs."

He continued that the meeting was not only highly secret; it was also very much exclusive in nature: "My source is very trustworthy; in the diplomatic corps, and always proved reliable. Only certain nations were advised of what happened at Stephenville: us, the U.K, France, Germany, Japan, Australia, Canada, Russia, and China. Now, I need to stress that we're *not* talking about the specific governments of these nations - or even ours - being officially briefed, but of certain players in government who know the truth of the UFO issue."

"So, what *did* happen at Stephenville?" asked Slade.

"Stephenville was a carefully handled and created hoax. It was pure reverse-engineering," said Drake, succinctly. "The stories of Colonel Philip Corso and Bob Lazar are definitely filled with distortions – mainly to confuse the true situation and to gauge public reaction – but they are, basically, fact."

As Slade knew, Corso was the co-author of a controversial 1997 book – *The Day after Roswell* - that suggested, during his time with the U.S. Army in the early 1960s, he, Corso, ran a program to clandestinely seed alien technology into the world of U.S. private industry, chiefly to try and determine if it could be duplicated and then used by the military. Lazar, an equally controversial figure, had claimed that, in the late 1980s, he was enlisted to work on the reverse-engineering of a number of alien spacecraft secretly held at the infamous Area 51. Just like Corso, Lazar had just about as many supporters as he did detractors.

Drake could see the realization in Slade's eyes: "Yes, Mr. Slade: there are *their* UFOs, and there are *our* UFOs. We even have a secret space program derived from all this, but that's another matter completely. I don't have *all* the details of the U.N. meeting, but what I know for sure is that the aliens have been putting on so much pressure to disclose that someone chose to try and do exactly that.

"The main craft, the one that caused such a concentration of reports, was pure back-engineering. The plan was to fly the craft repeatedly over Stephenville, deliberately send up a few reservists in F-16s to take part in a half-hearted chase – purely for witness effect, of course – and then carefully target the townspeople to see what their reaction was. Now, to the best of my knowledge, that op was planned and executed by the people that you and I, not to mention the rest of the country, need to win.

"The problem, however, is that keeping the other side at bay was never going to be easy, which is why your former friends at AQUA played such a big role and took over the reins from you. Both sides had their people in town, all trying to figure out how the mindset of the people had been affected: good, bad, or whatever. And both sides were eager to learn just about all they could from the case; mainly to see how they could benefit from the fall-out.

"And that is why Stephenville is the most significant UFO event of the 21st century – and maybe ever. It will dictate the future; *our* future."

"Okay, I get all that," said Slade. His voice began to rise: "But why me? Why am I here, right now?"

"It's all very simple, Mr. Slade: we want you to tell the story."

"To who?" asked Slade.

Drake laughed: "To who? To *everyone*."

-15-

It was coming up to 6:00 p.m. and Sarah Rollins was getting ready to head out to the Rotary Club in Dublin. To say that she was pumped about sharing what she knew with those UFO investigators who were on the breakfast news this morning would be an understatement. The radio had been promoting the event all day, too, and Sarah wasn't going to miss out. Unfortunately, missing out is *exactly* what Sarah was about to do, even though she didn't realize it at the time. She soon would, however; *very* soon.

Late on the night that Stephenville went crazy, Sarah was giving her terrier, Max, a last run around the yard before retiring to bed. All thoughts of trying to make Max pee one more time, however, went right out of the window when Sarah's attention was drawn to a low humming noise, seemingly coming from directly above.

It took only a second for her to realize what she was looking at: a huge, black craft – shaped like a cross between a triangle and a diamond – that sailed along the night sky at an incredibly slow pace and an extremely low level. Until, that is, it suddenly shot vertically into the darkness and was gone.

For a few minutes, Sarah continued to stare upwards, her mind numbed and shocked by what she had just seen. Even Max, who whined and whimpered at the feet of his owner, knew that something was up. Suddenly feeling very frightened and vulnerable, Sarah scooped up Max, raced inside, locked the backdoor, and checked the rest of the house was secure. And then she checked again.

Recently divorced and now living alone, Sarah had a friend install new locks on the doors and the windows just two weeks earlier – mainly to ensure that her jerk of an ex-husband, Bob, didn't try and put in an appearance of the unwelcome type. Sarah knew that the locks would keep Bob out, but as for whomever – or whatever - was flying that thing in the skies: probably not. It was a long, tense night as every creak and groan in the old house had Sarah's heart skipping beats and her muscles tensing.

What particularly troubled Sarah, however, was the worrying suspicion that she had actually been onboard that strange craft. Her dreams and nightmares were filled for days afterward with graphic imagery of unearthly creatures, bizarre medical experiments and, well, she just couldn't put her finger on the rest of it. Sarah was hoping, however, that maybe AQUA would be able to shed more light on that period of missing time, which was now tormenting and taunting her night after night.

Sarah had chosen not to share what she had seen with her friends and family – except for her best friend, Carrie, who was looking after Max tonight. When, however, the news broke about all the other reports, and then the press reported that those AQUA guys were coming to town, Sarah decided she had to tell someone. Unfortunately, something intervened; something that ensured Sarah never again spoke of what went down on that fear-filled night.

Just as Sarah was applying her lipstick, there was a loud, slow knock at the front door. Finally, she thought: it was the FedEx guy. She had been waiting for a package all day. There had been some issue with the delivery but, what the heck, late was better than never. Sarah ran to the door; she opened it quickly and eagerly. It was something she would forever regret doing. Standing in front of her was the strangest man she had ever seen. He was near-emaciated and had skin the color of milk. Even stranger, he was dressed in a decades-old style black suit and tie, and sported a 1950s-era fedora hat. The penetrating stare on his face reminded Sarah of a dog just about to bite.

"Miss Sarah," he whispered, in a bone-chilling pitch and tone that seemed part male and part female, "I understand you saw something a number of evenings ago; something over your dwelling."

"Excuse me: Miss Sarah? My *dwelling*?" asked Sarah, unsettled by this weirdo and his even weirder words. "You mean my house, right? How do you know that?"

The man ignored the questions, only to ask his own, as his bulging eyes bore deep into Sarah's: "Might I come in and speak with you?"

"Well, who are you?" she wanted to know.

"I am part of the study; the lights in the sky that people see," he replied, in a monotone fashion.

That bitch Carrie, thought Sarah: she must have contacted those UFO people and told them all about what I saw - *and* she gave them my address!

Sarah figured that people into UFOs were probably a bit eccentric, but this guy was beyond that. It seemed a crazy thing to even consider, but there was something about the man that was almost, well, *alien*. There was something else too: he was oddly persuasive, even to the extent that Sarah felt driven to apologize for her initial words and manner and invited him in.

"Please, have a seat," she said, motioning the man to the couch. "I suppose it was Carrie who called you, yes?"

"Carrie, yes," the man replied, repeating her words rather than answering the question.

She asked: "Would you like some coffee? Or a coke?"

"No."

"Well, would you at least like to take your hat off?"

"No."

"Okay, Mr.?"

"I am Mr. Bleak," the man whispered.

Bleak: what kind of name is *that*, Sarah wondered.

"So, how can I help your AQUA group, Mr., uh, Bleak? That's what it's called, right: AQUA?" Sarah asked.

The vaguest of all smiles possible appeared on Bleak's pale lips: "No, you misunderstand me, Miss Sarah. I represent a *different* group. It is *not* my wish to study your experience."

Sarah was becoming annoyed: "Then what, exactly, do you want from me? I thought this was about my sighting?"

Bleak leaned forward and gripped Sarah's hand: his touch was not just cold, but icy. "Oh, yes, it *is* about your sighting. But, what I want Miss Sarah, is for you not to tell *anyone* about it. I want you not to tell anyone, ever." Bleak gave Sarah a terrible grin.

Suddenly feeling extremely scared, Sarah looked at the front-door: it was around fifteen feet away and still unlocked. If she was lucky, she could get to the door, and onto the street, before the guy had a chance to move. As if reading her mind, however, Bleak gave a disturbing chuckle and said: "It would not be wise for you to try and run, Miss Sarah. It is not my desire to hurt you. But should you do *anything* but stay exactly where you are, I will surely end your life, *right now*."

Despite Bleak's threat, Sarah suddenly felt oddly calm, almost as if she was under some form of hypnotic spell or a magical enchantment, born out of ancient wizardry and witchcraft.

"Here is what you will do, Miss Sarah," said Bleak, as his eyes locked solidly onto hers. "You will stay at home this evening. You will not speak to anyone about what it was you saw that night. Do you understand the words I say?"

Sarah merely nodded, her voice subdued by fear or Bleak himself – perhaps even by both.

"Should you ever speak of that night, you will die. Should you ever speak of this meeting, you will die. Do I make myself understood?"

"Yes," Sarah croaked, weakly.

"Which reminds me: dogs provide you humans with so much pleasure," said Bleak. "And we wouldn't want anything to happen to Max, either, would we?"

"No," was all that Sarah could say.

"You are very wise, Miss Sarah. I only wish everyone on who I pay a visit could be so accommodating and helpful. All too often things end in tragedy, if you understand my words."

She did.

"Follow me to the door," ordered Bleak, as he stood up from the couch. "And take heed of my words, Miss Sarah. If you choose to ignore them, you will meet me one more time, after which you will never meet anyone again."

Sarah's lips were quivering so much that she was unable to respond with little more than a whispered mumble.

"I am pleased we were able to come to a unanimous agreement; my employers always prefer a positive conclusion. Good night, Miss Sarah. And please do not give me any reason to return."

Bleak walked slowly down the driveway to an old, 1950s-era Chevy. Just like Bleak's clothing and Fedora it was entirely black. That was the last thing Sarah remembered, before waking up in bed five hours later with a pounding heart, a pulsating headache, and her body drenched in sweat. And there was one thing that Sarah could not get out of her mind: Bleak's reference to "you humans." Did that mean Bleak was something more, or less, than human? Sarah prayed she would never find out.

As for Mr. Bleak, his work that night had barely begun.

-16-

It was close to midnight when Andrew Bridges finally left the Dublin Rotary Club. From his perspective, it was a job very well done. He and his colleagues had secured a massive amount of testimony from dozens of locals – all of who had provided Bridges with exactly what was needed: their personal responses to the Stephenville encounters. He unlocked his rental car, got in, turned on the interior light, and proceeded to pull out a few pages of the many reports that had been filed that night.

The words made it clear that Stephenville was a town now steeped in fear and paranoia: *"I was terrified...;" "We thought we were being invaded...;" "My kids can't sleep at night...;" "The military should be doing something about this...;"* and, *"What if the aliens are more dangerous than Bin Laden?"*

That was just the beginning. There were more than a few people who were deeply excited by the Stephenville affair; but – and this was the important point, from Bridge's perspective - there were even more whose nerves were on edge, and who were all looking for someone to take control of the situation. Bridges knew that if matters were handled very carefully it would be the project that would eventually take control, with him playing a central role in recreating the American way of life.

Very pleased with the outcome, Bridges turned on the ignition and headed for the Hampton Inn and Suites on Harbin Drive, where he was briefly staying. Such was the overwhelming darkness, Bridges failed to see the old black Chevy that followed him all the way to the Hampton, its headlights deliberately off.

It was to Bridges' eternal cost that when he pulled into the parking area of the Hampton, he chose to leaf through a few more reports – basking in a wave of self-congratulatory egotism. Had his head not been buried in all of those dozens of pages, Bridges would have noticed that the driver of the Chevy had just arrived, too, albeit at the other end of the car-park.

The driver, dressed entirely in black, quickly studied the layout of the hotel and the parking area. He got out of his car and took from the backseat a black briefcase. He then quietly closed and locked the door, and walked towards the entrance to the hotel, careful to avoid being seen by any night staff that might be on duty. He then waited in the shadows like a lion ready to pounce on an unwary gazelle.

Fifteen minutes or so later, and after puffing on a couple of Misty Menthol Ultra Lights and satisfying himself that all was going good, Bridges decided it was time for a comfortable bed and a nightcap of scotch and water. Just before he reached the doors, with his head down and his eyes focused on lighting and smoking one last cigarette before he headed inside, the black-suited man stepped into view. He deliberately walked into Bridges, ensuring that the base of his suitcase caught Bridges' left shinbone.

"Jesus!" cried out Bridges, as he dropped both his briefcase and that last cigarette, and as a sharp pain coursed through his lower leg.

"My apologies," said the man, in a tone that failed to offer even a modicum of emotion. "I didn't see you, sir; I am very sorry."

"Well, okay," said Bridges, "but watch where you're going next time; you could do someone an injury."

The irony of Bridges' words was not lost on the black-garbed character. Even he was able to manage a slight smile, one filled with satisfaction at a job well done and Bridge's fate forever sealed. The man hastened his pace and, after returning to his 1956 Chevy, fired it up and vanished into the night.

Mr. Bleak's work was over – for now.

By the time Bridges got upstairs, his leg was beginning to ache, and he wondered if that guy had bricks in his case. Bridges poured himself a large scotch and water, took a gulp, and then removed his pants. He inspected his leg: there was no bruise. What there was, however, was a tiny prick in his skin.

"Fucking great," said Bridges, out loud. He thought: the guy's case must have been damaged, and part of it had stuck him in the leg. Now he had visions of having to get an antibiotic shot in the morning.

No matter, his flight out of DFW and back to Arizona wasn't until 8:40 p.m. It was a flight that Bridges would never make. He chugged back the last of his scotch and water, washed his face, and went to bed -- for the very last time.

Around 2:20 a.m. Bridges woke up. He was cold and sweating, his breathing was labored, his arms were pounding, and his chest felt like it was caught in a giant vice. He struggled to turn over and reach the phone, which was on the stand on the other side of the bed. It was only a couple of feet away, but it might just as well have been a couple of miles. Every movement was torment and agony; Bridges felt like his heart was going to burst as he tried to raise his right arm and grab the phone. His mind told him he wasn't going to give up that easily, however. Too bad: his body was saying something entirely different.

In one final attempt to reach the phone, the life of Andrew Bridges came to a sudden end. His body fell backward, his eyes took on a glassy, doll-like appearance, and his heart delivered its final beat.

Just under a week later, the official verdict was that way too many cigarettes, combined with a sedentary, office-bound work environment for the last ten years of his career with the military, were the cause of Bridges' untimely death from a huge blood clot that had lodged in one of his lungs. As for that slight prick to the skin, "inconclusive" was the coroner's only word.

Mr. Bleak, however, knew better. It was not the first time he had been involved in wiping out someone in the UFO community. His deadly talents had been employed on far more than a few previous occasions. His most satisfying and successful silencing – one near-identical to that involving Andrew Bridges - occurred in the final months of the 20th Century when a decision was taken that a particularly bothersome UFO investigator had to be removed – for good.

In September 1999, a well-known UFO researcher and author, Jim Keith, headed out to the Burning Man Festival, a yearly event held around 120 miles north of Reno, Nevada in the Black Rock Desert. It's an incredibly popular celebration dedicated to "radical self-expression and radical self-reliance." The roots of Burning Man date back to the

1980s, when two men, Larry Harvey and Jerry James, set fire to an eight-foot-tall, human effigy on a stretch of San Francisco's Baker Beach – the reason, chiefly, to help Harvey put behind him the memories of a romance gone wrong.

Since then, Burning Man has grown to immense and arguably epic proportions, with its themes ranging from evolution to fertility and the American Dream, and its attendance figures reaching close to 50,000. Even the fiery effigy itself has grown in stature: to a towering 50-foot-tall creation.

Altered-states, massive firework displays, and a celebration of all-things-alternative are the combined name of the game at Burning Man. The sacrificial aspect of the event – namely, the burning of a man-like figure – is something that would take on a whole new meaning in the wake of Jim Keith's attendance.

While chatting with like-minded friends and souls on one of the stages at Burning Man, Keith slipped and fell to the ground, which was a significant number of feet below. It was only an *assumption* that Keith fell. Had anyone been looking closely amid all the stoned chaos and fun, they would have seen a pale-faced man in dark clothing give Keith a stealthily-delivered nudge off the stage, while stabbing his skin with a tiny needle.

Keith just about managed to make his way back home, despite being in significant pain. By the following morning, significant had been replaced by overwhelmingly excruciating, to the point where Keith had no choice but to call for an ambulance. He was quickly taken to Reno's Washoe Medical Center; today called Renown Health.

X-rays determined that Keith had fractured his tibia, better known as the shinbone. The only available option was surgery. Having been advised by the attending doctor that a local anesthetic was utterly out of the question, Keith's paranoia began to grow, and perhaps justifiably so.

Before he went under the knife, Keith told his nephew, Chris Davis – who had come along to the hospital to see how his uncle was doing – he feared if he was anesthetized he would never wake up. Incredibly, and tragically, that is *exactly* what happened.

The official story was that Keith's death – on the operating table, no less – was caused by a significantly sized blood clot that, having previously been lodged in Keith's lower-leg, became loose and upon reaching one of his lungs, killed him stone dead. The nature of the terrible event was quickly played down by the authorities. Anjeanette Damon, of the *Reno-Gazette Journal* newspaper, was told by the Washoe County deputy coroner that Keith's death was accidental and nothing else.

Keith himself had actually written – in his book *Biowarfare in America* – about certain toxins used by the military and the intelligence community that could make murder appear to be misfortune by creating huge blood clots in the lungs, which, ironically, just happened to be the very cause of Keith's death.

Jim Keith's death, however, had *nothing* to do with the U.S. military: Mr. Bleak and his deadly ilk were of far stranger origins, as were the toxins that Bleak skillfully ensured found their way into Andrew Bridges' bloodstream, and as more than a few further players in the Stephenville affair were destined to find out in due course.

-17-

For a moment or two, Slade was stuck for words, after which he asked: "What do you mean: you want *me* to tell the story, to *everyone?*"

Drake smiled and replied: "We – that's to say my colleagues and I - have seen your articles in the AQUA magazine, as well as the column you write for *UFO Journal*. You're a good writer, Mr. Slade; a *very* good one. You have a flair for relating the facts but keeping it entertaining, too, which is good. We're looking for someone who can tell the Stephenville story, and your writing style and knowledge of the UFO subject makes you an excellent candidate."

"Well, if that's what you want," said Slade, "why don't you just go to the *New York Times* or the *Washington Post?* Give it to them, and it'll be all over the news in no time."

"Actually, no it won't," Drake responded. "I doubt you'll find it surprising to learn that certain players on what I call 'the other side' hold a great deal of power and sway over both those newspapers – and over many others, too. I won't bore you with all the facts, but there is not a chance in hell of the Stephenville story – all of it, I mean – coming out, untarnished, unaltered, and in the way that *we*, and I hope *you*, want it, if we leave it up to the newspapers. So, we need another approach."

"Then why don't you do what I said before? Go to the FBI: tell *them.*"

"Since you're so intent on answers, Mr. Slade, I'll give them to you."

It was now coming up to midnight: the appetizers were long gone, and the last of the coffee was finished off more than an hour ago. The whiskey and cokes were still flowing, however.

"I agree," began Drake, "that the best approach, in a perfect world, *would* be to contact the FBI, tell them everything, and have them launch a full investigation and bring to justice those who are planning just about the worst *injustice* possible to our great nation. But it's not that easy."

"Why's that?" asked Slade.

"Because, any investigation will inevitably blow the whole UFO secrecy wide open. And when the secrecy is gone, disclosure will tumble out, just as sure as night follows day. The problem is that *we* are not ready for disclosure yet – the factors are still not in place for a smooth transition, in terms of how the public will handle it. And *they*, the others, aren't in a solid enough position, *yet*, to risk planning a coup d'état and a nationwide UFO deception without being absolutely sure they can succeed without any degree of failure. There's another problem too: we're not entirely sure who *they* are."

Drake continued that while certain key figures had been identified in the plan to enslave America, many others had not: "This is what we know for sure: there are people in the NSA, Defense Intelligence Agency, military, CIA – and yes, the FBI, too, and even in the White House – who are *extremely* loyal to the group and their plans. We know their names; we know what it is they're plotting. But, the overall group is buried so incredibly deeply that we're lacking in a complete picture of their size and scope.

"At first, we thought this plot, the overthrow of democracy, was just a bunch of guys sitting around a table chewing the fat and theorizing on an outlandish scenario. But, it didn't take us long to realize this was very far from what was going on. Can you imagine how shocked we were to find that, rather than being just ten or twelve people discussing ideas from a theoretical perspective, they already had a network of *hundreds* of people, in all arms of government, ready to move at their command?

"One might be a high-ranking official in the Navy. Another could be a particle physicist out at Area 51. Maybe a general in the Pentagon, an entire squadron of pilots, half a dozen Secret Service agents guarding the president, and so on. They all have their regular day jobs, families; they're regular Joes, on the surface, anyway. But, behind the scenes, they're all patiently waiting for the day when they get the signal to go. Each and every one of them will have an assigned task:

place the president under house-arrest – whether it's legal or not; shut down the Internet and the airwaves; have tanks on the streets

"That's the problem we face: they're like an ant nest; growing by the day, but essentially buried from view. Until we know, exactly, who we are dealing with – as well as the size and scope of the group – we only see a part of the picture. In a worst-case scenario, we barely see *anything*.

"Christ," muttered Slade. "They could be *anywhere, everywhere*, and we'd never know. And *you* can't make a move without the whole deck of disclosure cards crashing down on everyone before things are ready."

"Exactly," said Drake. "Until we know for sure who's running the show, who is onboard, how many, and where they are, we're limited in what we can do. The only saving grace is that they clearly don't have enough power yet to execute their program – if they did, it would likely be going ahead right now. But, that your AQUA colleague, Andrew Bridges, was running around Stephenville collecting all those witness-reports is a sure sign they're pushing ahead."

Drake added, in casual tones and while displaying a broad smile: "Oh, that reminds me: Bridges was found dead this morning."

"*Dead*? Is that a joke?" replied Slade.

"No joke, Mr. Slade: dead in his bed in a Stephenville hotel-room," said Drake. "They're already guessing natural causes, apparently."

"Who are *they*?" Slade pressed.

"First-responders, paramedics; whoever was on the scene first. Of course, though, it clearly *wasn't* natural causes."

"Your guys?" asked Slade.

Drake laughed: "No, nothing to do with us; I guarantee you that much."

Slade continued with the questions: "Who then?"

"Ah, well, that opens up yet another can of worms – one you will surely need to know about if you're agreeable to our book idea."

"Go on," said Slade, wondering what Drake had in store for him now.

"The Men in Black, Mr. Slade: the MIB. And no, we are *not* talking about FBI, CIA, or even Tommy Lee Jones and Will Smith. I mean, the *real* Men in Black."

"*What?*" replied Slade; his voice filled with skepticism. "You mean there really *are* strange little guys in fedoras and black suits running around putting the wind-up people?"

Drake's face looked grim: "Make no mistake; the Men in Black are *very* real."

"So, who the hell are they? Slade demanded to know.

"That's the big question," Drake answered. "I'll be honest with you: we don't know *who* or *what* they are. But one thing I know for sure: they're no joke. The UFO research community has pretty much got it right, though: the MIB tend to just make threats – sometimes vague and sometimes not quite so vague. But they very rarely take things any further."

"Except for when they do?" said Slade, in wry tones, pondering on the death of Andrew Bridges.

Drake nodded. "Yes, except for when they do. I can't give you any specific figures because we really don't know. But we suspect they've taken out people on both sides of disclosure; maybe ten or more in the last couple of years. In that sense, their agenda is pretty much unclear and most likely self-serving. Just like us."

Slade wanted an answer to one burning question: "But why Bridges? He was hardly one of the main guys in all this, was he?"

"True, Mr. Slade; very true: Bridges was a minor cog in a minor wheel. My guess is that someone – the MIB – was sending a message. As to what that message might have been? Well, maybe to let us and Bridges' people know they're not going to sit back and have disclosure dictated to them."

"But they've killed your people too?"

"Oh yes; make no mistake about that. These creatures don't take sides. I wish I could tell you we haven't had casualties too, as all of us would doubtless sleep sounder at night if that were the case. But we have. And that's one of the reasons we're suspicious of the aliens. They seem to want to scuttle Bridges' people. But, they're hardly helping us either."

Drake sighed and for a moment or two, sat silent. He then continued. "Three different groups, three agendas – two we're sure of and one we're not – and the future of the country hanging in the balance; that's where we're at. And now, you are, too. But let's get back to the book.

"Those we're fighting against, Mr. Slade, might have the newspaper industry wrapped up when it comes to *what* gets published and *how* it gets published, but we have our influences, too. One of them is the book industry. You may not know this, but government agencies sometimes work very closely with the book world, and particularly when it comes to getting a story into the public domain that will be to their benefit. It's not necessary for you to have all the details right now. But, I can guarantee you a major deal with a major publisher – and we have the contacts and the influence to have that book in millions of homes in months. Do you really think it was just down to chance that Whitley Strieber's *Communion* became such a best-seller?"

"You?" asked Slade.

"Not exactly, but colleagues and associates – put it like that."

"And the purpose is what, exactly?" asked Slade.

"We would like you to write a novel about everything you have seen, heard and done since this regrettable business with Stephenville began: the sightings, the story of the U.N. meeting, our friend Gladys, Bridges' death, the Men in Black, the plan for a faked alien invasion – and even me. You will, however, intimate – and intimate strongly – that the story you are telling is not fiction, but *fictionalized*. The reader needs to know that all of this is real, that it's all going on – *right now*.

"It needs to be done in a way that millions of Americans will be exposed to – and, more importantly, think about – what may be just around the corner. My people can't go public yet – for the reasons I explained. But *you* can give some warning. And which may even make Bridges' people back-off – to some degree - if they think they've been identified, which they surely will."

Slade was puzzled: "But what about the time-frame in all this? Who's to say we'll even have the book out before the shit hits the fan?"

"Well, that's the hard part. We've estimated that, even though Stephenville probably made it clear to them that achieving some kind of alien false-flag event is feasible, it may be a year or more before all the people, players and technology is in place. We may be wrong, of course, but we don't think we are.

"Think about it: this would be a mammoth plan, not just some overnight thing. Time, then, is hopefully on our side. You write the book – you'll be handsomely rewarded for doing so as soon as possible – and we'll do the rest: find the publisher, get the book out there, get you on the news, chat shows; the whole deal. Get the public and the media thinking. Then, if it does happen, at least people may see through the deception and stand up. We'll be doing our part, you'll be doing yours, and we have others, too, all helping to keep those bastards at bay. So, what do you say?"

Slade looked Drake firmly in the eye: "I say: you've got a deal."

"Tremendous, Mr. Slade," said a very satisfied Drake. "I warn you, however, that before all this is over you are going to see things the likes of which you have never seen before."

"Bring it on," replied Slade. "*Bring it on.*"

-18-

It was around 2:15 a.m. when Slade and Drake finally wrapped things up.

"We'll need one more meeting. I suggest lunch around noon, here in the hotel, and we can start things moving," said Drake.

"Define 'moving' for me, please," replied Slade, wanting a clear picture of what was going down.

"The first thing is that we need to get you back to Texas if we're going to stand any chance of exposing all this."

"Back to Stephenville?" asked Slade.

Drake smiled slightly. "Actually, no -- to Waxahachie."

"Waxahachie? What the hell's that got to do with all this?"

"Oh, far more than you can even imagine, Mr. Slade. We're going to get you into a place that will confirm just about everything you could ever want or need, and probably much more."

"In Waxahachie?" said Slade, somewhat doubtful that *anything* of significance had ever gone on in the town – except for ZZ Top's manager, Bill Ham, having been born there.

"Not exactly *in* Waxahachie, but *below* it; *far* below it, as you'll soon see," said Drake, in cryptic style. "But, that can all wait until tomorrow. I'll have a full briefing for you then. We'll have lunch here in the room; you never know who else might decide to join us in the restaurant – unannounced and sitting nearby, if you get my drift."

Slade got Drake's drift completely and immediately: after Slade's experience with the Department of Homeland Security guy in the restaurant of the Stephenville Holiday Inn, the idea of staying out of restaurants was suddenly very appealing.

"I warn you though, Mr. Slade, the Waxahachie excursion may turn out to be quite a difficult one. I trust your skills honed in the Marine Corps are still as good today as they were back then?"

101

"No problems there, Drake. I can handle myself just fine. And if I have to, how far do I go to protect myself and get what I need?"

"Mr. Slade," replied Drake, "whatever actions you have to take, however distasteful, will not come back to haunt you. *We* can tidy things up from our end. And *they* won't want to risk taking action against *you* – lest it blows their plans wide open."

"A 'get out of jail free card', Drake: that sounds good."

"It should, because I suspect you may well need it."

And with that, Drake nodded, made for the door and was gone - headed to wherever it was that government spooks head at 2:30 in the morning, thought Slade.

Two floors down, a tall, blond-haired man in his late thirties was lying on a king-sized bed, staring at the ceiling and carefully running through his mind the next day's activities. Very few people knew his name; those who did were usually headed for early deaths. He had three passports and three driving licenses: American, British, and Australian, and all courtesy of contacts in the ever-resourceful Central Intelligence Agency. Right now, he was using his British alias: Gary Mitchell. And he was here, in Washington, D.C., to visit a girl he had met in London the previous summer. That was the cover story: the *real* reason was to snuff out the life of a man he knew nothing about, except his name, what he looked like, and where he was staying. The man smiled to himself, knowing that just two floors above him was the target that, by tomorrow evening, would be leaving the hotel stone-cold and in a body-bag.

As a child, the man had lived, in poverty, in a tough part of Johannesburg, South Africa – Jozi, as it was affectionately known to the roughly one million people that called the city their home. He, however, had no affection for the place at all. Life in a rundown apartment, with no mother and just a violent, alcoholic father for what passed as company, was not his idea of fun. Fortunately, that all changed when the once skinny, fear-filled child reached sixteen. By then he was going on six feet tall and weighing in at a muscular 190 pounds. He took steps to ensure that he never again took a beating from the old man. He planned it carefully and brilliantly.

Every Saturday night was the same; his father would walk – or, rather, stagger – home from the bar around the corner, filled with just two things which, when combined, made for a volatile cocktail: whisky and hate. The old guy was not just a drunk, but the worst kind of drunk possible: the angry, spite-filled alcoholic whose only form of pleasure comes from making someone else's life miserable; but, not on this Saturday night. Not on *any* Saturday night, ever again.

The boy knew that his father wouldn't stand a chance; he was fifty-three and in poor shape. His yellowing eyes reflected the sorry state of his liver and his once toned stomach was now a blubbery embarrassment. It was going to be so easy. And it was.

To avoid taking the longer, safer route home, his father always took his life in his hands by snaking his way through the back-alleys and poorly-lit streets that cut ten minutes off the walk. Those same alleys and streets, however, were the feeding grounds of the hungry, the homeless, and those that would cut you just as soon as look at you. Amazingly, the old man had never once had a problem – probably because even the muggers and the psychos could see that he wasn't worth bothering with. They were right.

Since the bar closed at eleven, the boy calculated that around 11:15 his father would reach one particularly dark stretch of alleyway – one that only the most idiotic, or drunk, person would even think about walking along at that time of night. Idiotic *and* drunk, however, was guaranteed to ensure that all thoughts of personal safety would go right out of the window – which was very good news for the boy.

He had a weekend job at a local store and had spent the past couple of weeks putting a bit of spare money aside, specifically for two things: a pair of jeans and a sweatshirt; both black. The color was essential if he was to blend into the shadows as the drunk old bastard rolled on by. Sure enough, his father did exactly that.

It all happened very quickly and easily; effortlessly, even: "Hello, dad," the boy said, as he stepped out of the darkness that surrounded an old dumpster and with a maniacal smile on his face. His father, wasted as ever, managed a brief, puzzled and hazy look at his son, just before his throat was sliced open with a sharp, powerful blade. Death came quickly – and in red spurts, much to the boy's satisfaction.

The inevitable police investigation that began the very next day turned up nothing, beyond the probability that the killer had been one of the many street people that dominated the area. The case was quickly closed and labeled: *Unsolved*.

Two years later, the boy – now a man – joined the South African National Defense Force and spent the next couple of years serving in Pretoria, in South Africa's Gauteng Province. It was there that he proved his worth as an expert marksman, and someone whose hand-to-hand combat skills were the envy of his colleagues. And, then, one day, without warning, he got a phone call: would he be interested in serving his country by working for South Africa's National Intelligence Agency? The work would be difficult, dangerous, highly secret, almost always completely illegal, but very financially rewarding. It didn't take him long at all to accept the position; just seconds, as it transpires.

And it was that work which, after seven years spent with the NIA, ensured he developed a foothold with the intelligence services of three other nations: the United States, the United Kingdom, and Australia. All of which brought him to where he was today: stretched out on a Washington, D.C. bed planning the death of a man just thirty feet above him.

The man picked up the photo of Marc Slade and scrutinized it carefully. Just as was the case with his father, all those years earlier, it was going to be so easy. His contractors at the CIA were going to be very pleased. They were going to be significantly out of pocket, too, when it came to paying his fee.

The man placed the photo on the bedside table, turned off the light, lay back and closed his eyes. He pictured Slade's face, superimposed over his father's lifeless, bloodied body. Slade was as good as dead already.

-19-

There was nothing noteworthy about the room: it contained a large table, eight chairs, and a small refrigerator. The five people making their way to the room, however, were noteworthy in the extreme. Leading the pack was General Robert Fowler, practically marching into battle; such was his state of fury. Michael Harris, of the CIA's Science and Technology division, followed close behind, anticipating that a shitstorm of epic proportions was about to erupt. He was right. Harris had no idea who the other three were, except that he guessed he soon would. Right again.

As Fowler reached the room, he threw the thick, wooden door open with such force that it practically bounced back shut, barely missing Harris's head by an inch.

"Let's get on with it," Fowler hissed with fury, as he stood at the end of the table, his 220 pound, six-foot-four frame looming, in intimidating fashion, over the others, who were already taken their seats.

"Everyone knows each other but you, Harris," Fowler added, as he introduced Harris to Professor Marie Fawcett, a psychologist who worked in the field of profiling for the FBI, and who had been instrumental in helping the program figure out what makes the average citizen tick and how to rewire that tick; Miles Tanner, a senior figure in FEMA; and Harrison Knowles, one of the brains behinds the NSA's all-encompassing surveillance of the United States.

A secretary entered the room, holding a large tray containing water, glasses and coffee.

"Put it on the table and leave," Fowler said, coldly.

"Yes sir," the girl replied, carefully avoiding Fowler's piercing eyes. He waited until the door was shut, walked over to it, locked it from the inside, and began.

"As you know, the program is proceeding as planned. We now have exactly nine-hundred-and-seventy-three recruits – across nearly every government agency and the military. We've got infiltration at just about every level: White House aides, NORAD, Homeland Security, and, of course, FEMA and NSA," said Fowler, nodding at Knowles and Tanner. As if on cue, they smiled in dutiful, and practically fawning, fashion.

Fowler continued: "And the response at Stephenville showed that we *can* pull it off. But not yet: we need more people, far more people; people we can trust. In short, we need numbers. Getting them is not, we believe, a problem. But, getting the numbers quickly, and in a way that doesn't blow our cover, *is* a problem. As you also know, our time-frame of eighteen months from now, for when we go, is still on target, but there's another matter to be dealt with."

"Slade?" asked Fawcett.

"Yes, Slade," replied Fowler, "*fucking Slade.*"

"If I may ask," Harris chimed in, "how is it that just one man can cause us so much trouble?"

"It's *not* just Slade," Fowler answered. "Drake and his cronies – who should have been put out to graze years ago, and particularly that Gladys woman – are the troublemakers. It's only now becoming clear just how much influence they've got. You recall how they first thought we were just a couple of dozen people? Well, that's what *we* thought about *them*. It seems we both underestimated each other."

"Exactly what are you saying, general?" asked Fawcett.

"I'm saying our latest intelligence is showing they're *not* just a few old geezers trying to hang on to the past: they're a network. And we're now seeing evidence of exactly how significant that network is."

"And how big might it be?" Knowles wanted to know.

The general's face was a mixture of anger, frustration and concern: "*It's big.*"

"So, why aren't they making their move?" Knowles added.

"Same reason as we aren't: they don't have the power yet, and they can't afford risking disclosure until they're ready."

"They're our exact mirror-image," said Tanner, with growing realization. "So, general, what's their plan? And more importantly, what's *ours*? How are we dealing with it?"

"There's one very easy way to deal with all this," said the general. "One by one, we systematically wipe them out."

"I'm not sure that's a good idea," said Fawcett, worriedly.

"You have a better solution?" thundered Fowler.

Fawcett stayed noticeably silent.

The general continued: "We have someone on standby, in D.C., right now, to take care of Slade; the kind of guy who doesn't make mistakes and who won't alert any suspicions. As for the rest, yes, ideally, wiping them all out *is* the best option. But, the problem is that we can't just go around killing American citizens by the hundreds – and we're sure there *are* hundreds of them. For a start, it wouldn't take any time at all to see a pattern developing and, as sure as shit, we'd all be behind bars in no time."

He added: "One or two people, all made to look like an accident, won't rouse suspicions. Dozens or hundreds, it's not possible. We've *got* to come up with something else."

"That reminds me," said Fawcett, her voice brimming with curiosity, "what was the deal with Andrew Bridges? That was Drake's people? Clearly, with the timing, it was no accident."

The general stared for a moment, pondering on how to answer.

"Miss Fawcett," said Fowler, "you *are* aware there is another party involved in all this?"

"Of course, I am. You mean them?" she replied.

"Yes, I mean *them*: Bridges' death was most definitely *not* anything to do with Drake."

Fawcett responded: "The men in black?"

"Probably, but we can't be sure; we'll probably never know."

"This is getting insane," said Harris.

"Mr. Harris," said the general in forthright tones as he glared at Harris, "what is insane is letting our country fall apart. Our great land needs a shot of new blood; *our* blood. To ensure that America remains the dominant force throughout the 21st century, sacrifices need to be made. And in time people *will* accept them; just like America now

107

accepts 24-hour surveillance by Knowles' boys at the NSA. Bringing back the draft will send a message that we're not to be fucked with, a 10:00 p.m. curfew will remove scum from the streets, and a threat from E.T.s will just about seal the entire deal. There's nothing insane about that. It's about survival; you know that."

In slightly, and deliberately, threatening tones, he added: "Or, I *hope* you know that."

"I do, yes," said Harris, his mind now filled with thoughts of his own mysterious demise if he dared said anything else.

"Good. And that brings us to Slade. As far as the couple of insiders we have in place can figure out, Drake has this hare-brained plan to have Slade write a book – a novel – on Stephenville, with a less than subtle subtext that it's the truth. Under normal circumstances, we wouldn't care – UFO novels are a dime a dozen.

"But there's a big difference with Slade. Drake has given him the scoop on the U.N. meeting, on how the Robertson Panel got us to where we are today, specific names, and God knows what else he told him. We know Slade met briefly with Gladys Samuels, but we don't have a clue about what was said. And there's another matter of concern, too."

"And which is?" asked Fawcett.

"Waxahachie: the body."

"Holy Christ!" exclaimed Tanner. "Slade knows about Waxahachie?"

"Worse than that," replied the general. "We think Drake is trying to find a way to get Slade *in* there. Like I said, UFO novels are a dime a dozen. But with too many hard facts, too many real names and places, and some kind of statement from Slade's publisher, maybe the book isn't just fiction after all. And before you know it, some hotshot journalist is going to be on the trail, and we'll be facing exposure – *that* is where things are at."

"This is just bullshit," said Tanner. "This is just one man; get rid of the son of a bitch!"

"No, Mr. Tanner," replied Fowler, "this is *not* just bullshit, nor is it just one man. This is a highly organized group, one that is as dedicated as we are, and which will do what it has to do to protect

Slade and to ensure he gets what he needs to destroy us. Gentlemen and lady, we are officially in a state of war."

-20-

Right on cue, Drake knocked on Slade's door at noon. The man was as punctual and precise as he was mysterious.

"Greetings," beamed Drake, who was followed into the room by one of the hotel staff carrying two plates of sandwiches and a coffee pot. "And since it's now officially past noon, I brought us something else too," he added, holding up a small bottle of Jack.

Either the guy's the friendliest spook in D.C. or he's a drunk, thought Slade smiling. It scarcely mattered, though: Slade wasn't about to say no to a bit of the hard stuff, and particularly when it was at someone else's expense.

"Now, where were we?" said Drake, after the coffee and sandwiches were placed on the table, and they were left to their own devices. "I believe it was Waxahachie."

For the next forty-five minutes, Slade listened, amazed and transfixed, as Drake told him the story of the pulverized and preserved alien body held deep within the huge maze of tunnels that extended far below the town he had driven through so many times, but in which he'd never had any reason to stop – until now.

Two floors down and around one hour later, the man from South Africa was getting ready to end the life of the man who was, right now, sitting upstairs, sipping on a glass of Jack and listening to an incredible story concerning an alien on ice.

Ideally, he would have preferred to take out Slade on the dark streets of D.C., late at night, and have it look like the work of a mugger. That approach had worked out perfectly in Johannesburg with his father, so why should Slade be any different? Just because Slade was ex-Marine Corps didn't mean shit to the man. Unfortunately, and somewhat oddly, he thought, his target had not once left his room, aside from eating breakfast in the hotel. And, as skilled an assassin as the man was, even he couldn't end Slade's life and get away with it over cornflakes, orange juice and scrambled eggs. It was time for "Plan B."

It was a simple ruse that had worked perfectly on the three previous occasions he had employed it; today should be just the same. The man finished off his lunch of nachos and ice-tea, splashed his face with cold water, dried off, and put on his black jacket – which concealed a silencer-equipped pistol - and left the room. The clock was ticking ever faster.

The man chose to take the stairs, rather than the elevator – there was less chance of him being seen. That Slade's room was only two doors down from the stairs made things even better. As he opened the door from the stairwell to the corridor, the man peered carefully, assessing the situation. Not a soul was in sight; even better. He walked to Slade's room and took out of his pocket a twenty-dollar bill. He crumpled it up and knocked on Slade's door, the plan being to claim he was walking past and saw the bill on the ground, right outside the door. And, being an honest soul, he decided to see if the guest inside had dropped it as they dug their room key out of their pocket.

The beauty of this ruse was that, where money was concerned, most people would immediately accept it. And placing them off-guard, and having them focus on a bit of welcome cash was the perfect way to move in quickly for the kill. How easy.

Drake was just about to tell Slade of the specific plans he had to get Slade into the Waxahachie facility when there was a knock at the door. Drake, clearly in a good mood – one made all the better by the way things were progressing and a couple of hits of Jack – said: "Let me get it; I neglected to tell you I ordered us a superb dessert."

As Drake swung open the door, the man in the black jacket did something he had never done before: he hesitated. That sure as hell wasn't Slade. For a second, he turned his eyes towards the door number to check he had the right room. He did. It didn't matter: that one second proved to be both crucial and deadly. By the time his eyes caught Drake's again, the old man had already assessed the situation.

Seeing that something was up, Slade jumped to his feet. By the time he reached the door, it was practically over. In a move that amazed Slade, Drake delivered a swift and powerful blow to the man's throat. He staggered, panicking, as he fumbled for his gun. Drake grabbed the man's tie and swung him around, spinning him violently into the room and right into the way of Slade's pummeling fists.

The man, his nose now broken and bleeding, reached for his gun, but it was too late. Like a magician pulling a rabbit out of a hat, Drake himself pulled an impressive piece of weaponry out of his inside pocket and pumped two bullets into the man's chest. Drake's very own silencer ensured that no-one would come running to find out what was going on. The man gurgled briefly, and his eyes rolled into his head. As the lights went out, his final thoughts were of that long gone Saturday night in Johannesburg and his scumbag of a father. He had no regrets.

The man had been right: death *would* occur in this room today.

"Fuck!" said Slade, taking a deep breath. He had seen death many times on the battlefield, but this was something else. This was clearly a case of assassin vs. assassin.

Drake quickly closed the door – but not before first checking that pandemonium wasn't breaking out all along the corridors – and said, nodding to the floor: "Mr. Slade, *this* is what we're up against."

"From the way you handled yourself," said Slade, "I guess this wasn't the first time you've been in a situation like this?"

Drake smiled: "You guess right. Not bad for an old man?"

"Not bad at all."

"And that was a fine couple of right-hooks from you, Mr. Slade."

"I keep in shape," Slade smiled. "But what the hell do we do about this?" he asked, pointing to the dead, bloody corpse on the carpet.

"We bring in a clean-up crew," replied Drake, casually.

"Not the hotel's housecleaning?"

"Very amusing, Mr. Slade; no. We have our own people."

"You're telling me you can bring a crew in here and remove a dead body filled with lead, and all without anyone knowing?"

Drake smiled: "Well, no, not exactly. We have an association, shall I say, with the owners of this fine establishment. Like a lot of what you have seen just recently, Mr. Slade, this hotel is not all that it appears to be – *not at all*."

Slade asked: "Well, now what?"

"Now, we get you to a safe place and quickly. It won't take long for whoever hired this man to find out things haven't worked out quite as they planned. They know we won't involve the police, so there's nothing to stop them making a second attempt to kill you."

Slade put on his jacket, knocked back his Jack, threw everything into his suitcase and headed for the door.

"One moment, Mr. Slade; there's business to take care of," said Drake. He took out his cell-phone and dialed a number. It was answered by a man deeply familiar with the old man's deadly work. "This is room 915," said Drake. "I'm afraid I spilled something on the carpet. Could you send someone up?"

-21-

S lade and Drake stealthily exited the room. It was unlikely the assassin had an accomplice; both men knew that contract killers typically worked alone. On the other hand, it didn't hurt to play things carefully. Whereas Drake had dominated the conversation over the past two days, it was now time for Slade to take the lead. It had been more than a few years since he left the Marine Corps behind him, but the skills learned and honed in the service were ever-present.

"Keep behind me, Drake," Slade whispered, his right hand buried deep in his jacket pocket, gripping the assassin's gun – just in case.

"I can see you've done this before," quipped Drake.

"You know it," said Slade, as the pair kept close to the wall.

It was a tense couple of minutes from the hotel room to the lobby. Fortunately, everything ran smoothly; there was barely a soul in sight, aside from room-service and a woman trying to control two screaming kids. One would scarcely know that just minutes earlier a violent and deadly confrontation had occurred in this very building.

Drake said, "I took the liberty of using a company car this morning. Don't ask me why, because I don't know, but I had a hunch that we might see some trouble. We'll be safe in that; *no one* will be looking for anything but my car, if even that."

They took the stairs down to the parking garage. Unlike the hotel itself, the garage was a hive of activity, which was very good news. In the event the man *did* have an accomplice, it was highly unlikely he would try anything with ten or fifteen people around two families making their ways to their vehicles, a couple of maintenance guys on a break, and a group of businessmen heading out for the day. It was the ideal time for Slade and Drake to make their move – and quickly, too.

Drake's vehicle, parked on the south side of the garage, was a silver Toyota Prius. The walk was only a short one, yet each and every step was tension-filled as both men silently wondered if normality was about to be replaced at any moment by mayhem and murder. As it transpired, normality had the upper hand.

"Do you care for hybrids?" Drake asked Slade, as they reached the car.

"I guess they're good for the environment, but I'll stick with my Corvette. I bet I get more girls with the Corvette than I would with that," Slade joked, nodding in the direction of the Prius.

Drake smiled: "Probably so, Mr. Slade; probably so. And let's hope you get to prove the point for many more years to come. That means: we need to get out of here - *now*."

As Slade and Drake prepared to hit the road, General Robert Fowler received a phone call of the sort that he was most definitely not anticipating – or wanting.

"General, it's Briggs, sir."

"Is the job done?" asked Fowler, with urgency in his voice.

"I'm afraid there's a problem. We haven't heard from our South African friend; he's now fifteen minutes behind the planned check-in schedule."

"Christ almighty!" cursed Fowler.

"Yes, sir, I know. Even allowing for a five or ten-minute issue, he's still running behind. And we both know how precise he has been on previous occasions. It's not looking good."

"When was the last time you heard from him?" Fowler wanted to know.

"Only just a couple of minutes before he planned to leave his room, sir: that's what's worrying. He seems to have vanished at some point between leaving his room and getting to Slade's."

"Either that or Slade got word of what was going down and got to our man first," replied the general. "Christ, this is all we need. If Slade's still alive, we need to know what he's up to. He's too smart just to hang out in his room if the shit *has* hit the fan. Please tell me you have someone watching the hotel."

Briggs was silent for a moment, something which told the general the news was not going to be good. He was right.

"Sir," said Briggs, "we felt the best approach – to make sure that Slade didn't get a sense of what was going down – was to let the South African do his work, alone. Slade is not an idiot; he's Marine Corps all the way: he would have eyeballed any of our guys in a minute. We felt that backing off, and letting our friend do his work, was the best approach. Doing it that way always worked in the past."

"But not this time it didn't," said the general in hostile tones.

"No sir, not this time; it seems that's our mistake," replied Briggs, hesitantly.

Fowler's voice took on a tone that chilled Briggs to his core: "No, Mr. Briggs, it's *your* mistake, not *our* mistake. This is what you will do: you will utilize whatever resources are necessary, you will find Slade, and you will ensure that the task assigned to the South African is completed. By who, or how, I don't *want* to know and I don't *need* to know; I just want the job done. Do I make myself clear?"

Briggs swallowed hard: "You *do* make yourself clear, sir, yes. No more mistakes."

"No more mistakes: that's correct," said the general, before hanging up and letting loose with an ear-splitting tirade at no-one but himself.

Charles Briggs, one of the closest friends – or, more correctly, *supposed* friends - of the President of the United States of America, cursed quietly. He had to get on top of things and quickly – nothing could stand in the way of the program, no matter what. And the sooner that prick in the Oval Office is under house-arrest, he thought, the better: it'll be a great day when the new America is born. Briggs dialed a number: "I need to see you, one hour from now; the usual place."

"Best keep your head down, Mr. Slade," said Drake, as he put the car into drive and proceeded to pull out of the garage. "They, if anyone *is* watching, won't recognize this car. And they won't recognize me either," he added, pulling a black, wooly hat over his head, something that Slade couldn't fail to see the humor in.

"You look like an elderly mugger," Slade said.

"Well, in some ways, that's *exactly* what I am," replied Drake. "Here," added, "I have a spare; you might want to put it on too."

Slade pulled the hat on tight, lowered his seat, and stretched out flat. If someone *was* scoping out the place, keeping out of sight and in at least a bit of a disguise – until they were well away from the hotel - was the best thing he could do right now.

For around two hours, Drake drove north. The roads were monotonous, the gray, January skies were depressing, and the drizzle was endless. Drake finally signaled and took an exit off the highway; the landscape soon became far less concrete and far more forest.

"Where, exactly, are we going?" asked Slade.

"I have what you might call a home away from home, Mr. Slade. I use it for fishing, relaxing and emergencies. You, I fear, fall into the last category. I suggest we stay there until we can find a safe way to get you back to Texas; to Waxahachie. There's no way we can use the regular airlines now; you wouldn't make it through security. They'll have some trumped-up reason to have you detained, and then it would be goodbye to Mr. Marc Slade."

"You know there's a small airport not far from Waxahachie?" asked Slade. "Mid-Way Airport: it's right between Waxahachie and Midlothian. I've used it a couple of times."

"You're one step ahead of me, Mr. Slade," said Drake. "I was going to suggest we get you on a flight to Mid-Way: we can get you new I.D., as well as a cover story in case you're stopped."

Slade was impressed: Drake was on the ball.

Twenty minutes passed and, finally, the journey was almost over: Drake slowed down and took a left turn onto a small dirt road. Two minutes later, Slade could see a tree-shrouded, medium-sized wooden house, dead ahead. It looked like the kind of place mom and dad would take the kids to for a weekend of fun, not for hiding someone who now felt like he was starring in a real-life version of *The Fugitive*.

Drake brought the Prius to a halt, and the two men exited the vehicle; they both stretched their arms and legs. The grassy, muddy ground was damp and cold beneath their feet. It wasn't yet 4:00 p.m. but the stormy skies and the dense woods made it seem closer to evening. Slade carefully scanned the area – not just to take in its captivating lakeside beauty, but to check for any weak points, in the event that someone decided to try and finish the job that had been botched in a certain hotel room just a few hours earlier.

Had Slade looked a little closer into the heart of those dark woods, he just might have caught sight of a tall, thin man; one who was almost completely camouflaged by the overhanging, thick branches of an old, large tree. It was a man dressed entirely in black; he sported a fedora hat and stared intently at Slade and Drake. Whether it was a stare born out of concern or malevolence, only the man in black himself knew. The two men situated barely fifty yards away, however, would find out later that night.

-22-

“ “Sir, it's Briggs.”

“What is it, Briggs?” barked General Robert Fowler.

“Worse news, I'm afraid.”

Fowler took a deep breath: “Go on.”

“Sir, as you know, our South African contact failed to complete his task. And, as you also know, there's no sign of him – as in anywhere. Well, there's something else: one of our contacts in Drake's group overheard something a couple of hours ago about an altercation at the hotel, one apparently involving Drake and Slade. She doesn't know any more than that, but I guess it means they took care of the South African.”

“Jesus!” shouted the general. “Well, what about the body? And what about those I.D.'s he had? If I need to remind you, I helped expedite those. This, sure as shit, had better not get back to me.”

Briggs swallowed hard: “Sir, I don't think that will happen. We've already had a couple of people make a careful scan of the hotel. There hasn't been *any* police presence there at all, and there are no signs of anything unusual going down. That makes me think Drake and Slade got rid of the body.”

“And how might they have done that, in broad daylight, in a hotel?” asked the general.

“Well, we've heard rumors – granted, unsubstantiated rumors, but rumors all the same – that Drake's people have some sort of link to the hotel.”

“What do you mean: a *link*?” the general seethed.

“It sounds odd, but we think that the hotel isn't all it seems to be. We've got intelligence that it may have been used by Drake's people on previous occasions – mainly to entrap Soviet spies during the Cold War; that kind of thing. And it seems this is not the first time there has been a suspicious disappearance there. But, like with the South African, the police were apparently never informed."

The general's voice went quiet: "The hotel's being used as a lure and Drake's lot are paying the owners to turn a blind eye. Drake anticipated we might try and make a move on Slade, so he chose the place deliberately, in the event we *did* send someone along."

"Yes, sir; that's exactly how it appears to be," replied Briggs.

Fowler thought for a moment, then said: "Okay, now hang on; let's look at this carefully. We can make this work to our advantage. Drake obviously took steps to make sure the cops were kept out of the loop. That suggests there are people at the hotel working with Drake, and that, somehow, *they* got rid of the body while Slade and Drake headed to God knows where. That all means one thing: we're in the clear, as Drake obviously wants to make sure no-one gets to hear about it."

Briggs' tone brightened: "I agree, sir. If Drake even took the slightest step to getting the police involved, everything – disclosure - would come tumbling out. And, right now, he doesn't want that any more than we do."

Fowler smiled: "And that means, so far as we can tell, from their perspective and ours, the South African never existed."

"Yes, sir; and there is another matter too."

As the general sat and listened, Briggs told him that Drake's home had been under surveillance for the past few hours, and there was zero activity afoot.

"We had someone check the outside of the house – under the guise of delivering a parcel. No one's answering the door. We've made phone calls too – a telemarketing cover – but no answer. But here's the interesting thing: Drake's garage-door has a couple of small windows in it. Our man took a quick look and said Drake's car is in the garage."

"Shit!" exclaimed the general. "That means he could be driving around, anywhere, with Slade, and we have no idea of what kind of vehicle they're in or where they're heading. So we're back to being screwed."

"Not necessarily," said Briggs. "It seems that Drake has *another* place. It's up north; in the woods, on the edge of a small lake. A few years back he bought a cabin there; likes to go fishing. He goes there around two weekends a month. I'm guessing he and Slade could be there."

"Briggs," the general replied, in commanding tones, "I want that place checked out - *right now*. If they're there, I want the job completed. If they're not, have someone stay in the area, in the event they *do* turn up."

"It's already in hand, sir. I have two guys who can be there in just a couple of hours. It will be pitch-black in the woods then and..."

The general interrupted: "I don't need to know the details. Just get this mess over and done with – and quickly."

"Yes, sir," Briggs answered. He then added, in tentative tones: "In the event Slade and Drake *are* there, and things don't go well, we have another alternative, too."

"That is?" asked Fowler.

"Waxahachie."

Briggs outlined his thoughts: "The problem we've had so far is that things have very much been on Slade and Drake's territory: Slade barely stayed still in Stephenville and was way too visible there for us to take any action and get away with it. And with the hotel, Drake clearly masterminded that and, unfortunately, succeeded. It could be the same at his lake-house too."

"So you're suggesting what?" asked the general.

"I'm suggesting if Slade gets away from us here and makes it to Waxahachie – regardless of whether it's with Drake's help or not - we *allow* him to find his way into the tunnels."

"That's a hell of a risk, but go on," Fowler replied.

"I'm thinking we make it appear to Slade that we've backed off, to where it will look like no-one on our side knows about Drake's plan to get him into the Waxahachie facility. Yes, Slade will have his guard up, but if he doesn't see us, and he thinks there's a good chance he'll get to see what's hidden there, he won't be able to resist the lure. Then, when he's in the tunnels, he's in *our* territory. He'll be like a rat in a cage. We can have people already in there, ready to grab him or whatever."

"By God, that could work," said General Fowler. "We can have him the moment he's in the tunnels. And a couple of hundred feet underground, no-one would ever know. He'll be like a fish on the end of a hook."

"Either way, whether it's in the woods tonight, or in the Waxahachie tunnels, Slade is ours," Briggs said, his voice filled with warped pride.

-23-

"So what do you think of my home from home?" asked Drake, as he and Slade ate microwave chicken dinners and drank Jack Daniels - on a large couch in a living room filled with an impressive array of huge, mounted fish that Drake had caught in the waters of the lake just a couple of hundred yards away.

"Pretty good," said Slade, waving his glass in Drake's direction, by way of a toast.

It was hardly a conventional dinner, however. Keenly aware of the probability that those forces working against them would eventually find out about Drake's cabin in the woods, the pair chose to take time to recharge their batteries and get something filling inside them in near-darkness. The only illumination coming through the windows was the near-full moon that loomed overhead.

Both men knew that anything which might alert any potential, unwelcome visitors to the property had to be avoided at all costs. That included lights, television and outside activity. Fortunately, and as Slade was coming more and more around to realizing and appreciating, Drake was a man seemingly always prepared for any and all eventualities.

Night-vision equipment, an impressive arsenal of weaponry, motion detectors in the woods, no less than three cell phones, and a near-impenetrable cellar would all help to ensure that in the event of a face to face confrontation, there was a very good chance of keeping the enemy at bay.

With his dinner devoured and a couple of warming drinks inside him, Slade was in the mood to keep the momentum going: "So, what can I expect in Waxahachie?" he asked Drake.

"That's a very good question," Drake replied. "Much of it depends on how and where, exactly, we get you in."

"I thought you said there was one extra entrance point beyond the main building? Something fenced and disguised to look like a generator or something?"

"Correct," Drake replied. "It's made to look like something the city of Waxahachie put there, but it's actually the entrance point to a very deep shaft; one which leads into the tunnel system – and which will put you about two miles from the room where you'll find the answers."

Slade could see from Drake's expression that something was troubling him: "But you think there's a problem?"

Drake nodded solemnly: "The existence of the second entrance point is known to all our people. But, here's the problem: if *we* know of it, then *they* almost certainly do, too. I can easily see you ending up ambushed if we don't take things carefully."

"So what's the answer?" asked Slade, pondering on how he should best handle the situation.

"The answer," Drake replied, with a slight smile, "is the *other* entrance point."

"There's a *third* way in?"

"There is."

Drake explained that when, in the early 1990s, the construction of the originally planned fifty-four miles of tunnels that were to comprise the Superconducting Super Collider began, one of the major issues facing the team involved was the matter of water – chiefly, the concern of underground flooding. So, as a result, an extensive sewer and drainage system was installed, one which linked to the main sewer network that coiled its way around Waxahachie itself.

"And that, Mr. Slade, is our advantage and their disadvantage. The story was that the sewers were sealed when the project fell apart. I can tell you that was a cover story. With the things that are stored there, you can't afford to make mistakes. And having only one camouflaged way in and out *would* be a mistake – and a very big one, too."

"So, you're going to get me in from the sewers under Waxahachie, and *not* from the installation perimeter?" asked Slade.

124

"That's what I'm going to do," said Drake, in satisfied tones. "I can't guarantee you won't hit trouble, but I'm certain that very, *very* few people know of that extra entrance point."

Slade asked: "And where, exactly, will it take me once I hit the facility?"

"Well, I'll have all that for you soon – a full schematic – but I can tell you this: there are *other* tunnels that I am willing to bet my life most people, even those that know what's really going on below Waxahachie, know nothing about. One of those sewers will take you into a specific section of the thirteen miles of completed tunnels that's assumed to be completely bricked-up. I say assumed because that was the story deliberately spread to ensure those out of the loop didn't get to know of another entrance into the installation."

Slade replied: "Okay, that all sounds good."

"It won't be easy going, Mr. Slade; not at all. But, I'll provide you with the complete route that will take you to the room you want – but via a backdoor, rather than by ringing the doorbell, so to speak. In the event of an emergency, and in the event that the, ah, body, had to be removed, steps were taken for this backdoor to act as a fairly quick and safe solution. But, instead of using it to get something out, we'll be using it to get something in."

"And that something's me, right?"

"Right: we get you in; you take photos, files, anything you can get your hands on. Anything that looks useful, that we can use as leverage against them, and which will aid your book-writing."

"Leverage?" asked Slade.

"It's my view," Drake explained, "that if you can get something solid and undeniable, we can use that as a threat: we'll let them know if they try anything with their disclosure ruse, we'll go public first. And we'll threaten to do it right away, with what we have – thanks to you – regardless of the consequences. It'll be a bluff, of course. But, if nothing else, it might at least cause them to take a step back with their disclosure agenda."

Slade pondered on Drake's words for a moment, and then said: "This may sound a crazy question, but what about the body itself?"

Drake laughed: "I like a man with ambition, Mr. Slade! Are you thinking what I think you're thinking: stealing the corpse?"

"Yeah, I am; why not?"

"Well, the big problem is that it's preserved in a large, cylindrical tank; certainly not the easiest thing to walk away with."

"And what happens if I just happen to smash my way into it and wrap the body in a sheet or something? It's well-preserved, right?" Slade asked, taking the view that sheer, brute-force might be the answer.

"I don't advise that at all," said Drake, with a look ofey dokey concern on his face. "There's a part of all this which few know about. I know a bit of it, and I'll say one word: pathogen. Opening up that Pandora's Box would not be a wise move. I can only say any attempt to remove the body from its canister would potentially unleash a near-unstoppable killer across the planet."

Slade stared at Drake, his mind swarming with the old man's words: "You mean an alien virus; a plague?"

"Yes, a virus; one which could even spell the end of the Human Race."

Slade was about to ask another question when a sudden, electronic bleep stopped him in his tracks.

"That's one of the motion detectors," whispered Drake. *"Someone's in the woods."*

-24-

W ithin mere seconds of being alerted to the movement in the woods, both Slade and Drake were crouched down on the floor, in front of the couch.

"Good to see your marine instincts haven't left you behind, Mr. Slade," whispered Drake.

"Ditto," replied Slade, in muted tones. "Can you tell where they are?"

"Yes, I can," said Drake. "There are four motion-detectors out there. The one that got tripped is about fifteen feet to the left of the road leading here and about ninety feet out in the trees."

"They're following the most direct route, keeping in the shadows," observed Slade.

"Agreed."

Slade quietly slid along the carpeted floor to the living-room window and very carefully and slowly lifted his head. "Damn it," he whispered. "It's blacker than black out there."

"Here, take this," said Drake, as he slid a compact night-vision device across the floor. Slade reached down and picked it up. "Any luck?" asked Drake.

Slade placed it to his eyes and focused: "Not a damn bit. It's helping to about twenty feet out, but beyond that, nothing. The woods are too thick. And I've got a feeling that if we're dealing with professionals – and I'm sure we are – they're going to split up and try and take us out from at least a couple of different directions."

"Well, the only other way in," Drake added, "is the back door. I can keep a good watch on that, and we're well stocked with ammunition." With that, Drake crawled towards the kitchen, which backed onto the pathway down to the lake, and kept a low profile behind the large table that sat squarely in the middle of the kitchen.

Moments later, there was another bleep. Drake checked his hand-held motion-detector and, in low tones, said: "Forty feet out; moving to the right."

And, as if right on cue, another bleep confirmed Slade's worst fears: "Don't tell me, Drake; that one's to the left? Roughly the same distance out?"

"I'm afraid so. That means there are at least two of them; one for each of us. Whatever we do, let's not get killed here tonight, Mr. Slade."

"No chance of that, Drake," said Slade. He wasn't going to take his last gasps deep in the woods, riddled with bullets. But, with any luck, whoever was out there was going to do exactly that.

"Mr. Slade: stealth mode; no more talking. Good luck, my friend."

"You too, pal."

For around two minutes or so, there was nothing but a proverbial, deafening silence. It was suddenly broken. Not by the sound of gunfire, but by the slight but distinct creaking of the wooden boards that comprised the base of the porch directly outside the front door. This was it: Slade steadied himself, his finger carefully and precisely balanced on the trigger of his pistol. Someone was definitely prowling around.

In the kitchen, Drake was practically holding his breath: he thanked the Lord those creaky old boards out back had never been replaced. Just like Slade, he knew what was afoot: a two-pronged attack; one that would likely see the doors kicked open and a spray of bullets spread across just about everywhere.

Slade had experienced this so many times before in the Marine Corps: a sense of eerie tranquility before carnage and chaos erupted in all corners. No doubt, he thought, Drake was thinking just the same. He was. But carnage did not erupt; nor did chaos.

Almost simultaneously, there were two muffled screams; not from Slade and Drake but from whoever was circling the cabin. The sound of someone suddenly being thrown hard against the front door almost caused Slade to empty his weapon in seconds. At the last moment, however, he held back. Keeping his breathing in check and his mind focused, Slade crawled across the floor to the small window that overlooked the front porch, just as another cry echoed around the woods and another body-slam shook the room to its foundations. Then there was nothing.

Slade didn't know it right away, but a near-identical situation had just played out on the back porch. Drake, like Slade, was ready to do whatever he needed to do to keep on living. It turned out he didn't need to do anything. The panic-filled death cries of the man outside were of the type that Drake had come across so many times in his dark career. He already knew what the outcome would be, and particularly so when a violent thud suggested someone's battered body had just said "hello" to the exterior wall. Only silence followed.

Slade scurried across the living-room floor, through the small hallway and into the kitchen: "Drake, are you okay?" he whispered.

Drake gave Slade a thumbs-up from the far side of the darkened kitchen.

"Thank God."

In quiet tones, Drake said, as he crawled towards Slade: "It appears we have other visitors, too, and far more friendly ones, I think."

"Your people?" asked Slade.

"Could be; but I doubt it. I think someone would have got a message to me. And why aren't they now alerting us that everything's okay? No, I suspect there's more to this than meets the eye."

"Look, we can't sit here like this all night," said Slade, growing impatient. "I'm going to check outside."

"Right behind you," Drake replied.

Crouched down low, Slade slowly turned the back door knob. He thought: don't let it creak. It didn't. With his gun in hand and the door now open wide enough to where Slade could take at least a slight look outside, he scanned the porch area. Plant pots were knocked over, a hammock was practically destroyed, and a rocking-chair was lying on its side. Not a single person could be seen – anywhere.

"It looks like a battlefield out there," Slade said.

"Oh dear," replied Drake, who was, by now, seemingly, more concerned for his yard furniture than his life.

Slade then motioned Drake to the living room: "Let's check out front."

Slade and Drake took careful steps to the front door, keeping low and close to the walls as they did so. Neither man was entirely sure the threat was gone: all they knew for sure was that some serious shit had just gone down. That they didn't know *how* or *why* kept them on their guard.

"I have your back, Mr. Slade," said Drake as Slade tentatively opened the door.

The sight before him was one that Slade would never forget. Two of the strangest looking men stood opposite Slade, staring him firmly in the eye; almost as if they had been patiently expecting him to open the door. Neither exceeded five feet in height; both wore matching black suits and 1950s-era fedora hats, and their skin was vampire-white.

"Christ," said Slade, "you're...," his words trailed off, his voice suddenly snuffed out by amazement and disbelief.

"Yes, Mr. Slade, we are," said the man on the left.

At that point, Drake came rushing through the door and switched on the porch light.

"Mr. Drake, once again we meet in unfortunate circumstances," said one of the terrible things.

"Slade," said Drake in concerned fashion, "don't say another word and don't move."

Slade was sure that both men, as if in response to Drake's words, issued slight smiles; they were the kinds of smiles one might expect to see on the face of a sly, psychotic, serial-killer. For around thirty or forty seconds, Drake and Slade stared at the Men in Black while they did likewise in return. Such was the silence it seemed that even the local insect population had fled in terror at the presence of these pale-faced ghouls.

The stalemate was only broken when both MIB, in unison, walked backward down the porch steps to the muddy ground below and moved to their right. As Slade and Drake looked on, they could see, just at the beginning of the trees, two bodies; one placed on top of the other and both dressed in dark, military fatigues. The MIB grabbed the dead men quickly and firmly by their collars and began to haul them towards the thick woods.

"Wait! Wait a minute! Stop!" cried Slade.

They *did* stop. And then they slowly turned around. Their malevolent glares were enough to galvanize Drake into action. He grabbed Slade's right arm and gripped it tight: "Don't be a fool, man! Let them go. They have their agenda; we have ours. Nothing good will come from this if you push them."

One of the Men in Black, clearly approving of Drake's words, said: "Listen to your friend, Mr. Slade, and listen to him very carefully. This night, we saved your lives. We welcome your motivations in this matter. The motivations of those you and Mr. Drake oppose are *not* welcomed by us. That does not mean, however, that we are your friends. We are not. Our actions here tonight were for the benefit of the greater good. Not for you as individuals. Everyone is expendable at some point."

And, with that, the two Men in Black – Mr. Bleak and Mr. Storm – melted into the heart of the woods, dragging behind them the bodies of two men who, between them, had killed more than fifty people in the past thirteen years. They would kill no more.

As the two MIB finally vanished from sight, Slade looked at Drake and said one word: "Whisky?"

Drake grinned: "Whisky, Mr. Slade."

They returned to the living room and Drake told Slade all about the Men in Black. No, not Will Smith and Tommy Lee Jones, but the *real* Men in Black. And why Stephenville was so important to them.

-25-

The first thing Slade and Drake did on returning inside was to ensure that all of their available weaponry was loaded and close at hand. This was going to be a long, tension-filled night. They could have made a run for it – or, rather, a drive for it – but, as Slade pointed out: "If there are others out there, and they're out for our blood, too, then we'll be sitting ducks if we try and leave now."

Drake nodded: "Yes, the last thing we need is to get ambushed in the woods, trying to leave. The best thing we can do, right now, I think, is to stay on our guard, and stay inside. And let's close the shutters, too."

Fortunately, each and every window in the cabin had thick, shuttered windows; it took only a few minutes before they were all closed and locked. The cabin was now just about as fortified as it ever could be.

"I have to say," Drake added, "knowing what I know about the Men in Black, I seriously doubt there *is* anyone else out there. They're pretty systematic in everything they do, to put it mildly."

Slade didn't doubt that, He poured a couple of glasses of whisky, tossed in a few cubes of ice, sat down and asked Drake: "So what *do* you know about the Men in Black? I mean, what I just saw; they're not human, are they?"

Drake swirled the ice around in his glass, looked thoughtfully at Slade, and admitted: "We actually know very little about them, despite that – thanks to the movies – just about everyone's heard of them. We're not sure *what* they are. But, no, they're not human. I take it you know the folklore."

"Well, some of it," replied Slade. "I guess I kind of ignored a lot of it; I figured it was a lot of paranoid stuff mixed in with a bunch of UFO crazies trying to outdo each other in the weird stakes."

"Well," Drake said, in response, "the problem is that there *is* a lot of paranoia tied in with the Men in Black. And you *do* have the people that make up stories, and there *are* a few people in your field of studies who liked to play games with the subject. But, get rid of the hoaxes and the lies, and there's still a Men in Black phenomenon. You've *seen* them."

It was then that cold reality, and even a bit of shock, hit Slade hard: "You're right. I've seen the Men in Black; *real* Men in Black. Jesus." Slade went quiet for a few moments and then asked: "So, what *is* the deal with them?"

Drake took a sip from his glass: "Time for a late-night story, Mr. Slade."

As Slade listened, Drake told him the weird tale of Albert Bender. A paranoid hypochondriac with an obsession for all things paranormal, supernatural and occult, Bender, in 1951, created a UFO research group called the International Flying Saucer Bureau. Operating out of the attic of a creepy old house in Bridgeport, Connecticut, Bender spent his nights and weekends turning the IFSB into a major force in the growing UFO scene. Newsletters were mailed out by the hundreds, the phone constantly rang, and in no time at all the IFSB was very close to being the AQUA of its day. That is, until something deeply strange happened.

"Bender," explained Drake, "started to see these strange characters around town – usually late at night, such as when he'd walk back home from the cinema: all in black, '50s hats, and, so he said, glowing eyes. They'd materialize and dematerialize in his bedroom and finally warned him to get out of UFO investigations, forever, and to quit using Ouija boards and dabbling in the paranormal."

"And you *believe* this stuff?" asked Slade.

Drake looked astonished that Slade might even consider doubting his words: "Well, you've seen them, yourself. What do you think I think? *Of course*, I believe."

"The thing is that Bender *did* quit Ufology – in 1952," Drake continued. "His buddy, Gray Barker, wrote a book about Bender's experiences in 1956: *They Knew Too Much About Flying Saucers*. But Barker left out all the paranormal things that Bender claimed went on.

This is what led to the idea that the Men in Black work for the government.

"It was only when, in 1962, Bender decided to briefly – *very* briefly, I might add – come back into the UFO fold, and write his own book, *Flying Saucers and the Three Men*, that the weirder side of the MIB became apparent. Unfortunately, hardly anyone took notice of Bender's book and so the idea they were, quote, 'government agents' took hold."

"But they're not," Slade said.

"No, they're not.

"So what are they?"

"Here's what we know. Or what we *think* we know," conceded Drake.

"Obviously, as you've seen, Mr. Slade, the Men in Black are not the Grays. But, also obviously, they're not human either. Wouldn't you say they look like they're somewhere in between?"

"I guess," said Slade. "Are you saying those stories about alien hybrids – crossbreeds – are true?"

"Not necessarily, no. But we can't rule it out; which is why I mention it. What we know for sure is they are clearly linked to the UFO phenomenon: sightings, witnesses; even us, as you now know. But they're far more enigmatic than that. I can tell you that a still-classified study was prepared on this back in 1981 – by a Pentagon think-tank group – which is as valid today as it was back then. It suggests the MIB are a kind of police force."

"*A police force?*"

"Oh, I don't mean it in such simple terms, Mr. Slade. But, they do seem to turn up at times of critical importance – sometimes to intimidate and threaten people, and other times to silence them, as in permanently; as you've *also* witnessed tonight. The big questions are: are they in the employ of the Grays or are they working independent of them?"

"Fuck," said Slade, "how many sides are there in all this?"

"That's the problem, we just don't know. There are us and the people we're up against. There's the aliens we know for sure are here – after all, we've got their bodies and craft. So, their presence is not in doubt. But, these other guys – the Men in Black – we're just not sure. You could make the argument they're following the orders of the Grays. But, maybe it's the other way around. Or, maybe they're a rogue group, with their own agenda we don't really understand."

"Okay," said Slade. "Tell me what you think the Men in Black are."

"Very well," Drake replied, "but it does involve a few far-out concepts."

It was now into the early hours and Drake had saved the best – or maybe the downright weirdest – until last.

"Do you remember what that one Man in Black said to me?" asked Drake.

Slade nodded: "Yeah, something about seeing you again, in unfortunate circumstances."

"Precisely, Mr. Slade: I did have an encounter – that's a good way to word it – with a MIB back in 1977. A very unfortunate affair, hence his words: lives were lost; *many* lives. I won't go into all the details, but it was a violent altercation, not unlike tonight. But, I can assure you I have never met that MIB before tonight."

"But, he said…"

Drake interrupted: "I know what he said. And, in one way he *is* right. Whitley Strieber – a man whose work we have followed very closely – once said that the aliens seem to have a hive-like mind. You should listen to Strieber; he's on the right track. The Grays work like insects; and what one knows, they all know. I believe that's the same for the Men in Black. They're like worker-bees, but made out of a mold. And as with the Grays, what one MIB knows, they all know, too; hence his words tonight."

"They're all part of a single intelligence; one mind, and one big, collective memory?"

"Very astute, Mr. Slade; *very* astute," said Drake. "I believe the MIB to be little more than biological robots. They are the equivalent of a computer-program; a program designed to perform a specific task, which has access to a huge database of material and memories, but which is not self-aware – at least, not how we understand the term."

Slade understood: "They're like a virus protector weeding out a Trojan."

Drake nodded approvingly: "A very good analogy."

"So who's running the program?"

Drake shook his head and let out a deep sigh: "We haven't got a clue."

-26-

At the same time Slade and Drake retreated into the safety of the cabin to plan their next course of action, the two Men in Black were in the process of completing their own agenda – a far darker one.

Had Slade and Drake hung around long enough to see what happened next, they would have seen the MIB not just drag the two dead assassins into the woods. They would have seen them after a trek of about three hundred feet, reach a large black car. It was parked on the edge of the track-like road that led directly to Drake's cabin.

If anyone had been there - anyone *normal* - they might have wondered why someone had left a pristine, 1950s-vintage Cadillac sitting on the fringes of the woods in the middle of nowhere. There was nothing normal about this night, however. It was a night strictly *abnormal* in nature. Neither Mr. Bleak nor Mr. Storm cared about the thoughts of others or of what constituted normality, however. Their programming didn't allow them to care – about *anything*.

The trek to the car was made in complete silence. Mr. Bleak and Mr. Storm were not big on conversation; words were only ever necessary when dealing with the humans. As they reached the car, Mr. Storm dropped to the ground the body he had effortlessly hauled across the damp, forest floor for the past ten minutes. Mr. Bleak did likewise and took a set of keys out of his pocket and opened the trunk. Both bodies were tossed inside like rag-dolls. Mr. Bleak closed the trunk without making a sound.

Mr. Storm and Mr. Bleak, in eerie unison, got into the car and closed the doors. Mr. Storm placed the key in the ignition and the engine rumbled to life – in a way that only old, antique cars can. An eerie, green glow emanated from the dashboard. This was no regular car. And very much the same could be said for its driver and passenger.

They left the old woods behind them; their minds focused on their next terrible task.

After around seventy minutes of driving on the highway, Mr. Storm signaled and took the exit road. He then turned right onto a darkened street, one that was dominated by a burger joint and a gas-station. Both were closed. Not that it mattered to either Mr. Storm or Mr. Bleak: their vehicle ran on something far stranger than gasoline. And as for food: neither had a need for it or even an understanding of the concept of it. They passed by both places without a glance.

Eighty feet down the road, a large warehouse loomed into view. Its rundown appearance suggested it had long been abandoned. It had. Mr. Storm, Mr. Bleak and the rest of their kind had no need for a regular base of operations: they were constantly on the move; always staying one step ahead of those humans that sought their secrets.

Mr. Storm pulled up in front of the old, large, rusted doors that dominated the front of the building. In a few seconds, they began to open sideways. Mr. Storm drove slowly inside and brought the Cadillac to a halt around thirty feet into the building. He and Mr. Bleak exited their vehicle. Seven men - all dressed in the same outdated fashion, and all equally pale-faced, gaunt and seemingly free of any and all emotion - loomed slowly out of the darker than dark shadows.

In almost voyeuristic fashion, they stared intently as Mr. Bleak and Mr. Storm pulled the bodies from the trunk and dropped them on the concrete floor with sickening thuds. Two of the Men in Black – Mr. Dread and Mr. Cold – moved slowly forward. They had in their hands thick ropes, each around ten feet in length. Mr. Dread looped and tied one of the ropes around the neck of victim number one. Mr. Cold followed suit with number two. Such was their dispassionate nature they might just as well have been tying shoelaces.

Mr. Cold and Mr. Dread took firm grips on the ropes and heaved the bodies up a small flight of metal steps to the second floor of the warehouse. Having done so they tied the other ends of the ropes around a long metal bar, one originally constructed to prevent anyone from falling the twenty feet or so to the ground below. And then they slung both bodies off the edge. The only noise was the echoing, snapping of necks.

Mr. Cold and Mr. Dread proceeded back down the steps. The bodies of the two men swayed for a few seconds, before finally hanging motionless. For a moment, all of the Men in Black stared at their handiwork. Mr. Storm and Mr. Bleak were the first to move: they returned to their Cadillac, fired up the engine and disappeared into the night. Their colleagues, whose identical Cadillac's were also parked in the expansive warehouse did likewise. As for the doors of the warehouse, they were deliberately left open. This was not about hiding the bodies. Quite the opposite: the intention was for them to be found. This was a case of sending a message to certain, hostile forces in the U.S. Government.

Right after arriving at work the next morning, seventeen-year-old Brittany Shaw told her boss at *Ron's Burgers* that the doors of the old warehouse were wide open. Suspecting kids had broken into the place; Ron took a stroll over to see what was going on. He expected to see the remains of a beer-and-pot-party and a bunch of graffiti on the walls. What he didn't expect to find were two dead bodies hanging by their necks.

Within minutes, the local police were on the scene. Within the hour, it was all over the local news. And within two hours, General Robert Fowler had been informed as to exactly why the second attempt to have Slade and Drake taken out of circulation had failed: the bodies of the two men sent to do the job were in the county morgue.

As far as the police were concerned, and despite what ultimately turned out to be an investigation that lasted months, the case remained frustratingly unsolved. The men's identities couldn't be confirmed: their prints weren't in any U.S. database. Interpol couldn't help either. There were no incriminating additional fingerprints on the scene. There was no telltale DNA. Of course, there wasn't: Cold, Dread, Bleak, Storm and all the rest didn't have fingerprints or DNA. As for recent tire tracks or footprints, none were ever found. The state of the shoes of the dead men showed they had been dragged through muddy, wooded ground. But, that described near-countless square miles. And the rain that was now falling like a definitive deluge would likely wipe out any evidence, even if the right area of woodland was ever located.

But for General Fowler, the message was as loud as it was clear: mess with Slade and Drake and we mess with you.

-27-

Roughly four hours after the local media began reporting on the discovery of two corpses hanging by their necks in an otherwise deserted, old warehouse a couple of hours outside of Washington, D.C., General Robert Fowler was driving at breakneck speed through the streets of the nation's capital. His destination: a pleasant and picturesque park on the outskirts of D.C. On weekends, mainly during the summer months, the park was filled with children, young lovers strolling hand in hand, and picnicking families. Today, however, in freezing cold January, the park was just about as barren as it could be. It was, however, about to play host to very different visitors: the general and Charles Briggs.

Providing that the conversation was couched in terms that left things very much open to interpretation – something vital in today's world of overwhelming eavesdropping – the general was usually content to speak with Briggs by phone. But not this time; probably never again, even. The events of the last two days ensured that Fowler was not prepared to leave a single thing to chance, or himself open to more than a bit of phone surveillance.

As was his typical behavior, Fowler arrived at the park ten minutes or so ahead of the planned rendezvous time of 4:00 p.m. He paced around the near-empty expanse; his thick coat pulled tight, his hands buried deep in his pockets, and his anger levels and blood pressure rising by the minute. Practically on cue, Fowler locked on to a man – also sporting a heavy coat – walking towards him, around 300 feet away. It was Briggs. The general began to pace even more.

"By God, Briggs," the general bellowed, as Briggs got within twenty feet of him, "you'd better have a damned good explanation for what happened last night! This was supposed to be a clean operation. But now we've got the press and the television news, and even the police are in on it. That's twice now that you've failed to take care of

Drake and Slade. I mean, Jesus, we're only talking about an old man and a UFO buff. And you can't take them out the picture – *twice*?"

Briggs winced: he knew the general was right, as much as it pained him to admit it. The two men walk towards a small wooden bench and sat down.

"I want the whole story, Briggs, and I want it now!" the general raged.

Briggs took a deep breath: "Sir, I can't give you the full story, because we don't know what the full story is. All I can do is to tell you what we know so far."

"And that is?" asked Fowler, impatiently.

"We had two of our best men on the job. They were handpicked personally; both had been in Iraq and Afghanistan. Both were capable guys; knew how to get the job done. Yes, we screwed up. But not with the guys: they were perfect for the task."

"So what went wrong?" asked the general, in what were now noticeably lower tones, as he tried to calm both himself and his heart.

"We don't think Slade and Drake had *anything* to do with this."

"So who did?"

Briggs's face took on the look of a man filled with fear: "I think you know, sir."

General Fowler's head dropped; his eyes were focused on the grass beneath his feet, but they hardly even registered it: "The Men in Black."

"Yes, sir," replied Briggs. "The last contact our people had with the two, ah…"

Fowler interrupted: "No-one's listening except me, Briggs; you can speak openly."

"The last contact with our two hired employees was at 11:11 p.m. last night. They were in the woods, at Drake's cabin. The lights were off. There was no vehicle around; although apparently the property has a large garage, so that doesn't necessarily mean Drake and Slade weren't there. Their last words were they were going dark – radio-silence – and were going to check out the cabin."

"And they fully understood their orders?" asked Fowler.

"They did, sir, yes," said Briggs. "If Slade and Drake weren't there, they were to find a way in and wait for them if necessary until morning. If they turned up, get rid of them and have the bodies disposed of – something they had done very skillfully in earlier situations."

"And if Drake and Slade were already there?"

"Get rid of them with a minimum of fuss as possible. And get rid of the bodies; basically, the same scenario. Then that was it. But then no more contact."

"But you're inclined to think that Slade and Drake didn't get the upper hand; at least not without some help?" the general asked.

Briggs stood up, rubbed his hands together to try and lessen the chills running through them, and outlined to the general what he believed happened the night before.

"It's my guess, sir," said Briggs, "that Drake and Slade – even if they did succeed in killing our guys – would have got rid of the bodies locally; maybe even in that lake Drake spends all his spare time fishing in. What they *wouldn't* have done – simply because it doesn't make any sense – is to drive the bodies for about seventy miles, break into a warehouse, and string them up for all to see."

Briggs continued: "It's like this: Drake and Slade know we're after them. And we know they know, and they know we know, and so on and so on. All of which means they don't need to give us a sign they took our guys out. And, even if they wanted to, they wouldn't be so stupid as to head out immediately after killing them, in the event we had other people in the woods as backup. And why drive out to that warehouse and hang the bodies up for everyone to see?"

"It's a sign; a fucking sign," said Fowler.

"Yes, sir, it is," agreed Briggs. "It could be there's another group – a *human* group, I mean – involved in all this, too. It would have to be one we don't know about – and I find that unlikely. But, if not, that just leaves the Men in Black."

Fowler nodded: "There's one other option."

"The Waxahachie plan?" asked Briggs.

"Yes," said the general. "The last intelligence we had was that Drake was planning to get Slade in there. God knows what that man will try and get his hands on if he gets in. Briggs, I want you to have a team ready - in Stephenville, in Waxahachie, I don't care. But, as soon as there's even an inkling that Slade or that old fucker is in the area, I want that team in those tunnels – immediately. If that's where it has to go down, then that's where it has to go down."

"Yes, sir," said Briggs. He was about to add: "And that's a promise," but the events of the last few days had left Briggs wary of promising anything from now on. All he could do was hope.

The general looked up: "On your way, Briggs; I need to think."

"Okay, sir," Briggs replied, awkwardly, as he headed back the way he came, across the lonely windswept park, wondering what was going on deep in the general's mind.

-28-

G eneral Fowler sat with his legs apart and his hands in his lap, doing his best to figure out how to get a grip on the growing problem called Marc Slade. But, it wasn't just Slade – as one man - that was the problem, the general knew. It wasn't even the fact that Slade would be publishing a novel that might actually get people thinking a bit *too* much about what was going on behind the scenes when it came to UFOs and Stephenville – and possibly even in relation to Fowler's agenda for the entire United States.

The bigger problem was that Slade was the planned mouthpiece for a group of God knows how many people that probably rivaled his, Fowler's, own group in size. Killing Slade and Drake would be a good start, but that was the bigger problem: a start is all it would be. The entire group had to be made to vanish. That, however, was the trickier part.

The general would have thought about it for a great deal longer, and to a much deeper degree, had he not suddenly developed an unsettling sense of being watched.

As the hairs on his arms and neck stood to sudden attention, the general whipped around and stared intently into a dense clump of trees that stood about fifty feet away. It was a feeling he had felt so many times during combat. And it was a feeling he never, *ever*, ignored. Fowler peered into the trees, with his mind in a whirl and his heart hammering. There was something about those trees, about the way they swayed – as if they were calling him towards them. But that was crazy. What the hell am I thinking of?

The longer he looked at those spindly branches, however, the more Fowler became entranced by them. They seemed to beckon him. Twigs became fingers, reaching out for him, demanding his presence. The general felt his willpower melting away, like a bar of candy melting on a windowsill on a hot, summer's day. He slowly rose from the bench and began to walk, in a near-zombie-like stagger, towards the trees. His arms hung limply by his side as he did so.

As a sudden wind enveloped him, he heard the words: "Come to us." Fowler was helpless to do anything else. As he got within feet of the small, wooded oasis, the branches of the trees seemed to stretch out as if welcoming him with open, friendly arms. Although his mind was now under the control of something eerie and uncanny, Fowler still vaguely understood that what seemed pleasant and inviting was, in reality, manipulative and deadly. Nevertheless, he headed into the heart of the trees and stopped after about fifteen feet.

"General, greetings," said a whispered, unearthly voice.

It was those two words which seemed to awaken Fowler from his near-hypnotized state. He gasped as the clouds in his mind began to clear, and the trees returned to their natural states. They gave way to a man in a black trenchcoat and a black hat. His white face was dominated by a soulless smile.

For quite possibly the first time in his life, Fowler was rendered speechless. He knew what he was looking at, but seeing it – for an "it" was all that a MIB could ever be – was something else entirely. Fowler's heart pumped as if it was fit to burst; adrenalin flooded his body, and a sense of doom overcame him.

"You should be right to be frightened, Robert Fowler," the man in black said in quiet, sneering tones. "You have caused me and my kind much pain. And you plan equal pain for all of your kind. This can no longer be permitted."

"No longer permitted," said the general, almost drunkenly, his mind suddenly again held by the vice-like grip of the ashen MIB.

"General Fowler, you will please do something for me."

"Will do for you," Fowler parroted as if drugged.

"Hold out your right hand, general," said the black-garbed man. Fowler did as he was told. Into his hand was placed a black revolver and a single bullet.

"Please insert the bullet into the revolver and prepare it for firing," the cold and calculating orders continued. The general did as he was told.

"Now, general, place the barrel in your mouth, and slightly upturned."

Even though Fowler's mind was now a slave to the MIB, deep inside he was wrestling to escape the nightmare into which he had been plunged. He fought and fought to do anything *but* what the MIB demanded of him.

"In your mouth: *do it*," the man spat, showing, for the first time, a degree of emotion. It was emotion born out of pure hate and nothing else.

The general followed the order – just as he had dutifully followed every order given to him throughout the course of his prestigious, military career.

"Place your finger on the trigger, please, general."

Part of Fowler's mind was screaming "No!" The rest of it was hanging on to the Man in Black's every word.

"Now, pull the trigger; *pull it*!"

General Robert Fowler performed with perfection his last on-duty order – ever. Brain-matter, pieces of shattered skull, and a significant amount of blood exploded out of the back of Fowler's head as he fell to the floor. It was 2:43 p.m. And, for Fowler, it would never again be 2:44 p.m. It would never again be *anything*.

The Man in Black stared at the lifeless corpse of Fowler for a few seconds. He knew it would not be too long before someone stumbled upon the body; the sound of gunfire would guarantee that. The media and the police would likely put it all down to the stress of overwork. Fowler's colleagues would know otherwise. They would fear, and that was good.

The man turned to his left and left the trees and the cold, desolate park behind him. The MIB then did something that he and his kind seldom ever did: he smiled.

-29-

Sure enough, it didn't take long at all before word of General Robert Fowler's death began to circulate widely and wildly. His body was found barely ten minutes later by Mary Morrison, a school-teacher who had been walking her Labrador, Charlie, at the time and who couldn't fail to hear the firing of the bullet that ended the general's life so violently. Not surprising, since she was barely one hundred feet away when Fowler pulled the trigger.

While gripping Charlie's lead tightly with her left hand, Morrison took tentative steps – as in *extremely* tentative steps – to where she thought the shot had emanated. She was pretty much right on target. Since the landscape was flat and clear, and there appeared to be no-one in sight, Morrison was comfortable, to a degree, about trying to find out what happened. She did exactly that. After a few minutes and finally having made her way to the trees, Morrison caught sight of the general's body, sprawled on the grassy floor, and the gun just a couple of feet away.

Morrison froze in her tracks and did the only thing she could: she screamed. And then she screamed again.

Overcome by fear, Morrison dropped to her knees. Sensing her terror, Charlie began to whimper and licked Morrison's cheek vigorously. Trying to keep a steady hold on Charlie's lead, Morrison shakily took her cellphone out of her pocket and pressed three numbers: 9, 1, 1. In minutes, the police were on their way. Within fifteen minutes, the far side of the park had been turned into a definitive crime-scene; a locked-down, no-go area for anyone but the responding emergency services.

After being treated for severe shock by a paramedic, Morrison was questioned extensively by Detective Suzanne Wise, to who the case had been assigned. Had Morrison seen anyone unusual in the area? Not a soul. Had she seen anyone – *period*? No. And yet she was within easy walking distance of the crime scene, the day was clear – albeit dull – and the landscape was flat and largely open? Yes.

Detective Wise just knew this was going to be one of those far less than open-and-shut cases; the ones she hated. She cursed to herself – and even more so when the wallet extracted from the inside pocket of the man's jacket revealed who he was: only a high-ranking figure in the military who practically called the Pentagon his home. The night was going to be a long one.

In less than one hour after the body of General Fowler was found, the D.C. media was already onto the bones of the story. Word was circulating that "a senior Pentagon official" had been found "shot to death" in a local park. Newspapers, television and radio: they were all reporting on the shooting.

It was at 8:33 p.m. that Charles Briggs got the news that stopped him dead in his tracks. Or, rather, it stopped him dead in the middle of eating a *Subway* sandwich. It had been a long, tiring day and Briggs, living alone since his wife left him fifteen months previously, had no desire to cook or eat out that night. Even television didn't interest him. What did interest him was a six-inch Meatball Marinara. Tonight's, however, was destined to make him feel sick to his stomach.

Briggs was half way into his sandwich, with his feet stretched out on the recliner and a Heineken in his hand, when his cell rang. He looked at the screen: Jim Moss. Briggs frowned: Moss was NSA and part of the program. But he never called – ever.

Briggs quickly answered it: "Moss? What's going on?"

"You haven't heard?" said Moss, his tone giving away his anxiousness.

Briggs' stomach sank: bad news. "Heard what?"

"Fowler's dead. Shot dead in some park in D.C. Looks like suicide; blew his brains right out the back of his head."

Briggs' breathing turned shallow, and his pulse raced. If he had a mirror in front of him, he would have seen his face suddenly turn white.

Despite his growing panic, Briggs knew this was a time to get a grip. The last thing he needed was for anyone to find out that he,

Briggs, had probably been the last person to see Fowler alive. Suicide: no way, thought Briggs; there was *no way* the general would take that way out – and certainly not now, of all times. That is, unless, someone forced Fowler to end his life.

"What do we know?" asked Briggs, trying to get a handle on things.

Moss outlined the facts, most of which were gleaned from sources in the D.C. police department: "A woman heard the shot; out walking her dog. Found the body; major head trauma. *Major.*"

"But there were no witnesses to the shooting?"

"Nope, none we know of. The cops have no-one: suspects or witnesses, other than the one woman, and it looks like she's in the clear."

Briggs took a deep breath and readied himself for the answer to his next question: "Did the woman see anyone else in the park?"

"Not a soul; she didn't see anyone."

Briggs put his palm over the mouthpiece and exhaled loudly and deeply. Thank God for that. Hopefully, no-one would be able to I.D. him as being anywhere in the area at the time. And neither he nor Fowler had told their secretaries where they were going or who they were meeting with. He suddenly felt more secure.

"So what do you think?" asked Briggs.

"It's all bullshit, that's what I think," said Moss, in frank, concise tones. "All the evidence is suggesting suicide. But, can *you* see him doing that?"

"No, I can't. Look, I appreciate the call, but I have to get on this, right now. We've got to keep on top of it and make sure the damn cops don't stumble onto anything. If they wrap it up as a suicide, all well and good. But we need to know who's speaking to who, and what the word is. And we need to figure out who did this."

Moss replied: "I'm NSA: listening is what I do best. I'll keep you in the loop." He hung up.

Briggs tossed his phone on the couch and took a long swig of Heineken. The South African, the two guys hung by their necks up north, and now the general: all dead. Things were getting out of hand – and quickly, too.

Briggs walked to the window and peered through the blinds. The night was dark and the view near-impenetrable. He felt a chill: who might be out there? If someone got to the general, they could get to him, too. They could get to damn near *anyone*.

-30-

"I guess whoever was out to get us backed off, huh?" asked Slade, partially opening one of the blinds and taking a careful look outside. The woods were as dark and enigmatically mysterious as ever. The overwhelming silence was a fairly good indication they were alone.

"I suspect so," replied Drake. He looked at his watch: "It's just ten minutes to three. I don't doubt that whoever sent those characters, they know all too, by now, well that something's gone wrong. If I was running the show, I'd have had them calling in hours ago, confirming the hit."

Slade nodded: "Exactly. So, they know we're still alive and well. And they know, or they're reasonably sure, their guys are *not* alive and well. And they're probably thinking that even if there's the slightest chance we called the cops, sending out another team could see them exposed, which is the last thing they want."

"And which means just one thing," said Drake.

Slade finished the sentence for him: "They're gonna try a hit somewhere else; somewhere that doesn't tie them to this place – and probably not to D.C., either. Somewhere that's not going to raise any suspicions."

"Very astute, Mr. Slade," commented Drake, adding: "Be careful. With that mindset, they may well recruit *you*."

For the next couple of hours, Slade and Drake took turns to grab a bit of sleep here and there. Slade was impressed by Drake's stamina – he hoped he could say the same for himself when he was in his late sixties, if that's what Drake was. It was hard to get an accurate gauge on the man: he might even be mid-seventies, thought Slade.

By 6:00 a.m., the dawn light was slowly beginning to put in a welcome appearance. As Slade woke up from a thirty-minute power-nap, Drake said to him: "I think the best thing for us to do is to make a move and find somewhere less conspicuous and where we won't be noticed. It's at times like these that having four different identities helps a lot!" he winked at Slade. It was time to pack and get on the road.

Three hours later, the pair was seventy-three miles further north and booked into a cheap motel, the kind of rundown, seedy place where people go to hide, where the manager will turn a blind eye for a few dollars, and where afternoon liaisons of the unfaithful kind are regularly cemented.

The journey had been hassle-free: both men were skilled at recognizing a tail, but none was in evidence. A good sign, a bad sign, or something else, neither man was really sure.

Drake had signed in under the identity of "Charles Whittaker," a writer of shoot-'em-up-style western novels, who was looking for a few days peace and solitude and the chance to pen a couple of chapters for his next book. The guy on the front-desk couldn't have cared less. As for Slade, after Drake checked in, he made his way from the car to Drake's room via the hotel's rear door – no-one even knew Slade was on the premises.

"As much as I abhor fast-food," said Drake, "I think that's the best option right now," in direct response to his growling, empty stomach. "Pizza?"

"Pizza," Slade agreed. The thought of a few slices of something stodgy, filling and damn tasty, was just way too good to say "no" to.

Drake called the front-desk: there was a pizza place just two miles down the road. Did Mr. Whitaker want the number? Yes, Mr. Whitaker most definitely did want the number. Less than half an hour later, Drake and Slade were eagerly munching on what even Drake had to admit was a fine and tasty concoction: Italian sausage, roasted red peppers, banana peppers, and a topping of oregano, all on top of a thick crust.

As they ate their early lunch, Slade picked up the TV remote to surf the channels. Or, he would have done so, had the television not been on the local news channel – something which made both men practically freeze as they ate.

As Slade and Drake watched in complete silence, the news anchor was reporting on the discovery – only hours earlier – of two bodies hanging by their necks in a warehouse that, eerily, was barely forty minutes drive from the very hotel they were now hunkering down in.

"Holy crap," exclaimed Slade, "that has to be the two guys from last night!"

Drake stayed silent and merely nodded, his eyes and ears fixed intently on the screen, as the anchor, Debbie Kerr, revealed what the police knew – which was apparently not much, aside from speculating on the idea that this was some sort of Mob hit.

"Good," said Slade, finally snapping out of his silence. "If the police have nothing to go on, and they continue to follow their *Sopranos* angle, that will be to our advantage."

"Never had you down as a *Sopranos* fan, Drake," said Slade.

"Oh, yes. I got some of my best ideas from Tony Soprano," he laughed. "Seriously, though, our friends in black had to have been behind this. I think we can ascertain this was some sort of deliberate sign. Not meant for us, though, but for whoever sent those two hired-guns."

Slade said: "With that guy in the hotel, and now these two guys, all gone, whoever's on our tail is gonna take it very, very slowly from now on."

"And cautiously, too," added Drake, picking up his third slice of pizza. "We're not out the woods yet; not by a mile. But, I'd say the events of last night, and now this, are just the start."

"The start of what?" asked Slade.

"The start of something positive, I hope," Drake replied.

His prediction proved to be right on target. A little less than seven hours later, as Drake and Slade ate the last of the pizza – re-heated in the room's microwave – there was an even bigger development. It was, yet again, a development dominated by mysterious death.

-31-

ince both Slade and Drake had decided the best thing to do was keep quiet and out of sight for a few days – after which it would, hopefully, be safe to get Slade on his way back to Texas – there was little for both men to do than channel surf for the rest of the day and evening.

In addition, Slade tuned the room's radio into a local station, one which continually – to the point of near-saturation – reported on the discovery of the two dead assassins. Clearly, it was the biggest news in the area for a long, long time and, by God, everyone was going to know about it – like it or not. It was during the 6 o'clock news, however, that a breaking story surfaced, one which took matters to an entirely different level.

Slade, bored rigid, was flipping through the channels when he reached the local news and heard the words: "...but it's not clear if there is any connection with the discovery of two dead men in a warehouse in...," at which point Drake interrupted and said:

"I *knew* this was just the start!"

Wrong, Drake was not.

Slade was sprawled out on one of the two beds while Drake was perched on the edge of the other. Both listened intently. The body of an elderly man had been found in a Washington, D.C. park with a fatal gunshot wound to the head. It looked like suicide, but was being treated as suspicious, the reporting news-crew said.

Then there came a bombshell: although it had yet to be confirmed, two unnamed police sources had stated the body was that of one General Robert Fowler, a senior member of the U.S. military, one with a long and distinguished career. A "true American hero," said the newsreader, carefully adding that: "But, right now, the identity has not been fully confirmed."

"Well, well," said Drake, with a satisfied look on his face. It was also the look of a man considering his options and which cards to play next. "I was right: things *are* moving. And they're moving quicker than I thought."

"I guess that means you know this Fowler guy?" Slade asked.

"Yes, I should say so. Fowler is – or, I should say, *was* – one of the key figures in this twisted plot to overthrow the nation. And when I say one of the key figures, I mean almost at the top. For his people, this is like the JFK assassination was for the public back in '63. This is *huge*."

Drake's enthusiasm for Fowler's death was growing by the second, as were the implications for the battle ahead.

"So, tell me more about Fowler," said Slade.

Fowler, Drake began, had been in the "UFO game" since the early 1990s, when he was recruited into an Air Force Intelligence program, the purpose of which was to spread disinformation deliberately to the UFO research community – specifically to muddy the waters, confuse the truth about what lay at the heart of the UFO phenomenon, and have "everyone chasing everyone else's tail, while the real secrets stayed hidden."

The careful dissemination –which, admitted Drake, "was also a brilliant dissemination" – of bogus tales of crashed UFOs of "pickled aliens," and of "sensational bullshit coming out of Area 51," was "down to Fowler and his hand-picked lackeys."

Drake added: "But, it all worked so well because Fowler knew of the real dead bodies, of the real craft. And so weaving faked stories into the mix made people doubt the genuine ones. For more than a decade, Fowler was near the top of the chain on keeping the entire UFO issue buried in lies and distortions."

"And then something changed?" asked Slade.

Drake nodded: "That's precisely what happened: something changed."

"I knew Fowler quite well back then," Drake told Slade. "I viewed what he did, what we *all* did, as necessary, but I didn't agree with certain things he did that crossed the line. Yes, there were different agendas, but they came down to two things. The first was keeping people – the public, the media, and the UFO researchers - in the dark. The second was when they couldn't keep them in the dark: keep them confused; away from the facts, away from the things that could open up the whole thing – to everyone. But there was no attempt to control the public or change society back then. It was all about hiding the truth – and that was all."

"And what: he got power hungry?" Slade wondered.

"Well, not exactly. Fowler saw – more and more - the UFO subject as not just something that had to be hidden, but he also saw how it could be used as a tool of control. Have people fear the phenomenon. Have them manipulated by it. A lot of us didn't like where this was going. That's when things splintered, early to mid-2000s. This was right after 9/11, when everything was up in the air, the Patriot Act was passed, the NSA surveillance: Fowler saw how easy it was to put people in a state of fear.

"It was then that Fowler became less and less involved in creating disinformation to hide the truth about UFOs, but more and more involved in finding ways to use it to enslave people – and that word, enslave, isn't an exaggeration."

After a few moments of silence, Drake continued: "I suppose so many of us viewed his grandiose plans as a bit of a pipedream; until it became clear he had a growing network – a cabal, to be accurate – that could actually take on the government, possibly even oust the president himself and set up a kind of militarized government, driven purely by the promotion of fear.

"That's what we've been fighting, and his icing on the cake was going to be Stephenville: the case that leads to – in a winding way – martial law. But, now," Drake said, with a look of satisfaction and relief on his face, "maybe we can get things back on track."

"Without the head the body falls," commented Slade.

"True enough," said Drake. "But, don't underestimate these people. Fowler had a loyal, powerful group behind him. This may push them to make their move even quicker – out of pure anger, if nothing else, at what happened to Fowler.

"I'll say this to you, Mr. Slade," said Drake, in dramatic tones, "when the war is over, what we've seen today will be viewed as one of the major battles that decides the outcome. Yes, just one man is dead. But this could be our D-Day, this could be our Hiroshima. By God, I suspect we – and our friends in black – just might have the enemy on the run. If we can splinter these people, and with Fowler gone, I think we can turn things around. We might just save the day."

-32-

It was around 2:30 a.m. and Charles Briggs was lying in bed, staring at the ceiling, with both fists clenched. Two attempts to have Slade and Drake killed had completely failed. Instead, it was the general who was dead. And, just as bad – and maybe even worse - the media was now all over Fowler's supposed suicide. Christ.

Then there were the murders of the two assassins sent out to dispose of Slade and Drake. If the press made a connection between those guys and Fowler, the whole house of cards could collapse – and right on top of my fucking head, thought Briggs. And God knows where the body of the South African was. What had happened to *him*? How the hell had everything gone so spectacularly wrong – and in no less than just a couple of days?

At this point, for Briggs, the answers to the questions were far less important than something else: ensuring some damage control was quickly put into place. Despite the stress he was under, the darkness actually helped Briggs to focus his mind.

Briggs knew it was highly unlikely that Drake and Slade would run to the cops, either sooner or later. One of them, at least – and probably both of them – were implicated in the disappearance, and the likely murder, of the South African. Maybe even in the deaths of the two follow-up guys and the general himself, Briggs considered. And even if the killings *weren't* down to them, Briggs was as sure as he could be that they knew something of it all.

Neither man was stupid enough to risk getting detained by the cops, even if they were innocent. The last place Slade and Drake would want to be, Briggs knew, was in a jail cell – one from which he, Briggs, could probably get them pulled and handed over to Homeland Security for a bit of "safekeeping."

That meant they would likely be lying low - as in *very* low - at an out of the way location, and trying to figure out their next course of action, none of which would involve going public or getting the authorities involved. Good.

Despite the hour, Briggs phoned Jim Moss: if anyone could find Drake and Slade it was Moss and his people at the NSA.

Moss's phone rang out just once before it was answered; clearly, Moss, too, was having a sleepless night.

"What's the latest, Briggs?" Moss asked; his voice filled with a mixture of anticipation and trepidation.

Briggs's voice, on the other hand, was dominated by pure anger: "The latest, Moss, is that we are screwed. Three people are dead; one is missing, and two, certain people are *still* on the run. This is *not* how things were supposed to go down."

Moss jumped in quickly: "I might remind you that, with all the technology we have at NSA, we can only do so much. I might *also* remind you that we've been unable to track either Slade or Drake's cell-phones – a good indication they've destroyed them, as in completely. Plus, there has been no activity on either man's credit card or debit card. No activity at their homes. We have *nothing*."

"'Nothing' is not acceptable, Moss," Briggs hit back.

Moss tried to calm the situation: "Look, we both know they're keeping a quiet profile somewhere, even if we don't know where. And we know they're not gonna turn up on the doorsteps of the *Washington Post* or the *New York Times*. That gives us an advantage: namely, time."

"What about Drake's cabin?" Briggs interjected.

"Nothing there: we had a team there by daybreak. They found nothing, no-one. A couple of beat-up and busted doors and that was it."

Briggs exploded: "*Daybreak*? You had a team there by *daybreak*? It was my understanding you were supposed to have had people there within the hour if we didn't get the call that Slade and Drake were dead."

"That order was countermanded," Moss replied.

"And by whom?" shouted Briggs.

"That's above me," admitted Moss. "All I know for sure is that we didn't get the call last night that the job was done. And, for some reason, right after, there was a stand-down until morning."

"You find me the person that ordered that stand-down, Moss, and you find them quickly. If Slade and Drake *were* there through the night, we could have had them, right then; they were sitting ducks! Why wasn't I told about this?"

Moss' voice was filled with exasperation: "I didn't know you *weren't* told. Briggs, look, it was barely twenty-four hours ago. I don't have all the answers. If I need remind you, a shitload has gone down over the course of the last day. And, as I said, the order came from someone above – *way* above."

"Find the answers and find me that person!" demanded Briggs, immediately before slamming the phone down on Moss.

Briggs was as amazed as he was furious. He had assumed that if Drake and Slade *were* involved in the deaths of the two assassins, then they had likely fled the area right afterwards, and which was why they couldn't be found. Briggs vowed never again to assume anything – and certainly not in this game.

The idea of not storming Drake's cabin when it became clear that something had gone wrong baffled Briggs, as did the fact that no-one had kept him in the loop on that specific issue. Or, for a few seconds it baffled him. Then something else hit Briggs hard: what if whoever ordered the stand-down was deliberately trying to buy Drake and Slade some time, regardless of whether both men knew it or not?

Whoever countermanded the general's orders is going to pay, thought Briggs. But not before they spill their guts. Waterboarding wasn't just for terrorists. Briggs was going to get everything he needed, and if that required more than a bit of rough justice to get it, so be it.

If there were traitors in the project, they were as good as dead. Briggs lay back down on the bed: the body-count, he just knew, was going to get much higher – and probably all too soon.

-33-

It was now coming up to 4:30 a.m. and Charles Briggs - wide awake as a result of the adrenalin coursing through his pumping veins – continued to seethe over the inability of just about everyone to reel in Slade and Drake. And now the pair had vanished. Despite the stress and tension he was under, not to mention the distinct possibility that the group's plans were now in very real danger of going down the drain – and big-time, too – Briggs tried to think logically and clearly. He took a few deep breaths and followed the relaxation techniques taught to him by his doctor. It worked – to a degree. His mind began to clear, his pulse slowed noticeably, and clarity returned to his thought-processes.

The first thing that popped back into Briggs' mind was the suspicion that someone had deliberately allowed Slade and Drake to escape from the old man's cabin in the woods. It all seemed just too damned convenient that no-one turned up until morning to check out what had gone on – despite the fact that, as Briggs now knew, contact had been lost with two of their best assassins *hours* before. Mistakes like that don't happen, he thought. Unless they're not mistakes, of course.

It was bad enough that he was up against Drake's group – who now seemed to be getting the upper-hand. That there might be infiltrators or traitors in Briggs' very own organization was just too much. It had to stop. It had to stop *right now*. It was time to weed out the guilty. And Briggs knew just how to do it.

Unbeknownst to Briggs, and barely thirty miles away, Slade and Drake were sitting in yet another out-of-the-way motel, counting down the hours to what both men hoped would be the decisive battle of the war: Slade's clandestine flight to Waxahachie. Drake had pulled out all the stops in his efforts to get Slade into the heart of the facility. And he had done well; *very* well.

Within twenty-four hours, said Drake, Slade would have a new passport, a new driving license, and even a new Social Security Card, all in the name of Michael Voight, a non-existent veterinarian with a wife and two kids – also completely non-existent. And less than twenty-four hours after that, Slade would be making a flight, from D.C. to Mid-Way Regional Airport, followed by a short drive to Waxahachie.

"Getting you to the airport won't be the problem," said Drake, adding: "We've taken excellent steps to ensure that, even if I say so myself."

Slade could see that, despite the fact that Drake was clearly pleased with how things were progressing, he, Drake, was also showing signs of strain. And not just due to his age and having been awake for about twenty hours, thought Slade.

"Something wrong?" asked Slade, knowing that now – of all times possible – was not the time for secrets.

Drake, who had been staring at the carpet, looked up: "Not really; I know you're the man for the job. You've had the kind of training you need to get in and out of a place like that. You know your UFOs history, too. That's all I can ask for."

"So what's the problem?" asked Slade.

"Not knowing who to trust, that's the problem." Drake leaned forward: "I haven't told you this before, Marc," he said, to which Slade thought: And you haven't called me Marc before, either. "I'm someone who relies on facts, on figures, on data, on probabilities. But, I'm also someone who knows there's more to this world, to life, than just that."

"Getting a bit deep on me, Drake?" asked Slade jokingly.

Drake just about managed a slight smile: "I've learned that in situations like this, intuition counts. And it counts for a lot. I don't know if intuition is just a normal function of the human brain, or something more, something, well, *higher*."

"Don't be getting all religious on me," said Slade, with a faked laugh, and somewhat already concerned about where the conversation was heading – and at such a crucial time, too.

"No, no," Drake replied, but in a way that left Slade sure that something weird was going on in Drake's brain that only he, Drake, knew. But what was it? Slade was just about to find out.

Drake sighed. It was not a sigh born out of being content. Nor was it one that signified tiredness. To Slade, it seemed like a sigh prompted by a deep sense of resignation. He was right.

"I've had a long career, Slade, and I've done a lot of things for what I really do believe is the greater good. I'm not proud at some of the things I've done, but they were always necessary things; I know that. But, there's something else." Drake then paused, noticeably.

Slade leaned forward in his chair: "Well, come on. What?"

Drake sighed again: "I have this deep sense, a deep sense of what I can only call foreboding. That whatever the outcome, it's not going to go well for me. It's as if I can't see past these next few days. That even if we beat them at their game, my part's over."

"What do you mean, over?"

"I mean," Drake added, "have you ever had the feeling that your life is not your own? That it's fate calling the shots? That you can just tell the vultures are circling overhead, even when you can't see them?"

Christ, this *is* getting deep, thought Slade. "No, I never have," Slade quickly and forcibly replied. He lied as he said it, however. Slade, like most people, at one point or another, knew that intuition played a major role in life – whether from a good or bad perspective. This seemed to be Drake's moment.

Jesus Christ, what a time to pick!

The room was eerily silent for more than a few seconds, after which Slade broke the tension by pouring both of them a much-needed brandy. Drake looked up, slowly took the drink, swirled the ice around, and took a gulp. He smiled: "Thank you, Marc."

Slade did his best to give Drake a wide grin and said: "You're welcome." Slade couldn't help but wonder, however, if this was about to be Drake's swan song. Hell, working in intelligence for years, everyone takes a hit – fatal or not – sooner or later. Nevertheless, Slade was going to do whatever was necessary to ensure that Drake lived to see the outcome.

To hell with fate, circling vultures and intuition, Slade whispered to himself. He and Drake were going to blow those bastards out of the water. They were going to start to prepare the public for the *real* UFO story. And they were going to share another round of brandies. Definitely. So why did he feel like he was trying to convince himself, rather than Drake? Maybe there were storm clouds ahead for the old man.

-34-

The man – today he was calling himself "Mr. Edwards" – had been in Waxahachie for barely a couple of hours. It was unlikely that, in a town of its size, he would have stood out from the crowd. Even so, he was determined to keep a low profile. In his eleven years as someone hired to get the kinds of jobs done that most people wouldn't even think of touching, Edwards knew the critical importance of blending in with the masses.

As he sipped on his coke and ate his chicken salad sandwich and fries - in the cramped confines of a small mom-and-pop-style restaurant - Edwards scanned the room, carefully and completely. There was a mother and her two screaming kids to the left. To the right, a fat businessman was talking loudly on his cell phone, clearly filled with self-importance and determined to ensure that the rest of the customers got to hear about his latest deal. Whatever, prick. A group of teenagers was over by the window, laughing equally loudly.

How easy it would be, thought Edwards, to take each and every one of them out. A swift bullet to the head, a snap of the neck, the list was almost endless. He entertained himself by wondering: who first? It was easy: the businessman. Asshole. Mind you, those kids and their screaming ran a close second.

It felt good to have the power and the skills to dictate the future of entire lives – or the *lack* of futures, as was usually the case when he was needed. All of which brought Edwards back to reality. He quickly forgot about his fellow customers and focused on the man who was now in his sights: Marc Slade.

Only two days earlier, Edwards had received a call from a go-between that, it didn't take him long to figure out, represented some of the most powerful people in government. He hated those suit-types but could not deny that they paid well – as in, *extremely* well. In fact, the fee offered for taking out this guy Slade – who, he was told, would soon be en route to Waxahachie – was extreme, even by his standards. Of course, he quickly accepted it. Only a fool wouldn't.

In a meeting in a Houston, Texas hotel room Edwards had been provided with a background dossier on Slade, several clear and recent photos of him, and a list of names, addresses and phone numbers of just about everyone that knew him.

The guy who had provided him all the information was of the kind Edwards loathed: a lackey, a weasel, someone who wanted to be a big player and who liked to think he was a big fish in a big pond. You're wrong, buddy, Edwards thought: you're strictly small pond-style. He amused himself by thinking about what his new employers might say if that same go-between suddenly turned up dead. They might be relieved, he thought, with a smile. He decided to let him live.

A car was made available to Edwards. Half of the fee was handed over in a black, shiny briefcase. And a list of instructions – written in pen and running to three pages – completed the transaction. The balance of the payment was to be provided on proof of Slade's death. Edwards was expected to be in Waxahachie in no more than two days. It was all going to run very, very smoothly. He should have known not to jump the gun.

Only a few hours later, Edwards received yet another call. It was of a kind that he had never received before, and of a kind it was highly unlikely he would ever receive again. The caller was elderly, male, and made it clear that he knew all about the contract to take out Slade. As Edwards listened, the old guy made him another offer; a very different offer, one that turned things right on their collective head. As cool and as calm as Edwards was, even his jaw dropped ever so slightly.

"We understand that you have accepted a contract on a certain Mr. Slade, correct?"

Edwards simply answered: "Go on."

"Very simply, we would like to negotiate a *new* contract. I represent what we might call a consortium, a group of people that very much wants Mr. Slade to remain alive and intact. We're willing to triple your current fee. All you have to do is tell those who want Mr. Slade dead that you performed the task successfully."

Edwards thought for a moment and then asked, with a high degree of skepticism in his voice: "And they're just going to take my word for it?"

'Not at all: you will be provided with a photograph that will show Mr. Slade appearing to be dead. You will hand it over when you collect the balance of your fee, and you will tell them that you disposed of Slade's body in a fashion that will ensure it will never be found."

"And if they don't believe me?"

"They *will* believe you; they wouldn't have hired you if they weren't sure you could get the job done," was the matter-of-fact reply.

"And all I have to do is hand over the picture? No-one dies? I walk away with *their* fee and *yours*?"

"That's it."

"Someone must badly want this Slade guy alive."

"Yes, they do; *very* badly."

"You know that will make me a sitting target, don't you?"

"Yes, and for that reason, you'll be amply rewarded with a yearly payment of very generous proportions, and for the next five years. And, let's both be honest with each other, you and I both know you can take good care of yourself."

Edwards couldn't disagree with that: he was extremely good at laying low. He was even better at wiping out the enemy. Thoughts of a couple of years hanging out in Chile or Brazil – two of his favorite places – flooded his mind. If this whole thing wasn't too good to be true, he thought, we could have a deal here.

He asked the elderly voice down the phone: "What's the next step if I say, 'maybe?'"

"The next step, sir, is a meeting tomorrow, at noon."

"And where might that be?"

"There's a certain restaurant in town. We'll have a man meet you there, at 12:30. He'll take you to his car and then the deal will be sealed."

Edwards laughed at the old guy's confidence: "Will it really?"

"You work for money, sir; yes, it will be sealed."

The voice down the phone provided the address of the restaurant and abruptly hung up.

And, now, here was Edwards, sitting in that same restaurant, awaiting the arrival of someone who was going to – hopefully – significantly increase his bank balance and with not a single death in sight or bullet fired.

-35-

Sure enough, the visitor was right on-time. Edwards prided himself on having been able to nail the guy immediately. His entrance into the restaurant was just a bit too careful and cautious, and he scanned the room for just a bit too long. Edwards' steely eyes were already on the guy when he caught his attention. Edwards enjoyed the fact that he was already in control of the situation.

Rather than walk over to Edwards, the visitor exited the restaurant and casually looked over his shoulder as he did so. Edwards - with two guns secreted about his body - knew that this was a sign to follow. Fair enough: it was unlikely that anything was going to happen to him on the parking area of a busy restaurant at the height of a Wednesday lunch-hour.

As Edwards followed and opened the door, he saw the guy standing near a gleaming, white truck. He walked over and nodded. The only response was a nod in return and a motion to get into the passenger-seat

"Not on your life, pal; not on your fuckin' life," Edwards said, determined to keep running the show.

"That's how it has to be," said the guy, in low tones.

"No, it's not. This is how it's going to be: there's no-one out here but us. You tell me what this is all about, right here, right now, in the open. If I like what I hear, then it's a deal. If I don't, I'm gone and your man, Slade, is as good as dead."

In response to Edwards' words, the other guy stared back, thoughtfully while sizing up someone who was rapidly becoming his opponent.

"Very well," he said, as he closed the passenger door.

A scenario was carefully outlined to Edwards: at some point over the next three days, he would receive a phone call. In that call, he would be told to phone his employers and inform them that Slade was dead. When the inevitable request for proof was asked for, Edwards was to tell the voice down the phone that he had taken a photo of Slade's body and could provide it as that proof.

"I know all this," said Edwards, impatiently.

"I'm just making doubly sure you know the drill," the guy said, his voice giving away what was clearly a small amount of irritation.

Edwards noticed it: "Look, pal, I'm the one running all the risks here, not you. I might be up for this, but I don't like it. And I'm not stupid, and I don't need to be told twice: that old guy, he told me all this two nights ago. All I need is the photo of Slade and my money. You do that, right now, and Slade – as far as *they* are concerned – is dead meat. And they'll get the photo. Fuck me over, and I'll track every one of you down and your families, too. You understand?"

He got the message and handed over a leather case: "Here's your fee, all of it; plus the extra that was promised to you for your silence, as well as instructions on accessing the yearly payment you're also promised."

Edwards wasted no time: "Open the back of the truck."

The guy looked at him, incredulously: "You want to check it? *Now*? *Here*?"

"That's exactly what I want to do. *Open it*."

The man let out a deep breath, clearly frustrated, but did as he was told.

Edwards checked carefully throughout the case. Sure enough, it was all there. For a few moments, he thought about what he was about to do: accept a deal that would see him screw over one powerful group at the request of another. It was going to be dicey and dangerous, and he'd likely be on the run for the rest of his life. Still, he had pretty much done that for years, anyway. And what's the point of being alive without a bit of thrill and adventure?

His mind was made up.

"Okay, it's a deal."

The other man managed a slight smile and nodded. He said: "One other thing: here's the photo of Slade."

On looking at it, Edwards took out of the right pocket of his pants the picture of Slade that had been provided to him days earlier. He compared the two. It was definitely Slade. But, this photo, it didn't look like a staged image. This guy really did look dead. His eyes were glazed. He had clearly been garroted. Dried blood was all around the deep wound. Or so it looked.

After carefully studying the picture for around a minute, Edwards asked: "Are you sure this guy, Slade, is still alive? This looks pretty impressive for a fake."

"Don't worry about Slade. Just get this photo to you-know-who, and we'll do the rest."

With that, the mysterious visitor got into the truck. Offering only a nod by way of a goodbye, he was gone. Edwards, the assassin who would not now be assassinating anyone, after all, stood there for a few moments, wondering if he had just ensured for himself a future life of riches and luxury, or if he had sealed his death sentence. He wasn't overly bothered; he could take care of himself. He hoped.

As the man in the truck drove away, he dialed his cell. Drake answered the phone after just one ring.

"How did it go?"

"He's on board, got the photos, and he's going to deliver them according to plans."

"Excellent," replied Drake. "I'll inform Mr. Slade he has the ultimate cover now: he's dead."

Both men laughed.

Although they didn't mention it to each other, both hoped they would still be laughing when all of this was over.

-36-

eanwhile, just twenty-four hours earlier…
After knocking on Slade's slightly-ajar, motel-room door –
and not waiting for him to offer something by way of a
reply – Drake strode in, with a big smile on his face. Slade was busily
and carefully checking the schematics of the tunnels under Waxahachie
that led to the secret facility he would soon be penetrating. He looked
up, smiled back, and said: "Hey, man."

Slade was pleased to see that Drake's air of melancholy of the last
few days had lifted. Although, Slade didn't want to bring that to
Drake's attention – just in case it plunged him back into his previous
state. Best to say nothing, thought Slade.

"Mr. Slade," said Drake, now grinning broadly. "I have some very
good news."

"Really? What's that?" asked Slade, seriously wondering what
was good about *any* part of the situation he was in. After all, he had
been shot at, almost killed by the Men in Black, and was a target of god
knows how many government agencies.

"The good news, Marc, is that today is the day you die."

Slade's face changed from upbeat to puzzlement. "That's good
news?"

"It certainly is," said Drake. He put his hand into his jacket
pocket. For one moment, Slade wondered if Drake was about to pull
out a pistol. But that was a plain stupid thing to think, right? As it turns
out, it *was* a stupid thought. Drake had in his hand nothing stranger
than his cell-phone.

He pressed a couple of buttons and the line rang out. After just a
couple of rings it was answered. "Miss Macklin, will you come and
join us in Mr. Slade's room, please?"

173

Around three or four minutes later, there was yet another knock at the door. In walked someone that Slade presumed was Miss Macklin. Slade was impressed: thirty-something, hot, slightly gothic-looking, and full of curves in all the right places. Beats Drake's face, he thought. She smiled at him, in what was a slightly flirty fashion, or so Slade liked to think.

"Miss Macklin, Mr. Slade," said Drake, nodding at both.

"Hello, Mr. Slade," said Miss Macklin.

"Very nice to meet you...?" said Slade, already trying to get her first name.

"Miss Macklin will do just fine," she replied, slightly amused.

Slade wondered: does anyone around here use their real name?

"Please show Marc your box of tricks," said Drake, looking at Miss Macklin.

"The day's looks promising already," Slade quipped. All three laughed.

Miss Macklin bent down and opened the large, black case she had brought with her. Slade was more interested in the way her little black skirt rode up than he was in what was in the case. It turned out that the case was filled with make-up, prosthetics, paint, and just about everything you would expect to see in the special-effects department of any self-respecting Hollywood production company.

"Miss Macklin is going to turn you from one of the living into one of the dead," explained Drake, getting right to the point.

He outlined the plan to Slade: "Marc, this is going to be a potentially extremely dangerous assignment, at the very least. There are going to be some very dangerous people on your tail; *very* dangerous. I have a feeling, however, that there is one way we might succeed in lessening that threat."

"And what's that?" asked Slade.

"We get the word out – subtly – so it doesn't look faked or suspicious, that someone has taken you out. That someone has made you a non-entity. In other words: *Dead*. Okay, it's not going to have everyone back off, but if it convinces a few people – on the other side – that you're no longer a player in all this, it might buy you some time and ability to complete the mission."

"This is where Miss Macklin comes in, right?" said Slade, nodding at the case.

"Exactly," said Drake.

"Miss Macklin is going to end your life in this very room, right now – although only briefly, of course."

"Well, thank God for that," said Slade, who could not fail to be amused by the surreal nature of what was about to go down.

With that, Miss Macklin asked Slade to take a seat on the desk chair that was on the far side of the room.

"Make me look good," Slade said, as he smiled at his very own make-up artist. He thought that Miss Macklin let her return smile linger a bit longer than normal. That was fine with him. As Slade watched, fascinated, in the large mirror attached to the desk, Miss Macklin slowly began to transform him from a healthy man in his thirties to one of the recently deceased.

An application of something thick, greasy and foul-smelling turned Slade's skin a sickly, pale color. A dab here and there of something else added a few bruises to his faded skin. Then it was time for Miss Macklin to go for the jugular, so to speak.

Before she began, Drake jumped in: "I thought that if we're going to do this, we might as well do it right. Marc, you are about to be garroted."

Drake wasn't joking: within about twenty minutes, Miss Macklin had Slade's neck turned into a bloody mess. Slade couldn't deny it: it looked as if he had been brutally garroted. He was impressed – in a very strange way.

With the job done, Slade stood up, at which point, Drake said: "One more thing: a couple of photos."

"Please lay on the floor, Mr. Slade, on your back," said Miss Macklin, clearly relishing the moment. Slade was pleased to do as he was told. Miss Macklin took a Polaroid camera out of the case.

"Head back, please, slightly to the right, stare vacantly at the wall and open your mouth very slightly." Again, Slade followed the orders. Miss Macklin took a look through the viewfinder, suggested a few changes to the lighting and the positioning, and then took three shots.

Seeing the developed images sent a chill through Slade. He could see it had done exactly the same for Drake. His face made that very obvious.

"It's only makeup," said Miss Macklin, realizing the atmosphere in the room had suddenly shifted significantly.

Drake coughed and recomposed himself: "Marc, we're going to get these pictures to a few people who, when they see them, will hopefully get the word out that you're gone. That means you lying *really* low for the next few days."

"Got it," said Slade, his mind and eyes still on his dead form in the photographs. This was the closest he ever wanted to get to death until he was a very, very old man.

-37-

Mr. Edwards took out his cell-phone. He dialed the number that he had been given to call when the assignment to kill Slade was over. Despite being a distinctly cold and calculated character, even he found himself taking a couple of long and deep breaths before he dialed. He was used to killing people to order and for money. He was not, however, someone who had ever *pretended* to kill someone, and then screw over the very people who were paying him to complete the job. Not until now.

He could ponder on things all day. He could delay the inevitable call for another twenty-four hours. He could sit around, thinking about all kinds of scenarios. But, whichever approach he took, Mr. Edwards would still have to make the call, like it or not. Best to get it out of the way: whatever the future was going to bring, finding out sooner was preferable to him than later. One last deep breath and he dialed.

"Yes?" said the voice at the other end of the line.

"It's me; Edwards."

"Yes, Mr. Edwards," was the reply. It gave away no hint of emotion.

"The job's done," said Edwards, coming straight to the point.

"Really?" the man said, in tones that Edwards perceived as being distinctly doubtful. Damn it.

"What do you mean by that?" Edwards replied, his voice suddenly filled with anger. "You asked me to get the job done and I did it. What's the problem?"

The voice at the other end, Edwards was already thinking, sounded skeptical. That was not a good sign.

There was a noticeable, three-or-four-second silence on the part of Edward's employer, after which the man said to him: "There *is* no problem; providing you really did fulfill your obligation."

Edwards went on the defensive: "You calling me a liar?"

177

"Not at all, Mr. Edwards; I just want to know, for sure, that our money has been well spent."

Edwards played his ace card: "I have the photos you asked for."

"Well, that's good; that's *very* good. I want to see them - within the hour, at the place where you received your initial payment, the restaurant."

"Okay," said Edwards, adding: "Meet me outside. We then go inside, where plenty of people can see us."

"Very well," said the man. He hung up. This had *better* go well, thought Edwards.

The man at the other end of the line did not know it, but Edwards was only a five-minute drive from the restaurant. Better to be early than late, Edwards thought, as he rolled up way ahead of time. He got out of his vehicle and scanned the area. It was a quiet, normal morning. In about thirty minutes or so, the situation would be very different. The restaurant would start filling up with those looking for a tasty lunch.

About twenty minutes later, a large, black car pulled up, just five parking spaces from Edwards'. A tall, grim-faced, slim man, who Edwards estimated to have been about sixty years of age, got out of the car and walked towards Edwards' vehicle. There was no turning back now. He, also, got out and locked the car door behind him.

"You got here early, too," said Edwards, as the man closed in.

"Yes, I did. It's always advisable to plan ahead, don't you think?"

Edwards nodded.

"You have the photos?" the man asked.

"You have the money?" Edwards hit back.

"Yes, I do."

"Then, yes, I have the photos."

The old man's eyes widened and a slight smile crossed his face: "In that case, we had better go inside."

The restaurant had only been open for about ten minutes and, a waitress aside – who nodded with a smile as they walked in – the place was empty. Well, almost empty: the noise coming from the kitchen made it clear more than a couple of people were preparing for the looming, lunch-time invasion.

"I want to sit there," the old man said to the waitress, as he pointed towards a booth in the corner. Edwards instantly knew why he had picked it: right above the booth was a speaker from which the drone of country music was coming. The old man didn't want anyone overhearing what they were discussing. They sat down, both ordered ice-tea, and – when the waitress went to get their drinks – got down to the matter in hand: the murder of Marc Slade.

-38-

The old man stared at Edwards for a few seconds as if sizing him up. Edwards prided himself on being a ruthless, efficient character, but there was something about the man that gave even Edwards the chills.

So," the man began, in quiet tones, "you say Slade is dead."

Edwards felt his blood pressure and anger rise: "I don't *say* he's dead. He *is* dead."

"You apparently found him in very quick time, Mr. Edwards. I like that. But, how, exactly, did you do that? Our people weren't even aware he had reached town yet."

Edwards had anticipated a question along those lines. Reeling off a long and complicated story just might blow the whole thing wide open, he had suspected. So, the best option was to keep it short and to the point.

"Look, Mr.-whatever-your-name-is, I have my ways. I have my contacts. And I have my methods. You want someone found, I find them. You want them followed, I follow them. And if you want them killed, then I fuckin' kill them. I know *nothing* about you and what your game is. That works both ways: how I found Slade is down to me. You don't need to know. Got it?"

"If you say so," the old man replied, slightly amused, and not even giving away a single sign that Edwards' words had had any effect on him.

"I *do* say so."

As the waitress returned with their drinks, and took their lunch orders, Edwards thought: the next couple of minutes are going to be the most important ones of your life. He wasn't wrong.

After taking a sip of his tea, the old man said to Edwards: "Show me the photos, *now*."

Edwards pulled out from the inside pocket of his jacket an envelope. He said to the man: "There are three Polaroid pictures in there: different angles, different lighting. I figured you would want as much proof as possible."

"Yes, I do," the old man replied, his manner now downright menacing.

"Then take a look, asshole" hissed Edwards, as he thrust the envelope into the man's right hand. "Open it; see for yourself."

"When lunch arrives, and we won't be bothered again, I will do exactly that."

Edwards had ordered a burger while the old man had a plate of catfish. Although Edwards quickly tucked into his lunch right away, the man opposite him did not. He took out a handkerchief, wiped his hands, and then slowly and carefully opened the envelope. He looked around the room to ensure no-one was watching. They weren't. The rapidly-filling restaurant could not have cared less about what was going on between the two guys in the corner booth.

One by one, he removed the photos, each time ensuring that no-one else was in a position to see them. He studied them intently, back and forth, for about three minutes, all in complete silence.

Edwards wondered what was going on in the man's mind. He didn't have much longer to wait.

"Very impressive, Mr. Edwards; very impressive," the man finally said, adding: "And the body?"

"Gone," Edwards succinctly replied.

"To where, exactly?" the old man said, in a fashion that made it clear he wanted a straight answer.

Edwards was not about to give him one: "You don't need to know. No-one does, except me. But, let me put it this way: there's not a single chance in Hell of Slade's body ever being found. In fact, there *is* no body. There are *parts*, if you get my drift."

"I do," the old man replied, after carefully – and yet *again* - studying the images. He added: "I think that concludes the terms of our contract, Mr. Edwards."

Edwards' only response was: "Good."

The remainder of the lunch was spent in total silence, after which the old man paid the bill and the tip – both in cash – and the two exited the restaurant. Edwards followed the man to his car. The trunk was opened, and a large package was handed over to Edwards.

"It's all there, Mr. Edwards," the man said, as he handed it over.

As Edwards took hold of the package, the old man failed to release it. With both of them in somewhat of a stalemate, the man said: "I trust that we never have to cross paths again, Mr. Edwards, and particularly so regarding these photos. I also trust that we have definitely seen the last of Mr. Slade. Do I make myself clear?"

"Don't threaten me," Edwards spat," I got the job done, just like you asked."

"I hope so, Mr. Edwards; I definitely hope so."

As the man got back into his car, Edwards was already opening the package. Sure enough, it was all there. One more payment of a very nice amount – from Slade's people – and he would be out of town, and out of the country, in no time at all.

-39-

Mr. Edwards sat in his vehicle, thinking carefully about what had just happened; thinking *very* carefully. Sure enough, he had the money; more than enough. If nothing else, that told him the people paying him to have Slade killed had been successfully deceived. But, for how long would that deceit last? Edwards' thoughts then turned quickly to his second set of employers. Since they clearly wanted Slade alive, eventually – and maybe even sooner than later - someone would know that he wasn't dead.

Despite his plans to leave town – in fact, to leave the entire United States behind him, *forever* – Edwards couldn't quite pull himself away from the undeniable mystery that surrounded the hit-that-never-was.

There was something strange about this affair with Marc Slade; something *deeply* strange. Typically, Edwards' targets were people in politics, in big business, and in foreign governments. There was, he conceded, a certain world-famous actor whose death by a bullet to the head was not the tragic suicide that his mourning fans, the police, and the media thought it was. Edwards was particularly proud of that one, and even more so since the guy was a secret pedophile, something which had sealed his fate – and good riddance, too.

Slade, however, was something else.

Edwards's briefing on Slade was a significantly different from most of those that he had previously received when an assignment had to be carried out. There was nothing in it to suggest Slade was anything but a good, loyal American citizen, one who had served his country diligently, bravely, and dutifully – as had Edwards himself, before the lure of freelancing for shadowy, powerful figures took hold.

What stood out for Edwards were the references in the file to (a) Slade's interest in UFOs, (b) his work with AQUA, and (c) the likelihood that the best place to find Slade would be in the vicinity of that old Superconducting Super Collider, right here in Waxahachie.

Edwards knew enough from his time spent in the military that some UFOs – the ones that weren't the work of fantasists, liars, and bullshitters – were almost certainly the highly classified hardware of Uncle Sam.

He also knew, from what he had occasionally heard on the military grapevine, that there were true *unknowns*, as well. Edwards thought: was someone in government – or, maybe, in the private sector – wiping out UFO investigators? Had Slade stumbled on the evidence that so many people had, for years, been looking for and wondering about?

Edwards knew he should just take the money and walk away, and never look back. Damn straight! His instinct was screaming at him to leave. But, something felt different this time. Maybe, it was because he viewed Slade as someone not unlike himself: former military, decorated, and involved in something hazardous and who was only getting to see part of the full picture. But, the bottom line was that Slade was a decent, upstanding guy. And that was important, for one specific reason.

The one flaw in Edwards' character was that he had great trouble taking out the good guys. Give him some Mob guy, a crooked politician, a big-time drug dealer, or a cop on the take, and he was up for it, every single, damned time. Edwards, then, was that rarest of all rare things: a hitman with a conscience. He was certainly in the game of murdering for money, but only when he felt that snuffing out the life of the target would actually make the world a better place in the process – or so Edwards always secretly hoped.

Granted, Edwards knew nothing about what Slade was up to – all he had was an extensive bio on the man. But, he guessed that Slade was almost certainly a regular guy caught up in something spiraling wildly out of control - and big-time, too.

Edwards knew that his original employers wanted the man dead. And he knew that the hit was supposed to go down right here, in Waxahachie. That whoever was looking after Slade wanted him to appear very dead and very quickly, however, suggested to Edwards that the plan was for Slade still to come to Waxahachie, albeit under another guise. Edwards could not have known how close to the truth he really was.

It was then, as he stared across a stretch of sparse, sun-dried stretch of Waxahachie field that Edwards made his decision. Slade was one of the good guys; he, Edwards, wasn't going to stand by and see a bunch of suits take a man's life just for running around chasing UFOs, even if someone had decided it was all in the name of "national security."

Of course, finding Slade in a town the size of Waxahachie – about forty square miles and with a population of around 30,000 people – could be a near-impossible task. In fact, under normal circumstances, it *would* be. Except for one thing: Edwards' employers had told him the best place to hang out at was the site of the old Collider. That was Edwards' ace-card: he had a very good idea where Slade would be, and very soon too, even if he didn't know why.

And, Edwards wasn't stupid enough to assume that someone hadn't given thought to the possibility that Slade was still alive and that the photos were faked. That being the case, if Edwards *was* going to stay in town – and if he *was* going to help the man who he had been paid to murder – then he needed to tread very, very carefully – maybe even more so than Slade himself.

Edwards felt a chill of excitement as adrenalin surged through his body, just the way that it always did before a job was about to be done, and a life was about to be extinguished. But this job was very different. For the first time in his career, Edwards was turning the tables. Hell, he thought: I might even get to learn if the U.S. Government *does* have a bunch of rotting, old, dead, aliens stored away somewhere.

He did not know it at the time, but Edwards' thoughts would soon prove to be eerily and downright prophetic.

-40-

Edwards knew all too well how the likes of his employer – the one he had fucked over, not Slade's group – would almost certainly still have him in their sights. If he stayed around Waxahachie any longer, they were sure to smell a big rat – or even several. So, he had to give the *appearance* that he was leaving the town behind him. In a way, he was. What those guys didn't know is that Edwards would be back.

Leaving nothing to chance, Edwards waited until morning and left his motel. He then stopped off at four separate stores, before heading out of town. He figured that if he were being watched, this would be the best time for him to be seen. And, being seen meant he would be tailed, which was exactly what he wanted. He *needed* to be seen leaving. When he finally exited Waxahachie, those keeping an eye on him would see he really had packed his bags.

At the time, Edwards was living in Norman, Oklahoma; not too far – as the crow flies, at least – from the Oklahoma-Texas border. Although all of the instructions to take out Slade had come by phone, Edwards was ninety-nine percent certain that the people who hired him were fully aware of the existence of the small apartment from which he was currently operating. So, he took the best option that he considered available to him.

Edwards drove all the way back to Norman. Yes, it was a tedious journey from Waxahachie, but an essential one, if he was going to successfully maintain the ruse that he had left town – and left for good. It was late afternoon when he finally arrived back at his temporary home. Then, it was time for the next stage of the operation.

Edwards parked his vehicle and took his time heading down to the mailbox room, which stood adjacent to the complex's main office. He then made an elaborate job of washing and drying all his clothes in the laundry room. Again, Edwards figured that if someone was still keeping a beady eye or several on him, then it would bode well for those same eyes to see him carrying out those activities that occupied his mind and time when he wasn't killing people.

With all of that finally behind him, Edwards returned to his apartment and did something unusual: he squeezed his hand down the right side of the couch. There was just enough room for him to pull out a small, black, compact cell phone. It was a cheap TracFone, one that had been registered by – and to – a friend in "the business."

Edwards only ever used it for emergencies, and what was going down now was surely one of those. Edwards slipped it into his pocket and headed down to his car. He jumped in, started the engine and dialed.

A voice answered almost immediately: "Yes?"

"Bob, it's Michael," said Edwards, revealing his real first name to one of his most trusted contacts.

"Hey Mike, what's up?" said Bob.

"I need a car, tonight; nothing that can tie it to me. And I need you to come and pick me up, here at the apartment. We're going out to dinner. On the way back, you'll drop me off at that place you decide works best for me to collect the car. I'll need it for a few days. And it needs to be registered to anyone but me. Will that work?"

"It's late in the day," Bob sighed.

"But, will it work?" asked Edwards, his voice betraying a noticeable amount of frustration.

"Yes, it will work."

"Thanks, man! Seven o'clock for dinner?"

"Seven it is."

The evening ran smoothly: Edwards and Bob – who looked more like a school-teacher than a fellow assassin - ate at a local barbecue joint, after which Bob swung his vehicle around the back of the restaurant, and where an innocuous white Honda sat.

"Will that do you?" asked Bob, with a smile. It certainly did.

It was a gamble, but Edwards hoped no-one had seen the game-playing that had just gone on. Before getting out of Bob's vehicle, Edwards dipped down behind the driver's seat, changed from a white shirt to a black t-shirt, and put a black cowboy hat on his head. He then got out of the vehicle, grabbed a suitcase off the backseat, and opened the door of the Honda. Nodding his goodbyes to Bob, Edwards was soon on the road – in a car registered to someone else, with a phone listed to someone else, and with ID that, yes, identified him as someone else.

Hopefully, all of that elaborate play-acting – which, by now, had practically taken an entire day – had ensured that the people who wanted Slade dead were satisfied that Edwards really had made his way back to Norman and had stayed there. He hoped no-one had followed him and Bob to the barbecue joint. If they had, it could be game over when someone realized he was heading back to Waxahachie – albeit in highly clandestine fashion.

As he left Norman behind him, Edwards kept a watchful and wary eye on what was going on in the rear-view mirror. Headlights came and went. But no-one seemed to be sitting on his tail for a suspicious length of time. It was close to midnight when Edwards finally reached the Texas-Oklahoma border.

A few more hours and he would be right back to where all of this strange game started: Waxahachie. And, in his heart, Edwards knew that whatever might very soon go down, it would *end* in Waxahachie, too. As he crossed over into the Lone Star State, Edwards took another long, peering look into the mirror. Everything looked good. He knew, however, that appearances were so very often deceiving.

-41-

I t was around 10:30 p.m. when Drake's phone rang. He was so on edge - which was not characteristic of him at all - that he answered before the first ring had even finished.

"Yes?" he said. It was just one word, but the man at the other end could not fail to notice that Drake's voice was filled with anticipation, and even with a bit of trepidation. For a moment or several there was silence. Then Drake heard the words he had been waiting to hear – and for what had seemed like a near eternity.

"It's on; Slade is on. It's time to get things moving."

Drake replied: "Everything's good?"

"Well, as good as it can be, yes. It may not be as tough as we originally thought. Let me put it this way, there are people there – at Waxahachie – that, in the last few days, we've been able to convince them that *our* way – disclosure – is the *right* way. Some of them took a bit of persuading but not the others. The battle might just be going our way, Drake."

Drake exhaled deeply. That was good news. Actually, it was damned *great* news. The last couple of weeks – filled with disappearances, deaths, and the Men in Black – have clearly made certain players think carefully on where they want to be when the shit hits the fan, Drake thought.

The man continued to Drake: "It's hardly going to be an official visit and Slade will definitely still have to take the back-door route through those tunnels. But, there's a good chance – I'll fill you in on all the details later – that Slade will have the chance to see the bodies, and even photograph them. If we can get those photos into his book, into his novel, then that will get people talking."

Drake listened intently, as the man added: "The main thing is that we need to get the book out, send a signal to everyone, and sit back and see what happens. The press will bite; we'll see to that. The UFO crowd will debate on whether his story's real or not, but the main thing is that it will have the public thinking and the media digging. And we need all the allies we can get if we are going to get disclosure, in the way we need it."

Drake thanked the voice at the other end of the phone, hung up, and made his way to Slade's room.

"Come in," said Slade, as Drake knocked on the door and announced who it was.

"Marc, it's a go," he said, coming straight to the point. "You're going in."

"Waxahachie?"

"Yes, Waxahachie."

Drake told Slade exactly what he, Drake, had just been told, himself.

"Marc," Drake began, with a serious look on his face, "none of this will be easy, and it's likely to be not exactly the safest environment for you to be in. But, we have insiders – people who, like you and like me – want this secrecy to end. You'll have to take your chances on getting inside – the tunnels – but when you're in, we've got people who can protect you, get you to where you need to be."

"And that's…"

Drake interrupted, his face looking grim: "The bodies."

Slade looked at Drake, his face, too, taking on a serious appearance.

"Marc," said Drake, sitting down, "there's something you should know. It's all very well seeing an extraterrestrial on TV – *The X-Files*, *Star Trek*; whatever. Seeing a *real* one, in person, is very different. Dead or alive, it doesn't really matter. It causes culture-shock, immediately. There's not a person who has seen them that isn't severely affected the first time; it's impossible not to be."

Then, Slade realized: "You've seen them, haven't you: the bodies?"

Drake looked grimmer than ever: "Yes, I have."

"What's it like?"

"Seeing them? Fantastic and terrible, both at the same time; terrifying but amazing: it's hard to explain. I need to warn you, though, that it's not something you can prepare for - *ever*. It's going to change your world, and your life, forever. And I *do* mean forever. I will always remember where I was when JFK was shot. You'll always remember this; it won't ever go away."

"I get it," said Slade, although – inside – he didn't, not fully, anyway. He knew that it was only when he saw the evidence through his own eyes that it would hit home: we're not alone in the Universe.

Drake got up, poured both Slade and himself double whiskies and said: "We're likely to get a call very soon; probably early hours, for a nighttime flight to Waxahachie. We've got a good cover for flying at that time. It should, hopefully, all be okay. After all, your photos show you're dead."

Slade smiled, nodded, and sipped his iced drink.

"But, you must be on your guard at all times. Yes, there are people at the Waxahachie installation that want disclosure, and who want it soon. But there's an uneasy tension there: lines are being drawn. Sides are being taken: to disclose or not to disclose.

"You getting in there, seeing the evidence, photographing it, the novel – this is what we need. We, my people, can only do so much; we can't dump disclosure on the American people overnight. But your book – that can do so much for all of us."

Drake took a swig and added: "This book, your book, is going to be the most important UFO book, *ever*. It's going to be a best-seller, it's going to get the public talking, and it's going to ensure questions are asked at the highest levels. Questions are what we need. Questions will open more doors, a subtle acclimatization to the end-game."

"The end-game: this is the final countdown," said Slade, almost gravely.

"Yes, Marc, it is."

-42-

It was around 7:15 p.m. and Drake had just finished with a flurry of calls. It was all good news. Or, at least, as good as he was going to get at this stage in the game. He had spent the last few hours calling, and leaving messages with just about anyone and everyone who could offer input and answers on that most important question of all: were *they* – the other side – still convinced that Slade was dead?

Three days earlier, that was definitely the case. But, as Drake knew all too well, a lot could happen in a few days; a hell of a lot.

Drake's people had half a dozen or so people inside the National Security Agency who weren't just sympathetic with the plan to have disclosure become a reality, but who were outright supportive of it. They had done their absolute best to secretly access the NSA's finest eavesdropping technology and listen into the conversations of those that dearly wished to see Drake, Slade and company dead and gone.

The problem was that, when it came to the use of cell-phones and online media, the aforementioned other side was very good at covering their tracks. Conversations were scrambled, emails were encrypted, and messages were routed, re-routed, and for good measure, re-routed again.

The one positive thing in all of this was that Drake's NSA contacts had been able to pick up enough data that had them convinced the plan was running smoothly: as far as could be determined, the photos were still convincing the enemy that Slade was no more. There was, however, a negative side.

The one thing that had Drake worried was that while he had friends in the NSA who were willing to help in any way possible – at least, to where they could do so without risking their livelihoods, freedoms, and maybe even their lives – the *other side* had just as many people in the NSA, too. God knows what they had learned from penetrating his, Drake's, network. He hoped the answer was: not much. But he knew he couldn't be sure.

Drake's people took all the steps they conceivably could to protect themselves from cyber-penetration. They had, for example, all agreed that wherever and whenever possible, Slade's name would not come up in conversation. And, even if it did, it would be in coded form, thus preventing anyone from getting word on the fact that, far from being dead, Slade was very much alive and kicking.

There would, however, always be a weak spot; it would be just waiting to be exploited, no matter how hard they tried to plug it. Since, all the signs were that Slade was still being seen as a dead man, now was the time to strike; now was the time to push for disclosure like never before. All that meant now was the time to get Slade to Waxahachie safely, quickly, and stealthily.

Five minutes later, Drake knocked on Slade's door and told him that it was, for all intents and purposes, a case of now or never. Such was Slade's dedication to precision, and time being of the essence, within the hour the pair was on their way to a small, out of the way airport where there would be no going through security, no officials asking questions, and no screening. All there would be was a drive around the far side of the perimeter fence, where a security guard – also on board with the program – would open the back gates, Drake would drive in, and in minutes, Slade would take to the skies.

Drake was someone who always tried to look on the positive side, but he couldn't hide his nagging worries that if anything bad was going to occur, it just might be when Slade was at his most vulnerable: exiting the vehicle and making his way to the small, private plane.

Slade could tell that Drake was on edge. "Easy, pal," he said, as Drake did his best not to fidget in the backseat of the car, but failed. "It's all gonna go fine."

Drake nodded, not sure if it was for his benefit or Slade's.

As it transpired, there was no last-minute surprise; no interception at the gate, and no Men in Black. It was looking as if Slade was seen as being officially terminated. Unless, that is, someone was going to grab him when he was deep below the Waxahachie installation.

Drake knew very well that might be an all too real scenario, but thought it wise not to bring it up with Slade. But, he knew Slade was no fool – far from it – and had almost certainly thought of just such a possibility occurring too.

It was now around 9:30 p.m. The driver turned off the highway, traveled along a small road for about two miles. He then made a left, followed by a right. Within seconds car, driver, and passengers were confronted by a large metal fence and a heavily protected entrance point. Standing next to it was a man in a black jacket and black jeans. He nodded and walked over.

A back window quietly slid down. Drake leaned out and motioned the man to come over. He did.

"All good?" asked Drake.

"Yes, sir: everything's fine; no hassles, at all."

Drake and Slade exited the vehicle. Slade took his backpack from the trunk. He knew how to pack well when space – or, in this case, the lack of it – was an issue. Two guns, plenty of ammunition, several changes of clothing – all black, a necessity on a nighttime mission like this – two cell-phones, both of which would tax the finest of the NSA in accessing, and a digital camera and audio recorder, were pretty much all that he was carrying.

On-board would be a hot dinner (probably a microwave meal, but as long as it gave him the energy he would need, that was all that mattered), and snacks and water for the next couple of days – if that long was even needed. If possible, Slade wanted to get in, secure the evidence Drake needed, and get out again. Slade knew deep down it probably wasn't going to be that easy, but remaining upbeat was important.

Drake and Slade shook hands and nodded at each other. This was not the time for words. They could wait until things were over and when it was time for congratulations. Drake watched as Slade and the guard walked through the gate and across a large expanse of tarmac. Within seconds, and due to the lack of light, Slade melted from view. The game is finally on, thought Drake.

-43-

As Slade took to the air, he peered out of the window. The sky was dark. The ground was darker still – aside from the sparkling lights of the small, surrounding towns that grew ever smaller as the plane continued to climb. It wasn't long before he was high in the sky, knocking back a couple of whiskeys, and eating an adequate and average aircraft meal of chicken and pasta. After finishing, Slade tried to switch off, but he knew it was useless. After all, how *can* you switch off when you're faced with something as monumental as the prospect of possibly coming face to face with something from another world, from another solar system, and – just maybe – from an entirely different *galaxy*?

All that Slade could do was ponder on the events of the past few weeks, events that had begun so innocently, but which, by now, had radically altered his entire existence – and, undoubtedly, for the rest of his entire life.

Slade thought back to how it had all begun; all so innocently. He could scarcely comprehend how quickly things had changed since he had got that phone call from Sally Richardson, informing him of her close encounter down in Stephenville.

Looking back on things now, Slade knew he should have been more suspicious of AQUA's Brian Anderson, and particularly so when then the old guy did his damnedest to sideline Slade out of the Stephenville investigation, and hand it over to Andrew Bridges.

At the time, Slade had thought it was just down to the typical bureaucratic bullshit that dominates most UFO research groups. Now, he knew better; *far* better. Today, and with hindsight, it all made perfect sense: have the Intel crowd infiltrate the UFO community and manipulate it just about whenever, however, and whenever, *they* saw fit.

For Slade, everything changed when his cop friend, Kenny, had told him Homeland Security was on his tail. It seemed unlikely, unbelievable; impossible, even. And, yet, it was the absolute truth: for poking his nose into a series of Texan UFO sightings Slade was now public enemy number one – or, if not number one, he surely had to be pretty damn close to the top of the list, he thought.

The hysteria that took hold in Stephenville, the strange affair with that old woman, Gladys, and Drake - who Slade had, at first, viewed with downright distrust and suspicion, but who had grown into a firm friend in just a couple of weeks – only served to amplify the high strangeness that was developing rapidly.

And, there was no doubt that Drake had popped up at just the right time: with assassins and Men in Black – *real* Men in Black – on the loose, Slade knew that without Drake he would have been as dead as a duck caught in a hunter's sights.

Then there was the matter of the United Nations: Jesus, how high and far did this all go? Despite all that he had seen and done in the past weeks, Slade knew that whatever the complete picture was, he had barely scratched the surface of it. He suspected that even Drake – for all he knew – was probably unaware of the full, unexpurgated, facts.

But Slade knew that was exactly how things worked in the world of official – and *unofficial* – secrecy: tell someone just what they need to know to get their job done and leave it at that. That's the way it worked; Slade knew that from his Marine days.

And, now here he was, a man on the verge of potentially playing a leading role in changing the course of human history – yes, it really was that serious; Slade knew that all too well.

Slade wondered how the Human Race would react, when – or if – disclosure came. Would he, Drake, and who knows how many others, be thanked for blowing the lid off of the whole, secret, shebang? If those little gray fuckers were the good guys, yes, we probably will be thought of as heroes, Slade mused to himself.

But, what if – Slade thought - disclosure brings nothing but terror; unbridled fear? If there were dark sides to the UFO phenomenon – and, based on his years of investigation, Slade was absolutely sure there were – maybe the world's population would prefer they had been kept in the dark, rather than having the horrific facts thrust in their faces, against their will.

In all probability, Slade thought, exposure to the truth would provoke numerous responses: good, bad, positive, negative; they would all play major roles in the fraught world to come.

Slade tried to think of the day when it would finally happen: who would make disclosure? Which country would come clean first? Might it be down to a worldwide consortium? Or, would the situation be one filled with chaos, turmoil and near-anarchy? He didn't know; he *couldn't* know. No-one could. All that Slade knew for sure was that if the plan he, Drake, and the rest of his people, had put together worked, disclosure was surely coming.

There was, of course, the distinct possibility that Slade would not succeed in the operation that was now just mere hours ahead of him. If that did happen, his death – or, far more likely, his disappearance – would be chalked up to something akin to the deaths of untold numbers of people in Ufology, right back to the days of pilot Thomas Mantell in 1948.

People would debate on his passing, conspiracy theories would flourish. But, nothing would change. Slade knew that because nothing in Ufology *had* ever changed. In that sense, failure was not an option. Slade knew he had to succeed; he had to pull this off. Disclosure, no matter what the cost, had to come to the world.

With that, Slade felt suddenly, and slightly oddly, contented. He felt his eyes growing heavy, his limbs relaxing. He was soon in a dead sleep. His mind was free of all thoughts of aliens – dead, alive, or dressed in black. His body was recharging for the work – and the downright battle – ahead.

And, if he was going to survive this one, Slade needed all the recharging he could get – and then some.

-44-

The touchdown on the 6,500-foot-long runway at Midway Regional Airport was both smooth and quiet. Slade had woken up from his welcome sleep about twenty minutes earlier. He felt revitalized and ready for action – whatever the action might turn out to be.

As he peered out of the small window of the aircraft, into the darkness, Slade thought: Drake chose this place carefully and wisely. It was situated half-way between Waxahachie and Midlothian, just about a thirty-minute drive to both Dallas and Fort Worth, and less than ninety miles to Stephenville. It was, pretty much, central to everywhere in this strange saga.

Slade was impressed by something else too: Drake, or at least someone in his team, had the influence and power to ensure that Drake could bypass security at the airport. As the aircraft reached the gate, he noticed that a black sedan pulled up next to it. The pilot, whom Slade hadn't seen during the course of the flight, opened the cockpit from the inside and nodded at Slade. He returned the gesture.

That the pilot was in black fatigues emphasized what Slade had figured out immediately: this was not a regular flight. The pilot then opened the plane's outer door and silently motioned Slade to follow him. Slade stood up, took a deep breath, and made his way to the door.

Slade had a careful and cautious look around him as he exited the door and walked down the mobile steps that had been placed next to the plane. Aside from the subdued, night lights of the airport, darkness was the order of the day. The air was chilly and the sky filled with stars.

Slade made a quick scan of the sky. He didn't really expect to see anything out of the ordinary, but - based on what had gone on across the past few weeks - he would hardly have been surprised to have seen something large, unidentified, and piloted by something small, gray, and black-eyed.

Out of the sedan stepped a man who sported the same sort of manner, appearance and demeanor as Drake: he was elderly, immaculately dressed, and bore all the characteristics of someone sitting on decades-worth of unholy secrets – secrets that, just like Drake, he had no doubt killed to keep hidden.

"Good morning, Mr. Slade," said the man, looking at his watch and noting the time of 1:45 a.m.

Jesus, thought Slade, he even talks like Drake.

The man reached into the car, pulled the keys out of the ignition and handed them to Slade. He also provided Slade with a manila envelope. It contained the details of a nearby motel that Slade would be able to check into at any time of day or night, and various, sundry items, such as further maps and schematics of the Waxahachie installation.

They silently shook hands, after which the Drake lookalike boarded the aircraft. Slade got into the car and exited the Midway Regional Airport. He didn't wait for the aircraft to leave. Slade didn't know it at the time, but Drake and his band of mysterious buddies were not the only ones who knew that Slade had just landed and was now on the final countdown to disclosure – but, he soon would know.

The drive to the motel took only ten or fifteen minutes. The roads were quiet, the atmosphere was calm, and the ability to stretch his legs out, as he drove, was just what Slade needed.

Taking into consideration everything that had gone on up until now, Slade kept a careful, eagle-eye on his rear-view mirror. Of course, it was inevitable that vehicles – cars, trucks, pick-ups – would be out at this time of night. And they were. But, Slade prided himself on having honed his instincts to where he could spot a tail in mere minutes. He was pleased that he didn't get any such sense at all.

There was a good reason for that, one that Slade knew nothing about: there was no need for Slade to be tailed. The man who had a rendezvous with Slade was already at the motel; ready and patiently waiting for him to arrive.

Always on alert, Slade pulled up close to the sliding doors of the Parks Motel. He grabbed all his gear, opened the door, and immediately scanned the parking area. There was no-one else in sight. Good. On entering the motel, he could see what was, clearly, a bored, middle-aged guy reading a local newspaper.

"Hi," said Slade. "I have a reservation: Philip Werner."

The guy looked unimpressed and half asleep.

Slade pulled out the phony driver's license provided by Drake. This better frickin' work, Slade thought. It did. Not only did the bogus license pass muster, but so did the credit card. Slade wondered: How many people, and in how many outfits, does Drake have working for him?

The guy behind the counter gave Slade his key-card and uttered just a few, choice words: "Down the corridor, fourth on the left."

Within a minute, Slade was in his room, emptying his bags on the bed, and checking exactly what he had in-hand. He brewed a pot of coffee and stretched out on the bed. He knocked back a couple of cups and got into bed. Fortunately for Slade, he was one of those that coffee didn't keep awake.

He lay down and figured out how he was going to do this. He and Drake had decided that the best approach was to keep phone contact to an absolute minimum, even though Slade had a new phone, in the identity of the non-existent Philip Werner.

As for his assignment, Slade figured the best time to penetrate those old, deep tunnels would be late at night, or, like right now, in the early hours. Tomorrow night would be the night, he said to himself. Whatever happens is whatever happens.

Slade closed his eyes, his mind filled with thoughts of what tomorrow would bring, of what he might get to see, and of what the future might bring to just about everyone. Those thoughts were suddenly interrupted, however.

There was a knock at the door.

-45-

W hen someone knocks on the door at around 2:45 a.m., most people freeze for a moment. Is it the police turning up with bad news? Is it a burglar scoping the place, trying to figure out if anyone is at home? Worse still, is it some crazy axe-murderer?

Over the years, Slade's training had been honed to a fine degree; even in the most unpredictable and unlikely of all situations, his instinct, and his reaction were both immediate. For Slade, there was no wondering who it was or who it wasn't.

Slade treated the knock at the door as he would *any* such knock, on *any* such door, at that time of the night. That's to say, he sprung into immediate action.

Slade quickly rolled off the right side of the bed and slid to the floor. Next to him was his backpack. And, inside the bag was the thing even *he* didn't anticipate possibly having to use right now: his gun.

It was a testament to Slade's skills that before he even left the airport he had ensured that the gun was fully loaded and that the safety was off. No matter how much advance preparation had gone on – chiefly thanks to Drake – no-one knew how the next few days were going to play out. Maybe, Slade thought, I've just found out.

Slade quietly placed his hand inside the bag and pulled out the gun. He then crawled slowly and stealthily across the room and through the bathroom door. Slade stayed on his knees. Who knows, he thought: maybe whoever it is has an accomplice outside, on the car park. Someone might easily take a potshot at him, even with the curtains closed, chancing on the possibility of him standing upright and making for a very easy target.

Slade positioned himself on bended knee and shouted: "You better identify yourself – *right now.*"

There was a moment or two of silence, which was then followed by a few words that were not of the kind Slade expected to hear.

"Mr. Slade?"

"I said, identify yourself, pal," Slade replied tersely and firmly.

"I'm here to help Mr. Slade," the man said, in lowered tones, clearly concerned about the guy on the front desk hearing, thought Slade.

"You can help by doing what I told you to do: identify yourself." Slade could feel his anger and tension levels growing.

There was yet more silence, after which Slade got another surprise.

"The person I am, Mr. Slade, is the one who got you out of trouble; *big* trouble."

"How's that?" demanded Slade.

"I'm the guy who got the photos to those people who want you dead."

Slade decided to test the guy: "What photos?"

"Come on; let's not play games," said the voice behind the door. "The photos: *the* photos; the ones of you dead. I'm the guy who was paid to take you out and then got a better offer. Does that clear it up for you?"

To an extent, it *did* clear things up. Slade's mind raced: if it *was* the guy who Drake had told him about – the assassin turned non-assassin – then he was taking a hell of a chance if he had a change of heart and planned on killing Slade in a motel room, even if it was now getting close to 3:00 a.m. There were far better, and easier, ways to take him out – all without risking getting caught and arrested.

"Okay, I'm listening," said Slade.

"I'm here to help," said the voice. "Yeah, I know; it's not what you're expecting. You think I'm here to finish the job: I go from accepting the gig, to canceling it, and then accepting it again, right?"

"No, wrong," replied Slade. "I don't think you would be so fuckin' stupid."

"No, I would not. I'm here to help – really."

Slade decided the only way to figure out what the hell was going on was to confront the man. Playing this game wasn't getting Slade anywhere. And, right now, time was not a commodity to be wasted.

"Back away from the door and place your hands on top of your head," ordered Slade.

Slade heard the sound of a frustration-filled sigh.

"Done?" he asked.

"Done."

Slade quietly made his way to the door and took a quick glimpse through the spy-hole. Sure enough, the man had done as he was told. Even in that short moment, Slade had been able to size up the guy: about Slade's age, built, and someone who could take care of himself.

If the guy was on the level, this was all going to go very easily. If he wasn't, the fight was likely to be a tough one.

"Move against the far wall," Slade said.

Slade flipped the lock and opened the door quickly. He had his gun trained on the guy's forehead in a millisecond.

"Impressive, Mr. Slade," said the man, with a slight smirk on his face.

Slade was not in the mood for humor: "You think this is funny?" He added, tersely: "Get inside."

As Slade backed into the room, ensuring the man was in his sights at all times, his mysterious visitor slowly and cautiously walked forward. In just a few steps he was in the room.

"Close the door," Slade said, motioning with his free hand.

They stood opposite each other, staring. Slade broke the ice: "So, you're here why, exactly?"

The man's annoying smirk appeared again: "I'm the guy who's going to help you find the aliens."

-46-

S lade prided himself on being not just a good judge of character, but someone who could figure what made a person tick, and where they were coming from, in an instant. He also prided himself on the fact that, so far, his instincts had never let him down. But there was something about this guy that had even Slade puzzled.

Despite the fact that Slade's instinct should have been screaming: "Get away from this guy!" Slade felt that the man was honest. The surreal nature of the situation wasn't lost on Slade: here was the guy who, just a few days earlier, was all set to take Slade out of circulation, forever. Now, Slade was contemplating working with him to blow wide open what was arguably the world's biggest conspiracy.

The guy clearly recognized the downright weirdness himself. He said to Slade, who was staring silently at him, gun in hand: "So, what happens now? Do we stand like this all night, me over here, you over there?"

Slade replied, with the gun fixed squarely on the man's forehead: "You'll understand if I'm skeptical of all this."

"Sure, I get it," the man conceded, nodding. He added: "Maybe if I tell you a few things that might help."

"Maybe," said Slade, his voice betraying no emotion whatsoever.

"Can I at least sit down?"

Slade nodded.

For good measure, Slade tossed the man the small bottle of Jack Daniels he had brought with him. The man caught it skillfully, took a seat, and then took a swig.

"You not having one?" he asked.

Slade moved forward a few steps and reached out for the bottle. The index finger of his right hand was poised to pull. His instinct, however, told him it wasn't necessary. Slade didn't betray his thoughts, but he was puzzled by his lack of concern. He took the bottle from the man, sat on the chair by the door, and poured himself a glass. He filled a second glass and passed it to the man.

"Okay," said Slade, taking command of the conversation, "what's your deal?"

The man sat back in his chair, took a deep breath, and took another gulp of Jack. He began by outlining what Slade already knew from Drake's intelligence data. He admitted that, yes, he killed for money – and lots of it, too.

He also told Slade something that Slade didn't know: that, unlike so many others in his line of business, he was very careful and selective about who he took out of circulation – and, more importantly, who he *didn't*.

The man further explained that he was always careful to undertake deep, background investigation on the potential target. And, what he found out about Slade troubled him, but in a positive way. Had Slade been someone who was out for American blood, or to commit terrorist attacks on U.S. soil, he wouldn't have thought twice about taking Slade out, permanently. But, something bothered him; it bothered him a lot.

"What was that?" asked Slade, taking a drink.

"You don't have the background I would have expected, when it comes to someone who wants you gone. By all accounts, you're loyal to your country; you've got a military background and no criminal record. I'm used to getting rid of scum: men with dark skin and beards, if you get my drift."

Slade did, exactly.

The man continued: "Big business types that screw the little guy over and that someone else wants wasted; some wannabe dictator in South America; someone from the Mob; a guy who wants the piece of shit who raped his wife gone – *these* are the types I take out jobs on. You're *none* of those."

The man then proceeded to tell Slade that the background data on him was one of the things that led him to accept Drake's offer to forego the assassination and, instead, help make it look like Slade had already been wiped out.

He told Slade of his own – albeit, admittedly, brief – exposure to the UFO phenomenon, which was when he *officially* served Uncle

Sam, rather than in the *unofficial* status that he often found himself in today.

"So, it's all about aliens, right? You want to keep me alive so you'll get to know the truth about Roswell?" asked Slade.

The man laughed. "Well, that and, like I said, it might sound strange, but I'm a guy who only kills when I see it benefitting my country or if I'm wiping out scum that deserves wiping out. I don't see that getting rid of you serves *any* purpose – beyond keeping whatever *they* know about UFOs from *us*. Plus, your guy's money helped me make up my mind, too."

At least the guy seemed to be speaking honestly and placing his cards on the table, thought Slade, before replying: "Here's how it goes: you show me it's worth me having you onboard, we do this together. I get any sense of you having another agenda, and you take a bullet, How's that?"

The man had that annoying smirk again: "Okay, I get it."

"Good," replied Slade. "So, what's your name?"

"Edwards," the man said.

"Real name?" Slade wanted to know.

"Real enough," was the only reply he got.

"Okay, Edwards," said Slade, "it's time for you to prove yourself."

"And how do I do that?"

Slade tossed Edwards a stash of papers – they were the schematics of the Waxahachie base. Slade looked at his watch and said: "It's 3:20; we're going to do a bit of scouting around. Take a look at a tunnel or several. Understand?"

Edwards nodded. He understood all too well. It was time to search for, and damn well find, Uncle Sam's aliens.

A t the very same time that Slade and Edwards were going from near-arch enemies to becoming almost comrades in arms, a flurry of activity was erupting in various installations, facilities, and offices across the United States. It was activity that ranged from the good, to the bad, and to the downright ugly.

Although Slade and Drake had an agreement to avoid cell-phone contact at all times – unless it was deemed absolutely essential - Drake had his own ways and means to keep tabs on how things were going. Thanks to the bogus credit card that Slade had been given, Drake could, at least, see that Slade had checked into the motel – Drake's connections at the NSA had kept him fully informed on that side of things.

Drake sighed with relief, as he sat in his own hotel room on the outskirts of D.C., far away from prying eyes and ears. Or, rather, he *hoped* he was far away from intruders.

That Slade had made it to his first destination was good: it suggested to Drake that even if there was someone on Slade's tail, they certainly hadn't taken any action against him yet. It wasn't Slade's *first* destination that Drake was particularly worried about, though. It was that certain, *second* destination, the one buried deep below ground in a certain Texan town.

Drake hoped that something positive, something world-changing, was going to come out of all this. Drake also hoped – and prayed, which was something he rarely did – that Slade was going to come out of this intact. Not everyone was of that particular mindset, however.

Barely an hour's drive from where Drake was hunkered down, a phone rang out at a safe-house used by the CIA. No names were used; they were not needed: both men knew who they were speaking to, and both knew the importance of remaining incognito at a critical time like this.

"Bad news," said one.

"Jesus, what now?" replied the other.

"We've got intelligence that Slade might not be so dead, after all."

"What the *fuck*? What about those pictures? I was told your people had confirmed they showed Slade dead. What the hell's going on?"

"All I know is that the guy we hired to hit Slade may have double-crossed us."

"Double-crossed us: how, for Christ's sake?"

"By taking a big, cash payment from Drake's group; that's how. We now know for sure that someone close to Drake paid Edwards a lot of money, right after he showed us the photos."

"They're doctored photos, then?"

"No, our guy was adamant the photos were real, which can only mean one thing: the pictures were staged, make-up, fake blood; that kind of thing."

"Damn those people! What now?"

"Now, we go after Edwards. The good thing is that we kept watch on him: he left Waxahachie after he took our money. But, get this: he came back."

"Came back?"

"Yeah, can you believe that shit? We think he's going to help Slade."

"Help him? This is getting way too fuckin' complicated!"

"I know, but don't worry. Here's the plan: we let Edwards lead us to Slade. We wait until they're in the tunnels – we know that's the most obvious route for them. Then, when they're a good distance into them, we hit them, and we hit them hard."

"I want both of those assholes to take their last breaths in those tunnels."

"I'm on it."

Both phones slammed down, almost in unison.

Meanwhile, 120-feet below Waxahachie, a stressed-out security guard named Bradley Woodward paced around, outside the lab which, he knew, was home to the kinds of things most people would kill to see – and some had.

Woodward was a man with debts; *significant* debts of the mortgage and divorce-settlement kind. That's why when an old man, with a D.C. accent, knocked on his front door three nights earlier and offered to financially clear his slate – and also throw in something substantial as an extra – Woodward didn't just listen, but accepted the offer with barely an afterthought.

All that Woodward had to do in return was to ensure that in the event an uninvited visitor turned up – Slade, of course; although Woodward was given no names – he, Woodward, would ensure that the man got into the fortified room that Woodward was, right now, standing in front of.

Although Woodward, as a guard, wasn't cleared for even two percent of what went on at the facility, he knew far more than most suspected. Woodward knew how to work the staff, and he kept his ears to the ground, picking up every nugget of data, every scrap of gossip, and every morsel of conversation that he could.

Word was circulating that something was going down; something *major* and something very soon. There were rumors of some kind of shadow agency planning on penetrating the base and blowing the whole thing wide open. That was fine with Woodward: he knew what he was guarding, and he knew where it came from. He also wanted people to know – for *everyone* to know.

Woodward was pretty sure that whoever the old guy was, and whoever the mysterious visitor might be, it was all connected to the rumors and whispers flying around. He smiled to himself and thought: it's about time the rest of the world got to know about the bodies, about the ships, and about the biggest secret of all: the forty-three *living* extraterrestrials that lurked in the lowest level of all – the one where very few dared, or even wanted, to visit.

-48-

By the time Slade and Edwards got on the road, it was close to 3:30 a.m. It was, to say the least, a tense time as the two walked along the corridor from Slade's room to the lobby, then to the car- park, and, finally, to Slade's vehicle. Very wisely, he ensured that Edwards was always around five or six feet in front of him and that Edwards' hands were in view at all times. Slade's time in the Marines had shown him the perils of not being constantly on-guard in potential, combat situations.

Slade clicked his remote and motioned Edwards to the passenger door: "Get in and put your hands on the dashboard."

Edwards shrugged and shook his head, but did as he was told. Slade very carefully got in the driver's side, never taking his eyes off Edwards. Now was not the time to make mistakes or get overly confident. Slade fired the ignition and hit the road, steering with his left hand and keeping his gun firmly fixed in his right.

A look of amusement crossed Edwards' face: "You *can* trust me, you know. I get it: I was hired to take you out. But, that's history. I *am* on the level."

"*Maybe*," said Slade, still finding the entire situation one in which it was difficult to relax and easy to see a potential danger point at any given moment.

"Get out the schematics," said Slade, as they hit the main street through town and headed towards the home of the former Superconducting Super Collider. Edwards, again, did as he was told: he leaned over his shoulder and picked up the envelope that Slade had tossed onto the backseat of the car.

"There's something I should tell you," said Edwards, his voice filled with an air of intrigue.

"Why am I not surprised?" Slade quipped, as he started to finally relax and the feeling that any minute now Edwards might go for his jugular began to subside. "Okay, what?"

"There was a reason I was picked for the job on you. It wasn't just random," said Edwards.

Slade shot back: "Meaning?"

"Meaning that I know Waxahachie; I know it *very* well. I did another job – years ago – taking care of someone on the collider project. Well, he was supposed to have been on the collider project, but now I'm not sure – maybe UFOs."

It was Slade's turn to be amused: "Taking care of?"

"Car accident: you know?"

"Yeah, I know." He knew all too well. "So, what's the point?"

"The point is that this way – the schematics, the way in that your people have given you - is the most obvious route. We'll get hit as soon as we get in those tunnels. Even if just one word of all this has got out, they'll be waiting for us; I guaran-fuckin-tee you, they'll be down there already, armed and positioned."

Slade knew that Edwards was right, but if he was to get into the base, access the lower levels, and find the evidence that, in a roundabout route, just might force the hand of disclosure then there really was no alternative.

The tunnels had their entrance point in a small, innocuous-looking field around half a mile from the facility. That was the only way in, aside from marching through the main gates and the front door, which was hardly going to work. He said as much to Edwards.

Edwards glanced over at Slade, grinned, and said: "You know what? That's *not* the only way in."

Slade almost did a double-take and quickly swung into the parking area of a closed *Olive Garden*. He looked at Edwards for a moment and said: "You wanna run that by me again?"

Edwards, clearly relishing the moment, but also hopeful that Slade would finally come to trust him fully, told Slade how, on what Edwards tactfully referred to as "the previous occasion," he had been given extensive details on the guy he was to hit. Why he had to hit him,

Edwards never knew. And when he found out the guy was selling secrets to "the other side," he didn't care either.

It turned out that the man in question had worked in a deeply sensitive part of the facility; it was one that – with hindsight – Edwards now believed probably had far more to do with the UFO issue than it did with the futuristic collider program. After all, he mused, the collider program never really got off the ground, so the chances were that this was all a cover for whatever his *real* role was.

"We'll never know now," said Edwards, who, Slade thought, was keen to steer Slade away from any and all questions about the man's identity. That was fine, thought Slade; what happened in the past was done and gone. It was right now that mattered.

"Don't take the exit to the collider," said Edwards, "just keep on moving."

Slade didn't take kindly to what sounded like an order: "*I'm* running the damn show, Edwards; not you."

"Okay, okay," replied Edwards, who secretly found the back and forth sparring entertaining.

"Good," said Slade, his voice firm and forthright: "What's this all about?"

Edwards explained that roughly another half a mile or so up the road – and also in what looked like a regular field - was a farmhouse, a dilapidated one. Or, rather, said Edwards, it was *made* to look dilapidated.

"When I was here last," said Edwards, "they had a guy in there, kind of a caretaker. His whole job was to keep watch over the farmhouse. Or, to be accurate, keep watch on what was *under* the farmhouse."

"What might that have been?" Slade pushed for answers.

Edwards smiled: "Another way in – and a way out, too."

Suddenly, things were looking much brighter, thought Slade. It was still important for Slade to flex his muscles, however: "Don't fuck with me, Edwards; this better be legit."

"*It is!*" he hissed. "This is the break you need; that we need. They're not stupid; they'll be planning to deal with you at either the gate or the regular tunnels. I mean, Christ, probably half the town of

Waxahachie has heard the rumors of the tunnels. But, I'd bet my life they're not gonna anticipate us knowing anything about the *other* entrance. And even if there's anyone there, we can take care of ourselves."

Slade knew that Edwards had got that much right. If this was the break Slade had hoped for, then the backdoor route might just be what was needed to blow the whole UFO issue wide open, once and for all.

As they sat on the *Olive Garden* car-park, Slade looked at Edwards and said: "Right, you better give me the directions to that farmhouse. One way or another, we're getting in - *now*."

-49-

W ithin barely a minute of leaving the *Olive Garden* car park, Slade and Edwards were taking a slow and careful drive. It was along a road that, hopefully, would prove to be the much-needed gateway to the government's underworld of the alien kind. The skies were still dark and filled with black clouds. The shadowy fields, on both sides of the road, were foreboding.

"We're right on it now," said Edwards, as he pointed to his left and added: "It's about a quarter of a mile, on foot, across that field."

"Okay," replied Slade. He looked around for somewhere to leave the vehicle. In a few moments, he found it: a closed-down gas station that was advertised as being up for sale. It had clearly seen better days since the windows were boarded up, and grass and weeds had broken through the tarmac.

Slade had a quick glance in the rear-view mirror. There was zero traffic. And: nothing was coming towards them either. They were alone. Now was the time to act. Slade turned off the headlights and coasted slowly onto the rundown property. He figured the best thing to do was to take a look behind the station and see what was there.

It was a wise decision, one that was solely born out of instinct – something which Slade never ignored. Sure enough, there was the perfect place to leave the car: a small concreted area that allowed for the parking of three vehicles. Not only that, the area was 100 percent obscured by the highway.

Slade turned off the ignition, looked at Edwards, and said: "Let's go."

It was important that the pair traveled light enough to ensure they could outrun any potential adversaries they might cross paths with. On the other hand, going *too* light-handed just might prove disastrous. Four silencer-equipped handguns, a large supply of bullets, night-vision equipment, cameras, a compact camcorder, and a couple of bottles of Gatorade, were all that they needed.

Slade motioned Edwards to crouch down. "I know!" hissed Edwards. "I *have* done this before!"

"Just wanted to remind you who's calling the shots!" Slade grinned.

Edwards thought: "Whatever."

Like darkened crabs, they scuttled across the side of the gas-station parking area, leaving nothing to chance.

As they reached the edge of the highway, both men paused and carefully studied the long road they were about to cross. Aside from the wind, the entire area was silent.

"Let's go for it," whispered Slade. Edwards nodded in reply. The black-clad duo stayed low and sped across the highway, rolling and disappearing into the denseness of the field as they reached the far side.

"That's the way we need to go," said Edwards, pointing in an easterly direction and to an area that, at this time of night, was pretty much out of view.

"You're sure?" asked Slade. "We don't want to fuck up now."

"Yeah, that's it; no question about it," Edwards answered. "That's our way in."

Staying low, silent, and out of view, were only achievable by taking things carefully and slowly. The result was that, although Edwards said the farmhouse was roughly around a half a mile from the highway, it took more than double the time they would have normally anticipated to get there.

Of course, there was a small road that led to the farmhouse from the highway, but both men agreed that it would be madness to follow the most direct route – one that stood every chance of ending in complete disaster, maybe even death. At this stage, there was no sense at all in jumping the gun. Slowly and steadily were the only ways to do it.

"I see it!" said Slade, finally, as he carefully raised his head above the overgrown, unkempt field. He pointed to a modestly-sized building at a distance of around two hundred meters.

"Yep, that's it," said Edwards, smiling at a job well done – so far, at least.

They took a decision to approach the farmhouse not just cautiously but separately. Slade took the left side of the building while Edwards took the right. The good news was that the field shielded the pair pretty much up until a point of about eighty feet before they reached the farmhouse.

All was quiet and dark. Just maybe, thought Slade, it was *too* quiet and dark. Although Slade didn't know it at the time, Edwards was thinking exactly the same.

Slade's career in the Marines had taught him all he needed to know about making a stealthy approach on a potentially hostile target. As much as he wanted to get inside, this was no time for rash decisions. This was a time for a well thought out, concealed assault; one that, if there was anyone inside, would result in Slade and Edwards being the only ones to walk away intact.

As they exited the field, almost completely on their stomachs, both men could see that the place didn't look lived in. The small amount of light that indicated dawn was soon approaching revealed flaking paintwork, torn-up wooden steps that led to the front-door, and an old, rusted truck that had seen better days.

Edwards said this was all part of the process of ensuring that the second entrance to the underground facility looked just about as innocuous as it could be. It was time to find out.

-50-

The old, weathered porch ran all the way around the farmhouse and stood about four feet off the ground. Slade signaled Edwards to make his way up its right side while he did the same on the left. A two-prong attack might be expected, thought Slade, but there was no choice at this stage of the game.

Having crawled across the small, open stretch of ground that stood before the old house, Slade carefully placed his bag of supplies on the porch and quietly pulled himself up. As he reached the porch and placed his feet upon its rotting surface, there was a sudden creak, one that briefly filled the air and echoed eerily.

"Damn it!" cursed Slade, concerned that he might just have given the whole game away. For more than two minutes, he lay silently and unmoving. Fortunately, there didn't seem to be anything out of the ordinary afoot. There were no tell-tale noises outside; no detectable sounds coming from the inside, nothing at all. But, was that a good thing?

On one hand, the complete silence was a relief. On the other hand, however, there was always the possibility that someone might be biding their time, practically enticing Slade and Edwards inside, at which point all hell might break loose.

Whatever the answer, sitting outside – as dawn intruded more and more upon the rapidly fading darkness – wasn't going to get them anywhere. They had to strike, as in *now*; as in *right now*.

Slade got into a crouching position and quietly made his way to the back of the building. As he did so, he caught sight of a shadow coming his way. Instinct meant that, in a second, Slade's handgun was ready to inflict fatal damage. Fortunately, it was – as Slade had hoped and surmised – Edwards.

"Jesus, man," whispered Edwards, "you could have blown my fuckin' head off!"

"But, I didn't," replied Slade, his face displaying a cold smile.

Neither man thought that charging headlong through the front door was the wisest approach. There was a far better way: the left-side window was completely smashed. All that was needed was a few slices of a knife to cut down the tattered blinds and they could be inside.

Neither man was convinced that they were safe, however.

"This all looks *way* too damn easy," said Slade.

"I know it," Edwards answered. "Like we're being led here; drawn in."

Slade nodded, grimly. He added: "You know what? We don't have much of a choice. What's going to happen is going to happen."

Within moments, the blinds were on the floor and Slade and Edwards were inside; they were standing in an empty room; one filled with a choking combination of dust and what smelled like a dead animal. Both men gagged at the stench and held their palms to their noses.

"And this is all a dupe to hide what's going on below us?" asked Slade, his voice now louder, and his mind filled with more and more doubts. For a moment, he wondered if Edwards had lured him here with the intention of killing him. That theory soon went out of the window, however. After all, Edwards could have got that job done any time in the last few hours. Why wait until now?

"I have a bad feeling about all this," said Edwards.

"You're not the only one, pal," Slade shot back.

Sensing that – good or bad – they were totally alone, Slade and Edwards let their bags drop to the floor and knocked back mouthfuls of Gatorade.

"So, do you have any idea where this entrance point is supposed to be?"

"Yeah, I do," answered Edwards. "The pantry."

"The pantry?!" exclaimed Slade. "Does anyone still use that word?" he asked, incredulously.

Edwards smiled: "I guess they would have done in 19th-century shitholes like this one."

It didn't take the pair long to find it. Upon opening the battered door, they were confronted by a variety of old boxes, cans, and a few old, rusted knives and forks, all scattered across the floor of the cramped room. Maybe, thought Slade, they had been strategically placed to create just such an impression. What looked like abandonment and decay just might not have been, after all.

The two looked around, for anything, in the slightest, that might give them a clue as to what their next step should be.

"Well, if the pantry *is* the place," said Slade, "there's only one way to look, and that's down."

He dropped to his knees and tapped the floor with his knuckles. The sound that resonated was a dead giveaway: *the floor was clearly hollow*.

Slade took out his flashlight and carefully scanned the floorboards. In moments, he had what he was looking for.

"Look at this!" he said to Edwards, who bent down beside him. In the far corner of the pantry, there was a large latch. A second one was positioned directly opposite it. Slade flipped both latches and he and Edwards held tight onto one each and pulled.

To the amazement of Slade and Edwards, a small section of the pantry floor – that spanned the width of the small room, and a length of about four feet, came loose. As they pulled the section completely free, a blast of cold air hit them. Wherever it was coming from was below their feet; almost certainly *way* below their feet.

For a few moments, the two men looked at each other in complete silence.

It was Slade who broke the ice: "Ready for a bit of exploring?"

-51-

Peering into the cramped opening proved one thing: whatever was down there was enveloped in darkness. That there was a sturdy, metal ladder affixed to what was clearly a tall wall, however, suggested the probability that the distance to the next level was probably fairly significant.

Slade had an idea. He grabbed a battered and rusted can of beans that sat on its side on the floor of the pantry. Edwards stood in silence as Slade dropped the can into the inky darkness and quickly lowered his head into the opening, hoping to hear the echo of the can hitting concrete. To Slade's amazement, he heard nothing. Either the floor below was cushioned in some fashion or the distance was far beyond what either man had imagined. There was only one way to take things further.

"Here," said Edwards, as he passed his flashlight to Slade.

"Thanks, man."

Slade placed it into one of the pockets of his pants. He turned around and slowly lowered himself onto the rungs of the ladder. The air suddenly got even colder.

"Take my hand," Slade said to Edwards, as he stamped down hard on the step that his boots were balanced on. The last thing Slade needed was for the steps to give way and for him fall to his death. Nothing moved. That was a good sign. Whoever had constructed the steps had clearly done a good job.

Slade took a few more steps down, and pulled the flashlight out of his pocket. He flicked the switch. Slade uttered two words only: "Holy shit."

"What is it?" Edwards asked, his voice clearly showing concern.

"I can see for maybe sixty feet down; maybe a bit more. But, I don't see any floor; it's too damned dark. Jesus, this thing could go on forever."

Slade took a few more steps down, and Edwards quickly followed behind. The problem for both men was that the steps were encased in something that resembled a metallic well. In other words, it was as if they were descending in a somewhat cramped, claustrophobic, vertical pipe.

"We should count the steps," suggested Edwards, as his eyes slowly became accustomed to the small amount of illumination that the flashlight offered.

"Good idea," said Slade.

It seemed like forever before the descent was finally over, during which the two decided to remain tight-lipped and as quiet as possible. God knows who, or what, might be waiting for them below. It was only when they finally reached a small concrete floor that both men realized just how far down they had come. Based on the distance between each step, they estimated a descent of somewhere around 340 feet.

Edwards, who was still on the steps, and about twelve feet above Slade, quipped that it was like taking a trip down into the pits of Hell, except without the fire and the guy with horns and a forked tail. Slade could hardly disagree. As he shone the flashlight in front of him, Slade could see a small metal door, no more than five feet in height. At the base of the door was the can of beans, bruised and dented.

"Please don't let it be locked," Slade said, knowing that if it were, the only way out would be the way they came. And, although both he and Edwards were in excellent physical condition, a 340 foot, vertical climb would be a tough job for anyone. Slade held his breath and turned the metal handle. It opened.

Slade turned off the flashlight and tentatively pushed the door open. He slowly exited the cramped, funnel-like tube they had just descended. He used the door as a shield while Edwards dropped to the floor-space that Slade had just left behind.

For a few moments, the two men stood in complete silence. That old adage about a "deafening silence" was right on target: the lack of even the remotest bit of noise was as bizarre as it was surreal.

Finally, Edwards broke the ice: "I guess we forget how much background noise we have all day, huh?"

"Yeah," Slade replied, as he flipped the switch on the flashlight again, wondering – just like Edwards – what, or who, they would be confronted by.

As Slade scanned the scene before them, it became instantly clear that they were in a large tunnel, one that had a height of around thirty feet and a width of roughly twenty feet. Both the walls and the floor were concreted. In a couple of places, there was clear evidence of tire tracks.

Edwards suggested someone had been driving a forklift truck in the tunnels and had left the marks while spinning the truck around, no doubt loading and unloading...well, *something*. Slade agreed.

Here and there, a few empty, wooden crates could be seen. There was the occasional, discarded soda can and candy wrapper. Clearly, no-one had been in the tunnel for a very long time – or so it appeared, at least.

As they got their bearings, Edwards pulled another compact flashlight out of his backpack. With two flashlights being better than one, they could now see that the tunnel was infinitely long. The beams faded long before the tunnel did likewise. There was no choice but to start walking. Whether it was a walk destined to take them to the truth of the UFO phenomenon or to a battle to the death with some rogue arm of government – or maybe both – neither Slade nor Edwards had any idea.

"You know what's interesting?" asked Slade, as they began to carefully make their quiet way along the tunnel.

"What's that?"

"The old tunnels that were built here for the super collider only went down to a depth of about 200 feet. I've seen the schematics. Hell, it's even on Wikipedia. So, you know what that means, right?"

Edwards knew *exactly* what Slade was saying: the super collider tunnels had been constructed on top of an already existing, secret facility.

"Christ, how far down does this place go?" Edwards asked Slade.

"Maybe what you said about hitting Hell wasn't so far off the mark," Slade replied. It was a comment that silenced both men for more than a few minutes.

A s they continued to walk along the vast, dark tunnel, it became apparent to both Slade and Edwards that all was not as it seemed to be – or even should be. Slade had assumed that some of the tunnels – specifically, the ones that had supposedly been constructed for the collider program – had been commandeered by those that were running the UFO program.

After all, converting the tunnels into self-sustaining, fortified labs and workplaces would not have been difficult. And, of course, since the construction of the collider tunnels was done with the knowledge of the people of Waxahachie, the world's media and the government, then it would be all too easy to hide the secret in plain sight. Everyone would buy the collider story, without realizing that some of the tunnels would have a very different purpose.

It was a great theory; but, as Slade had to admit, it had a major flaw: the tunnel that he and Edwards were now walking along was around 140 feet *below* the long-abandoned collider tunnels. To have openly dug even deeper tunnels – with the world's media looking on – would surely have set off alarms somewhere and would have resulted in major questions being asked.

But, here was the most baffling thing of all: Slade had in his possession extremely detailed schematics of the collider, of the old tunnels, and of the portions of the facility that had been constructed before the plug was pulled on the program. None of them gave *any* indication of another facility already in place, or even being secretly constructed at the same time.

There was, as Slade saw it, only one possibility – it was a possibility almost as unbelievable as it was incredible. It was time to share a few thoughts with Edwards.

"You know what I think?" said Slade.

"What's that?" asked Edwards.

"Okay, here's the deal: we're in a tunnel, more than 100 feet under the collider. Right?"

Edwards nodded: "Right."

"But, how in hell did someone build this section without anyone knowing? I mean, come on: we're not at the North Pole or the Amazon Jungle. We're in Waxahachie, for chrissake!"

"So, what are you thinking?" asked Edwards.

"I'll tell you what I'm thinking," Slade shot back. It was a theory that left Edwards near-dumbfounded.

"Here's what I think we have," Slade began, after taking a chug on his Gatorade. "It's obvious this place wasn't built in the nineties, when the collider program began. And, there's nothing to suggest *any* extensive, deeper digging was going on here in the fifties, sixties or seventies; we would know about it. You see where I'm going?"

"Go on," said Edwards, cautiously.

"I'm thinking this place isn't just old; this is *centuries* old. I don't think we – that's us, the Human Race – built this. Okay, there's tire tracks and shit lying around everywhere, so maybe we've remodeled it, revamped it. But, what if where we are, right now, has been here – under everyone's noses – for who knows how long, maybe even before Columbus?"

Edwards looked doubtful: "You're kidding, right?"

"Hell, no!" Slade shouted. "You think someone can get away with digging down 300 feet, in Waxahachie, at any time in the last century and we wouldn't know about it? *Everyone* would know."

Edwards had to admit that Slade made a good argument.

"I don't think we built this," said Slade. "I think we inherited it or commandeered it. Hell's bells, maybe we're even *sharing* it – with *them!*"

Another thought began to come together in Slade's mind. It sounded like wild sci-fi. He hoped it was, but he suspected it was all too terrifyingly real. He outlined it to Edwards:

"Humor me: what if, right now, we're in something that's just a small part of something even bigger? What if there's a damn network of these things all across the country – a fuckin' alien maze, hidden from sight? Everyone's looking for UFOs above us, and trying to figure out whether they come from this star or that star. But, what if they've got a permanent presence here?"

Edwards felt a chill go through his entire body: "All the time, right below us?"

Slade nodded; his face was bleak: "All the time, right below us. *Everywhere*."

Both men had to admit it made perfect sense. Slade remembered how the late Dr. J. Allen Hynek had said that the problem with the UFO mystery wasn't the *lack* of reports, but the *overabundance* of them. Hynek couldn't accept that thousands of advanced entities would keep flying back and forth, from some faraway star system, on a daily basis. Perhaps, thought Slade, Hynek's biggest flaw was that he had never considered the possibility of a permanent presence among us – or, as now seemed to be the case, *below* us.

"Maybe the government's first exposure to the aliens wasn't Roswell, or by a planned landing and meeting in the desert somewhere," suggested Slade. "Just maybe, we *stumbled* on them when we started digging underground, rail-tunnels, mining operations; that kind of thing."

It was a shocking scenario for both men to try and wrap their minds around. Our unearthly visitors were infesting the lower parts of our planet, surfacing at night to do God knows what: abductions, use cattle in bizarre experimentation, maybe even kidnap people and never return them.

Slade had heard all those crazy stories coming out of Dulce, New Mexico, about underground bases and hostile aliens doing all sorts of nightmarish experiments on imprisoned U.S. citizens. Now, he wasn't sure it was all so crazy, after all...

-53-

The possibility – maybe, even, the *probability* – that the Waxahachie installation was built on an ancient, underground site, constructed centuries ago by extraterrestrials of undetermined origin and intent, nagged on the minds of both Slade and Edwards as they continued to carefully, and slowly, walk the huge tunnel.

By now, the pair had been walking for more than an hour, and all they had seen were the walls of an endless tunnel and a floor littered with evidence that, at some point, this had been a hive of activity. Right now, it was something akin to a ghost town. Slade had a thought. It was not a good one. How could it be, hundreds of feet below ground, and in the middle of God knows what?

Slade glanced over at Edwards and said: "I've got a theory: what if this place, this tunnel, isn't just abandoned or closed down?"

Edwards looked puzzled: "I don't get it. What do you mean?"

Slade motioned Edwards to stop. The two of them leaned against the huge, cold concrete tunnel and Slade laid it on the line: "This place looks abandoned, right?"

"Right," Edwards replied.

"What if this place isn't just abandoned or no longer needed. What if they – I mean our people – were forced out; made to leave? Think about it, there's shit lying around here everywhere. It sure as hell looks like somebody was in a real big hurry to get out of here!"

Edwards looked around and had to admit Slade had a good point. Edwards hadn't given it much thought, beyond the fact that the place was empty and clearly not in use. But, yeah, he now thought, a good case could be made that the aliens had forcibly removed our guys – a *very* good case. The big question was: why?

Slade outlined his scenario: "Let's say someone – government, intel, the military – found out years ago about the underground network and set about trying to contact the builders."

"The aliens," said Edwards.

"Right, the aliens," replied Slade. "Let's say the government – or whoever is running this – thought the best approach was to do a deal with E.T. You know that's a long-running theme in Ufology, right?"

Edwards did know it: for decades there had been rumors of some type of Faustian pact having been done with an alien race during the Eisenhower administration. But, it was all story, no hard facts. Until now, that is…maybe.

Slade continue to unravel his theory: "Suppose there was a deal: we agree to hide their presence from the world, they do whatever the hell they're doing, and maybe, even, we work together. Well, if the aliens have underground installations all across the United States, maybe the best way to keep things under wraps would be for us to build our classified installations – Area 51, S-4, even this place – directly *above* theirs. It's a working environment that'd allow for direct working contact between both sides, and they would have literal camouflage – in the form of our installations. No-one would be able to penetrate the aliens' installations because they would have to get through ours first – and a massive security presence is gonna prevent that from ever happening."

Edwards admitted it made good sense. There was, however, one thing that hung over them ominously: the matter of why this section of the facility was seemingly abandoned. Slade was on a roll and expanded further:

"I think that maybe, at some point, there had been a falling out – in simple terms. We were kicked out, forced out. Perhaps, what's left is a kind of uneasy truce, where both sides are working for their own ends, but at times it serves each side to work with the other. Just maybe, something bad went down here."

"If that's true," said Edwards, "it would mean we're right in the middle of a fuckin' alien base which is a no-go area for us."

"That's exactly what it might mean," Slade said.

"At first," Slade continued, "I thought we were being allowed to get in here – that maybe Drake had some insiders who were making sure we get in, get the evidence, and get out again. Okay, we haven't seen anyone, but it doesn't mean they're not here. But, I'm thinking, now, that the reason we're all alone and there hasn't been a single attempt to stop us, or even help us, is because everyone is shit-scared to come down here – *all of them*."

"Oh, *shit*," Edwards muttered.

"There's something else, too," said Slade. "And it gets worse."

"Can it get any worse?"

"Oh yeah," said Slade, gravely. "If our guys are gone – or, at the very least, are here, somewhere, in a secondary role - then that means *they*, the aliens, are in control. And what the hell will happen if they find us wandering around here? We need a plan…*and fast*."

They continued on, ever deeper into the tunnel.

-54-

"We've been walking for about an hour, and probably doing a speed of about three miles per hour," said Slade. "That puts us *way* past the perimeter of the Waxahachie facility. And, it's a straight tunnel, no exits, no doors, nothing.

"I'm pretty sure I know what we're in: a tunnel that's eventually going to connect to another. There's no point in building a huge tunnel for the sake of it. This is a connecting point to somewhere else; it has to be."

"So, we keep going?" asked Edwards.

"Yep, we keep going."

Slade's instinct finally paid off. After approximately another forty to fifty minutes of walking, both men came to a sudden halt. At a distance of around eighty or ninety feet, they could see a doorway built into the left side of the wall. They looked at each other; no words were needed. Both men carefully extracted their handguns from their bags and, as they quietly walked towards the door, prepared for the worst.

As they reached the door, the first thing Slade and Edwards noticed was that it had seen better days. The handle was partially crushed, and a large dent dominated the lower part of the door. Something had tried to force its way in - but what?

There was no choice: it was a case of either take the door or keep on walking for what might be hours or even days.

For what was just a couple of seconds, but which seemed almost a lifetime, Slade and Edwards stared at the door, assessing the damage, and trying to imagine what might be on the other side.

"Fuck it," Slade suddenly said. "We can't stand here all day." He pushed down hard on the damaged handle. As Slade did so, he also pushed forward. The door, to the surprise of both men, opened near-effortlessly, albeit with a loud, metallic groan. Slade and Edwards breathed deeply and peered into the darkness ahead, wondering what was about to await them.

What they found was a long corridor, perhaps ten feet wide by eight feet high. There was something very strange about it, however. The entire corridor – floor, ceiling, and walls - was made of a purple substance that had the texture of plastic, but the toughness and coldness of steel.

Edwards took out his knife. With Slade holding his flashlight, Edwards tried to make a mark on the wall. The blade didn't even come close to scratching it. Time and again, he and Slade tried their damnedest to make a mark, but no luck.

They looked at each other, realizing that wherever they were, they had just left normality, and the world they once knew, far behind them.

Slade looked Edwards square in the eye: "You're good with this, right? You know we have to go on, whatever happens."

Edwards nodded: "Sure, we've come this far; no turning back, whatever happens."

They shook hands tightly and pressed on.

Negotiating the corridor was not a problem; it was, however, downright eerie. After all, they had nothing but a couple of flashlights to help them on their way, and all they did was to light up about fifteen feet of the eerie, purple surroundings that dominated their every view. Slade was about to say something when he came to a sudden stop.

"Hear that?" he asked Edwards. He had heard it.

"That was footsteps," Edwards hissed. Slade nodded.

Somewhere, further down the darkened corridor, and outside of the small area of illumination that the flashlights provided, there was…someone else. Slade had an idea.

"Keep walking until I say stop," Slade whispered. "And keep listening."

After about twenty steps, Slade motioned Edwards to halt. Sure enough, for a second or two after the pair came to a halt, the sound of footsteps could be heard. That is, until they ceased, too. The same thing happened three more times, across around 300 feet.

"Somebody's jerking us around," said Slade. "You up for action?" he asked Edwards.

"You know it," Edwards shot back.

Both men charged headlong into the darkness, their flashlights wildly, and almost psychedelically, lighting up portions of the walls and ceilings as they did so. Both men had their handguns ready. If there was going to be a firefight, they were damned well going to win it – or go down fighting.

As it turned out, there was no firefight to the death. There was something else; something far more terrifying than facing death by a hail of bullets hundreds of feet underground. It was the end of the corridor, perhaps thirty feet ahead.

But that was not all. There was someone standing against what was clearly another door, facing them. There was, however, something that was amazing and awful in equal measures. Despite the poor light, Edwards and Slade could see that the shadowy, silhouetted person was barely four feet tall.

"Holy fuck," said Slade.

Edwards found that he was unable to reply.

-55-

Barely a second or so after Slade and Edwards caught sight of the small entity against the door, there was an ominous and unforeseen development: the flashlights of both men went suddenly dark. Completely out of the blue, and unanticipated, the pair was now plunged into total darkness.

Out of instinct, more than anything else, both men hit the ground, keeping their guns firmly fixed in the direction of the door, even though now they could barely see each other, never mind the door and the thing that was standing in front of it.

They were breathing hard; too hard, as it transpired. Slade suddenly remembered how Drake had warned him that encountering the "others" for the first time was – for everyone – a traumatic, shock-inducing experience. Slade thought: hell, the old guy wasn't wrong. He fought to slow his breathing, as did Edwards, who was also clearly affected by what they had just seen – albeit briefly.

For two minutes or thereabouts, they lay silently on the corridor floor, and with their guns never moving from their target. Eventually, Edwards whispered: "Did you *see* that?"

"I saw it," replied Slade.

"Jesus, they're real," was all that Edwards could add, his voice filled with wonder and astonishment.

Slade didn't reply, but he knew that what they had seen, even if it had been for just a second or two, was not of this world. It was one thing to read about such things, and to investigate them. It was, however – as both men now knew – something else, entirely, to actually encounter some part of the phenomenon up close and personal.

Suddenly, and without any warning, illumination was inexplicably restored to both flashlights. Slade thrust the beam into the darkness and directly against the door. Edwards did likewise. There was nothing there, nothing at all; just a door. The creature was gone. But to where?

They certainly hadn't heard or seen the door open. Maybe a side door: they stood up, and moved slowly, and tentatively, forward.

It took the two only a handful of seconds to walk the forty or so feet to the door. As they reached it, they became even more confused and concerned. Not only was the small creature gone, but there appeared to be no way, whatsoever, it could have escaped.

The walls, the floor, the ceiling: they were seamless, all running and melting into one. That left just one possibility: it had somehow gotten past Slade and Edwards in all the chaos of the darkness and then exited the way they had entered. But, as small as the thing was, there was absolutely no chance of it having done that.

"I guess it could have dematerialised," quipped Edwards. His panic was beginning to subside, even though his heartbeat wasn't. For both men, that instant of fear was being replaced by adrenalin-fueled excitement and drive.

Slade couldn't argue with Edwards' words: "Yeah, beam me up, Scotty, and all that shit."

After standing around, debating on what to do next – or, maybe, what not to do – Slade finally said: "Okay, whatever that thing was, it's gone. We're not going to figure anything out standing here in the dark, twiddling our flashlights." He pointed at the door.

"I figured that would be next," said Edwards.

Slade slowly took the handle of the door – which, in sharp contrast to the corridor, looked to have been the creation of nothing stranger than human hands. He gripped tightly and pushed down.

As he opened the door wide, Slade held his breath and figured Edwards was doing exactly the same. He was. Slade half expected to be attacked by hordes of savage, little fuckers from some god-awful, nightmarish world. It was for this reason he had his finger balanced carefully on the trigger of his handgun; it was right at that point where even just the lightest bit of extra pressure would send a high-powered bullet slamming into anything that came lunging forward. Even if they're alien, thought Slade, they can surely die, just like us. Or, so he hoped.

As Slade and Edwards passed through the doorway they were confronted by something mind-numbing, something that simply could not be, but which was there, right in front of them. They found themselves standing on a steel balcony, around twenty feet wide and seven feet deep that overlooked what appeared to be a gigantic aircraft hangar, about fifty feet below them. But, there were no aircraft in sight. At least, no aircraft built by human hands.

Scattered, in haphazard fashion, across the massive hangar – which was easily the size of a couple of football fields - were seven circular shaped, silver colored objects. They ranged in diameter from around twenty to forty feet. You could wrap it up however you wanted to - vehicles, craft, or machines - but there was only one accurate way to describe them: *flying saucers.*

The eeriness of the situation was made even more powerful by the fact that there was not a soul in sight. The entire place was filled with a classic, deafening silence and a sense of menacing emptiness.

"Fuck me," said Edwards, his voice deathly quiet. Such was his astonishment, he repeated it, twice.

Although there was a portable staircase leading from the balcony to the ground, neither man thought to use it. They just stood and stared. Flying Saucers *are* real. And the fuckin' government – or some rogue arm of it – damn well knows it. And who knows for how long?

Slade looked down and noticed that he had been pressing down so hard on the steel rail encasing the balcony that his knuckles had turned white.

He turned, and was just about to say something to Edwards, when a booming voice, clearly coming from directly below the balcony, echoed in Slade's and Edwards' ears: "Mr. Slade, perhaps you and your colleague would like to come down? That's why you're here, after all; to see our collection of little toys, correct?"

Slade and Edwards looked at each other and then peered slowly over the balcony.

"**I**t's perfectly safe," said the smiling man, who stood about fifty feet below Slade and Edwards. After all they had been through and seen in the last few days, neither man was prepared to leave anything to chance. Almost in unison, both quickly trained their handguns on the elderly, stooped man dressed in a white lab coat, and who sported a shock of equally white, thinning hair.

A look of amusement crossed the old man's face: "Really," he repeated, "there's no need for weapons. It's just you and me; time for a chat."

Slade and Edwards looked at each other, puzzled, and with frowns on their faces. As if reading their minds, the man said: "What were you expecting: a James Bond villain and hordes of troops racing around?"

It turned out that was *exactly* what both Slade and Edwards were anticipating. Drake had made it sound like just about every step might be their last. And yet from the time they hit the old ranch house, descended into the huge tunnel, and finally reached their destination, there had been no drama, at all. No bullets flying around, no attempts to have the pair put in handcuffs; in fact, nothing. What the hell was going on? It was time to find out.

The old man motioned them to come down, which they did – cautiously. Slade was determined to ensure that he ran the show. That meant, basically, aiming the gun directly at the man's face, from a distance of about six inches.

Rather than being intimidated, the man merely smiled. He said: "Mr. Slade, please, relax. No-one is here to hurt you; no-one's going to kill you, or lock you up."

He turned his attentions to Slade's partner: "And you are?"

"Edwards," came the terse reply.

"Ah, yes," the man responded, as a grin crossed his face. "I hadn't anticipated that. You're the turncoat; decided not to take Mr. Slade out of circulation when money and your conscience got the better of you, correct?"

"Something like that," Edwards answered, irritated by the man's smug nature.

"Yes, I've heard a lot about you," the man shot back, making Edwards wonder what the hell he meant by that.

"And who, exactly, are *you*?" asked Slade, his voice now brimming with anger.

"I'm the man who is going to give you all you'll need to get us on the road to disclosure."

"I want a name," Slade demanded.

"I'm sorry, but that won't happen," said the old man. "But, I *will* tell you all you need to know."

The man motioned the pair to a small office on the far right side of the hangar. Neither Slade nor Edwards could stop themselves from staring, almost open-mouthed, at the squadron of silver saucers as they made their way.

The old man had seen such responses dozens of times before, maybe even hundreds. He had, after all, worked for the group for forty-four years. He never got tired of seeing the reactions of those who found themselves, for the first time, right in the midst of the absolute proof that the Human Race was not alone in the Universe.

"Please, sit," he said to Slade and Edwards, offering them very welcome mugs of steaming hot coffee.

"Look, Drake said that...," Slade began.

The old man quickly interrupted him: "I know what Mr. Drake said, but he doesn't know everything. In fact, you might be surprised exactly how much he *doesn't* know. Before we get to the matter of what's going on *here*, it's important you understand the nature of what's going on with the bigger picture; what's going on at other places like this all across the United States – and not just the U.S."

"Meaning?" asked Slade, still showing hostility towards their aged informant.

The man leaned forward, sipped on his coffee, and said: "Let me tell you a story."

"What we have here, what we have everywhere, is a war: two sides, two factions, two agendas. Yes, there are a few crossovers here and there, but it comes down to two approaches to the extraterrestrial problem: there are those who wish to disclose, to tell the whole story to everyone. And I do mean to everyone.

"Then we have the other side, those that will do all they can to maintain the secrecy, to maintain the status quo. We have a silent war going on. It's not quite as straightforward as I suspect Mr. Drake described it to you, however. Not his fault; he doesn't know it all."

"And you do?" asked Edwards.

The old man's penetrating eyes flashed from Edwards' to Slade's and back again: "Yes, it happens that I do," he said, in cold, quiet, and ominous fashion.

Slade and Edwards listened carefully to what the elderly whistleblower had to say: "Imagine a war that is constantly on the verge of erupting, but which never quite does. Imagine a situation where you have different people – powerful people – jumping from one side to the other as it suits them; playing both sides, trying to figure out who they need to be allied with when the storm begins - and then changing back again.

"And, in the meantime, you have people vanishing, people riddled with bullets, suicides that probably aren't suicides, car accidents that aren't car accidents and...well...you see where I'm going. I'm sure Mr. Edwards knows; that's your territory, correct?"

Edwards glared.

The old man ignored Edwards' look and continued: "There's a silent war, which involves the military, the government, the intelligence community, private industry, private corporations, the money people who really run the planet, and even the Vatican.

"And it extends to right here, to this very facility we're in right now. There was a very good reason why you were directed to follow the route you came. Poor Mr. Drake thought he was doing the right thing, but if you had followed his instructions, you would have walked right into the heart of what I call 'the other side.'"

"The aliens?"

"Not at all," the old man responded. "I mean the other side in this strange war; those working to stop disclosure. The welcome there would have been far, far different. Put it like this: I doubt you would be breathing by now. And that's the big secret: we have the equivalent under here - and elsewhere – of a 1950s-era Cold War, each side trying to destroy the other, but neither able to do so out of fear of what might happen: sudden, unplanned disclosure.

"We have control of this side; they have the other, both following their own agendas."

"And where do the aliens fit into this?" Slade wanted to know.

"Ah, yes," the man said. "That's a different story entirely."

-57-

As Slade and Edwards sat and listened, the old man told them the summarized version of the U.S. Government's involvement with the others, as he insisted on repeatedly calling them. Indeed, in the time available, a summary was all that was conceivable.

"Despite what you might have heard," the man began, as he slowly sipped on his second mug of coffee, "Roswell really was the first, hard evidence of their presence. Those stories of pre-Roswell crashes: hoaxes or disinformation; we encouraged both. Now, we knew something was going on; had been going on for years: sightings, pilot reports, and things like that.

"There wasn't much we could do during the war – World War Two – as we were focused on destroying the Nazis. But, post-war, that's when things changed: missing aircraft and pilots, radar encounters, sightings of strange things in the sky; it all began to increase. Then, out of the blue: Roswell. That changed *everything*. And, you might be surprised how quickly things changed."

"What do you mean by that?" Slade asked.

The old man sighed, and Slade was sure that a tell-tale look of fear briefly overwhelmed their elderly informant. He continued: "Roswell told us that someone, or *something*, was flying around, skulking around, watching; *spying* on us. We responded quickly: set up a committee, autopsied the bodies, tried to figure out the technology that had fallen in our lap."

"Majestic 12?" interrupted Edwards, demonstrating to Slade that he knew more about UFOs than Slade realized.

The man laughed: "No! God, no. Only fools and the gullible believe in that. MJ12 was pure disinformation; it was run to keep certain people in UFO research away from, and off the track, of the *real* group. Certain researchers spent *years* chasing down that yarn,

239

something which certain *other* people were very happy with, as it kept those some researchers tied up in knots and out of our hair."

He added: "But, yes, there *was* a committee: created solely to deal with the problem of the others."

Slade butted in: "Why do you keep referring to them as the others?"

The old man visibly paled.

"I – we, I should say – call them the others because even after all the years since Roswell happened, we have no hard proof they are what they say they are: aliens."

Edwards looked puzzled and asked: "Well, what else could they be?"

The man replied: "You tell me: we know they are highly deceptive and manipulative. We also know that the key to their travel is inter-dimensional, basically jumping from one reality to another, but all co-existing at the same time.

"It's hardly surprising, then, that even within the groups that have looked into all this – and for decades – there's a thought that these things don't just use multi-dimensions to travel, but that that's their natural environment, rather than another star-system.

"There's another group – a small think-tank in the Pentagon – that, for years, looked at the theory of time-travel; us from the distant future, rather than alien. And you've heard the demonic theory, too?"

Slade nodded. He knew all about the "aliens are stealing our souls" scenarios.

"That's another one that a small group studied for decades – they're *still* looking into it. The problem is that we have a lot of theories, but no hard evidence of what these things are or what they want with us.

"Then, there's the idea that they're from right here: an ancient terrestrial, subterranean race, forced to share the planet with us. In one way, it makes sense: we know they have entre networks, underground, right here, on Earth. There's one right below us. Maybe, that's because this is *exactly* where they're from."

Edwards and Slade both took a gulp of coffee and listened as the man added: "Everyone in the UFO community thinks we're hiding this, and we're hiding that, and that we have a handle on the entire situation. The truth, however, is the exact opposite: we *know* we're being visited and that some of the operations of the others seem benign; but some, meanwhile, seem outright hostile. Mostly, they're just manipulative and deceptive.

"We have several dozen corpses from a handful of crashes, plus more than a few craft, some of which were – you might say – donated. A few, even, captured. But, really, that's *all* we have: nothing solid to say what they are, where they are from, or what they want. Those are the important issues that, even now, decades after Roswell, we can't answer. That's why we want disclosure: to try and tell people, in a responsible fashion; get it out and have people prepared for the day when we either get good news or bad news."

"And what news do *you* think we're gonna get?" Slade pushed.

The old man looked grave and said softly: "They're looking after number one: themselves. Let me put it like this: you eat beef?"

"Yeah," replied Slade. Edwards nodded and thought he could do with a good, well-done steak right about now.

"Do you hate cows?"

Slade shook his head.

"I don't believe the others hate us," said the man, "but that doesn't mean we're seen as anything other than cows. We're someone's commodity. *Their* commodity. And they're in control of the situation, while we don't get to see the full picture, the final agenda."

For a few moments, all three sat in silence.

"You must have learned *something* about them," said Slade, adding: "These stories about pacts, alliances, agreements; that kind of thing."

Again, the old man laughed. "Forget all those stories about pacts and treaties; it's a joke. These things don't make pacts; they don't ask permission. They don't need to because of one important and terrifying reason: we *can't* stop them. They can do *what* they like, *where* they like, and *when* they like. And, if you think about it, the idea of them sitting down with us – at the White House or somewhere and literally signing a treaty with a pen – is ridiculous. Oh, there has been contact, but not of the kind you think, Mr. Slade."

"What do you mean?" Slade asked.

Again, a look of fear came over the old man's face. He took a deep breath and continued.

"The first time you have contact is terrifying, complete terror, fear; a sense of losing your sanity. Imagine your mind flooded not with an alien voice speaking English, but with images and concepts; ideas that are then somehow translated into something you can understand. I know I'm being vague, here; but it's extremely difficult to explain.

"In fact, more than a few people couldn't cope with it: there are significant numbers of people in these programs who take the suicide option. Those on the programs who liaise direct with the others are mentally tuned into it; they have prepared themselves. They're very skilled and not everyone can do it successfully. I imagine it's rather like what a schizophrenic goes through every day – but, here, the voices, or the imagery, are real. And what we know, really, is only what they want us to know. That's why we have such an uneasy situation about disclosure."

The old man firmly fixed his eyes on Slade and said: "Your friends in those disclosure groups – Bassett, Greer, and all the rest - they think when the day comes we're going to spill the beans on the secrets of the Universe. We might have a handful of crashed saucers and bodies, but what we don't have is what everyone thinks we have: answers.

"So, your job – with your planned novel that, I understand, Drake will be putting in the hands of a major publisher – is to present everything you see today into the public domain. Drake will see everything is done to make the book a bestseller and you'll present the facts to the world in a hypothetical 'what if?' scenario. It will get people talking – hugely. That's the first step to, hopefully, our next step."

The old man smiled: "And that brings us to something else: it's time for you to take a tour of what, exactly, we have here."

He stood up, walked to the door, and motioned Slade and Edwards to follow him.

It was *that* time.

-58-

The old man had provided Slade and Edwards with a fascinating – and undeniably controversial – history of the UFO phenomenon, as well as fragments of what was afoot at, and way below, the Waxahachie installation. It was only now, however, that the enormity of the situation was really beginning to hit home. And big time, too.

After all, it was one thing to be told what was going on hundreds of feet below the Lone Star State. It was, however, quite another thing to see the hard evidence, up close and personal. And, that, incredibly, was exactly what was about to happen.

When they first arrived, neither man could fail to see the squadron of saucer-shaped vehicles that sat in the massive hangar-like structure. But, even so, at the time, they were at a considerable distance from the vehicles. That was all about to change; as were the lives of both Slade and Edwards – forever.

As they exited the small room, the two glanced at each other. They wore near-identical expressions. They were a mixture of awe, anticipation, trepidation, excitement and, if they were honest with themselves, a degree of fear. Slade remembered that Drake said it would not be easy to cope with the enormity of encountering alien life, firsthand. He thought: whatever happens, happens.

Slade could see from his face that Edwards was clenching his jaws and gritting his teeth. Tension enveloped the air in the eerily silent building. The uneasy, overpowering silence was added to by the fact that the floor of the facility appeared to be made out of some strange form of hard, rubber-like surface that completely muffled – or even *absorbed* – the sounds of the boots of both men.

"Stay close at all times," said the old man.

"Huh, these things are dangerous?" asked Edwards.

243

"In a way," said the man. Even his face was now filled with a degree of concern. He explained why: "We've had some of our people who spent too much time on these programs becoming, ah, affected."

"Define affected," said Slade, immediately wondering how much was being withheld from the pair.

"Well, there's good evidence – but we're not exactly sure why – that certain people seem to pick up on fragments of the memories of the others, when they're inside or around the craft for lengthy periods."

The man's face became even more fear-dominated: "We've never been able to figure out the reason, but it's as if some sort of energy - a thought- or memory-based energy of theirs – is tied to the energy of the vehicle itself. The longer you're in its presence, the greater the risk is of becoming directly linked to the memories of the others. And you do not want that, I assure you."

"We've had people in psychotic states," said the man, "after a few weeks of working on these things, these vehicles: hearing voices, seeing supposed images of the others' home-world, the kinds of things that could drive you insane – and have."

He saw the look of concern on the face of both men.

"You'll be fine," he said. "We're limiting you to about five minutes for each craft. There has never been a single case of anyone – *ever* – getting affected after just that amount of time."

The man's forced, unconvincing smile hardly helped Slade and Edwards from thinking there was more to these craft and their creators than met the eye; *much* more.

The first vehicle that the trio approached was made amazing not by its size, but by its total *lack* of size. Completely circular in shape, smooth, and lacking in any markings or evidence of how it was constructed, it was barely about twelve feet in diameter, and less than two feet thick. Its color was akin to that of polished silver. It sat atop a sturdy, metal, four-legged stand.

"Touch it," said the man, nodding in Slade's direction.

As Slade moved towards it, he quickly looked up at the old guy. His face was one of pure terror. Slade thought: Christ, what the hell do they have here? He tentatively reached out his hand.

As the index finger of Slade's right hand ran along the upper side of the craft, he was shocked to find that the texture was not at all what he expected. The sensation was not just weird; it was *beyond* weird.

Slade expected to feel some kind of metal beneath his finger. What he actually encountered was something that *looked* like metal but that had a texture which reminded him of wet cement. Suddenly, it felt as if some invisible, wet substance was coiling around his hand, even though the surface of the vehicle had clearly not changed. He pulled away instantly, as an odd sense of malignancy swept over him.

"What did you feel?" asked the old man, his tone filled with urgency and concern.

"It felt wet! And hostile, took a grip of me, fuckin' grabbed my hand!"

"Yes, everyone experiences that," said the man. "We're not fully sure why."

"Not fully or totally clueless?" Slade shot back in loud, angry tones.

"Very astute, Mr. Slade. No, we don't know why – at all."

"You could have *warned* him," Edwards boomed. "What did that thing do?"

"Don't worry. I was just thirty-one when I first experienced it. Look at me: I'm an old man now. There are no lasting effects. I promise you. I can't tell you how many times I have come into contact with it and felt it."

The man continued: "I had a reason for what I did. I apologize."

"And that was?" Slade demanded, angrily.

"It's important you understand the concept of what 'alien' really means. It doesn't just mean things, entities, from some other world or galaxy. This isn't *Star Trek*. Their minds, their technology, even the surface of the craft I had you touch: *everything* about them is alien to anything we can relate to. These aren't just someone else's equivalent of NASA. When I say these creatures are alien, I mean they are so far beyond us, in every sense, that they become almost unfathomable; incomprehensible.

"When disclosure occurs, everyone on the planet will be faced with what you have just experienced – and much more, too. The psychological effect on you, Mr. Slade, was clear. And all you did was touch the craft, a craft made...somewhere else. You're a trained military man, and even you were shocked and unprepared by your first exposure. We are preparing to expose *billions* of people to what you have barely begun to see - but which you *will* in the next couple of hours.

"I'm telling you all this, showing it to you, to get you used to the concept of how radically everything is going to change – *everything* and *everyone*."

-59-

"It's regrettable that our time today is limited," said the old man. "I said you'll get to see all you need to, and you will. But, I have a few concerns, if things go on too long, and you outstay your welcome."

Both Slade and Edwards frowned.

"What do you mean by that?" asked Slade.

"I mean, that we got you in here just fine. We anticipated that using that old entrance was the key to getting you in. My main concern, though, is just how easy it was for you. I really thought you might face some trouble. That you didn't is making me think there's someone – someone on the other team – that wants you dead, and the best way to achieve that is to get you down here, out of the way of just about anyone and everything."

"So, you're thinking we're okay here, right now, but when we get back into the tunnels and try and leave, that's when the shit's gonna hit the fan?" Slade said.

The old man looked grave: "That's exactly what I think. This portion of the facility is fortified – and that's a good term to use. The people we're up against won't risk a major firefight down here – too many questions. But, I have to admit, I can't guarantee your safety when you leave here and try and get back to the surface."

"That's when you think we'll get hit?" Edwards wanted to know.

"I do," he answered.

Slade and Edwards listened as the man continued: "There are two other things I need to show you. The first is the technology, the propulsion behind these things."

"What's the second thing?" asked Slade.

"The others," the man replied. "And I don't mean a few rotting corpses from Roswell, floating in formaldehyde."

Both Edwards and Slade felt a chill go through them. They were going to meet aliens, extraterrestrials, things from another world. Christ.

"I warn you, Mr. Slade, and you too, Mr. Edwards, this will not be easy; not at all. There aren't going to be any handshakes, no Texas-style 'howdy' welcomes. Try and imagine making conversation with a four-foot-tall cockroach, one with a mindset totally different to ours, completely alien. That's what you're going to see. Again, it won't be easy. Okay?"

They nodded. Slade and Edwards were increasingly seeing that all of their preconceptions about what it meant to encounter an alien were rapidly going out of the window.

"This way," said the man, as he almost scurried towards a larger, saucer-shaped craft positioned close to the right-hand wall of the huge hangar. It was, roughly, fifty feet wide and about seven feet thick. Unlike the smaller craft they had just seen, this one was sitting firmly on the floor – no doubt because of its excess weight, thought Slade.

As they closed in on the object, it became clear that this one was hardly in what could be called pristine condition. On the lower side of the saucer was a gaping hole, about four feet wide and high.

The old man saw Slade and Edwards peering intently at it. He said, with pride in his voice: "One of our very few successes at bringing one of their craft down. Not easy, I assure you: their technology is far in advance of ours. I wish I could say it was down to skill. It wasn't: just pure luck. Over Montana, June 1971; I remember it well."

The man looked into the eyes of both men, intently. He uttered a mind-blowing, life-changing question: "Would you like to see what a UFO looks like inside?"

Slade and Edwards grinned at each other like a couple of kids opening their presents on Christmas morning.

"This way, gentlemen," said the old man. "Take a look."

Slade took the lead, kneeled down, and peered in through the violently torn open portion of the craft.

"What do you see, Mr. Slade?" the man asked.

For a few moments, there was only a deafening silence, as Slade said nothing and did nothing, aside from slowly moving his head to get a better view. Finally, after about a minute and a half, he backed away.

"Check it out," Slade said to Edwards. The latter eagerly bent forward. In less than ten seconds, he pulled out, a look of deep puzzlement on his face.

"Did you like what you saw?" the old man asked, with a knowing smile on his face.

"There's nothing," said Slade. "It's empty – completely frickin' empty."

"Is it, really?" the old man said, in almost taunting fashion.

"Yes, that's *exactly* what it is," Edwards chimed in. "What's the game?" he added, his voice filled with suspicion.

"Maybe, it's not so empty, after all," said the man.

Slade and Edwards wondered what was coming next.

-60-

The old man motioned Slade and Edwards to the wall, where there was a small table and four chairs. They sat down. Their mysterious informant was the only one not wearing a look of complete bafflement.

"What did you see?"

Slade was in no mood for games: "You *know* what we saw. A large, circular empty room, completely silver in color, that's it." He looked over at Edwards: "Right?"

"Right," said Edwards, with a nod. "There was nothing."

"Actually, there was," said the man. "There was *everything*."

He looked at Slade: "How well do you know your UFO history, Mr. Slade?"

"Pretty well," he replied.

"More to the point, how well do you know your UFO books?"

"Just as good," Slade said.

"Do you remember when a certain UFO book was published in 1997, to coincide with the fiftieth anniversary of Roswell?"

Slade knew just what the man meant: "You're talking about the Corso book: *The Day After Roswell?*"

"I am," the man responded. "Are you familiar, Mr. Edwards?"

"Vaguely," said Edwards.

"As you know, Colonel Philip Corso told a controversial story – a very controversial story – of supposedly back-engineering the Roswell wreckage for the Army and then seeding it into private industry to strengthen and massively advance our own technologies.

"Much of what Corso had to say was pure bullshit, absolute garbage. What I can say to you is that it was orchestrated; even we're not sure who by, though. It wasn't us, and it wasn't them. And it definitely wasn't the others."

"*Another* player in town?" asked Slade.

"Almost certainly," said the man, impressed at Slade's quick response. "But, cut through all the bullshit and the elaboration – which, we think, was done to test the disclosure waters – and there's one thing that Corso was right on the money about."

Slade jumped in: "And that was?"

There was a moment of silence before it all became clear.

"Corso," began the old man, "was absolutely right when he said the Roswell crew and the craft had a symbiotic relationship. Each was part of the other. We can't prove it, but in some strange way, these craft are...*alive*."

"Alive?" said Edwards, in doubting tones.

"Is it really that strange?" replied the man. "After all, our own technology is advancing, intelligence-wise, by the day. Perhaps, there's a point in every technologically advanced civilization when machine-based self-awareness inevitably occurs."

"These things, these craft, are self-aware vehicles?" asked Slade.

"As best we can tell, yes," said the man. He then got to the crux of the matter...

"The reason why you don't see anything in the craft as simple as a control panel, levers, pedals, and the kinds of things *we're* dealing with, goes back to what I said about the others: they are alien to the point of being *beyond* alien.

"They don't need the kind of things we rely on. Can you imagine an alien intelligence, one with a symbiotic link to the craft, that literally *thinks* the craft to turn left, that *thinks* it to accelerate, that *thinks* the atoms of the craft to change and allow for a doorway to appear in the side of the vehicle? That's what these craft are: intelligent entities in their own right, directed and flown by an alien civilization so strange and advanced that it has become part-direct machine interface."

The man continued: "One of the reasons why there has been so much secrecy surrounding this program – or, these programs, to be correct – is because, for years, we weren't able to get these things into the air."

Again, he looked at Slade: "Despite what you may have heard – much of which was Cold War disinformation to keep the Russians confused about how many advances we were making, compared to them – we had zero success in flying one of these things ourselves until 1968, despite Roswell being back in '47.

"Trying to train a pilot to use their mind to maneuver a craft is not at all easy," said the man, with a slight degree of sarcasm in his voice. "It took us, literally, years to get one of these things even just a few feet off the ground."

"And today?" asked Slade.

"Today? Put it this way, the number of people who can successfully interface with these objects – these *things* – is nowhere near the number you might imagine. They are prized personnel; extremely prized."

Slade was just about to say something else when the old man beat him to it: "Now, it's time for the next step of the briefing."

"We're going to see someone get this crate fifteen feet into the air?" asked Edwards, with a laugh.

"Not quite, Mr. Edwards. It's time for you to meet the others."

Only silence followed, as the sheer enormity of what was – *right now* – about to occur hit Slade and Edwards like a bullet to the brain.

-61-

"So, where are we going?" asked Slade.

"Right there," replied the old man, pointing to the far end of the hangar. "You see that light- blue doorway?"

Slade nodded.

"That's where they are; right behind that door."

"You really aren't joking, are you?" said Edwards, clearly shaken to the core, even *before* encountering the others.

The man didn't smile when he said: "No, I really am *not* joking."

"So, what can we expect?" asked Slade, knowing that preparedness was always the name of the game.

As they made the minute or so walk towards the door, the man said – in response to Slade's question – "I wish I *could* prepare you, but I can't. Oh, I can tell you what they look like, how they act, and what you're going to see, but it still won't prepare you. I'm sorry, but there's no way for you to understand it than by experiencing it."

"Kind of like the first time you ride a bike, or jerk off?" said Edwards, hoping that cracking a joke just might ease the tension.

The man managed a slight smile: "You're really not far off, Mr. Edwards, not far off at all. You can imagine all you like, but the best approach is just to walk through the door and deal with it."

"How long will we be there for?" asked Edwards.

"Minutes, I daren't risk any longer. You just need to see this is all real, that's enough. We need to get you in and then out again."

As they got to the door, Slade felt his heart start to thump. No doubt, Edwards' heart was doing exactly the same. It was. For all their training and military combat, it was difficult to deal with something like this, something so...*unearthly*.

"Before I open the door," said the man, "there are a couple of things I *do* need to tell you. Number one, stay next to me; *right* next to me. They will recognize me, and they'll recognize – in their own way – that if I'm with you, you're not a threat."

"And if they *don't* recognize we're friendly, then what?" asked Slade.

"Where we're going is like walking into a lion's den: it would be all over before you even had a chance to blink. But, just stay by me; that's all I ask.

"There are, however, several other things: while they operate in our gravity fairly easily, we came to learn early that wherever they're from, the gravity and atmosphere is somewhat different. Not significantly, but you *will* notice it."

"Notice what?" asked Slade.

"That they can create their own gravitational fields, anywhere and everywhere they want."

Edwards looked at the old man: "Anti-gravity?"

"Well, kind of, yes, in simple terms. You'll find it strange as you enter: your body will feel slightly heavier, it will be slightly harder to breathe, and the temperature is very warm. The best way I can describe it is as tropical."

Slade looked incredulous: "Wait a minute, are you saying they've terraformed parts of our planet, to make it more like theirs?"

"That's *precisely* what they have done. We might have a strange working relationship with them, an uneasy relationship, but one where there's a mutual understanding of a kind. But, down here, they *own* it. The lower parts of our planet are *theirs*, not ours. And that's worldwide."

"They're *altering* our world," said Edwards in hushed tones.

"Yes, Mr. Edwards, they are. So far, it's only at places like this, purely, it seems, to make things easier for them to operate. If that's *all* it is, perhaps there's not a problem. But, there have been discussions along the lines of: could they do this worldwide, everywhere?"

"What's the answer?" asked Slade, anticipating the reply was not what he wanted to hear.

"The answer's not good: we see no reason why they *can't* do it. But, for whatever reason, the good news for us is they *haven't* done it…*not yet*."

"Two other things," said the man, "we believe that, wherever they originate, their atmosphere is pretty dim and a pale green color."

"How'd you know that?" Slade pushed.

"Simple: that's how all of their underground installations are constructed: artificial, dim, green-lighting. And one last thing: the smell, their atmosphere. When you walk in, you'll be hit by something quite unpleasant, rather like burning plastic. You'll just have to deal with it, I'm afraid."

The man looked at Slade, then at Edwards, and back at Slade. He asked: "Are you ready?"

Slade and Edwards looked at each other, nodded, and high-fived. Almost in unison they replied: "Yes."

"Then, let's go," said the man, whose deep breath and shaking fingers neither Edwards nor Slade could fail to miss, as he keyed in a five-number code on a small box affixed to the huge wall.

After a slight hissing noise emanated from the box, there was a clicking sound and the large, metal door opened, ever so slightly. A space of roughly two inches allowed the old man to take a grip of it. For a moment, Slade thought the clearly nervy man was using the door as support. Just maybe, that *was* what he was doing.

-62-

Even with the door just barely open, the smell of burning plastic that the man warned them about filled the nostrils of Slade and Edwards; it was sickening. He slowly pushed the door open, motioning both men to stay behind him, but slightly off-center.

"You need to be seen, and keep your hands open and at your sides at all times," the man whispered.

With the door now wide open, Slade and Edwards were just about able to peer into the strange and unsettling environment ahead of them. The man walked slowly through the door, with Slade and Edwards just a careful, quiet step behind.

Sure enough, just as they had been told, the atmosphere on the other side of the door was of a sickly green color. The humidity was almost stifling; Slade wondered how the old boy could stand it. Such was the heat and the atmosphere, the entire room – god knows how big it was – was filled with a hazy, dense, wet mist. It made seeing anything beyond about ten feet in front almost impossible. It was almost like being in some nightmarish jungle.

Suddenly, Edwards lurched forward and Slade grabbed him.

"You okay?" asked Slade, concerned as to what was going on.

"I felt dizzy, like I was gonna pass out."

"It's the gravity," said the old man. "It won't pass, but it won't kill you either. Just try and steady your nerves. Stay calm."

Edwards thought: stay calm? Who the hell is he kidding?

Slade could feel it too, now: his chest was heavy, and his boots felt like someone had dropped a ton of lead in them. He felt like he was wading, rather than walking. He was claustrophobic and nauseous. But, this was no time to back out.

Slade took a deep breath, to the extent that he could, and gave Edwards a thumbs-up – who did likewise. The old man saw what happened and nodded with a smile. It was a smile swiftly replaced by a look of pure fear. He motioned both men to stop. For a second or so, they wondered why. They didn't have to wonder for long, however: the others were about to make themselves known.

As all three men peered into the stifling fog, they could just about make out the shadowy outlines of four small creatures, perhaps four feet tall, maybe slightly more. Slade could feel the adrenalin kicking in, Edwards did his best to fight the sense of lightheadedness that threatened to overwhelm him. The old man stood frozen, awaiting the creatures that, for decades, had terrified him as much as they had amazed and awed him. After a few seconds there was movement.

All Slade could think about was Ray Bradbury's novel, *Something Wicked This Way Comes*.

Drake was right, after all, thought Slade: he felt like he was in the ocean, about to be eaten by circling, hungry, merciless sharks. Edwards moved back, ever so slightly.

"Don't move!" the old man hissed. "They'll interpret it as a possible threat."

Edwards struggled to keep his feet fixed to the floor, while his mind screamed: run!

Then, in all their terrible glory, the four creatures slowly surfaced out of the swirling mist and stood in front of the trio. Edwards felt himself visibly, and uncontrollably, shaking. Slade clenched his fists, despite the old man's warnings to keep his hands by his side.

The others had arrived.

The old man glanced at Slade and Edwards, both of who were clearly in states of near-shock. He remembered his first time; it was always like this, for everyone. The two men stared, dumbstruck, at what stood before them.

They looked as Slade had assumed they would: short, large-headed, and black-eyed. But, seeing them in person was very different to checking out the front-cover of Whitley Strieber's *Communion*.

They appeared far less like the smooth-skinned, placid ETs of alien abduction lore, and far more like incredibly old, wrinkled and wizened goblins of fairy-tale lore that eat children in the woods by night. Their grey faces were deeply lined and creased, their cheeks sunken and shadowy, their heads bulbous. Their naked, emaciated forms suggested to Slade that whatever they *were*, healthy they were *not*. Although their eyes were utterly black, Slade got a distinct sense of hostility emanating from the others.

Suddenly, one of them, in lightning speed, raced forward, grabbing the old man's shoulders with bony, scrawny fingers. The man motioned to Slade and Edwards not to move, anticipating that the ex-marines just might decide to take on the terrible thing that stood before them.

It seemed like forever, but, in reality it was just seconds: the menacing dwarf let go of the old man and moved swiftly back into the safety and camouflage of the mist. The three remaining others moved forward and proceeded to surround the men in a triangular pattern. This wasn't good, thought Slade – knowing all too well that this echoed some of the ambushing techniques he'd learned and honed in the military. Edwards was thinking exactly the same.

Just as the two men were prepared to take action, the trio of whatever they were retreated too, carefully keeping Slade, Edwards, and the man who had gotten them into this mess, in view at all times. In seconds, they were mere shadows in the swirling mist. In just a few more seconds, they weren't even that. The others had come, changed the lives of Slade and Edwards forever, and were gone, back into the mysterious, hazy, terraformed world of their own creation.

"What the hell was that about?" whispered Slade.

"In simple terms, they read my mind: who you are, your mission, why you're here. They can pull images, thoughts, from the human mind – and vice-versa. That's how they communicate with us: images, thoughts; never spoken words."

"And they're cool with us?" asked Edwards.

The old man actually managed a laugh: "I seriously doubt they have any concept of the word 'cool,' Mr. Edwards, but let me put it this way: you're still alive."

Suddenly, the air was filled by a low, animalistic moan that echoed around the room, and which was made all the more threatening by the fact that, whatever the source, it was clearly lurking in the shadows and out of sight – for now.

Slade and Edwards stared at the old man, who was noticeably trembling. He turned and said to them: "That's our sign to leave – now. *Right* now. Do what I do and make your way to the door by walking backwards; don't take your eyes off that mist."

All three shuffled to the door. The man fumbled awkwardly with the lock, his nerves betraying what had earlier been an air of confidence and control. Suddenly, the door opened and all three practically tumbled back into the huge hangar. The old man slammed the door and keyed in a new code to ensure it was firmly locked.

For a few moments there was just silence. It was finally broken by the old man: "Welcome to hell."

-63-

It took all three men ten or fifteen minutes to recover from the strange, unearthly environment behind the door. They leaned against the wall of the hangar as waves of dizziness, leg cramps, and nausea came and, thankfully, finally went, as their bodies reacclimatized.

"You can probably now see why we try and avoid spending time in there, with the others. Luckily, they can tolerate *our* atmosphere and gravity much better than we can *theirs*."

His eyes scanned the faces of both Slade and Edwards: "So, how are you feeling?"

Both men went to say something, but then realized that the sheer enormity of the situation, coupled with the life-changing effects, meant it was difficult to say anything. The man understood: "Don't worry, your silence speaks more than you can imagine. The important thing is you've seen the craft, you've seen the others, and you know the history.

"When all of this appears in your novel, Mr. Slade, it'll send a signal to those that we're fighting against that the real story is starting to come out. There are significant numbers of people who'll read the book and know – from personal experience - that your description of the base, and what's behind that door, is exactly how it is. They will know you've been here, and that will scare the hell out of them."

Slade nodded, still focused on what he and Edwards had just encountered.

"All, I ask, for now," said the man, "is that in the story, you place this installation, the whole Waxahachie connection, somewhere else. Everything else, keep it exactly as it happened. But, this is a gradual process; we can't have the world's press, and those in government who're outside of all this, poking their noses around too soon, or all descending on Waxahachie. It's got to be step by step, and your novel is the first wave."

Slade replied: "Got it. So, what now?"

"Now is the tricky bit," said the man. "We have to get you and Mr. Edwards out of here."

As they reached the small office where the initial conversation occurred, the man said: "Take a seat, please, and I'll just be a moment."

The man exited the office and, with Slade and Edwards watching him carefully through the large glass window that dominated the front of the office, pulled out his cellphone. He dialed a number and in seconds was deep in conversation. But, with who? That was the big question.

Both men could see that he was wearing a look of deep concern on his face.

"You get the feeling there's shit going down?" asked Edwards, glancing at Slade.

"Yeah, and more, too."

As the old man started to pace around, with the phone jammed against his ear, Slade added: "This just doesn't look good, at all."

Slade was right on target.

The man reentered the room: "We've got problems. The old farmhouse – the way you came in – we've got word there's a drone, unmanned, circling the area. There are also two cars parked at the end of the road that leads to the farmhouse. Someone clearly knows what's going down here, and they probably have a good idea of what you've seen. We can't send you back that way; it'll be suicide. And I suspect the route Drake gave you is swarming with their people."

"Then, we are *so* screwed," said Edwards.

"Not quite," the old man replied." "There's another option. Not a particularly good one, but under the circumstances, it's the only option left."

"Well, let's hear it," said Slade, anxious to get out of there and get the job completed.

"I'm afraid you're not going to like what you're about to hear," said the man.

Slade sighed: "Just get on with it."

The man began: "When, back in the early fifties, we found out what the others were doing down here, one of the things we discovered was that their mining abilities were, truly, incredible. But, we also found something else: during the course of constructing their installation - and for reasons we don't know and that aren't actually that important right now – there were significant numbers of tunnels they left abandoned and unused.

"At one point, there was talk of us using them as a place where, in the event the Soviets launched a first strike, some continuation of government could occur – a safe haven for the president and his staff; that kind of thing. The problem, of course, was having the president so close to the others – something we didn't want. So, it was shelved.

"But, here's the important thing: those tunnels still exist. The others – so far as we know – have never used them, and we don't either; we're still not really sure how extensive they are. Except for one thing: one specific tunnel – which we modified - has an elevator shaft that goes directly to the surface; brings you out in a field maybe three quarters of a mile from where you got in: the farmhouse.

"You can be in that tunnel in an hour at most – just go further down the tunnel you came in on, and you'll see a large, iron door with a yellow sign on it that reads *Hazardous Waste*. That's just a diversion to keep any uninvited visitors away. Get behind that door and it opens up into a large tunnel; very large. Keep walking and you'll finally reach the elevator shaft. I'm confident that the other side knows nothing of this."

"*Fully* confident?" asked Slade.

The man paused, then said: "*Fairly* confident."

"Fuck it," said Slade, "if it's that or end up dead at the farmhouse, or under lock and key at Guantanamo, we haven't got much of a choice, right?"

"Unfortunately, no you don't," the man replied. "I can only do so much without drawing attention to this place, and before we know it the press and god knows who else will be here."

Slade looked at Edwards: "Then, let's get moving."

The pair stood up, grabbed their bags, ensured their handguns were fully loaded, and made their way towards the doorway that led to the tunnel they originally entered by. The old man followed.

They shook hands with the old man, whose mind and life were dominated by secrets of the kind that Slade thought no-one should be burdened with, and turned to leave.

The old man had a final, few words: "Good luck, to both of you. Things are going to get bad down here when the confrontation begins – and it will. You're best away from it all. Do what needs to be done Mr. Slade; get that book written. Get everyone thinking. The first step's the hardest of all, but we need it."

-64-

S lade and Edwards retraced their steps, finally reaching the huge tunnel that they had spent hours wandering along. After all the mind-screwing things they had seen and done, however, it seemed a lifetime ago. As they entered it, Slade looked to his right, and peered into the distance of the tunnel: a small part of him was still wondering if they could fight their way out at the farmhouse. But, he knew there was no time to lose. It wasn't much of an option, but the new tunnel seemed to be the only viable, survivable option.

"Let's get moving," said Slade, having one last look behind him.

'Can you believe all that shit we saw?" Edwards asked, his mind spinning with images of the others and their strange, semi-alive craft.

"Before all this began," said Slade, "hell, no. Yeah, I was pretty sure it was true – the UFO phenomenon, I mean – but some sort of deal with these things, underground areas out of bounds to us, terraforming? Jesus. I would never have thought it. It's a frickin' nightmare! No wonder no one knows how to tell the story to the people. But, let's forget it for now. The main thing is that we get the hell out of here – and fast."

Time was definitely of the essence, so they broke into a jog, something which was definitely guaranteed to shave off significant minutes, in terms of making it to the exit point. The sound of their boots hitting the concrete echoed loudly in the crypt-like environment. Luckily, it really did seem like they were all alone. We better be, thought Slade.

Finally, they reached what was clearly the door that the old guy had referred to: it was large, metal, and – the clincher – there was a slightly torn and tattered sign indicating that hazardous substances were on the other side.

"Let's hope he was telling the truth about that sign," said Edwards, whose mind was going down the same path as Slade's: what if they had been set up, that this was a trap all along? It seemed unlikely: after all, if it was a ruse, why show them the craft and even the others? For all their suspicions, this was the real deal – a real chance to tell the world what was going on. And, besides, they had no choice but to follow the path they were now on. It was that or they were dead in the water.

Slade walked up to the door and checked it out carefully. It was very slightly ajar, maybe an inch or so.

"Look at this," he said to Edwards, "the door's covered in rust, and check that out." He pointed to the top of the door, which was coated in spider-webs. "He wasn't wrong," Slade continued. "This place has been abandoned for years."

Slade pulled on the door-handle, but nothing happened. He pulled harder and there was a loud screech of metal on concrete.

"Give me a hand," said Slade.

Edwards took a firm grip on the door and both men pulled. The clearly warped door finally opened enough to allow both men to squeeze through. For a minute or so, as they reached the other side, they stood in silence, trying to figure out if they really were alone. The only noise was that of their own heartbeats. As soon as they could be sure that no-one else was around, they turned on their flashlights and scanned the area. Clearly, the old man had been good to his word: the place was derelict, there were old filing cabinets, chairs, tables, mountains of old papers, coffee mugs, plates, and more all strewn across the floor.

There was, however, something that made Edwards and Slade deeply suspicious: the place wasn't just abandoned. It looked like it had been abandoned in a hurry, a perilous hurry. They wondered: what the hell had happened here? The place was in chaos. The deathly silence only added to the ominous atmosphere and sight before them.

"Maybe the others decided to take back a bit of what was theirs," offered Edwards.

"Yeah, maybe," replied Slade, trying to assess the situation and figuring what their next step should be. Really, though, there was *nothing* to assess: if they wanted to keep breathing and living, they had to keep on going.

Around two hundred feet into the tunnel, the pair was stunned by the sight of literally dozens of off-shots from the main tunnel. None of them were higher than five feet and were all built into the sides of the tunnel. Clearly, they had been constructed to allow access to something smaller than the average human: the others. That was the only, real possibility. They were in the equivalent of a gigantic, abandoned, alien, ant's nest.

"Jesus," said Slade, aiming his flashlight into the darkened tunnels, "these things could go on forever."

Both men took hold of their handguns, fully aware that something could come charging out of any of the dozens of tunnels at any moment. They crept past each one carefully, and holding their breath as they did so. The only things they saw were more tunnels, and more evidence of some violent altercation having occurred years – probably decades – earlier.

Finally, the small entrances to god knows where came to an end and Slade and Edwards were faced with nothing but a lengthy, completely enclosed, tunnel ahead of them.

"It can't be much further," said Edwards, after nearly an hour of walking. It wasn't: ten minutes or so later, the beams of their flashlights no longer dissolved into the darkness. Instead, they bounced off a large, steel door. As they got within about twenty feet of the door, they could clearly see it was part of a large elevator.

Slade put his fingers to his lips, motioning Edwards to stay silent. The last thing they needed was to push the red button that opened the elevator door and find themselves walking into a trap. They turned off their flashlights and the tunnel was plunged into absolute darkness. Slade quietly moved forward and found the button. Delaying things would achieve nothing: he pressed it and quickly moved back into the darkness.

For a few seconds it seemed like the door wasn't going to open; Slade felt his mouth go dry. Edwards cursed to himself. Finally, with a somewhat disturbing groan, the door slid to one side. The interior light was out, but, as their eyes became accustomed to the darkness, they could see the elevator was clearly empty. Slade turned on his flashlight and they slowly and carefully walked inside.

-65-

Two seconds into the elevator, the door closed behind the pair. Unlike a regular hotel elevator, this one didn't have multiple buttons for several floors. Instead, there was just one button for up and one for down. That meant when they hit "up," there was no going back. It would take them directly to the surface, to the single access point in the field the old man had described.

"Ready?" asked Slade.

"You bet," said Edwards. "Go for it."

Slade pressed the button and the jerking sensation of moving upwards kicked in. The journey was hardly smooth: the elevator shook, shuddered, and groaned as it made its way up.

"When do you think this was last used?" asked Edwards.

Slade looked at him: "I don't even wanna think about that."

Finally, the elevator came to a lurching halt. Both men had their handguns trained on the door. There was no room to hide, so they assumed kneeling positions, just in case there were uninvited visitors on the other side. The door opened torturously slowly, something which put both men in an agonizingly high state of alert. They were met by one thing only: silence. They got to their feet and carefully peered around the door.

All they could see were two things. There was a lighted corridor to their right, which looked like it extended for a couple of hundred feet. In front of them were twelve concrete steps that led to a small access hatch above their heads. No doubt, this was the exit to the field that the old man divulged.

Edwards flicked the wall switch and killed all the light in the corridor and immediately outside of the elevator. They were in darkness again, which was probably a very good thing. Slade climbed the steps, pulled back cautiously on a sliding lock, and raised the hatch by just a few inches.

Immediately, a shot rang out. What was undeniably a high-powered bullet whistled past Slade's right ear, causing him to lose his balance and almost crash to the floor. Edwards raced up the steps and pulled the hatch down, locking it tightly.

"You okay?" shouted Edwards.

Slade gave him a thumbs-up and got to his feet. "It's a fuckin' ambush!"

"I just *knew* it was too good to be true," raged Edwards.

Back down the steps, Slade flicked the wall switch again, illuminating their only remaining option. Peering down the corridor he sighed, "Come on, let's check it out."

The corridor ran for about three hundred feet. To the dismay of both men, there were no exits off the corridor – not a single one. This wasn't good. They were hemmed in

"We sure as hell can't go back down in that elevator," said Slade. "There's gotta be someone waiting for us there, too. This is exactly what they wanted: both of us, caught in between, with nowhere to go. Fuck!"

Just when it seemed the end was in sight, there was light at the end of the tunnel – literally. When they reached the end of the corridor, there was a nearly identical set of concrete steps leading to yet *another* exit. Both men stared at it wordlessly.

"Do you remember him saying anything to us about a second hatch?" asked Slade.

"No, I don't," said Edwards. "He definitely said there was only one way out."

"Right. So, if *he* didn't know about it, then maybe whoever is out there doesn't know either. Okay, where we will come out is only a couple of hundred feet away from the other exit. It's still dark out there – 4:30. We can be out there and on them before they know what's happened. I *know* we can!"

"Let's do it," said Edwards.

Both men were operating on adrenalin and nothing else: it was do or die. Once again, it was lights out as Slade slowly climbed the steps.

He slid the lock and pushed up the hatch with his flashlight, doing his utmost to keep himself out of anyone's potential firing line.

Slade waited and waited – and then waited even longer. There was nothing. More importantly, there was no one. Another thumbs-up told Edwards things looked encouraging. Slade hauled himself out of the hatch without a sound.

As he reached the surface, Slade instantly saw that he was in a large field, just as the old man had told him would be the case. The air was cold, and the sky above was filled with stars. He motioned Edwards to follow.

The two of them stealthily crept towards what they estimated to be the location of the original hatch. They took no chances, crawling along on the frigid, dried out ground. Whatever purpose the field had once served, it was clearly no longer in use. Plus, if the land belonged to a farmer, he surely would have stumbled on both hatches years ago. So, where the hell *were* they? No time now to ponder on the answer. This was a fight for survival.

As they drew close to the original hatch, Slade and Edwards could see the shadowy forms of two men squatting within twenty feet of it. Both were dressed in black and were clearly armed. Slade and Edwards continued towards them at a snail's pace, intent on taking out both men with as little hassle as possible.

Slade motioned Edwards to concentrate on the guy on the right, while he kept his sights fixed on the one to the left. Both had silencers attached to their weapons. This was no time for some Rambo-like, gung-ho charge across the field. That might be how they do it in the movies, but this was real life. This situation was highly dicey and deadly. Slade and Edwards did what they had to do.

Neither of their targets knew what hit him. Both were taken down by precisely aimed, single bullets to the head, which violently spun them around and threw them to the cold, dry ground.

Slade and Edwards were still not able to let their guard down. They stayed low and slow in the shadows as they crept across the huge field, towards apparent streetlights past the tree line. It was a trek that took about twenty minutes, during which the possibility that each step might be their last was never far from their minds. As they reached a two-lane road, Slade was finally able to get his bearings: they were still on the vast Waxahachie installation, albeit far on the north side. Right in front of them was a high, barbed-wire fence.

Slade tossed his knife at the fence. It was not electrified. They used the cutters from their kitbags to make a sizeable hole in the fence big enough for both men to crawl through. As they made a break for freedom, the glaring headlights of two vehicles suddenly spotlighted their location from only a couple of hundred yards away.

"Shit, they're onto us," Slade growled.

Edwards grabbed Slade's arm and looked him squarely in the eye: "Slade, get your ass out of here! Dealing with two-bit security goons is a walk in the park for me! You have to write this up! You have to tell the story –what we saw, what's down there, what's going on. All of it – every last, nasty detail! *You* have the support behind you to get it published and spoil their plans. You have to go straight from this godforsaken field to some safe place where you can get all of this down on paper! It's up to you – only you!"

"No way, pal; we're in this together. Two of us with our skills are way better than just one."

Edwards' voice calmed: "Listen. We're on foot, they're not. They'll be on us in no time. We can't afford that. What we have been trying to achieve here trumps everything else! I was hired to take you out, forschrissakes! I'm glad now I didn't! But I still have a debt to pay – to you. If they get their slimy hands on you, all of this will have been for nothing. So, go! *Now!* And don't look back – I promise you, those assholes don't stand a chance against me."

Slade grabbed Edwards' hand and shook it vigorously. His last words to Edwards: "Next time I see you, drinks are on me!"

"You betcha!"

Slade scrambled through the fence, raced across the road, and vanished into the inky darkness of the field on the opposite side of the road. Just for a few seconds, he looked back. Two trucks with high beams on were hurtling across the field towards where he left Edwards.

Slade turned around to continue his escape. After about a minute, the violent sound of a hail of bullets split the night. Then there was silence. Nothing but silence.

"Shit! I should have stayed! He was a sitting duck!"

All of a sudden he heard a deep male voice yelling, "Write that book, buddy! Write it! I told you I had it covered. I want a signed copy next time I see you!" Then a V-8 engine roared to life, and four oversized cross-country tires were spitting out a plume of gravel and dust.

Son of a *bitch*! Edwards had done it! He made it, and both of them were going to live to tell about it. Slade watched the truck smash through the barbed-wire fence, shimmy onto a side-road, and zoom off into the darkness. Edwards was on the road to safety.

Slade raced across the field, swallowed by darkness. He was ready to fulfil his part of the deal with Drake – to write that book. A book that would mark the turning point for all sides involved in this long contest. It would also mark the beginning of a new chapter in the book cataloging the history of human civilization. Hell, it would start a whole new library!

-66-

FOUR MONTHS LATER...

Just before midnight, with a north Texas thunderstorm winding down outside, Slade put the final touches to his novel: *The Stephenville UFO and Alien Disclosure*. He swallowed the last remaining shot of his whisky and leaned back in his office-chair, looking at the ceiling but really looking through it and far beyond it. Beyond here and now.

Slade's mind returned to that night in the dry, cold field, where he and Edwards made good their escape. Slade had neither seen nor heard from him since. Nonetheless, he truly wished him well in whatever he was doing – which, hopefully, included taking out of circulation more of those assholes who were trying to prevent disclosure.

Slade never heard anything more from Drake, either: the one man who, more than any other in this strange saga, he had come to call a friend. Even so, it was clear that Drake was still pulling significant strings in the background.

In the days since Slade had fled Waxahachie, he had been offered a huge monetary advance from one of New York's premier publishing houses. His editor – a woman whose previous job had been as translator at none other than Langley – made it very crystal clear they had a mutual friend who very much wanted his book published.

On top of that, there had been a strange spate of mysterious deaths in the defense industry, the Pentagon, the NSA, Air Force Intelligence, certain private corporations, and the CIA. All within the last two months. The media monkeys were doing their best to convince everyone it was the work of a Middle Eastern terrorist cell. Slade knew better: this was Drake and his group at their best, expertly deleting all powerful players who were still foolishly hell-bent on stopping the disclosure movement.

Besides, Slade obviously had a cadre of guardian angels – expert but unseen protectors. For instance, there had been no knocks on the door from the FBI. Nothing but utter silence surrounded the Waxahachie installation. As for the few deaths that might otherwise be associated with Slade, clearly all had been deftly disappeared. It absolutely *had* to be due to Drake and his efforts. One day, Slade knew he would have the chance to thank him.

Shutting down his laptop, Slade stared out the window into the lingering drizzle sparkling against the streetlights. Sure, there were going to be trying times ahead: *very* trying times, maybe even *terrible* times. He knew very well that his integrity and veracity would be questioned at every step as the major news networks booked him, interviewed him, even afterwards as they *interpreted* what he had said in their interviews. So what? He was only playing out his role in this end game, all choreographed by his editor and Drake.

He knew damned good and well he absolutely *had to get all of the information* – every single snippet of it – into the public domain, even if it might appear in fictionalized form. The world has to know what is going on: warring factions, ruthless murders, disclosure vs. non-disclosure, hired assassins, rogue groups in the government and the intelligence community. So much to throw into the spotlight and pull from behind the heavy curtains. At the very heart of all of it are those strange, hardly understood beings – not creatures – from some other world that have lived among us, only far underground, for who knows how long and why.

So much for this long evening, thought Slade. Now another wild rollercoaster ride starts up with the publication and promotion of the manuscript. Laptop put to bed and one bottle of bourbon killed, he moseyed off toward the cabinet where he kept his liquor. Grabbing a fresh, unopened liter and an equally fresh glass, he headed for the bedroom. Just as he turned off the lights in the front of the house and was heading for the stairs, the phone rang. He glanced at his wristwatch – one fucking thirty? Who the hell calls anyone at one fucking thirty? On a weeknight? No name or number in the caller ID. "Private caller."

Great. He made a mental note to get a new cell phone and number and not to give it to anyone except people whose names and numbers he would recognize on caller ID. On a whim, he punched the key to answer and barked out a less than happy greeting: "Who the hell is this?"

"Mr. Slade! So nice to hear your voice! And you sound absolutely full of vim and vigor! How is the book progressing?"

Slade was momentarily stunned to recognize Drake's familiar accent. But Drake's numbers were listed in Slade's contacts, so what's with the cloaked caller ID?

"Mr. Drake! I'm sorry if I barked at you – I had no clue this was you calling."

"Ah, no matter, Mr. Slade. Occasionally I feel the need for a new cellular company, or a new phone. You know how easy it is for electronic trails to be detected and tracked to their sources."

"Yep, indeed I do. Come to think of it, I was just thinking a new number and carrier might be a good idea myself. You asked about the book – I just shut down the laptop a few minutes ago after tweaking the last chapter. I suppose my editor will still want to go over a few adjustments with me, but the lion's share of my part is now completed. I already uploaded the manuscript to her secure FTP site so she can start on final edits as soon as she wants."

"Wonderful news, Mr. Slade! Bravo! This has been a remarkable journey for you, I would imagine, since our first encounter. You have certainly kept up your part of the bargain all along the way, and you have my deepest gratitude for that!"

"Well, it has been a year I will remember for many years. For many reasons."

"Yes. I understand. Many reasons. But Mr. Slade, I have called you about another issue. Do you have a few minutes now?"

"Shoot! What's up?"

"Well, your landmark book is now completed and awaiting only the final adjustments for publication. Soon, you will likely rarely have no more than 10-12 hours at a time free to you for several months as you promote the book and .... ehmm .... juggle a myriad of fiercely competing journalists and news anchors as they clamor for your presence and full attention."

"You make it sound so...appealing. I'm not sure I am ready for that level of intrusion in my life, public or private!"

"Well, Mr. Slade, the price of celebrity. I have been thinking about offering you the use of a private – very remote, one might say "hidden" – vacation cabin. A place where you could definitely get away from all of it, recharge your batteries. Gird your loins for the ensuing months of travail and aggravation."

Slade hesitated. A Trojan horse? Or looking a gift horse in the mouth? Which equine metaphor to choose. Drake had never been stingy, but he had never really been generous. In fact, if he was offering *before* asking, what he wanted to ask must be greater than access to a remote cabin.

"With all due respect, Mr. Drake, what is on your mind? Forgive me, but an offer like this at this late hour and out of the blue – my spidey sense tells me that there is more to it?"

Chuckling, Drake replied, "Of course, my boy! There is *always* more to it, isn't there? Can't we agree that you and I at least acknowledge that fact from experience? I am sincere, that the cabin is totally at your disposal, *private* disposal I might add, in case you would appreciate a small holiday from the level of efforts of the last year or so. No strings attached, of course. But I do want to offer you something more."

Ruh Roh, thought Slade. Here it comes. "Okay .... What do you have in mind?"

"Now that your long awaited book is now on the brink of publication, we feel that you are ready to take the next step, so to speak."

Slade's mouth suddenly went dry. *The next step?* What next? Jumping out of the space shuttle? He was mulling over potential scenarios of what "the next step" might look like when Drake continued.

"I am not able right this moment to provide you much detail in this regard, especially over this cellular connection. What I propose is that you take my offer of the private cabin, make it your own for a week or so. We will stock it with all the necessities and several additional indispensable items. There is a four-wheeler at your access, to explore the woods and nearby habitats. There is also a boat and ample fishing gear, in case you are so inclined. It is a lovely setting deep in old-growth forest area, in the northern Appalachian ridge. We will arrange, of course, for your flight connections and rental car to and from. The cabin is equipped with electricity, running water, and internet access. I think you will find it a rather nice little retreat in an intoxicating locale. No one but you, deer, wild turkey, perhaps a black bear or two, smaller denizen. No lights to interfere with a first-class view of the heavens at night."

Despite his innate suspicions and distaste for staying anywhere other than his own cave, Slade was close to drooling over the description. After the last year, getting away from everyone and everything sounded like a blessing. Better than winning the lottery. "What do I have to do if I accept – sorry, I know that sounds … distrustful."

Again chuckling, Drake answered. "One of our operatives will contact you personally at the cabin, three to four days after you arrive there. You do need some down time, Mr. Slade. You've more than earned it. Now that our initial opus is soon to be released, there are more irons in the fire, so to speak, that well afford closer attention. I believe at least one of those irons will induce you to consider partnering with our organization again, to shine the spotlight on important facts and events that have for decades, in some cases centuries, gone unnoticed or undisclosed."

Slade was intrigued, to say the least. If he had been told explicitly what he eventually witnessed in the last year, he would have shrugged it off as wild-eyed fantasy. Who knows what other mysteries Drake's organization monitors? "Can you tell me a little more about where this is?"

"Rather not, Mr. Slade. I can provide you with details tomorrow morning, if you accept. Best not to be too specific right here, right now."

"I get it. Sure. Okay. I could use a little vacation. What should I bring along? Other than clothes and the usual essentials, of course."

"Pack as you would for a typical vacation. There is already a computer at the cabin, but if you want to bring your laptop – BYOD, I believe they call it in the IT world – feel free. Anything else that will make you feel comfortable while away for a little R&R! Can you be ready to leave by, say, 8:45 a.m. tomorrow?"

Slade ran through the list of things he would need or need to do. Other than get some cash, which he could do at an ATM, he could easily be ready by that time. "Okay – I will be ready for a lift to the airport by no later than 8:45. Good talking to you, Mr. Drake – I am looking forward to hearing more from you. Very soon."

"Yes, Mr. Slade – excellent! I am sure you will find this next phase of our partnership most intriguing. Good night!"

Call me curious. Or call me a glutton for suspense. I don't know – everything this past year worked out all right – for me, anyway. Nothing feels like I am going down the wrong tunnel.

How many guys get invited to look behind the official curtains on things that pretty much no one even realizes are being hidden? Drake didn't say anything about ETs or space ships. How weird could this be? I can look after myself. No worries.

And he didn't even tell me I had to write another book!

The Stephenville UFO Case:
FACT VS FICTION

KEN CHERRY

A HISTORY OF STEPHENVILLE

George B. Erath, a native of Vienna, Austria, came to America in 1832. He was a surveyor, soldier at San Jacinto, Texas Ranger, Republic of Texas congressman, member of the Legislature of the State of Texas, and a major in the Confederate Army. In 1849, Erath surveyed the town of Waco. One hundred years later, in 1949, the *Waco Tribune Herald* stated: "George B. Erath had more to do with the actual settling of Central Texas than any other person."

Between sessions of the Congress of the Texas Republic, prior to 1846, when Texas became a state, Erath continued surveying. Erath saw the possibilities in the valley land, which Spanish and Mexican predecessors had named "el bosque," which means, "the forest." Thus began the march of settlement up the Bosque River.

In May of 1854, the heirs of John Blair, who died in the Alamo, received a land patent which had been secured by John M. Stephen. On January 12, 1855, the heirs of John Blair made a warranty deed to John M. Stephen for the land which eventually became the town of Stephenville.

According to the *Memoirs of George B. Erath*, written by Erath's daughter, Lucy: "In the latter part of May, 1855, McLennan and I led a party of 30 pioneers into the territory now Erath County. John M. Stephen, who owned the land where Stephenville now stands, was among them."

She continued: "The settlers agreed to choose their homes there and in the country around about; so we laid off the town of Stephenville; finishing laying it off on the fourth of July. This settlement was then the farthest west of any on the water of the Brazos."

At this time, John M. Stephen, who had come from Burleson County, made an agreement that he would give land for the county

281

courthouse and building lots for his fellow settlers and for several churches, if the town was named Stephenville and was designated the county seat. The State of Texas accepted this agreement, and in 1856, the County of Erath was organized with Stephenville as its county seat.

In 1858, the population of Stephenville was estimated as being 766. There were two stores and a hotel, which was much needed to house buffalo hunters. The buffalo ranged within three miles to town, and so did the Indians.

When the Civil War ended, war veterans returned to their homes to find desperate conditions. Life on the western edge of the frontier was hard, manufactured goods were scarce; home-grown and home-made articles became a necessity. The Pony Express was the only communication link to the rest of the world. Overland freight to Erath County came by ox wagon from Houston. Transportation was by horseback, horse and buggy, wagon, or on foot.

Today, Stephenville is the Erath County seat and is located about 70 miles southwest of Fort Worth, Texas. Agriculture is Stephenville's leading industry, and Erath County is the state's leading milk producer with approximately $140 million in production. Five of the ten leading employers are manufacturing firms with the remainder in education, retail, and healthcare services. Tarleton State University provides further economic stability with over 10,000 enrolled students and 844 employees.

In March 1992, the Texas State Comptroller released a state report which ranked Erath County as the fifth best county among 205 rural counties in the state for economic development for the previous five years. Stephenville was listed in a book compiled by Norman Crampton and published by Prentice Hall, titled *The 100 Best Small Towns in America*.

Stephenville offers a variety of recreational areas including two public parks, two public swimming pools, two golf courses, fourteen tennis courts, a movie theater, six football stadiums, two rodeo arenas, a bowling alley, a youth center, and a historical museum.

There are also two major lakes within a forty-mile radius and many excellent areas for hunting and fishing. Stephenville offers many annual events including livestock shows, arts & crafts festivals, rodeos, basketball tournaments and the Tarleton homecoming.

STEPHENVILLE UFO INVASION

"**S**tephenville, Texas – In this farming community where nightfall usually brings clear, starry skies, residents are abuzz over reported sightings of what many believe is a UFO.

"Several dozen people – including a pilot, county constable, and business owners – insist they have seen a large silent object with bright lights flying low and fast. Some reported seeing fighter jets chasing it.

"'People wonder what in the world it is because this is the Bible Belt, and everyone is afraid it's the end of times,' said Steve Allen, a freight company owner and pilot who said the object he saw last week was a mile long and half a mile wide. 'It was positively, absolutely nothing from these parts.'"

The Associated Press, January 14, 2008.

"Major Karl Lewis, a spokesman for the 301st Fighter Wing at the Joint Reserve Base Naval Air Station in Fort Worth, said no F-16s or other aircraft from his base were in the area the night of January 8, when most people reported the sighting.

"Lewis said the object may have been an illusion caused by two commercial airplanes. Lights from the aircraft would seem unusually bright and may appear orange from the setting sun.

"'I'm 90 percent sure this was an airliner,' Lewis said. 'With the sun's angle, it can play tricks on you.'

"Officials at the region's two Air Force bases – Dyess in Abilene and Sheppard in Wichita Falls – also said none of their aircraft were in the area last week. The Air Force no longer investigates UFOs."

CNN, January 15, 2008.

"Stephenville's latest close encounter is weirder than any light in the sky.

"Stephenville is under assault – not by Martians, but by people hunting them.

"The phones haven't stopped ringing at Steve Allen's trucking company in nearby Glen Rose. He's the guy who was out Jan. 7 watching the sunset at a friend's house near Selden when they all saw some weird flashing lights.

"Now he can't work for all the calls from London and around the world.

"Some of the callers are scarier than space aliens.

"'I'll be OK,' he joked Tuesday, 'as long as I don't get abducted.'"

Star Telegram, January 15, 2008.

"Dozens of eyewitnesses have reported seeing a mile-long UFO being pursued by fighter jets last week in the small town of Stephenville, Texas. 'It was very intense bright lights…and they spanned a wide area,' said one woman.

"NBC News spoke with County Constable Lee Roy Gaitan, who offered a somewhat different description. 'I saw two red glows,' he said. 'I never seen anything like that, never.'"

The Raw Story, January 15, 2008.

"The U.S. military has owned up to having F-16 fighters in the air near Stephenville on the night that several residents reported unusual lights in the sky. But the correction issued Wednesday doesn't exactly turn UFOs into Identified Flying Objects.

"Several dozen witnesses reported that they had seen unusual lights in the sky near Stephenville shortly after dusk Jan. 8. One sighting included a report that the lights were pursued by military jets. Military officials had repeatedly denied that they had any flights in the area that night.

"But that position changed Wednesday with a terse news release:

"'In the interest of public awareness, Air Force Reserve Command Public Affairs realized an error was made regarding the reported training activity of military aircraft. Ten F-16s from the 457th Fighter Squadron were performing training operations from 6 to 8 p.m., Tuesday January 8, 2008, in the Brownwood Military Operating Area (MOA), which includes the airspace above Erath County.'

"Major Karl Lewis, a spokesman for the 301st Fighter Wing at the former Carswell Field, blamed the erroneous release on 'an internal communications error.'

"That still left unanswered the question of what F-16s might have been doing that would look like a line of silent, glowing spheres. Maj. Lewis said he could not give any details."

Dallas Morning News, January 23, 2008.

"A lot has been said as of late on the apparent trend of UFO reports being treated with more respect by mainstream media. This trend seems to have begun with the O'Hare Airport sightings, and reached fruition with the recent Texas sightings near Stephenville. Now there is a report from researcher Michael Salla, who claims to have insider information that confirms a series of meetings on alien contact held in secret by a group sanctioned by the United Nations. These meetings are reported to have spanned three days, beginning on February 12. Supposedly, three United States Senators have asked for further meetings on the subject. The primary concern of these meetings was dealing with public reaction to an announcement that alien contact has, or will soon occur."

About.com, March 4, 2008.

PRESIDENT REAGAN, UFOS,
AND "STAR WARS"

In March 1983, President Ronald Reagan announced his plans to create a futuristic defense system designed to ensure the western world remained free of nuclear attack by the Soviets. While the Strategic Defense Initiative was its official title, the project is far better known by its nickname: *Star Wars*. The idea, which finally got off the ground in 1984, was a decidedly far-reaching and alternative one.

Essentially, the plan involved deploying powerful laser-based weapons into the Earth's orbit that, in essence, would provide a collective shield that could skillfully and decisively destroy any incoming Soviet or Chinese nuclear weapons. The program was not just ambitious: it finally proved to be *overly* ambitious.

Ultimately, the Strategic Defense Initiative program collapsed under its own weight and a lack of adequate technology to allow it to work in the fashion that Reagan had enthusiastically envisaged. Nevertheless, it wasn't entirely abandoned: during the Clinton administration it became the Ballistic Missile Defense Organization, and is today known as the Missile Defense Agency.

Although the MDA is a vital component of America's defense and security, it's a far cry from the *Star Wars*-like SDI-based imagery of hundreds of laser-firing weapon-systems positioned high above the United States. But, in its very earliest years, SDI *was* seen as a winner by many.

But was it really the Soviets that Reagan was worried about? Ever since the SDI program was announced, rumors have circulated to the effect that it was a far stranger enemy that was plaguing the mind of the president, an enemy that wasn't even human or fully understood, in terms of its origins and motivations. SDI, the theory goes, was planned to take on not an internal threat, but an *external* one: an evil, extraterrestrial empire, no less.

It's a notable fact that President Reagan made a number of intriguing statements relative to the UFO phenomenon in the mid-1980s – when SDI research was at its height - and specifically from the potential threat it posed to each and every one of us. It all began in November 1985, at the Geneva Summit, when Reagan was deep in discussion with Soviet Premier, Mikhail Gorbachev.

The subject: trying to find a way to reverse the arms-race and decrease the threat of a global, nuclear holocaust. According to formerly classified memoranda generated by the Department of Defense in 1985:

"Reagan said that while the General Secretary was speaking, he had been thinking of various problems being discussed at the talks. He said that previous to the General Secretary's remarks, he had been telling Foreign Minister Shevardnadze (who was sitting to the President's right) that if the people of the world were to find out that there was some alien life form that was going to attack the Earth approaching on Halley's Comet, then that knowledge would unite all the peoples of the world.

"Further, the President observed that General Secretary Gorbachev had cited a Biblical quotation, and the President is also alluding to the Bible, pointed out that Acts 16 refers to the fact that 'we are all of one blood regardless of where we live on the Earth,' and we should never forget that."

Barely four weeks had passed before Reagan publicly raised the UFO issue yet again. This time it was before an entranced throng at Fallston High School, Harford County, Maryland. He told the packed crowd:

"I couldn't help but – when you stop to think that we're all God's children, wherever we live in the world – I couldn't help but say to [Gorbachev] just how easy his task and mine might be if suddenly there was a threat to this world from some other species from another planet outside in the universe.

"We'd forget all the little local differences that we have between our countries and we would find out once and for all that we really are all human beings here on this Earth together. Well, I guess we can wait for some alien race to come down and threaten us, but I think that between us we can bring about that realization."

And Reagan was far from done with alluding to the world that, just perhaps, there might be an extraterrestrial threat waiting in the wings to assume control of the planet. It was September 21, 1987 when, before none other than the United Nations' General Assembly, Reagan told a captivated audience:

"In our obsession with antagonisms of the moment, we often forget how much unites all the members of humanity. Perhaps we need some outside, universal threat to make us recognize this common bond. I occasionally think how quickly our differences worldwide would vanish if we were facing an alien threat from outside this world.

"And yet, I ask you, is not an alien force already among us? What could be more alien to the universal aspirations of our peoples than war and the threat of war?"

SENATOR BARRY GOLDWATER
AND DEAD ALIENS

B orn in 1909, Barry Morris Goldwater was a Major-General in the U.S. Air Force, a Senator for Arizona, the Chairman of the U.S. Government's Senate Intelligence Committee, and the Republican Party's nominee for President of the United States in the 1964 election. Indeed, it was on May 2, 1964 that Goldwater received no less than 75 percent of the vote in the Texas Republican Presidential primary.

Had Goldwater won the election (he lost it to Lyndon B. Johnson), it's not at all out of the question that the full and unexpurgated facts concerning what the world of officialdom really knows about the UFO phenomenon might have come tumbling out.

Goldwater had a fascination for the UFO issue, and, throughout his life and career, made more than a few notable comments and observations on the subject. The bulk of them revolved around his attempts to determine the truth about longstanding rumors that something of a UFO nature (and something of deep significance, too) was secretly held at Wright-Patterson Air Force Base, Dayton, Ohio. The location of whatever this "something" may have been has variously been termed as "Hangar 18" and the "Blue Room."

On March 28, 1975, Goldwater wrote the following, highly thought-provoking, words to a UFO researcher named Shlomo Arnon:

"The subject of UFOs is one that has interested me for some long time. About ten or twelve years ago I made an effort to find out what was in the building at Wright-Patterson Air Force Base where the information is stored that has been collected by the Air Force, and I was understandably denied this request. It is still classified above Top Secret."

Goldwater continued to Arnon: "I have, however, heard that there is a plan under way to release some, if not all, of this material in the near future. I'm just as anxious to see this material as you are, and I hope we will not have to wait much longer."

The UFO research community sat up and took notice of Goldwater's words. In 1979, Goldwater made another comment on this particularly intriguing issue, this time to UFO investigator Lee Graham. Goldwater told Graham: "It is true I was denied access to a facility at Wright-Patterson.

Because I never got in, I can't tell you what was inside. We both know about the rumors."

In October 1981, Graham received another letter from Goldwater. It read: "First, let me tell you that I have long ago given up acquiring access to the so-called blue room at Wright- Patterson, as I have had one long string of denials from chief after chief, so I have given up. In answer to your questions, one is essentially correct. I don't know of anyone who has access to the blue room, nor am I aware of its contents and I am not aware of anything having been relocated." Very significantly, Goldwater added: "To tell you the truth, Mr. Graham, this thing has gotten so highly classified, even though I will admit there is a lot of it that has been released, it is just impossible to get anything on it."

And, as the years progressed, so did Goldwater's comments on what, of a UFO nature, might be held somewhere at Wright-Patterson AFB.

On more than a few occasions, the subject of UFOs featured heavily on Larry King Live. On one occasion, in 1994, the person King had on his show to talk about UFOs was none other than Goldwater himself, who told King:

"I think at Wright-Patterson, if you could get into certain places, you'd find out what the Air Force and the government does know about UFOs. Reportedly, a spaceship landed. It was all hushed up. I called Curtis Lemay and I said, 'General, I know we have a room at Wright-Patterson where you put all this secret stuff. Could I go in there?' I've never   heard

General Lemay get mad, but he got madder than hell at me, cussed me out, and said, 'Don't ever ask me that question again!'"

If the outcome of the 1964 presidential election had been very different, and if the events of May 2, 1964 had led to Goldwater becoming President of the United States, it's not at all out of the question that Goldwater – as the newly-elected Commander in Chief – would have demanded access to what was really held on, in, or even under, Wright-Pat.

In another reality, 1964 could have been the year in which the Human Race learned it is not alone.

THE REAL MEN IN BLACK

For decades – or perhaps even for centuries, some firmly believe – the infamous Men in Black have been elusive, predatory, fear-inducing figures that have hovered with disturbing regularity upon the enigmatic fringes of the subject of Unidentified Flying Objects (UFOs), coldly nurturing, and carefully weaving, their very own unique brand of horror and intimidation of a definitively other-world variety.

The preferred tools of terror of the MIB are outright menace, far less than thinly-veiled threats, and overwhelming, emotionless intimidation. And they are relentless when it comes to following their one and only agenda – that is, to forever silence witnesses to, and investigators of, UFO encounters. Unfortunately, it has to be admitted, they have been highly successful in achieving their unsettling goal, too.

Indeed, and without any shadow of doubt whatsoever, the long and winding history of UFO studies is absolutely littered with fraught, frightened and emotionally-shattered figures that have been forever menaced into silence by the Men in Black, and who, as a result, have firmly distanced themselves from the UFO controversy, vowing never, *ever* to return to the fold.

Like true vampires from some strange, outer edge, the painfully-thin, white-faced and sunken-cheeked Men in Black appear from the murky darkness; they then roam the countryside provoking carnage, chaos, paranoia and fear in their notorious wake, before duly returning to that same shrouded realm of unsettling weirdness from which they originally oozed forth.

Very often reported traveling in groups of three, this definitive trinity of evil seemingly has the incredible ability to appear and vanish at will, and is often seen – in the United States – driving 1950s-style black Cadillac's, and – in the British Isles – 1960s-era black Jaguar's, both of which are almost always described as looking curiously brand new.

Despite the passing of the decades, and of the many and varied changes in fashions, the preferred mode of dress of these bone-chilling characters never, ever alters in the slightest, at all: it always consists of a well-preserved black suit, a black Fedora- or Homburg-style hat, black sunglasses, a black necktie, black socks and shoes, and a crisp, shining white shirt. Very little wonder, therefore, that they have been given the wholly notorious name with which they are, today, most famously – or perhaps infamously – associated.

But who, or far more likely, *what*, exactly, are the Men in Black? In the 1997 blockbuster movie, *Men in Black* and in its 2002 sequel, that starred Hollywood crowd-pullers Will Smith and Tommy Lee Jones, the MIB were firmly, and highly entertainingly, portrayed as being the secret-agents of a Top Secret, covert arm of the U.S. Government, whose sole role it is to hide from the general public the dark truth about a huge and intricate alien presence on the Earth. But, how much truth is there to the mega-bucks movie that spawned so much interest in these bizarre figures?

While *some* MIB are, without doubt, the all-seeing eyes of clandestine departments of at least several governments – including both the United States and the United Kingdom – the vast majority of these curious characters appear to be of a very different breed altogether. According to numerous, fantastic witness testimony and countless case-studies secured since the early years of the 1950s, the *real* MIB may very possibly be alien entities themselves, carefully and secretly working to ensure that we never successfully uncover the sensational truth about their presence, or the long-term goal of their strange and unearthly agenda, upon our very own planet.

On the other hand, however, some students of MIB history, lore and legend suggest that these non-human creatures are utterly occult-based, supernatural beings that originate in, inhabit, and with disturbing regularity surface from, strange and enigmatic netherworlds very different to that of our own, personal 3-D reality.

On a very similar path, a variety of individuals suspect strongly that the real Men in Black are nothing less than definitive demons – the literal, deceptive minions of none other than the lord of the underworld: Satan himself. The intriguing fact that many of those that have been cursed by visits from the Men in Black have dabbled in occultism, with Ouija-Boards, and in devil-worship, is perceived as further evidence by some that the MIB may have origins that are far, far removed from the enigma-filled world of outer-space and highly-advanced extraterrestrials from the stars.

Meanwhile, there are those investigators of the UFO phenomenon who have put forth a truly fascinating, unique and near-revolutionary theory that has nothing whatsoever to do with aliens, flying saucers, or even the realm of the occult.

It is a definitively jaw-dropping theory that posits the Men in Black may, incredibly, be time-travelers from humankind's far-flung future. Their role, it has been suggested, may be to ensure that we remain forever in the dark about the shocking facts of what is really afoot: namely, that our "aliens" are actually us, albeit from a time centuries, or even thousands of years, from now.

Whatever their point – or points – of origin, however, there is one thing that we can say with complete confidence and certainty about the Men in Black: they *are*, most assuredly, amongst us, and there is absolutely nothing positive, warm or welcoming about their presence at all.

UFOS AND MURDER

Immersing oneself in the world of the unidentified flying object can be exciting, illuminating, stimulating, and enlightening. That very same world, however, is filled to the brim with cold-hearted killers that will not think twice about taking you out of circulation, if such action is deemed absolutely necessary. And not all of those cold-hearted killers are human.

There are cases upon cases of missing aircraft, vanished and dead pilots, suspiciously-timed heart-attacks, murders made to look like suicides, the use of mind-control techniques to provoke quick deaths, the many links between the UFO phenomenon and the November 22, 1963 assassination of President John F. Kennedy, the termination of numerous scientists with secret UFO links, journalists hung out to dry (as in *forever*), the terrifying human equivalents of so-called cattle mutilations, and fatal illnesses provoked by close proximity to unidentified aerial craft.

In the very year that the UFO phenomenon entered popular culture, 1947, there was a grimly impressive catalog of deaths. When, in June of that year, a flying saucer reportedly exploded over Maury Island, Tacoma, Washington State, no less than two military personnel and two media men died under questionable circumstances. Less than two weeks later, the infamous event at Roswell, New Mexico occurred – an event that is dominated by suspicious suicides and mysterious deaths.

Six months later, Captain Thomas Mantell, of the U.S. Air National Guard, was killed after pursuing in the skies over Kentucky what many UFO researchers believe to have been a spacecraft from another world. Twisted wreckage and a dead pilot were the only pieces of evidence left for investigators to scrutinize.

Then, in May 1949, the life of the first U.S. Secretary of Defense, James Forrestal, came to a literal, crashing end when he plunged to his death from a window of the Bethesda, Maryland, National Naval Medical Center. Rumors abound that Forrestal's classified, government work gave him unique access to the U.S. Government's most guarded UFO secrets of all – secrets that Forrestal was intent on disclosing to the world, had his untimely and suspicious death not got in the way.

Four years down the line, in November 1953, no less than six pilots lost their lives or vanished into oblivion as a result of their UFO pursuits. Karl Hunrath and Wilbur Wilkinson were two men obsessed by UFOs and who mysteriously disappeared on November 10. Claiming to be in contact with human-like aliens, they took to the skies of California to meet with their extraterrestrial friends – never to be seen again. In less than two weeks later, four more pilots were gone: this time they were U.S. military pilots, each and every one involved in UFO incidents in the Great Lakes area.

In 1959, one of the most controversial of all UFO-related deaths occurred: that of flying saucer investigator and author Morris K. Jessup. While the official story is that Jessup's death was suicide (he was found dead in his car in a Florida park), there are solid grounds for believing that it was far more than that – nothing less than a case of full-blown murder. The reason: to keep Jessup away from certain UFO secrets that powerful players wanted to be kept hidden.

Without doubt the most sensational story that suggests a link between a suspicious death and flying saucers is that of President John F. Kennedy, who was assassinated on November 22, 1963 at Dealey Plaza, Dallas, Texas. As incredible as it may sound, the JFK killing is *littered* with spies, spooks and secret agents who were deeply linked to the UFO phenomenon. Was the president shot to prevent him from going public with what he knew of alien visitations? Don't bet against it.

In the late 1960s, and even more so in the mid to late 1970s, numerous farmers across the United States reported that their cattle were being mutilated in horrific fashion: organs, blood, and tissue were removed by unknown entities. Strange lights were seen in the sky. UFO encounters abounded. But, it may not just have been animals that were mutilated. There are more than a few reports on record of *human* mutilations – from the 1970s onwards and all just about as grisly as their cattle-based counterparts. Are we being used as food by hostile and malevolent aliens?

Eerily paralleling the November 1953 affair of Karl Hunrath and Wilbur Wilkinson, in October 1978 a young Australian pilot named Frederick Valentich disappeared over Australia's Bass Strait. That Valentich vanished shortly after seeing a UFO at *extremely* close quarters has given rise to the theory that he was the victim of nothing less than a cosmic kidnapping.

Moving on, from the early part of the 1980s to the 1990s, dozens of scientists working for GEC-Marconi, in the United Kingdom, died under very dubious circumstances. Many were linked to President Ronald Reagan's Strategic Defense Initiative (SDI), which was known far more famously by its nickname: "Star Wars." That SDI was alleged to have been created to deal with a possible attack by hostile aliens led to an astonishing hypothesis: the Marconi scientists were murdered by extraterrestrials, utilizing advanced mind-control technology, to prevent the SDI project from coming to fruition.

Then there is the 1999 death of UFO/conspiracy author/researcher Jim Keith, who penned such books as *Black Helicopters over America*; *Casebook on the Men in Black*; and *Saucers of the Illuminati*. Was Keith's death really just a tragic accident? Or did dark and manipulative forces conspire to have Keith taken out of circulation?

Collectively, the above accounts and reports are just the beginning of a long list of untimely deaths in the field of Ufology. Indeed, the number of people involved in research of the UFO variety, and who have died under mysterious circumstances, is now in the *dozens*. There is something so secret, so shocking, and so terrifying about the flying saucer phenomenon that it requires the permanent silencing of those that get too close to the truth.

THE AREA 51 CONTROVERSY

In 1989, a highly controversial man, named Robert Scott Lazar, went public with a series of sensational claims that continue to reverberate to this very day. A self-admitted maverick scientist, Lazar asserted that, for a brief period in the late-1980s, he was employed in a scientific capacity at an incredibly secret, deeply-protected installation situated in the harsh wilds of the Nevada Desert. Its name was S-4, a section of the infamous Area 51. The program to which Lazar had been assigned was, he said, one of astonishing proportions and profound implications.

Reportedly, it was a clandestine operation to evaluate, comprehend, and ultimately duplicate, an impressive fleet of spacecraft of non-human origins that had, quite literally, fallen into the hands of the U.S. Government – or, perhaps more accurately, into the hands of an elite, scientific, body of officialdom, possibly one that was not even answerable to the presidential office itself.

Whether obtained as a result of malfunctions, crashes, accidents or even generous donations from the aliens themselves, Lazar never did find out. But, regardless of *how* they got there, they *were* there, laid out before him in the secret hangars of S-4: a veritable armada of flying saucers of the precise type that the U.S. Government had officially, and for decades, confidently assured both the general public and the media were merely the stuff of fantasy, hoaxing and misidentification.

The bulk of Lazar's work was focused on trying to understand, back-engineer, and ultimately replicate the power-source of the amazing, split-level craft – which was, reportedly, a super-heavy element not found on Earth: Element 115.

The biggest problem for the surprisingly small body of personnel assigned to the program – maybe twenty at most – was that the successful duplication of Element 115, on our world, was simply not feasible, given the then-state of scientific expertise. As a result, much of the investigation was definitively trial-and-error-based, undertaken by personnel who fully understood the implications of what they were dealing with, but who were not necessarily sure how to deal with it, or even how to fully comprehend it.

What of these claims about fantastically-advanced craft at Area 51, supposedly fueled by a super-heavy element that cannot be found on Earth: Element 115? Do they stand alone? "Sure they do," say the skeptics. Well, no they don't.

It's here that we have to turn to the equally strange story of a young Welsh man named Matthew Bevan, who, in the mid-1990s, doggedly tried to crack the UFO secrets of Wright-Patterson Air Force Base's so-called Hangar 18. Bevan did so by hacking into the base's computers – something that got the then-teen-terror into scalding hot water with both British and American authorities.

One part of Bevan's experiences – recorded officially, and for posterity, by Scotland Yard during the course of its series of interviews with Bevan immediately after his 1996 arrest – focused upon him having hacked his way into files and systems at Wright-Patterson that appeared to describe a craft astonishingly similar in design to one of those reportedly seen by Lazar.

As Bevan stated, on one particular system at Wright-Patterson that he very cleverly accessed, he came across a stash of emails in which there was a discussion about some radical aircraft being developed at the base. This wasn't a normal vehicle; rather, it was very small, split-level, with a reactor at the bottom and room for the crew in the top section.

When Scotland Yard's Computer Crimes Unit asked him if he saw anything else on the Wright-Patterson computers, Bevan replied that yes, he did: nothing less than classified information on an anti-gravity propulsion system powered by a heavy-element.

The police wanted to know if Bevan had downloaded any such information, printed it, and then secretly circulated it to colleagues within the UFO research field. Bevan assured them he had not. Not entirely convinced by Bevan's words, Scotland Yard asked the same question again, again, and, just for good measure, *once again*, until they were as satisfied as they conceivably could be that Bevan was speaking truthfully.

Clearly, the nature of the aircraft that Matthew Bevan described to Scotland Yard in 1996 sounds *very* similar to those which Bob Lazar claimed secret access at Area 51 in 1988.

SUPERCONDUCTING
SUPER COLLIDER HISTORY

"Five-thousand miles southwest of Geneva, just outside Waxahachie, Texas, are the remnants of a super collider whose energy and circumference—true to American sensibility—would have dwarfed those of CERN's Large Hadron Collider. Nobody doubts that the 40 TeV Superconducting Super Collider (SSC) in Texas would have discovered the Higgs boson a decade before CERN. The collider's tunnel would have entrenched Waxahachie in a topographical oval that curved east before the southern Dallas County line, then running southwest under Bardwell Lake and curving north at Onion Creek. Since Congress canceled the project twenty years ago, on October 21, 1993, Waxahachie has witnessed the bizarre and disquieting history of its failure."

Texas Monthly, October 2013.

"The Superconducting Super Collider (SSC) that would have graced the rolling prairies of Texas would have boasted energy 20 times larger than any accelerator ever constructed and might have been revealing whatever surprises that lay beyond the Higgs, allowing the U.S. to retain dominance in high-energy physics. Except the story didn't play out according to script. Twenty years ago, on October 21, 1993, Congress officially killed the project, leaving behind more than vacant tunnel in the Texas earth."

Scientific American, October 2013.

"Like CERN's Large Hadron Collider on steroids, the Superconducting Super Collider was to be a huge underground ring complex beneath the area near Waxahachie, Texas, that would have been the world's most energetic particle accelerator. Construction on the site began in the early 1990s, but only got so far as 14 miles of tunnel being bored before Congress shut the project down due to the exploding costs of the project. What began as a few-billion-dollar marvel was quickly projected to cost over $11 billion after construction began and, combined with a lack of public knowledge or support, quickly smothered the complex in its infancy.

"Today the site looks like a decrepit office park dropped in the middle of nowhere on the surface, while the tunnels were stripped of any equipment and filled with water to preserve them. However if you can locate the buildings above ground, you can still find portals to the miles of drowned burrows."

Atlas Obscura, 2014.

"Construction began in 1991, and by 1993 workers had dug over 30 km of tunnels. In order to bore through the sandstone and limestone beneath Waxahachie, a 15 foot diameter tunneling machine was created that literally chewed through the bedrock. Most of the ring tunnel would be a smooth-sided tube, but the giant particle detectors required cavernous galleries that had to be blasted out of the rock."

Damn Interesting, 2006.

"In 2006, Arkansan multimillionaire Johnnie Bryan Hunt bought the complex for just $6.5 million in the hope of turning it into one of the largest and most-secure data storage facilities in America. Hunt's unique selling point for Collider Data Center was its location and infrastructure. The collider sits on an independent power grid capable of delivering 10 megawatts of power (and up to 100 megawatts if needed), and it has its own dedicated fiber optic line. Its two warehouses can support floor loads of 500 pounds per square foot, perfect for the enormous servers that Hunt intended to buy. The entire complex is clear of flight paths and out of hurricane, tsunami, earthquake and flood zones."

Amusing Planet, 2010.

KEN CHERRY

CATTLE MUTILATIONS AND UFOS

Since at least 1967, the United States has been beset by a disturbing phenomenon: cattle mutilations. Exactly who, or indeed what, is responsible for the widespread killing of cattle under very bizarre circumstances is far from clear. On many occasions, farmers, police officers, and veterinarians throughout North America have come across cases where cattle have been subjected to unusual surgical procedures, such as having organs expertly removed and being completely drained of blood – and also in the exact locations where both UFO and unmarked, black helicopter activity is prevalent, too.

This has inevitably led to suspicions that extraterrestrials are engaged in a covert, and possibly sinister, program that may relate to the attempted introduction of a lethal virus of truly cosmic origins into the human food chain. The destruction of the human species in a *War of the Worlds* style scenario may not be the only way to systematically wipe us out, adherents of such theories suggest.

A report from the files of the Federal Bureau of Investigation, dated February 2, 1979, lends credence to the possibility that the mysterious helicopters are implicated in the cattle mutilation mystery to some degree; but suggests that the mutilators may have a far more down to earth point of origin, and may be utilizing the UFO mystery as a convenient cover for clandestine bacteriological and biological warfare activities:

"For the past seven or eight years mysterious cattle mutilations have been occurring throughout the United State of New Mexico. Officer Gabe Valdez, New Mexico State Police, has been handling investigations of these mutilations within New Mexico. Information furnished to this office by Officer Valdez indicates that the animals are being shot with a type of paralyzing drug and the blood is being drawn from the animal after an injection of an anti-coagulant."

The FBI's report continues: "It appears that in some instances the cattle's legs have been broken, and helicopters without any identifying numbers have reportedly been seen in the vicinity of the mutilations. Officer Valdez theorizes that clamps are being placed on the cow's legs and they are being lifted by helicopter to some remote area where the mutilations are taking place and then the animal is returned to its original pasture.

"Officer Valdez is very adamant in his opinion that these mutilations are the work of the US Government and that it is some clandestine operation either by the CIA or the Department of Energy and in all probability is connected with some type of research into biological warfare."

In her book *An Alien Harvest*, Linda Moulton Howe documents her investigations into cattle mutilations, phantom helicopters, and unidentified flying objects. An Emmy-award-winning television producer, Howe has presented a large body of evidence that she believes is an indication that the three subjects are inextricably linked. Moreover, she offers the possibility that extraterrestrials derive some form of sustenance from the removed body parts of the unfortunate beasts.

But if extraterrestrials *are* responsible for these grisly attacks, then what role is played by the phantom helicopters? A number of researchers have mused upon this puzzle, including Tom Adams, a long-time student of the cattle mutilation mystery. He suggests that:

"The helicopters are of military origin. The government of the United States possesses a very substantial amount of knowledge about the mutilators, their means, motives, and rationale. The government may be attempting to persuade mutilation investigators and the populace as a whole that perhaps the military might be behind the mutilations, a diversion away from the real truth."

PILOTS AND ALIENS

S trange and amazing things were afoot in the night skies of Tehran, the capital of Iran, on September 19, 1976. Those things revolved around nothing less than the pilot of the Iranian Air Force practically going to war with a potentially hostile unidentified flying object. Not surprisingly, a U.S. Government file was created on the event.

Even less surprising, most of that file has vanished as mysteriously as did the UFO itself, all of those years ago. For at least some insight into what happened on September 19, we are reliant upon one of just two pieces of evidence that *have* surfaced, via the Freedom of Information Act. The first is a three-page paper titled *Now You See It, Now You Don't!* It was penned by Captain Henry S. Shields of the U.S. Air Force. The second is a three-page document from the Defense Intelligence Agency. The latter reads like sci-fi. Astonishingly, it is nothing of the sort.

According to the paperwork at issue, it was not long after midnight on the 19th when people living in the Shemiran area of Tehran reported seeing strange, unidentified lights maneuvering directly overhead. Phone calls were quickly placed with local police and military authorities at Shahrokhi Air Force Base.

An hour or so after the first call reached staff at the air base, a McDonnell Douglas F-4 Phantom aircraft was scrambled to try and determine the precise origin of the enigmatic lights. And that's when things got very interesting, as the following, extracted from the Defense Intelligence Agency's report, reveals:

"At 0130 hours on the 19th the F-4 took off and proceeded to a point about 40 NM north of Tehran. Due to its brilliance, the object was easily visible from 70 miles away. As the F-4 approached a range of 25 NM, [the pilot] lost all instrumentation and communications...When the F-4 turned away from the object and apparently was no longer a threat to it, the aircraft regained all instrumentation and communications."

Rather notably, the documentation adds: "The size of the radar return was comparable to that of a 707 tanker," which would have put its length in excess of 140 feet and its width more than 130 feet.

Despite the brief malfunctions to his aircraft, the pilot was not dissuaded by the actions of this unearthly, and uninvited, visitor. He diligently headed off in hot pursuit. That's when a chase practically became an aerial dogfight. According to the DIA: "The object and the pursuing F-4 continued on a course to the south of Tehran when another brightly lighted object, estimated to be one-half to one-third the apparent size of the moon, came out of the object" (Ibid.).

This smaller UFO didn't just exit its mother-ship: it headed straight for the F-4 at violent, breakneck speed. The pilot, reacting quickly in the face of something decidedly unknown, "...attempted to fire an AIM-9 missile at the object but at that instant his weapons control panel went off and he lost all communication."

Seconds later, noted the DIA, the two UFOs joined as one and shot away. Not into the night sky, as you might imagine, however, but towards the ground. There was no crash, however, which is what the pilot was anticipating. Rather, the pilot of the F-4 reported that, even at an altitude of 15,000 feet, he could see the object illuminating the desert floor, seemingly having made a perfect touchdown. Aliens, quite possibly, had just landed in Iran.

Given that the territory below was pitch black, the on-site investigation did not begin until the following morning, when the pilot was flown by helicopter to the area where the UFO had landed, which happened to be a dry lake bed. Whatever the true nature of the UFO - the Iranian military investigators who were also brought to the site concluded - it was now long gone.

When one takes into consideration all of the aspects of this extraordinary case – such as the ability of the UFO to disable both the weapon- and communication systems of the Phantom F-4 – there's a good likelihood that a lengthy file was prepared on the matter by U.S. Intelligence.

Back in the 1970s, Iran and the United States were on far friendlier terms than they are in today's fraught world: from the 1960s to the 1970s, no less than 225 Phantom F-4's were sold to the Iranian Air Force by the U.S. government. It makes perfect sense that the Americans would have been deeply disturbed by the ease with which one of their very own aircraft was overwhelmingly prevented from taking decisive action against the UFO hurtling towards it.

The U.S. military would surely have wanted to get to the bottom of who, or what, commanded such aircraft-disabling technology. So, what does the military's file on the matter say about it all? Well, aside from the three pages of raw intelligence, from which the quotes above were word for word extracted, we have nothing. That's not to say, however, that nothing is all there is to find.

UFO researchers Barry Greenwood and Lawrence Fawcett spent a great deal of personal time and effort digging into the matter of the Iranian Air Force incident of September 1976. They noted that the Defense Intelligence Agency papers on the case specifically stated that, "more information will be forwarded when it becomes available."

Unfortunately, for those of us outside of officialdom, at least, such has not yet happened. There are, however, good indications that a substantial file was created on the event and which remains hidden from public view.

In the words of Greenwood and Fawcett: "Reliable sources within the government have told us that the Iranian case file was about one and a half inches thick, yet absolutely no admission to having this file has come from any government agency with a possible connection to the case."

And there ends the remarkable story. As for that huge file, well, the words of Greenwood and Fawcett in relation to it were made in 1984. Three decades later, there's still no sign of the documentation surfacing any time in the near future.

A NASA ASTRONAUT SPEAKS OUT

Gordon Cooper was one of NASA's so-called Mercury Seven astronauts. In NASA's own words on Mercury: "Implementation was initiated to establish a national manned space flight project, later named Project Mercury, on October 7, 1958. The life of Project Mercury was about 4 2/3 years, from the time of its official go-ahead to the completion of the 34-hour orbital mission of Astronaut [Gordon] Cooper."

Not only was Gordon Cooper an astronaut and an American hero, he was also someone who had a firm belief in the existence of a UFO phenomenon of extraterrestrial origins. Cooper's belief was so strong that he shared his thoughts on the matter with the highest echelons of the United Nations – not once, but twice.

Sir Eric Matthew Gairy held the position of Premier of the island of Grenada from 1967 to 1979. In 1977, two years before he finally left office, Gairy began to enthusiastically lobby none other than the United Nations to create an agency, office or department designed to "collate, coordinate and corroborate information" on UFOs and extraterrestrial life.

In October 1977, Gairy said in a noteworthy and memorable statement to the United Nations, on the specific subject of UFOs: "I think it is accepted that these things do exist. I think we now want to know the nature, the origin, and the intent of these saucers. Some people think they have come to do good. Some think they have come to dominate human beings."

Significantly, Gairy also cited several cases where a number of "aircraft have been put out of commission, but not destroyed, after attacking saucers." According to Gairy's personal and particular, comforting train of thought on this specific aspect of the UFO phenomenon: "That confirms my thought on their positive intent: I believe they are coming here to help mankind because man is so self-destructive."

As a direct result of Gairy's near unique prompting to the United Nations, on November 9, 1978 NASA astronaut Gordon Cooper submitted memorable words of encouragement and support in the form of a letter to Ambassador Griffith, Mission of Grenada to the United Nations. Cooper was unequivocal and concise, as his words, recorded in official Department of State files, clearly demonstrated.

Cooper stressed that the establishment of any such organization along the lines suggested by Gairy would require it to have the ability, scope and staffing to capably, and scientifically, study the UFO subject to a truly significant and previously-unparalleled degree.

In specific terms of the aliens themselves, that Cooper solidly accepted were now visiting us, he told the United Nations that: "We may first have to show them that we have learned to resolve our problems by peaceful means, rather than warfare, before we are accepted as fully qualified universal team members. This acceptance would have tremendous possibilities of advancing our world in all areas. Certainly then it would seem that the U.N. has a vested interest in handling this subject properly and expeditiously."

Despite the very best efforts of Cooper, Sir Eric Gairy's ambitious *X-Files* style ideas never amounted to anything of real, meaningful significance. Cooper was far from being done yet, however, when it came to trying to alert the Human Race to the unearthly UFO presence that he believed was directly among us -- and had been for decades, and perhaps even longer, too. As evidence of this, in 1980, Cooper made a number of notable, public statements on the UFO controversy.

When questioned in that year by *Omni* magazine on the subject of his 1951 encounter, Cooper outright confirmed and reinforced its reality, adding in truly significant tones, given his standing and experience with the U.S. Air Force, and later with NASA, that: "From my association with aircraft and spacecraft, I think I have a pretty good idea of what everyone on this planet has and their performance capabilities, and I'm sure some of the UFOs at least are not from anywhere on Earth."

Then, in 1985, when UFOs were once again briefly on the agenda of the United Nations, Cooper offered the following, significant words that were recorded for posterity by the Department of State: "I believe that these extraterrestrial vehicles and their crews are visiting this planet from other planets, which are a little more technically advanced than we are on Earth."

Once again, however, despite the important and almost unparalleled fact that none other than a retired, and greatly respected, NASA astronaut and American hero was personally endorsing and highlighting the theory that some UFOs may represent alien spacecraft, the United Nations failed to act to any meaningful or worthwhile degree.

To some players within the public UFO research community at the time, this admittedly disappointing outcome was perceived as prime evidence that the United Nations was dissuaded from pressing ahead with its very own UFO study program, by even more powerful and shadowy forces buried deep within the Machiavellian realm of international officialdom.

UFOS: THE CIA'S ROBERTSON PANEL

O n December 2, 1952 the CIA's Assistant Director H. Marshall Chadwell noted in a classified report on UFO activity in American airspace: "Sightings of unexplained objects at great altitudes and traveling at high speeds in the vicinity of major U.S. defense installations are of such nature that they are not attributable to natural phenomena or known types of aerial vehicles."

Believing that something might be afoot in the skies of America, Chadwell prepared a list of saucer-themed recommendations for the National Security Council:

1.　The Director of Central Intelligence shall formulate and carry out a program of intelligence and research activities as required to solve the problem of instant identification of unidentified flying objects.

2.　Upon call of the Director of Central Intelligence, Government departments and agencies shall provide assistance in this program of intelligence and research to the extent of their capacity provided, however, that the DCI shall avoid duplication of activities presently directed toward the solution of this problem.

3.　This effort shall be coordinated with the military services and the Research and Development Board of the Department of Defense, with the Psychological Board and other Governmental agencies as appropriate.

4.　The Director of Central Intelligence shall disseminate information concerning the program of intelligence and research activities in this field to the various departments and agencies which have authorized interest therein.

Forty-eight-hours later, the Intelligence Advisory Committee concurred with Chadwell and recommended that "the services of selected scientists to review and appraise the available evidence in the light of pertinent scientific theories" should be the order of the day. Thus was born the Robertson Panel, so named after the man chosen to head the inquiry: Howard Percy Robertson, a consultant to the Agency, a renowned physicist, and the director of the Defense Department Weapons Evaluation Group.

Chadwell was tasked with putting together a crack team of experts in various science, technical, intelligence and military disciplines and have them carefully study the data on flying saucers currently held by not just the CIA, but the Air Force too – who obligingly agree to hand over all their UFO files for the CIA's scrutiny. Or, at least, the Air Force *said* it was all they had.

Whatever the truth of the matter regarding the extent to which the USAF shared its files with Chadwell's team, the fact that there was a significant body of data to work with was the main thing. And so the team – which included Luis Alvarez, physicist, radar expert (and later, a Nobel Prize recipient); Frederick C. Durant, CIA officer, secretary to the panel and missile expert; Samuel Abraham Goudsmit, Brookhaven National Laboratories nuclear physicist; and Thornton Page, astrophysicist, radar expert, and deputy director of Johns Hopkins Operations Research Office – quickly got to work.

The overall conclusion of the Robertson Panel was that while UFOs, per se, did not appear to have a bearing on national security or the defense of the United States, the way in which the subject could be used by unfriendly forces to manipulate the public mindset and disrupt the U.S. military infrastructure *did* have a bearing – and a hell of a major one, too - on matters of a security nature. According to the panel's members: "…although evidence of any direct threat from these sightings was wholly lacking, related dangers might well exist resulting from A. Misidentification of actual enemy artifacts by defense personnel. B. Overloading of emergency reporting channels with "false" information. C. Subjectivity of public to mass hysteria and greater vulnerability to possible enemy psychological warfare."

There was also a recommendation that a number of the public UFO investigative groups that existed in the United States at the time, such as the Civilian Flying Saucer Investigators (CFSI) and the Aerial Phenomena Research Organization (APRO), should be "watched" carefully due to "...the apparent irresponsibility and the possible use of such groups for subversive purposes..."

The panel also concluded that "...a public education campaign should be undertaken" on matters relative to UFOs. Specifically, agreed the members, such a program would "...result in reduction in public interest in 'flying saucers' which today evokes a strong psychological reaction. This education could be accomplished by mass media such as television, motion pictures, and popular articles. Basis of such education would be actual case histories which had been puzzling at first but later explained. As in the case of conjuring tricks, there is much less stimulation if the 'secret' is known. Such a program should tend to reduce the current gullibility of the public and consequently their susceptibility to clever hostile propaganda.

"In this connection, Dr. Hadley Cantril (Princeton University) was suggested. Cantril authored '*Invasion from Mars*,' (a study in the psychology of panic, written about the famous Orson Welles radio broadcast in 1938) and has since performed advanced laboratory studies in the field of perception. The names of Don Marquis (University of Michigan) and Leo Roston were mentioned as possibly suitable as consultant psychologists.

"Also, someone familiar with mass communications techniques, perhaps an advertising expert, would be helpful. Arthur Godfrey was mentioned as possibly a valuable channel of communication reaching a mass audience of certain levels. Dr. Berkner suggested the U. S. Navy (ONR) Special Devices Center, Sands Point, Long Island, as a potentially valuable organization to assist in such an educational program. The teaching techniques used by this agency for aircraft identification during the past war [were] cited as an example of a similar educational task. The Jam Handy Co. which made World War II training films (motion picture and slide strips) was also suggested, as well as Walt Disney, Inc. animated cartoons."

WAR OF THE WORLDS

Mercury Theatre on the Air performed Orson Welles' radio adaptation of H.G. Wells' classic sci-fi book *War of the Worlds* on October 30, 1938, specifically as a Halloween special. The program was broadcast from the 20th floor of 485 Madison Avenue, and was ingeniously presented in the form of a regular show that was repeatedly interrupted by a series of disturbing and escalating news stories detailing gigantic explosions on the planet Mars that were rapidly followed by frantic reports of the landing of an alien spacecraft near the town of Grover's Mill, New Jersey.

As the broadcast progresses, more Martian war machines land and proceed to wreak havoc throughout the continental United States. The Secretary of the Interior informs the pain-stricken populace of the grave nature of the ever-growing conflict, and the military launches a desperate counterattack against the burgeoning Martian assault. Frantic reports describe thousands of people fleeing urban areas as the unstoppable Martians head towards New York City. "Isn't there anyone on the air?" pleads a desperate broadcaster in suitably dramatic and chilled tones.

Of course, Welles had merely intended the show to be an entertaining radio rendition of *War of the Worlds* and nothing more. However, those listeners who were unfortunate enough to have missed the beginning of the production–in which Welles was very careful to say that the broadcast was simply a piece of fictional entertainment and absolutely nothing else–really did believe that a Martian attack on the Earth had begun, and that the end of civilization was possibly looming on the dark horizon.

Indeed, newspapers of the day stated that large-scale panic followed in the wake of the show. And although later studies suggested the hysteria was far less widespread than newspaper accounts initially suggested, many people were indeed caught up in the initial cosmic confusion.

It has been suggested by conspiracy theorists, such as the late William Cooper, that the *War of the Worlds* broadcast was actually a psychological warfare experiment secretly sponsored by elements of the U.S. Government to try and accurately determine how the population might react to the presence of a hostile alien menace, albeit an entirely false and officially manufactured one, rather like a "War on Terror" for the *X-Files* generation.

Although the majority of those who have studied such claims have outright dismissed them, the scenario of Government officials conspiring to unite (or, perhaps, enslave) humankind under one banner, as a result of an intergalactic alien threat, was discussed extensively in a controversial publication titled *Report From Iron Mountain*.

The late writer, Philip Coppens, states: "In 1967, a major publisher, The Dial Press, released *Report from Iron Mountain*. The book claimed to be a suppressed, secret government report, written by a commission of scholars, known as the "Special Study Group," set up in 1963, with the document itself leaked by one of its members. The Group met at an underground nuclear bunker called Iron Mountain and worked over a period of two and a half years, delivering the report in September 1966. The report was an investigation into the problems that the United States would need to face if and when 'world peace' should be established on a more or less permanent basis."

And as the *Report*, itself, noted: "It is surely no exaggeration to say that a condition of general world peace would lead to changes in the social structures of the nations of the world of unparalleled and revolutionary magnitude. The economic impact of general disarmament, to name only the most obvious consequence of peace, would revise the production and distribution patterns of the globe to a degree that would make the changes of the past fifty years seem insignificant.

"Political, sociological, cultural, and ecological changes would be equally far-reaching. What has motivated our study of these contingencies has been the growing sense of thoughtful men in and out of government that the world is totally unprepared to meet the demands of such a situation."

Upon its first appearance in 1967, *Report From Iron Mountain* ignited immediate and widespread debate among journalists and scholars with its disturbingly convincing conclusion: namely, that a condition of "permanent peace" at the end of the Cold War would drastically threaten the United States' economic and social stability.

Although subsequently identified as nothing more than an ingenious hoax written by Leonard Lewin, who had both conceived and launched the book with the help of a select body of players in the peace movement–including *Nation* editors Victor Navasky and Richard Lingeman, novelist E. L. Doctorow, and economist John Kenneth Galbraith–the controversy surrounding *Report From Iron Mountain* refuses to roll over and die.

Long out of print, the *Report* suddenly began to reappear in bootlegged editions more than twenty years after its original publication, amid claims that its contents were all-too-real.

Colonel Fletcher Prouty, a national security aide in the Kennedy Administration (and the model for Donald Sutherland' character, "X" in Oliver Stone's hit-movie *JFK*), continues to believe to this very day that the report is indeed authentic, and he specifically referred to it within the pages of his memoirs. Notably, in a 1992 Preface to Prouty's memoirs, no less a person than Oliver Stone, himself, cited the *Report From Iron Mountain* as explicitly raising "the key questions of our time."

After the book's initial publication, it was reported that then President Lyndon B. Johnson had deep suspicions that the late President John F. Kennedy had authorized the publication of the *Report*. Moreover, Johnson is famously alleged to have "hit the roof" upon learning of its publication.

In 1992, *Iron Mountain* author Lewin filed a lawsuit for copyright infringement against Willis Carto, a white supremacist, for allegedly publishing the now-discontinued, bootleg editions of the book. Interestingly, Mark Lane, an author who has written extensively on the Kennedy assassination and who served as Carto's lawyer, stated that *Report From Iron Mountain* may indeed have been a real government document and, therefore, could not be seen to have any bearing upon current United States copyright laws.

Similarly, a May 1995, front-page article in the *Wall Street Journal* reported that extreme-right fringe groups continued to quote *Report From Iron Mountain* as "proof of a secret government plot to suppress personal liberties and usher in a New World Order dominated by the U.N."

ALIENS IN THE WOODS

Between the nights of December 26 and 28, 1980, a series of almost science-fiction-like events occurred in Rendlesham Forest, Suffolk, England; a densely treed area adjacent to the joint Royal Air Force / U.S. Air Force military complex of Bentwaters-Woodbridge. Essentially, what many believe took place over the course of at least several nights was nothing less than the landing of a craft from another world, out of which small, humanoid entities reportedly emerged.

The vehicle was tracked on radar, deposited traces of radiation within the forest, succeeded in avoiding capture, duly made good its escape, was the subject of *intense* secrecy on the part of both British and American authorities, and created a wild controversy that rages and swirls to this very day.

One of those who has commented, deeply so, too, on this particularly mysterious case is a man named Larry Warren – a U.S. Air Force witness to the UFO-landing at Rendlesham Forest in December 1980. Warren, at the time a member of the Air Force Security Police, has stated that his own, personal encounter occurred late on the night of December 28. It sounds just like something straight out of *Close Encounters of the Third Kind*. Warren's experience was hardly Hollywood fiction, however. Rather, it was incredible, unearthly fact.

As the evening unfolded, rumors flew around the base about the nature of the UFO encounters of the previous two nights. Military personnel – possessed of sophisticated scientific equipment and hardware - were reportedly swarming around the dense, dark woods, seemingly deeply anticipating the return of the UFOs. Wild animals, such as deer and rabbits, were seen fleeing the forest in unbridled terror, clearly spooked to their collective cores by something menacingly unknown in their midst. And, at the height of these

319

extraordinary events, Warren and a number of his colleagues and friends were ordered to head into the very heart of those spooky woods. As for why: they were just about to find out.

The mystified group carefully made its tentative-but-intrigued way through the trees, until a clearing was finally reached, on the other side of which was an open expanse of field -- that, ominously, seemed to be illuminated by a form of weird, glowing fog. The tension in the air began to mount even more. As Warren and his colleagues slowly moved closer, they could now see there were already approximately forty personnel in the field -- some armed with cameras, others weighed-down with sophisticated motion-picture equipment, and a few even possessed of Geiger-counters.

The reason why suddenly became graphically and almost unbelievably clear: from the direction of the North Sea a small, aerial ball of red light came flying, which proceeded towards the unearthly fog, then duly stopped, hovering right above it. In an instant, there was a near-blinding flash. When Warren's eyes acclimatized to the situation, he could see that both the ball of light and the fog were now utterly gone. In their place, however, was something even more remarkable: at a distance of only about twenty feet from the shell-shocked Warren and his comrades was a pyramid-shaped craft that was clearly mechanical in nature, and that appeared under intelligent control. That was nothing compared to what happened next, however.

A large ball of bluish-gold light appeared from the right-side of the UFO and moved slowly away from the craft, to a distance of about ten feet from the stunned airmen. Within the ethereal ball were three entities, three non-human intelligences from some unknown realm: *aliens*. The ball then split into three cylinder-style creations, each containing one of the three beings, which were attired in silvery suits, had large heads and displayed significantly-sized, cat-like eyes.

According to Warren, some sort of communication -- possibly telepathic -- took place between the creatures and a high-ranking U.S Air Force officer, after which Warren and his colleagues were ordered to return to their trucks and await further orders - which is precisely, but perhaps somewhat reluctantly, what they did. The encounter in the woods, for Warren at least, was over. But there was something even stranger waiting on the horizon for him. It was something destined to take the man not back into Rendlesham Forest but *under* it.

It was around 6:00 p.m. on the following night when Warren, on-base but by then off-duty, received a telephone call. The mysterious voice on the line gave no indication, at all, of his identity, but ordered the bemused Warren to be in the dorm parking lot in twenty minutes, where he would see a dark blue sedan waiting for him.

Wondering what was going on, like a good soldier, Warren followed the orders, and sure enough: there was the car, waiting to take him to destinations unknown. He was motioned to the back door of the sedan by two silent men in dark suits – definitive shades of the dreaded Men in Black, perhaps – and got in the car. But something was wrong; in fact, something was *very* wrong.

An eerie, green glow filled the vehicle, and a strange feeling suddenly overcame Warren. Somehow rendered into a near-semiconscious, befuddled state, and unable to speak clearly or move properly, Warren later speculated that perhaps he had been secretly drugged in some unfathomable fashion. Regardless of how such a situation was achieved, however, Warren was now as helpless as a terror-stricken deer caught in full-beam headlights.

The next thing Warren recalled, in his semi-sedated state, was being taken to another location, followed by what he described as a definite descent that affected the pressure in his ears. The inference was clear: rather than being on-base, Warren was now in the process of being transferred to somewhere deep below it. And with his mind altered, and his body unable to fight back, Warren's involvement in whatever was about to happen next was more or less assured.

Warren, granted in somewhat of a distinct stupor, saw rooms filled with high-tech equipment and computers, and was motioned towards a massive door. On walking, on distinctly unsteady feet, Warren next found himself in a darkened room, to the left of which was some type of opening, access to which was prevented by a Plexiglas window.

"I stepped into the confined area and felt as if I was no longer on Earth," Warren later recalled. "I found myself looking into a gigantic, dark cavernous space. It reminded me of the interior of the Houston Astrodome in a strange way. Beads of humidity rolled down the other side of the seamless glass." Notably, Warren also recalled seeing a craft, resting in a corner of the huge installation, looking *extremely* like the one which he had encountered in Rendlesham Forest on the previous night. Lights in the darkness and distance, Warren was informed by those carefully guiding his movements, represented a huge tunnel under the base that led out to the harsh, cold waters of the North Sea.

Warren was then directed to a large, translucent screen, through which he could see the shadowy silhouette of a small-sized living entity, although it was impossible to make out any specific physical details. But, there was something very strange and undeniably unearthly about the creature, or whatever it was: Warren began to sense words and imagery in his mind, all of which gave every indication the being knew intimate, personal details of Warren's life and character. The creature also informed Warren, again via some form of mind-to-mind contact that it originated within a realm of existence that he, Warren, would never be able to comprehend.

Notably, further data was imparted to Warren by the unknown entity in front of him to the effect that he was indeed in a secret facility far below the base, that the underground installation had existed since the 1940s, and was expanded upon in the 1960s, thus allowing the creature and the rest of its kind access to the facility via the huge tunnel system that reportedly had both entry- and exit points approximately a mile off the coast of the English town of Lowestoft, Suffolk. Warren was also advised that other such secret bases existed across the entire planet; their purpose, however, was never quite made clear.

UNDERGROUND INSTALLATIONS

T he Alternate Joint Communications Center, located within Raven Rock Mountain, Pennsylvania, is situated only seven miles from Camp David, the presidential country retreat. Constructed in the early years of the 1950s, the installation – also referred to as Raven Rock and as Site-R - is designed to allow for at least *some* form of continuation of government in the event of a nuclear strike upon the nation's capital.

Whether Raven Rock, itself, can withstand a direct strike, however, is a distinctly out-of-bounds issue with those in-the-know. Nevertheless, the location is reported to be an impressive and near-futuristic one. Indeed, buried deeply within the mountain, it can comfortably house up to at least 3,000 people for a considerable period of time - overflowing, as it apparently is, with an abundance of food, fresh water and clean air. Not bad at all, providing you happen to be on the *inside*, rather than the *outside*, when the gigantic mushroom clouds start blooming and blossoming. And it's an installation that is thoroughly steeped in overwhelming official secrecy.

As a prime example, on May 25, 2007, the Federal Register - the official journal of the government – stated in a Department of Defense policy document titled *Conduct on the Pentagon Reservation*, which dealt directly with Raven Rock Mountain: "The use of cameras or other visual recording devices on the Pentagon Reservation is prohibited...It shall be unlawful to make any photograph, sketch, picture, drawing, map or graphical representation of the Pentagon Reservation without first obtaining permission of the Pentagon Force Protection Agency, Installation Commander, or the Office of the Assistant to the Secretary of Defense for Public Affairs."

China has been the target of claims that it too, in very recent years, has greatly expanded its plans to construct secret installations, either underground or burrowed right out of dense hills. The most noticeably-visible such place is that which has become known as the Sanya Base, located on the southernmost tip of Hainan Island, in the South China Sea.

Although many Western military analysts believe the facility to be a secret installation designed for the construction, maintenance and storage of an ever-growing armada of Chinese nuclear submarines, rumors suggest that the Sanya Base amounts to nothing less than China's very own Area 51.

That vast tunnels – more than sixty-feet-high – have been photographed in and around the base, and that are said to expand into gigantic caverns that run far below the green hills above, only amplifies the rumors.

Moving onto Russia, vast, underground installations have been constructed deep within the Yamantau and Kosvinsky Mountains in the Urals. Rudimentary construction at both sites was confirmed in the late-1970s by National Reconnaissance Office-controlled spy-satellites. Today, matters have progressed significantly, and data recently collected by further U.S. satellites suggests additional expansion of both places in the last few years has been widespread and intense.

The Kosvinsky site, for example, is now protected by around 1,000-feet of granite. It is a self-contained hub capable – rumor has it - containing housing in excess of 50,000 individuals. As for the Yamantau base, one U.S. intelligence source has suggested, it is equal the size of the Washington area within the Beltway.

Then there is Kapustin Yar, a secret Russian site dedicated to the research, development and deployment of rocket-based technologies, which, having been established in 1946 is located in Astrakhan Oblast, between Volgograd and Astrakhan. Rumors coming out of Russia and via data collected from NRO spy-satellites points towards continued massive, underground digging and construction at Kapustin Yar.

Better known as the Russian Area 51, Zhitkur is a highly secret, and incredibly well-guarded, installation built below a seemingly innocuous, small town in the region of Volgogradskaya Oblast. In the very same way that rumors, accounts and whistleblower testimony suggests recovered alien spacecraft are being studied and test-flown at Area 51, Nevada, similar tales surround Zhitkur.

Stories emanating from former employees of the base tell of top secret studies of crashed UFOs – or, as we should perhaps term them, Russian Roswell's. Darker accounts reveal the Russians are hard at work to try and develop deadly, terrifying, super-viruses at Zhitkur that will have the ability to lethally target specific races of people, while leaving others completely free of deadly infection. But, all of those rumors are overshadowed by accounts similar to those emanating from Kapustin Yar – that extensive, tunnel-boring activity is the order of the day at Zhitkur.

In April 2011, extensive digging began at none other than the White House – specifically in the vicinity of the famous West-Wing. Ostensibly, the media was informed, the work was strictly renovation-based, and focused upon repairing and upgrading sewer systems, water-pipes, and electrical systems. Such proclamations, however, were viewed somewhat skeptically by certain elements of the Washington press corps.

Although the East-Wing of the White House sits atop a hardened bunker designed to survive a nuclear attack on the nation's capital – it's called the Presidential Emergency Operations Center – the idea that the new work on the West-Wing was somehow linked to PEOC, and that elaborate tunneling was being undertaken to expand, strengthen and deepen the facility, was openly scoffed at by White House officials and spokespersons. Some journalists that followed the story suggested the White House scoffed just a little bit *too* much.

ET ABDUCTIONS

On the night of September 19, 1961, Betty and Barney Hill, a New Hampshire couple, were driving home from vacationing in Canada when they were subjected to a terrifying experience. Despite viewing some form of unusual aerial object in the night sky, and what appeared to be living entities that could be seen through the craft's portals, until their arrival back home, the Hill's had little indication that there was far more to the encounter than they realized. It later transpired, however, that approximately two-hours of time could not be accounted for.

After months of emotional distress, sleepless nights, and strange dreams pertaining to encounters with unusual, otherworldly beings, the couple finally sought assistance from Benjamin Simon, a Boston-based psychiatrist, and neurologist. Subjected to time regression hypnosis, both Betty and Barney recalled what had taken place during that missing 120-minutes or so.

Significantly, they provided very close accounts of encounters with apparent alien creatures that took the pair onboard some form of alien vehicle and subjected them to a series of physical examinations – a number of which were highly distressing in nature.

The experience of the Hill's later became the subject of John Fuller's now-classic book, *The Interrupted Journey* and a 1975 movie of the same name. Although claims have been made that the phenomenon long pre-dates the Hill affair, it was certainly this incident that paved the way for the massive interest in abductions and missing time phenomena that ultimately developed in the 1980s and 1990s.

While abduction cases continued to surface now and again in the 1960s, and more so in the 1970s, it was without doubt the 1981 publication of Budd Hopkins' book *Missing Time* that really thrust the phenomenon into the public arena, big-time. Then, with the 1987 appearance of Hopkins' *Intruders*, the phenomenon gained further publicity.

By now, there was a growing, widespread belief within the ufological research arena that extraterrestrials from some far-away world were engaged in a secret program to kidnap, experiment on, and exploit the Human Race – possibly for reasons relative to genetic manipulation, and the creation of hybrid entities of a definitively half-human/half-alien nature.

And, even though this particular theory continues to be championed beyond all others when it comes to abductions, it is far from being alone.

Whitley Strieber's 1987 best-seller, *Communion* – while certainly not dismissing the extraterrestrial hypothesis for abductions – demonstrated that even if aliens were at the heart of the abduction puzzle, there was far more to them than mere extraterrestrial scientists engaged in some other-world research project.

Communion, as well as Strieber's subsequent titles, delved into potential connections between the Grays of UFO lore and the realm of the dead, the similarities (as had been noted by acclaimed ufologist Jacques Vallee in his *Messengers of Deception*) between modern-day abductions and encounters in centuries past with magical, ethereal entities like fairies, and much more of a thought-provoking nature.

As time has progressed, so have the theories behind what may be present at the heart of abductions and the missing time mystery. Before his untimely death in 2009, Mac Tonnies was busily chasing down what he called the "crypto terrestrials". In Mac's mind, our mysterious abductors might not be from the stars, after all. Rather, he opined, they might very well be a very ancient terrestrial race – albeit one that exists alongside us in deep stealth.

Tonnies said: "I regard the alleged 'hybridization program' with skepticism. How sure are we that these interlopers are extraterrestrial? It seems more sensible to assume that the so-called aliens are human, at least in some respects. Indeed, descriptions of intercourse with aliens fly in the face of exobiological thought. If the crypto terrestrial population is genetically impoverished, as I assume it is, then it might rely on a harvest of human genes to augment its dwindling gene pool. It would be most advantageous to have us believe we're dealing with omnipotent extraterrestrials rather than a fallible sister species."

Then there was the research of the late Dr. John Mack, who cited in his published works the intriguing and disturbing testimony of a number of abductees who believed the predatory, black-eyed beings that are so associated with abductions were actually trying to steal their souls, rather than their DNA.

Then there is Jim Penniston. Formerly of the U.S. Air Force, and one of the key military players in the famous UFO encounter at Rendlesham Forest, England in December 1980, Penniston – in 1994 – underwent hypnotic regression, as part of an attempt to try and recall deeply buried data relative to what occurred during one of Britain's closest encounters. Very interestingly, while under hypnosis, Penniston stated that our presumed aliens are, in reality, visitors from a far-flung future.

That future, Penniston added, is very dark, in infinitely deep trouble, polluted and where the Human Race is overwhelmingly blighted by reproductive problems. The answer to those same, massive problems: they travel into the distant past – to our present day – to secure sperm, eggs, and chromosomes, all as part of an effort to try and ensure the continuation of the severely waning Human Race.

SECURITY FOR SENSITIVE INSTALLATIONS

A lthough the private-security company that appears in the pages of this novel – Black Stone - is purely fictional, it does have its real-life counterpart, on which Black Stone is based.

G4S Secure Solutions (USA) is an American security services company and a wholly owned subsidiary of G4S plc. It was founded as The Wackenhut Corporation in 1954, in Coral Gables, Florida, by George Wackenhut and three partners (all of them former FBI agents).

In 2002, the company was acquired for $570 million by Danish Corporation Group 4 Falck (itself then merged to form a British company, G4S, in 2004). In 2010, G4S Wackenhut changed its name to G4S Secure Solutions (USA) to reflect the new business model. The G4S Americas Region headquarters is in Jupiter, Florida.

After early struggles (including a fistfight between George Wackenhut and one of his partners), Wackenhut took sole control of his company in 1958, then choosing to name it after himself.

By 1964, he had contracts to guard the Kennedy Space Center and the U.S. Atomic Energy Commission's nuclear test site in Nevada, which included Area 51. The following year, Wackenhut took his company public.

In the mid-60s, Florida Governor Claude Kirk commissioned the Wackenhut Corporation to help fight a "war on organized crime," awarding the company a $500,000 contract. The commission lasted about a year, but led to more than 80 criminal indictments, including many for local politicians and government employees.

Following the murder of a British tourist at a rest stop in 1993, Florida contracted with Wackenhut to provide security at all state rest stops.

The company's work includes: permanent guarding service, security officers, manned security, disaster response, emergency services, control-room monitoring, armed security, unarmed security, special event security, security patrols, reception/concierge service, access control, emergency medical technicians (EMT) service, and ambassador service.

Like other security companies, G4S targets specific sectors: energy, utilities, chemical/petrochemical, financial institutions, government, hospitals and healthcare facilities, major corporations, construction, ports and airports, residential communities, retail and commercial real estate, and transit systems.

Having expanded into providing food services for U.S. prisons in the 1960s, Wackenhut - in 1984 - launched a subsidiary to design and manage jails and detention centers for the burgeoning private prison market. Wackenhut then became the nation's second largest for-profit prison operator. In April 1999, the state of Louisiana took over the running of Wackenhut's 15-month-old juvenile prison after the U.S. Justice Department accused Wackenhut of subjecting its young inmates to "excessive abuse and neglect."

U.S. journalist Gregory Palast commented on the case: "New Mexico's privately operated prisons are filled with America's impoverished, violent outcasts - and those are the guards."

The GEO Group, Inc. now runs former Wackenhut facilities in 14 states, as well as in South Africa and Australia. Some facilities, such as the Wackenhut Corrections Centers in New York, retain the Wackenhut name, despite no longer having any open connection with the company.

Frequent rumors that the company was in the employ of the Central Intelligence Agency, particularly in the 1960s, were never substantiated, but George Wackenhut, who was obsessive about high-tech security gadgets in his private life, never denied the rumors.

ABOUT THE AUTHOR

Ken Cherry is a fifth generation Texan and a US Marine Corp veteran who served from 1966 to 1970 in the Vietnam era. Ken attended the University of Texas at Arlington Business College and graduated Summa Cum Laude in Finance and Economics.

Ken is a 42 year member of MENSA and the retired former owner and principal of a regional Texas investment firm. Ken and his wife, Pat, are married 49 years.

Ken was the Texas State Director for MUFON (the Mutual UFO Network) for over 10 years. At the time of the Stephenville event he headed up a team of investigators and scientists that conducted extensive research and analysis of the mass sighting for an entire year. Unknown to most people after the widely reported sightings in January of 2008, the UFO returned in October of that year. Interviews with numerous witnesses and analysis of radar reports yielded the same results. A UFO - not a conventional aircraft - had returned to the Stephenville area as reported by reliable witnesses.

Cherry is the founder and President of EPIC-Extraordinary Phenomena Investigations Council, an organization which investigates and presents information on all manner of Extraordinary Phenomena. He is also the founder, host, and executive producer of the popular EPIC VOYAGES radio show on inceptionradionetwork.com

Ken Cherry's media credits History channel's UFO Hunter's, Larry King Live, NBC's Dateline, Discovery Investigates, Texas Monthly magazine, Fort Worth magazine, and countless radio, newspaper and television news interviews.

Other Books by Glannant Ty

All titles available at www.glannantty.com

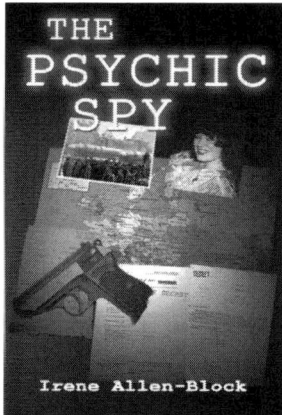

The Psychic Spy
by Irene Allen-Block

Eileen Evans, a beautiful young woman and talented psychic who is unwittingly recruited by MI6 to join their new top secret Remote Viewing program "Blue Star" during the heart of the Cold War in the 1970's and 80's. Eileen quickly finds herself embroiled in excitement and danger as she quickly becomes a "psychic spy" for British Intelligence.

$14.00

- **Paperback:** 320 pages
- **ISBN-13:** 978-0-9861675-0-8

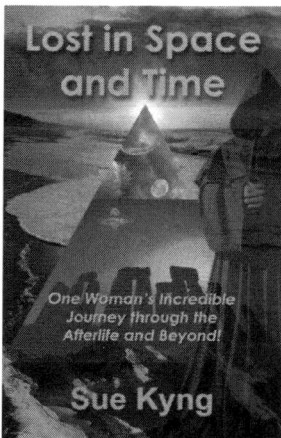

Lost in Space and Time
by Sue Kyng

Sue Kyng has spent a lifetime entertaining audiences on both stage and screen, when a medical emergency brought her to the edge of death and gave her a unique view of the other side of existence. Here she met JACOB, an enigmatic monk who would become her spiritual teach er and confidant. Through Jacob's guidance, Sue would come to a greater understanding of mankind's place in the universe.

$14.00

- **Paperback:** 330 pages
- **ISBN-13:** 978-0-9861675-3-9

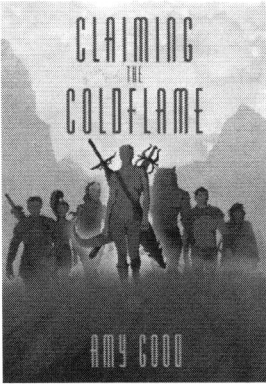

Claiming The Coldflame
by Amy Good

Bleda is a young Driakatana woman living a quiet life in an island village in the land of Areth, until a series of fantastic events changes the course of her life. After learning of her supernatural origins, Bleda embarks on a journey to unravel the mystery of her past life while searching for The Coldflame – the world's most powerful weapon that can bring peace back to an unstable world.

Claiming The Coldflame is an epic story set in a magical world filled with fascinating races and terrifying creatures, and where good and evil battle for the ultimate control of the planet.

- **Paperback:** 436 pages
- **ISBN-13:** 978-1500999896

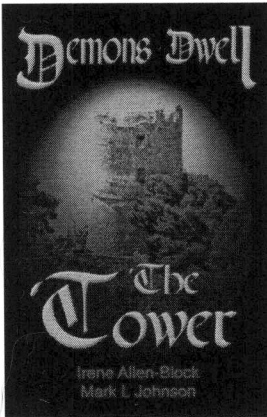

$16.00

Demons Dwell: The Tower
by Irene Allen-Block & Mark Johnson

A hidden evil torments a young couple in a small Italian village along the Amalfitana Coast and threatens to destroy their once peaceful lives. As the dark forces close in around them, help arrives in the form of two paranormal investigators delve into a one hundred-year old mystery while dealing with little known supernatural forces, and quickly find themselves plunging into the very heart of darkness.

"The Tower" is a frightening tale set in an idyllic part of the world where evil lies hidden from the bright Mediterranean sunshine, and old world.

- **Paperback:** 322 pages
- **ISBN-13:** 978-0-9861675-1-5

$14.00

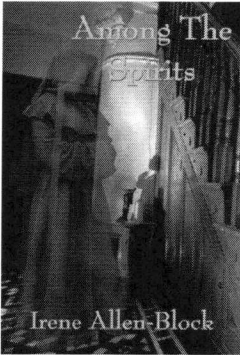

$14.00

Among The Spirits
by Irene Allen-Block

Irene Allen-Block discovered at a very early age that she wasn't like the other children she played with while growing up in England — she could see and communicate with spirits! This would lead Irene down a unique and sometimes lonely path of self-discovery.

Filled with laughter, tears and frightening visions of the other side, Among The Spirits is a personal story of one woman's spiritual journey as she travels through the world of the strange and paranormal.

- **Paperback:** 302 pages
- **ISBN-13:** 978-0-9861675-2-2

$18.00

The Demdike Legacy
by Barry Durham

An murder in a quiet English village in Lancashire re-ignites a legacy of witchcraft thought to have died out four hundred years before, when the Pendle Witches were hanged at Lancaster Castle in 1612. Now it seems that someone is intent on finishing the job started four centuries earlier. As the death toll rises, the descendants of the original Pendle Witches are forced out of hiding, and assist the police in hunting down the killer.

The Demdike Legacy is a thrilling mystery that combines modern-day detective work with historical witchcraft and old-world spiritual practices.

- **Paperback:** 472 pages
- **ISBN-13:** 978-0986167546

28968119R00191

Made in the USA
Middletown, DE
02 February 2016